caught up in the
RAPTURE

sheneska jackson

simon & schuster
new york · london · toronto
sydney · tokyo · singapore

SIMON & SCHUSTER
Rockefeller Center
1230 Avenue of the Americas
New York, NY 10020

SIMON & SCHUSTER and colophon are registered trademarks
of Simon & Schuster Inc.

Designed by Brian Mulligan

Manufactured in the United States of America

ISBN 0-684-81487-0

To Miss Etna, for loving me the best you could
and better when you knew how

acknowledgments

Much respect to Michael Levin, the first person outside the little voice in my head who told me I could do this. Thanks for being right.

Total gratitude to my agent, Felicia Eth, for knocking on the right door and a special Thankyouverymuch to my editor, Marvelous Mary Ann Naples, for opening the door and letting me in. A dainty high five to Miss Laurie Chittenden for being so sweet. You guys are all that, plus tax. Believe it.

Finally, a special shout-out to all my family and friends, without whom I'd have no one to impress. Love you all. Thanks, peace, and I'm out.

—Sheneska

are you listening, god?

I'm just about sick and tired of all this sneaking around like I'm some two-year-old child. I mean, look at me. I'm twenty-six years old and still breaking out in a cold sweat because I'm afraid Daddy won't let me go out tonight. He's probably going to say something like I need to be in church where God can reach me better, or he'll break out into one of his holy chants. "Oh Lord, save this child," he'll say, closing his eyes and holding the palm of his hand to my forehead. "Make her see the error of her evil ways. She's headed for destruction in them streets, Lord. She don't know no better. You gotta save her." The Reverend Deems has a definite flair for the dramatic. By the time he's finished, I'll feel so guilty and ashamed that I'll get dressed in one of my homey little white dresses and follow right behind him to the summer revival at Holy Sight Baptist Church. Or at least that's what usually happens, but not tonight. Tonight I've got big plans, and nothing, not the good Reverend Deems, not even the Almighty Himself, is going to stop me.

I mean, my goodness, to hear Daddy talk, you'd think I was some sort of low-life tramp who hangs in the street all night. But to tell the truth, I'm just like every other young woman these days. I wanna hang out with my friends, go places, see things, meet people—hell, have a little fun before I'm too old or too ugly or too tired from working or too depressed over what I don't have or too spooked by all the things I do have. And dang it,

I'm entitled to a little fun. I get up every morning and go to school, make good grades, then rush off to my part-time job at Bullock's. Then I come home and clean up everything Daddy didn't have time to because he had to rush off to choir rehearsal or go to the hospital and pray for someone he doesn't even know or go help out at some other church auxiliary function. Next it's homework or studying for the next test or research, and if I'm lucky, I'll get about fifteen minutes to sneak a listen at Luther or En Vogue before I hear the clink-clink of Daddy's keys at the front door. What a life.

Okay now, let's see. I've got my hot curlers, my makeup kit, my good panties that I keep hidden in a pillowcase just in case Daddy comes peeping into my underwear drawer on one of his surprise scavenger hunts. He claims he'll be looking for a pair of his socks that might have gotten mixed up with my things in the laundry, but I know he's really trying to see if I have what he calls "demon material" hidden in there. Once he opened my drawer and found a romance novel and an Ice Cube tape, and I swear I thought the man was going to have a stroke. He went off into one of his holy trances and for the next month I was by his side every night at Holy Sight, praying for redemption. That man is too much. You'd think he'd be grateful. I mean, I could be a whole lot worse. I'm a college student, at UCLA no less. I work, I'm dependable, I'm smart, I can take care of myself, I'm kind to people, ambitious, clean, neat, careful, and have a high tolerance for putting up with bullshit or else I'd be out of his dang house by now. I could have turned out like some of the rest of these stupid girls running around here. I could have dropped out of high school, had about four or five babies, be on welfare, and sit around the house watching *The Young and the Restless* and *Oprah* all day. But nooo. I'm trying to do things the right way, and look at me—still sneaking around trying to think of a good lie to tell the good reverend so he won't be suspicious.

Now where did I put those lace stockings? I've gotten so adept at hiding things from Daddy that I can barely remember where the heck anything is when I need it. Oop, here they are, under my mattress right next to my birth control pills. Ha, if Daddy knew I was taking the pill? I don't even want to think about how he'd react. His baby having sex? And she's not even married? Lord have mercy. By the time he would get finished with me, I'd be ripping out my own uterus. But it's not like I really use them anymore. The only time I took them for their intended purpose was when Dakota set me up with one of her cousins because she said I needed to be broken in. I was twenty-one years old and still a virgin and to Dakota that was like some sort of Guinness world record. Dakota's a dick-happy, borderline tramp, but hey, she's my best friend and I love her. So of course I did like she said and gave my virginity away to Boston, her stupid cousin who looks like a Bob Marley reject, with his long, messy dreadlocks that hang down to his butt and that goofy smile that makes him look like he's high all the time.

I did it partly because it was the thing to do and partly because I wanted to know just what the heck Dakota and everybody else was so crazy about. The whole experience lasted less than fifteen minutes, and I swear that boy didn't know the true meaning of deodorant or the pleasures of a long hot shower, but then again it was the middle of summer in L.A. and even the best of us get a little funky in one-hundred-degree weather. I had waited twenty-one years to do it so of course I thought my first time would be extra special, but it was nothing that I thought it would be. In fact it was pretty painful. Dakota said that it was just because it was my first time and since I hadn't done it before, I was just too tight and that it would take at least three or four times before I would experience any real pleasure. So Boston and I spent the majority of that summer twisted around each other, rubbing, poking, trying to get me to feel what everybody said I was supposed to be feeling, but it just didn't work. By the time I started my next semester at UCLA, I just gave up. The whole situation was just too dang awkward. I mean Boston was cool and everything, but he just wasn't my type, and I'm not one to put up with anything for too long that doesn't satisfy me to the fullest. Except for Daddy and that's just because I have no other choice.

Dakota says I'm weak when it comes to Daddy, but she just doesn't understand. "You need to leave the nest, Jazz," she tells me just about every other week. "You need to break away, do what you wanna do for a change. You're twenty-six years old and still running around trying to please him like he's going to put you on punishment or tell God to strike you down in a bolt of lightning."

"I know, I know," I tell her, but she just doesn't get it. She never had these type of daddy-daughter problems. I envy Dakota, I really do. She may not be the smartest sister, but she has her freedom. It seems like we're exact opposites, but I guess that's why we are the best of friends. I remember the first time we met at the beginning of twelfth grade at Harriet Tubman High. It seems the older I get, the more I like to reminisce about my last year of high school. Up until that time, life had been pretty boring, but twelfth grade was a time of change. In twelfth grade, there was Dakota.

It was the second week of school and by that time everybody had formed their cliques and posses and as usual, I was left by the wayside. Just another geeky-looking fat girl, with a face full of freckles, who was neither in style nor really wanted to be. While all the other girls were wearing their cropped tops and biker shorts, Guess? jeans and bomber jackets, I was in my homey, pleated skirt, penny loafers, and starched, white, button-up blouse—looking neat and pure and like a virgin. Makeup was a no-no, according to Daddy, and my red, shoulder-length hair was plaited in one fat braid down the middle of my head. And pants? Please. The only pair of pants Daddy ever let me wear were some cream-colored slacks that he only let me put on in the winter or if it rained and got really cold, which was hardly ever in sunny Los Angeles.

Needless to say I was nowhere near the "in-crowd" and by that time I had convinced myself that I didn't even want to be. Oh sure, I envied the hot mommas, with their basket-weave braids, long sculptured nails, and tight designer jeans, walking around campus in their boyfriends' football jerseys or ditching school to hang out at Taco Bell or better yet, sneaking over to one of their boyfriends' houses to play grown-up games. But by the time the twelfth grade rolled through most of those girls were walking around with swollen bellies, spent most of the day cutting classes and smoking in the bathroom, or had dropped out to take care of their kids or might as well have dropped out because they had nowhere near enough credits to hope to graduate by the time June popped up. For them school was just a fashion show. A place to hang out, see who was wearing what, talk about those who weren't wearing the right thing, and screw a few football players so everyone would think they were so cool because they were doing the nasty.

That life wasn't for me. I was on a mission. I wanted to go to college and not just any college, a good college, so that I could make something of my life and get out of South-Central Los Angeles. And if I earned Daddy's respect along the way, that would make it all worthwhile. I spent class breaks and lunches by myself mostly, sitting on a bench underneath a shade tree by the girls' locker room with my head in a book. That was my private hideout. A place where I could get away from all the wanna-bes and the laughter and insults from all the boys about my less-than-perfect figure and out-of-style clothes. That's where I first met Dakota.

Dakota was the new girl in school and of course nobody liked her because of that. I had walked over to my hideout and there she was, invading my space. She had on a pair of faded blue jeans with holes in the knees, a white T-shirt, and a pair of high-top Jordans. She was sitting on the edge of the bench, trying to hide a lit cigarette behind a *Vogue* magazine. I sat down on the other end of the bench, quite upset that my space had been violated, opened my English book, and started reading. The fumes from Dakota's cigarette engulfed me and although I wasn't in the practice of bothering people who weren't really bothering me, I had no intention of letting this foreigner who had so boldly invaded my hideout choke me to death with smoke.

"Skuse me," I said timidly. "I can't breathe."

She took one last drag from behind her magazine and put the cigarette out in silence without even looking in my direction.

That upset me even more, because she didn't even know me and already she was being rude. Who are you, anyway? I wanted to ask her, but I already knew. I had heard some girls gossiping about her earlier. They said she had gotten kicked out of her other school for ditching and for smoking in the bathroom. They said she was weird and I could tell they were right. It didn't take a genius to know there was something different about this girl. Nothing really weird though, just different, odd. Whatever it was, it was getting on my nerves and I didn't want her around. The bench and shade tree were my places of solitude, and I wasn't going to give them up for some new girl with a pack of Newports and a *Vogue* subscription.

"If you wanna smoke, there's a secret spot behind the gymnasium. Nobody ever gets caught over there," I told her.

"Look, I put the cigarette out, okay? No harm, no foul, honey," she said and finally looked at me. She was cute in an offbeat kind of way. In fact, she looked like she could fit right into the in-crowd if she wanted to. "I'm Dakota. Don't ask me my last name 'cause I don't have one," she said and laughed. "So who are you?"

"Jazmine Deems," I answered, trying to figure out if she was really interested or just making small talk. Ten minutes later, I guessed that she must have really been interested or either bored to death, because I swear the girl talked my ear off. By the end of lunch, I practically knew her whole life story.

Her parents, who she called by their first names, were musicians. Earth, her mother, was a drummer and River, her father, a bass player. They made most of their living doing session work for various blues artists and often went on tour across America and overseas, leaving Dakota here in L.A. by herself. That didn't seem to bother Dakota, though. "They're free spirits," she told me. "They do their thing and I do mine."

While Dakota's family weren't exactly the Huxtables, from what she told me they were pretty close. Their home was always filled with the sound of music like Ray Charles, Aretha, and B.B. King. All you heard at my house was some generic gospel group singing the same "Glory, glory, praise the Lord, Hallelujah" crap that amounted to nothing but a bunch of screaming and hollering. Not singing. The only group I really liked was BeBe and CeCe Winans, and I had to beg Daddy to let me play them at home because he insisted they weren't a real gospel group. He came home from church one evening and I had BeBe and CeCe blasting, filling myself with the spirit, and before I could catch my breath from the high note I had just belted out, he popped the tape from the stereo and flung it into the back of my head. "No secular music in this house, girl!" he screamed and began to pray and call the Lord.

"But that's the Winans, Daddy," I pleaded between his shouts of "Oh sweet Jesus" and "Lord have mercy on this poor child's soul." He finally came around though, after the church sponsored a bus to take the choir to see BeBe and CeCe and Take 6 at the Wiltern Theater. After that, he changed his mind, but I still could only listen to selected songs. Once I tried to sneak in a cut of M.C. Hammer's rap song, "Pray," but that tape ended up hitting me upside the head too. So I decided just to stick with the Winans, Take 6, and occasionally, Anointed.

Dakota enjoyed gospel music too, and after a week or so, she and I became tighter than Laverne and Shirley. I never invited her over to my house though. Daddy would have a fit if Dakota pulled out a cigarette in his holy house, and knowing Dakota she would do it just to start a controversy. That was Dakota, always pressing the boundaries. That was the way she was brought up. "Be who you be," she always says. "And never settle."

I remember the first time I went to her house. Her mother was walking around in a bikini singing some old Chaka Khan song. She was dancing around like she didn't have a care in the world. Dakota chimed in, off-key as usual, but didn't care, and I just sat on the couch watching the two shake and prance in the middle of their living room. "Come on, Jazz," Dakota said and grabbed my hand and pulled me up. Before I knew it, I was getting down right with them. It was so fun. *"I'm every woman, it's all in me,"* I crooned. Then Earth and Dakota stopped and looked at me and I felt so embarrassed. I thought I was doing the right moves, but the look on their faces made me sit my fat behind right back down.

"Girl!" Earth screamed. "Where'd you get pipes like that?"

"I didn't know you could blow, Jazz," Dakota added.

"Oh, I sing every once in a while in the young adult choir at church, but mostly at home, when Daddy's not around." That was an understatement to say the least. I loved to sing. Church is where I first fell in love with music. From the age of six, I had been singing in the choir and by the time I was ten I was given my first solo. I had that church jumping. By the end of my selection, five ladies had caught the holy ghost and three had passed out. That was the first time I knew I had a gift, the first time I really felt God within me. I was amazed how the sound of my voice could excite people, move people, make them *feel* something. That was my first taste of power and from then on I couldn't live without music. Couldn't imagine a world without a song, a lyric, an octave, a chorus.

After that, I sang at any opportunity I could get, and the opportunities were endless. There was always somebody getting married at church, or a funeral, a baptism, or a revival, and if not I'd just wait till Daddy left home, grab my hairbrush, stand in front of the mirror, and belt out whatever song came to mind. It was usually "Amazing Grace," and I swear I found every way but the right way to sing that song. Sometimes I'd sing it in my chest voice, which is pretty low, then at the end of the first verse, I'd switch to my head voice, and boy, if I wasn't extra careful, I'd end up catching the holy ghost myself.

The power of my voice was almost scary to me. I mean, the way it made me feel and all. I couldn't understand what God was trying to do. Why did he give *me*, this little fat girl, such a gift? I often felt God was trying to tell me something, but exactly what, I didn't know. But other times, it felt like a curse. Daddy was always dragging me off to some church function so I could sing, which was okay at first, but after a while it was as if it was Daddy's voice. I had to do with it what he wanted, and if that meant going to the hospital and singing for some stranger who was on the church's sick and shut-in list, then that's what I had to do. After a while I started making up excuses. I faked colds, the flu, strep throat—you name it, I faked it, but only if I really didn't want to sing or if Daddy got on my nerves in an extreme way, which was usually the case.

Through my voice, I could gain power over Daddy. If I knew some big church event was coming up and he wanted me to sing, I'd survey his actions toward me for about a week and if he irked me in the slightest way— I suddenly came down with something.

Dakota was the first to take my mind off gospel and introduce me to secular music. Her parents had a collection of albums and cassettes with everything from Nat "King" Cole to Public Enemy, Prince to Fleetwood Mac. Dakota taught me everything. How to curse, wear makeup, how to dress, do my hair, boys, the nasty, how to dance. She even taught me how to lose weight. "You're much too pretty to be warbling around here like a water buffalo," she told me and put me on a strict diet of less than eleven hundred calories a day, until my five-foot-five, one-hundred-and-sixty-pound frame dwindled down to a svelte one-hundred-and-twenty-five-pounds. That was the hardest thing I ever had to do in my life, but I must admit I had been out of control. Between Daddy and school and the mean little whispers everyone blurted out behind my back about how my thighs rubbed together when I walked or the rolls of fat that shook around my waist, all I wanted to do when I got home was raid the fridge, which was always stocked with potatoes, grits, pork chops, ice cream, four or five different kinds of cheeses, and strawberry-flavored milk. My favorite, though, was chocolate, and to this day I believe the stuff is addictive. I used to need at least three servings a day of some sort of chocolate. M&M's, fudge cake, chocolate chip cookies—you name it. I was sprung on the stuff. But Dakota ended all that. "You can't be hanging out with me looking like a moose, honey. I'm sorry," she said. "Now if you think you're being the best you can be, fine. But if not, honey, make a U-turn and find a different way."

So that's what I did, and by graduation day when the principal called my name to come up and accept my valedictorian award, I felt young again. Not like some old, fat dork who couldn't wait to get her hands on a pack of Ding Dongs. I practically floated up the stage and Dakota, my savior, gave me a standing ovation. She was the only one. Daddy sat coldly in his seat, but I didn't care. Dakota stood by herself clapping and crying and before long the rest of the senior class joined her, pumping their fists in the air and growling like they were on *The Arsenio Hall Show*. I knew then that I had arrived.

That night Dakota's parents treated the two of us to a concert. I told Daddy we were going to see a young gospel group and he agreed to let me go if I promised to be home by eleven-thirty. Dakota and I had the time of our lives. We pulled up to the Forum in her parents' gaudy, yellow El Dorado and stepped out like we were royalty. Dakota had done my bright red hair in a mound of Shirley Temple curls that she pulled back on one side with a hot pink comb and let the rest fall over my right eye. She let me borrow a pair of black leather pants and a pink-and-white top that plunged down between my breasts, showing just the right amount of cleavage without looking slutty. On my feet were a pair of hot pink pumps that I tried my best to balance myself upon without looking stupid. Dakota had on a skin-tight black dress with gold trim and a pair of big, gold hoop earrings that hung down to her shoulders. Her short and wavy jet-black hair was freshly cut on the sides and in the back and the top was swooped over to the side like silk. She made both of our faces up with the Fashion Fair makeup kit her mother had let us borrow. We knew we were looking tough and so did everybody else. When we got inside we stood around for about half an hour so everyone could see how cute we looked. When we were satisfied that we had been seen enough, we took our seats in the first row of the sold-out arena. Everyone was buzzing, talking, laughing, seeing who was who, and sipping drinks. There were black people, white people, in-betweens, all smiling and getting along as if they'd known each other all their lives.

The women wore all sorts of shiny, glittered outfits that ranged from the very expensive to the downright gaudy. Nobody really cared though. They were too busy enjoying themselves and sipping their cocktails. And the men, woo! Fine, simply fine. Especially the black men, in their suits and baggy pants and fresh haircuts. I love a man with a freshly cut head. It was so exciting to see black men looking like they had something. And of course, Dakota was going crazy. Before we had even gotten adjusted in our seats, she was all in the face of some light-skinned guy with hazel eyes. They looked sort of cute together, him in his beige Armani suit and her in those spiked suede pumps. They looked like they were engaged, the way they carried on together. He whispered something in her ear and she broke out laughing. "You're so silly," she cooed and brushed her hand over his. He left after that and came back with two drinks and another handsome guy, equally suited in black and gray. "This is my friend, Craig," he said and handed us the drinks.

"Thanks," I said, trying to look cool and unimpressed by the fine hunk of a man standing by his side. "I'm sorry, I didn't get your name."

"Oh, this is Jeff," Dakota broke in. "Jeff and Craig, this is Jazmine, my best friend."

"Nice to meet you, Jazmine," Craig said and flashed an unforgettable smile, and I swear it was all I could do to keep from puckering up my lips and kissing that angel. "Look, we're gonna get back to our seats before the show starts, but if you guys are up to it, we can go out for a drink afterward, okay?"

"Oh sure, we're up to it," Dakota said, coolly. "We'll meet you two in the lobby later."

What, Dakota? I thought. The show won't be over till at least ten-thirty, and if I'm late Daddy will go off. When they walked away, she turned to me as if she had been reading my mind and said, "Shut up, Jazz. You're grown now and it's about time you had some damn fun. Besides, I'm driving and unless you plan on walking home in those hot pink pumps, this night won't be over till I say it's over."

Before I could even open my mouth to protest, the house lights went off and the crowd began to cheer. A single spotlight lit up the middle of the stage as the sound of music began to fill the arena with an easy, slow groove. I could feel the crowd getting excited. Then a low, silky, smooth voice began to moan offstage. The crowd could barely contain themselves. The lady behind me began shouting, "Go on girl, sang that song." Then the man next to her stood up and started hollering too, "Sang, baby, sang it!" And then it happened. Anita Baker walked into the spotlight, standing less than five foot three, but seeming larger than life. *"You're my angel, oh angel."* That's all it took. By the end of the song the whole house was on its feet, clapping, swaying, and singing along with Anita. I was in awe. I sat straight up in my seat the whole time, barely able to move, unwilling to take my eyes off her. At that moment, I knew what I wanted to do. I wanted to sing. I wanted to get onstage in front of thousands of people and touch them deep down in their souls the way Anita touched me. I wanted to make people yearn, make their hearts bleed, move them, make them go home and make love, make them smile, make them *feel*.

By the time it was all over, I was so excited I didn't know what to do. I hugged Dakota and broke out into tears right there in the first row. "What's wrong with you, girl? You messing up your makeup. You sick or something?"

"No," I said, "I just wanna thank you, D. Tonight was the best time I've ever had."

Dakota looked at me for a long time and I knew she knew what I was thinking. She always did. "You know you're just as good as Anita, honey. And you know I wouldn't tell you nothing that wasn't the truth." And that was no lie. Dakota was straight to the point, forget feelings. She said what she thought and if you didn't agree—oh well. "But dry them tears, honey, we got some freak daddys waiting on us," she said and gave me another hug, then grabbed me by the arm and practically dragged me out of my seat.

The four of us ended up in Hollywood at Roscoe's Chicken and Waffles, but I couldn't eat. Partly because I was so excited that I had made up my mind about what I was going to do with the rest of my life, and partly because it was already past twelve o'clock and I knew I was gonna catch major trauma when I got home—whenever that would be. Besides, I had just gotten my figure together and I didn't want to blow it with a bunch of greasy chicken and fattening waffles. But it looked too good and I couldn't help eyeing Craig's plate as he drenched his waffles with three cups of syrup. "You're not one of those salad eaters, are you?" he asked and stuck a forkful of waffles in his mouth.

"No, I just don't have much of an appetite right now," I lied.

"Are you *sure*?" he said, picking up another forkful and twirling it around in front of my face. "I don't mind sharing."

"Well, in that case, put some hot sauce on that chicken wing and hand it over," I said, feeling no shame.

Dakota and Jeff sat across from us feeding each other as if they were really in love or something. Dakota picked up a piece of waffle with her finger and swirled it in syrup before sticking it deep into Jeff's mouth. She laughed as he sucked her finger and all of a sudden I felt this overwhelming urge to throw up.

Craig was cool, though. He told me he and Jeff had just started working for the sheriff's department and had been best friends since their college days at Cal State Northridge. I was fascinated. Most black men I knew were too busy running from the police, and college never even occurred to the guys I'd known. But then again, aside from the stupid jocks in high school and Dakota's friends, I didn't really know that many men to begin with. "So what made you want to be a police officer?" I asked.

"Well, I didn't, really. But after graduating from college with a degree in business that I found didn't mean shit, especially for a brother, I didn't have too much of a choice. It was either this or working in the mailroom over at Pacific Telesis, and I tell you one thing, I didn't spend five years in college to come out making fifteen thousand dollars a year as a mail boy for the man. So I said fuck it. Gimme a badge and a gun. This way if I don't get any respect from the man, at least I have the authority to blow his fucking head off and collect thirty thousand a year for my troubles."

"Man, chill out, Craig, you gonna scare the girl," Jeff said and wrapped his arm around Dakota's shoulder.

"No, no. Let the brother talk," Dakota said, wiping her mouth and flipping chicken crumbs off her lap. "The brother's only telling it like it is. Hell, a black man's gotta do what a black man's gotta do." Dakota loved these kinds of conversations. It was almost like she hated white people, although she had been brought up around them all her life. But she didn't really hate them. Hate was something Earth and River had refused to teach their daughter. They insisted she love everybody equally regardless of race, but they also taught her to speak her mind and stand up for what was right. That's why no one in their family goes by their last name. "Deems? You think that's your real last name?" she asked me once. "That ain't your last name, honey. That's just some name the slave master gave to one of your ancestors when they bought them and put them to work on the plantation. River's last name used to be Blackman. *Blackman.* Massah just looked at River's great-great-grandfather and said, 'Let's see here, you sho-nuff black and I guess you sort of a man, although I ain't gonna treat you like one, so I guess I'll call you Black-man, boy.'"

Dakota has always been passionate about these matters and sometimes she gets so excited that veins pop out on her neck and her voice gets so loud, you think she's about to haul off and hit somebody. But the next minute, she'll be laughing and joking and talking about how fine that white boy Tom Cruise is.

I boldly checked my watch and gave Dakota the old evil eye. I guess Craig could see I was getting impatient because he offered to give me a ride home.

"Go on, girl, I'll call you tomorrow," Dakota said and I knew that meant: "Get lost because I'm about to get me some tonight."

"Are you sure it's no problem, Craig?" I asked, unsure if I should go off by myself with a stranger I barely knew.

"Sure, no problem. I gotta get home myself, anyway. My shift starts in about three hours."

"You mean you have to be at work in three hours?"

"Yep. So if I fall asleep behind the wheel of my patrol car, I'm gonna blame it all on you for keeping me up so late." He smiled that cover-boy smile, and I figured he was safe enough and dang sure cute enough to take me anywhere. Matter of fact, the way I was feeling at that moment, if he had asked me to go to the moon, I would've chipped in on the plane fare.

We got into his convertible Mustang and I swear he looked so good behind the wheel, I thought I would die. "Where to, sweetheart?"

Sweetheart, *sweetheart*, that sounded so good to my ear. "Baring Cross Street," I said.

"Oh, you live in the hood, huh?"

"I guess you could say that," I said, feeling sort of embarrassed now because of what I thought he had probably heard about South-Central. Or should I say, what the media has told everyone about South-Central. If you look at the news all you hear about are the bangers and the slangers. You never hear about a girl like me going to school and trying to make it. And anyway, where the heck is South-Central? You can't find it on a map. South-Central is just a catchall name the media made up to classify neighborhoods with a majority of black residents. Man, I was getting pissed just thinking about all this.

"I've got a lot of family in South-Central too," he said.

"Oh really?" I said, feeling relieved that at least he could relate. Then I almost gagged. This wasn't how the night was supposed to end. I was supposed to go back to Dakota's and change into my own clothes before I went home. Now Daddy's gonna really flip when he sees me in these pants. And oh Lord, my hair and makeup, and on top of all that, it was two-fifteen! Then I looked back over at Craig, who was humming the words to some rap tune I'd never heard before. Baby was fine. Clean-cut fine. Caramel-colored skin, clean shaven, and that diamond earring in his ear was just too sexy.

He must have felt me staring at him because he started to blush. "How old are you?" he asked, throwing me off guard.

"You tell me," I said, testing him, but he didn't take the bait.

"Do I look stupid? You women always trying to catch us guys with that how-old-do-I-look routine. No way, baby. You tell *me*."

"Okay, okay. Eighteen."

"Eighteen!" he said and stripped the gear on his stick shift. "You've got to be joking, right?"

"No, I'm serious," I said, thrown off by his obvious shock. "And how old are you?"

"Twenty-five and not in the habit of dating teenagers."

"Well, don't sweat yourself, babe. This wasn't a real date."

We drove the rest of the way in silence and by the time he pulled up in front of my house, I was ready to jump out of the car, but chose to take my time because I was in no hurry to rush into the wrath of Daddy, who no doubt would be waiting on me, belt in hand, prayer in mouth.

"Look, I didn't mean to sound so put off about your age. It was just a big shock. You act at least twenty-one and I never would have thought you were only eighteen."

I chose not to say anything. If he wanted to apologize, he'd have to do it all by himself.

"Look, what I'm trying to say is that I really enjoyed your company tonight, and if you don't mind, I'd like to call you sometime."

"Well, why don't you give me your number and I'll think about it."

"Oh, so it's like that."

No, it really wasn't like that, but if I gave him my number and he called when Daddy was home, I'd have a lot of explaining to do. "Yeah, it's exactly like that."

He pulled out a card from his wallet and handed it to me. "Use it," he said and looked at me as if he didn't know whether to kiss me or pat me on the head.

"I'll think about it," I said and got out of the car. Dang it. I should have kissed that angel, I told myself, and took a deep breath before walking to the door. I was about to get the crap knocked out of me, I thought, and let myself in.

But when I walked in, the house was dark. I fumbled around for the light switch and turned it on. On the coffee table was a yellow stick-it pad and I didn't even bother to read it. Daddy always left a stick-it note when he would be away at the hospital, praying over some poor lost soul. I almost felt upset that he wasn't home. Church always came before me. I hurried out of my clothes and got in bed. I laid there and prayed for about twenty minutes. "God, please help me start a singing career. Not for the money, not for the fame, but so I can touch people with my voice." Daddy always said everybody was put on earth for a reason, and for the first time in my life I knew my reason. I wondered if Momma had felt the same way when she decided to become a singer. That thought surprised me. I hardly ever thought about Momma anymore. If it weren't for old photographs, I wouldn't even know how she looked. I was so young when she died, too young to miss her, but for the first time in my life I felt a bond with her. For the first time in my life I wished she was still alive. I closed my eyes and rolled over to finish my prayer. "And, oh yeah, God—I'm gonna marry Craig. Amen."

That was eight years ago and look at me now. Twenty-six years old and still waiting for my eighteen-year-old dreams to come true. But enough reminiscing, where the heck is my strapless bra? I swear, I don't know whether I'm coming or going. And where the heck's Daddy? He ought to be on his way home by now. The revival starts at eight o'clock. I stopped what I was doing, put my hand to my chest, and took a deep breath. What I need to do is sit down and relax and think of a good lie. Now let's see. I had a stomachache last Sunday, so I can't use that line again, and the week before, I told him I lost my voice, and. . . . My train of thought was broken when the phone rang out. It never fails. Every time I get a moment to myself it starts ringing.

"Hello," I said, abruptly.

"Jazz, where the hell are you? The party starts in an hour and you still haven't gotten your black ass over here to get dressed."

It was Dakota, going off as usual. I don't know who's worse, her or Daddy. "I know, girl, but Daddy isn't home yet and you know I can't leave without telling him where I'm going."

"Forget the reverend. This night is for you, Jazz. Do you know how many strings Earth and River had to pull to get us tickets for this party tonight? I hope you're not getting cold feet, and please don't tell me you're gonna back out now."

"No, Dakota, I just gotta wait for Daddy. You know the deal." Of course she knew the deal. We go through this every time we get ready to go somewhere. And every time, Dakota tells me to forget Daddy and just leave, but I can't. As long as I'm living under his roof, I have to play by his rules. I mean, he is footing the bill for college, and although I do work, I don't make enough to move out on my own and pay a car note, groceries, credit card bills, and utilities. So I'm stuck. "Dakota, I'll be there as soon as I can, so just lay out my black velvet dress and pumps so everything'll be ready when I get there."

"Do you have your demo tape?"

"Yeah, it's right in my purse."

"You sure?"

"Yes, D, I'm sure, dang." She can sure be a worrywart sometimes. But I love her and if it weren't for her I would have never gotten that demo tape finished. Her parents helped me out by setting up a recording session for me at this small studio in West Hollywood a few months ago. Her parents had the hookup on all sorts of things like that. They'd been in the business for so long that they knew just about everybody who's anybody, and practically everyone owed them a favor. They were good people, though. Once Earth found out that I was serious about singing, she gave me all sorts of tips, and River even helped me write the songs I sang on the demo. They had been more like parents to me than my own daddy, and sometimes, I can't tell who I love more.

"Just get your ass over here quick, fast, and in a hurry. Don't blow this, Jazz, I'm serious. Get back."

Dakota always accused me of dragging my feet when it came to my singing career. And I can't blame her really. I thought Dakota was going to flip out when I told her I was going to go to UCLA. She said I was just wasting my time, but I knew what I was doing. I couldn't just walk in one day and tell Daddy his valedictorian daughter was going to blow her education on some fantasy about being a singer. He'd flip. I had to take it slow. But after I got my bachelor's in liberal arts, I decided to go on ahead and start work on my master's. That really got Dakota pissed. I guess the decision to put off my singing career to work on my master's was just another delay tactic—an excuse. But I'm scared. I mean, what if I can't cut it? What if I never get a contract? Or worse, what if I do get a contract and nobody buys my records? I can't deal with the possibility of putting all my hopes and aspirations out there for everyone to see, then taking the chance of nobody liking or believing in me enough to take that ultimate chance on me. These thoughts sent me to sleep with a stomachache many a night. But two months ago, I really began to pray on it. "God," I said, "if this is what you really want me to do with my life, then show me the way. Make a path for me, dear Lord. Guide me in the right direction and if it is your will, I will do whatever it takes to fulfill your master plan. You've blessed me with a glorious gift, dear

Lord, and if you just show me the way, I promise I'll do the right thing."

I guess God heard me, because the next day, Earth called and told me she had some open hours at a studio and to come on over and lay down a couple of tracks. And today, Dakota called me up at work and said she had two tickets to Black Tie Records' annual executive party. "Everybody who's anybody will be there tonight," she told me, as if I didn't already know. "Network, girl, network," she said.

Black Tie Records is the foremost record company for black musicians. If I could just get my tape into the hands of somebody, anybody, at that company, I'd be set. Maybe they'd like it, maybe they'd think it was garbage, but at least then I could say I tried—I really tried.

My heart stuttered when I heard Daddy storming through the house. Oh shoot, I thought. Get it together, girl. Get it together. He busted through my door without knocking, as usual, and stood there taking up the entire doorway with his big butt. I thought once I lost my weight that he'd take the hint and follow my lead. No such luck. He looked bigger than ever in that bland gray suit and off-white tie. Ugh! If he's nice to me, I'll hook him up with a nice silk tie from the accessories collection at the store. And if he doesn't put up too much of a fight when I tell him I'm not going to church tonight, I'll even get it for him tomorrow.

"Child, what you doing in that nightgown? We got to be at the church in fifteen minutes. Now come on, girl. Get a move on."

"Daddy, I'm going to have to miss tonight."

"Oh no you don't. Get on up here. You need to cleanse your soul, girl. Jesus been looking down on you and I know He don't like what He sees. I know I don't."

"What are you talking about, Daddy?"

"You been missing too much church. You ain't been in two whole weeks, and don't think I don't know what time you been tipping your fast little tail in here at night. Bullock's closes at ten o'clock and you been walking in here after eleven. Now don't give me no grief."

"Daddy, please. You know it's been hectic as I don't know what at the store with all those summer sales going on. I can't just walk out at ten o'clock. I gotta stay until the store is cleaned up and ready for opening the next morning."

"The Lord don't take excuses, Jazmine. You could at least have the decency to go fellowship in the name of your Father."

"Daddy, I just can't tonight. With all the work at the store, I haven't had any time to study, and tomorrow I have an exam in Pan-African studies. I gotta hit the books, Daddy. But I *promise* I'll go with you tomorrow."

He didn't like it but he agreed to go alone. But first he came over and knelt down beside me. "Shut your eyes and bow your head and give the Lord his due." While he knelt next to me praying, I wondered if he had always been like this. I know he wasn't always saved. I'd seen old pictures of him and Momma before she died and he always looked happy in them. He never seems happy now. I don't care how many Sundays he gets in front of that congregation and professes the word of God, he still comes home looking lost. In the pictures, he'd usually have on dark shades with a drink in his hand and his arm around Momma. They always seemed to be enjoying themselves. Then after she died he started preaching. I guess we all have different survival techniques. Daddy's doesn't seem to be working for him, though.

He finally got up and headed out. And with a final, "Lord have mercy on this poor child's soul," he was gone.

Round one goes to Jazz!

I slipped on some leggings and tied my nightgown in a knot at my waist. Then I grabbed the phone and dialed Dakota's number. "I'm walking out the door."

chapter two

the strength of
street knowledge

"Well, I'm the X-Man
Rappin' on the streets of South-Central,
Got my pockets fulla money
And my lungs fulla Indo.
Smokin' on the bud,
And I'm feelin' kinda high,
With two bitches in my '64.
It's time ta ride.
Hey yo, Bone,
Tell these mothafuckas what tha fuck is up.
Hey yo, T, it's time ta rip shit up."
"Yeah, it's T-Bone.
Creepin' while ya sleepin', mothafucka.
Got my nine pointed ya ass,
You thank ya lucky?
Yo—Who I be,
I be what ya see.
Just the T to the B to the O, N, E.
I'm gonna pass the rhyme to my mothafucka, Rich.
Yo Rich, flow the fuck up in this shit."

"Yo, X. Where the fuck is Rich, dude?"

"Yo, man, I thought he was sitting up there on the porch. Yo, Rich!—Rich! Get yo punk-ass over here, man."

He does this shit all the time. Whenever we get ready to rehearse, Rich ain't nowhere to be found. Look at his stupid-ass, all hugged up with that hood rat Eyeisha. That bitch don't come around until we get ready to practice and then she be steady distracting Rich—the one who needs the most help. I swear, if that fool wasn't in a wheelchair, I'd chin check him—her too, for that matter.

"Yo, man, chill out, I'm comin'," Rich said, spinning around in his chair. "Say baby, push me on over there before I have to get out this damn chair and kick this nigga's ass," he said and laughed.

Yeah right. Kick my ass? Him and what army? And look at this ho, pushin' this fool like he some kind of king. How stupid does she look, in them cheap, swap-meet clothes—green-and-purple biker shorts and a blue tube top. She ain't nothing but a joke, and I swear, her butt is too big for spandex. And that hair, or should I say, whose hair? She ain't foolin' nobody with that fake weave hanging all the way down to her butt. I remember when she didn't have enough hair to hope for. Now can't nobody tell her she ain't Jayne Kennedy. And I'm not even gon' get started on them fake dagger nails and blue contacts she got stuck on her eyeballs. Bitches. I swear, if I didn't love Rich like a brother, I'd tell him to get rid of that two-bit ho. But I guess when you're stuck in a wheelchair for the rest of your life, you take whatever stank bitch you can get.

"A'ight, man," Rich said and wiped the sweat off his face with the blue rag he always keeps in one of his hands. It was only eighty degrees, but in South-Central, eighty feels more like a hundred, especially when you gotta keep looking over your shoulder for the next jacker or gang banger trying to roll up and take you out. It's sorta strange though. It can be eighty degrees and hot as a mothafucka, but still the sun don't be out. It's like the whole city be covered in a fog. I hate kickin' it over here at Rich's house these days. This whole part of town don't do nothing but remind me about what I keep trying to get away from—gangsta life. We a'ight here though, I guess. We grew up in these streets, even ruled these streets back in the day. Manchester and Hoover was our territory. Didn't nothing go on in this hood that we didn't either instigate or bring to a conclusion. I guess that's why Rich still lives over here. At least here, he's still considered the man. Wheelchair or no wheelchair. Rich squinted his eyes at the sun and said, "Let's take it from the top."

"Hell naw, man," T-Bone said, looking even more pissed off than I was by Rich's lazy attitude. "I'm about to go to the crib and get ready for tonight. You take it from the top, with your sorry-ass. You need the practice more than we do, anyway," he said walking across the yard to his El Camino. "Yo, X, I'll meet y'all at the party around nine," he said and jumped in his ride, turned up the thumps, and boned out.

"Yo, man, fuck that punk," Rich said after T-Bone rolled off. I could tell he was sort of hurt by what T-Bone had said. T-Bone was always talking about how Rich's rap was weak. "I don't even know why we let that fool in the group," T-Bone said to me one time. "He don't write his own lyrics, his timing is off, and every time we get ready to go over something, Eyeisha comes around butting her fat-ass into everything. We need to get rid of his cripple-ass if we ever gon' get some place with our music."

Everything he said was true, but T-Bone knew as well as I did that we couldn't just get rid of Rich. Rich was the one financing everything. They don't call his ass Rich for nothing. That nigga been slangin' 'caine big-time for the past ten years and the cops hardly ever sweat him 'cause he's in a wheelchair. I guess the cops don't know a wheelchair can't stop no black man when it comes to making money.

All that equipment around back in the garage was bought by Rich. We'd never be able to hook up them funky beats without all that shit in there. Top-of-the-line stuff too. MCI 16-track tape machine, Macintosh SE30 computer, Harrison 3624 console, DAT machine, MIDI-controlled keyboard, tube mics—the whole hookup.

Hell, without Rich we wouldn't be where we are today, which is nowhere, but still I gots to give props where props are due. And besides, if it hadn't been for Rich, I wouldn't even still be on this earth, let alone trying to be some kinda rap star.

To tell the truth, T-Bone and Rich really can't stand each other. They only put up with each other 'cause I have to constantly remind them that we boys. Ever since we been in junior high, the three of us have been boys.

We been in so much shit together that all three of our black asses should be six feet under. And that ain't no joke.

We all met in seventh grade at Molden Junior High over on Seventy-seventh street, the heart of Cross Street gangsta Crip territory, but we didn't stay there for long. The streets were calling us like church bells and just like every other little nigga in the hood, we gave in.

Baby Pooh, Rich's older brother, was the leader of Cross Street and by the time we were thirteen, we all had been jumped on the set. That was some scary shit for three little snot-nosed kids, but there was no one around to tell us "no."

All of our parents were jokes, or I guess I should say, all our mothers, 'cause there's no such thing as a father in the hood. My moms was killed in a car crash by some stupid, drunk, white asshole when I was just six years old. I don't really have much memory of her besides the fact that she would always sing "If I Could" by Nancy Wilson to me when it came time for me to go to bed. After she passed I got stuck with my Auntie Joyce, who never did give too much of a damn about me. I guess she felt I was a burden, especially since she was only twenty-one when she had to take me in. But she was Momma's only living relative, so you would think she would have some pity on me, her only nephew. But not Auntie Joyce. That's one mean bitch. So I started breaking out on my own and wound up in a gang. No, a family is more like it.

T-Bone's momma still walking the streets over on Slauson and Western with her shopping cart full of newspapers and bottles and shit. She got some kinda mental problem or something. It ain't unusual to roll down Western and see that fool standing out in the middle of the street butt naked. T-Bone don't like to talk about her though. I guess he's embarrassed. That's a damn shame if you ask me. At least his momma is still alive.

Rich's moms was strung out on the pipe until she died, when Rich was sixteen. He took it pretty hard too, 'cause the crack she overdosed on was from a stash he had hidden in his bedroom. His moms got a hold to it and smoked herself right into her grave.

I can tell he still miss her. I guess that's why he always latching on to these hos—any ho who'll give him some play. You'd think he'd recognize by now that all these bitches want from him is his money. Look at him.

Now, I know I ain't no Billy Dee Williams and shit, but Rich is one ugly mothafucka. Pitch black—damn near purple, with them big-ass lips that look like he been sucking on strawberry Now n' Laters 'cause they all red in the center. And that drippy Jheri Curl. I tried to tell the brother that curls are played, but he act like curls are still the bomb. Hell, even Ice Cube got rid of his curl. But you can't tell Rich nothing. He think he know so damn much but don't know shit. That's why them bitches be ganking his sorry behind for his dollars. You'd think he'd of caught on by now, but not Rich. He be so glad to get some pussy that he do just about anything to keep it. Buying them skeezers clothes, getting their hair done, nails done, taking care of all they kids. Stupid, just plain stupid. Me and T-Bone be trying to tell him, but he just don't wanna listen.

And T-Bone ain't no better. He think he fine as wine. He got that light skin, green eyes, and good hair that all the bitches be going crazy for. But he just as stupid as Rich. Every time one of them hos tell him she pregnant, he start dishing out money for 'em to get an abortion. That last bitch he was going out with told him she was pregnant with his baby two days after he fucked her. And what did that fool do? Hand over four hundred dollars so she could go take care of it. I tell you one thing, if that bitch was pregnant then I'm the president of these fucked-up United States. All that skeezer did was take that money and go put a down payment on that new Nissan Sentra she rollin' in now. T-Bone caught up with her one day on Crenshaw after she had stopped seeing him and asked her what was up. And she had the nerve to tell him the truth. She straight said she was usin' him and that she took the money and spent it on herself. Straight up like that! Now I don't know what the hell she did that for, 'cause T-Bone nutted up and broke all the windows out her car and slit all four of her tires. Now any sane person would have thought the relationship was over. But I be damn if the two of them fools ain't still together to this day.

I just don't know what the fuck is up with these people. A nigga like me ain't going out like that. Ain't no bitch gon' use me like I was born yesterday. That's why I try to stay one step ahead of 'em at all times. Now if Kelly ever tried to do some shit like that to me, I think I'd have to serve her up a nice black eye. But she'd never do nothin' like that. White bitches never do. They be too busy trying to take care of your ass, so happy to have a brother they don't know what to do.

Kelly's one of those rich, sheltered white girls, who when they finally get on their own, go crazy and try to eat up as much black dick as they can get their hands on, then try to play hide-and-seek with their parents so they never find out. Kelly's cool, though. I been kicking out in the Valley with her, at her condo in Encino, for the past six months. It's been good to be out in the Valley away from all the bullshit in the hood. Plus she does just about everything for me—cook, clean, fuck me when I wanna be fucked, and shell out the cash like it was water. But I swear it'd be nice to have some black pussy every once in a while. That white shit is cool when you first get it, but nothing compares to a sister with a big butt and big, juicy lips. Screwing Kelly is like screwing a pole sometimes. She's always on some kinda diet, and I swear if she puts one more plate of salad or tofu on the dinner table I'm gon' throw that shit. I need me a sister. Somebody with some meat on her body and who knows how to cook real food like fried chicken, macaroni and cheese, corn bread, and collard greens.

But I guess I can't complain too much. Kelly's been footing the bill ever since I quit my five-dollar-an-hour job as a runner for Perkins' Construction Company. I couldn't concentrate on writing lyrics and hold down a job at the same time. And besides my black ass is dark enough without baking for eight hours a day out in the hot sun. Ever since I shaved all the hair off my head it seems I can't get no kinda break from the sun. I would let it grow back, but Kelly likes it too much. And now that I let my goatee grow in, she been all over me. I guess I'll keep everything the way it is. It's the least I can do for her.

I wish Rich would follow my lead and cut that trifling Jheri Curl off, but I guess that's asking a little bit too much. He had that curl ever since the day I first met him. But I guess I do love the little ugly mothafucka. Hell, I owe my life to him.

If the three of us could just go back to acting like brothers, then we could take this rap thing to the top of the charts. But nothing's been the same since that night Rich got shot.

We was all hanging out at our spot, Chee Lin's liquor store over on Crenshaw and Florence. T-Bone had rolled up three fat-ass joints, the good shit—Indo—and Rich had just come out the store with two overflowing brown paper bags. One had a bag of barbecue skins, Louisiana hot sauce, three forty-ounces, and some Wrigley's. The other bag had the usual Friday night party flavor—a bottle of gin and a liter of orange-flavored Super Socco.

Everything was pretty quiet out on the streets for a Friday night, except for the prostitutes switching back and forth and a couple of bad-ass kids riding around on skates knowing good and well their mommas were gon' beat their asses when they got home 'cause the street lights were already on. It was almost too quiet, and if it wasn't for the funk of urine coming from the alleyway, the graffiti on the side of the store, the potholes dotting the main street, and that traffic light that had been busted for the past five weeks, I wouldn't have known where I was.

We had just come from a picnic some of our homeboys had given over at Baldwin Hills Park. We threw down on some serious ribs and hot links, potato salad, and corn on the cob. I musta kicked Rich and T-Bone's asses about a hundred times in dominoes. Neither one of them fools can hang with me when it comes to some bones. Everything was chillin'—real chillin'. Then some fools from West Coast Brims rolled through in a candy apple red Cadillac. I don't know who them fools thought they were, rollin' up on us like that. We were about fifty deep, I mean all the Cross Street Gang was on hand, and of course everybody was strapped.

T-Bone was the first to recognize them Brims and when he did it was on. "Yo, man, ain't that them West Coast fools rollin' by?" he yelled. Everybody stopped what they were doing and took a look, then automatically reached for their terminators—.45s, 9s, Uzis, Glocks, Rich was even packing a sawed-off shotgun. All the girls took off running, dragging their babies and screaming like the world was about to come to an end.

T-Bone ran out into the middle of the street and started screaming, "What's up, fool? Y'all want some? Y'all want some!" But the Cadillac just kept on rollin'. I guess we had scared them off when all fifty of us stood along the curb with our pieces drawn and aimed. After they turned the corner I stuck my 9 back in the top of my pants and went back to the domino table. But T-Bone just kept standing in the street screaming. "Fuck them punk mothafuckas. They better recognize. This Cross Street hood. Cross Street, mothafuckas."

We boned out shortly after that. Everybody was all spooked and shit. The girls were all crying and scared that them West Coast fools were gon' come back and start shooting up everything. I picked me up another hot link and jumped in Rich's ride. This kinda shit always happened when the homies tried to get together and have a little fun.

T-Bone was still going off in the car as we drove to the liquor store. "We ought to roll over to the Westside and take them fools out, X," he kept saying. Finally, Rich just told him to shut the fuck up. "You all talk, T," Rich said. "What was yo scary-ass gon' do if them fools got out and started firing? Nothing. Not a damn thang."

"Both of y'all need to shut the fuck up," I said. "Just hurry up and get to the store so I can get me a drank." I was tired of hearing all that shit. There we were, three grown men still waiting for the chance to take another brother out. And for what? The set, the fucking Cross Street Gang? All that shit was getting pretty old. I didn't know about Rich and T-Bone, but I didn't want to be fifty years old and still shooting up brothers 'cause they had on the wrong color or lived in the wrong part of town. A nigga can't make no money like that.

By the time we got to the liquor store, everybody had calmed down. I was already feeling my body getting edgy from the mix of Super Socco, gin, and weed, and after a few minutes I had the munchies, big-time. Rich was sitting on the driver's side of his midnight blue Suzuki Samarai taking a forty to the head. Me and T-Bone were standing outside on the passenger side jammin' to the music coming from the Alpine pull-out Rich had just installed in his new ride. I think it was a cut from NWA—no, it musta been Eric B. and Rakim. I really don't remember, but whatever it was, it was funky. Anyway, we was all chillin' like villains in our blue dickeys, crisp white T-shirts, and white Puma tennis shoes with fat blue laces. We always dressed like O.G.'s on Friday night.

"Yo, man, I'm ready to roll," Rich said and started up the engine.

"You just ready to get home to that stupid bitch you got waiting on you at the crib," T-Bone said and took another toke off his joint.

For some reason, I was ready to go too. Something just didn't feel right, but I didn't know what it was. Then I saw that damn Cadillac stopped at the corner with the motor running. "Yo, T. Ain't that them same fools from the picnic?" I said, throwing down the bag of skins. My eyes fixated on the car as it began to move slowly toward us, but for the life of me, I could not move. "Yo, T, T, T-Bone!"

It all happened so fast, but at the time it seemed like everything was going in slow motion. The next thing I knew, gunshots fired and I heard the front windows of the liquor store smashing and falling to the ground. I looked over toward T-Bone, but all I could see was the back of his head as he ran behind the store and down the alley. I looked back toward the street and saw the red Cadillac with the back window down and a semi-automatic shotgun hanging out. By that time the car was almost directly in front of me, but I choked. I just could not move.

The next thing I remember was waking up at Martin Luther King Hospital in the middle of the hallway with all kinds of people walking past me, looking at me like I was some kinda freak. "What the hell is going on?" I asked, but was ignored. I finally took off one of my Pumas and threw it at the back of some cocky-looking black man in a white coat. "Would somebody tell me what the fuck is going on? Where the hell is Rich and T-Bone and why the fuck does my head feel like somebody's been using it to tear down buildings?"

"First of all you need to relax, young man," the guy in the white coat said. "You must have banged your head on the pavement really hard because you've been unconscious for at least the past forty-five minutes. Now I'm going to have a nurse bring you some painkillers, but you need to calm down and relax."

"Where the fuck are my homeboys? Where the fuck is Rich?"

"Look, son, I don't know who Rich is, but you were brought in with another young man by the name of Stacey Alexander."

"That's Rich, man."

"Well, Rich, as you call him, is in the operating room as we speak. He sustained six gunshot wounds to the spine, stomach, and chest areas. He's going to be in there for a good while, I believe."

"Naw, man. Naw, I gotta see my homie, man. Where he at?" I attempted to get up off the cot, but as soon as I sat up straight, I blacked out again. When I woke up the next time I was still laying on the cot, in the middle of the hallway, but I was joined by two other guys who were on cots on the opposite side of me.

"Fridays and Saturdays are always the busiest around here," some old white lady in a uniform and one of those stupid-looking paper hats said. "I call it drive-by night. That's all we get in here on the weekends. Young kids caught in cross fire, drug dealers shot up in a drug deal gone bad, and gang bangers. We don't have enough rooms for all these thugs, so we keep 'em out here. It's a crying shame."

The black man in the white coat walked by just as I was fully regaining consciousness. "Yo, man," I called out to him. "What's up with my home-boy? He a'ight?"

"Oh, I see you came back to us, huh?" He pulled out one of those mini flashlights and stuck it in front of my eyes. "How does your head feel now?"

"Man, forget about my head. What's up with Rich?"

"Well, Stacey is in ICU. He lost a lot of blood, but looks like he's gonna make it." I could tell he wasn't telling me everything. He took a deep breath and looked down at the floor. "Stacey, uh, Rich, may not be able to walk again. Right now he's paralyzed from the waist down, and I've seen enough of these cases to know that it's hardly ever reversible."

"Man, what the fuck you talkin' 'bout? That nigga can walk. Can't no bullet stop Rich. He gon' walk again, man. He gon' walk."

That was over six years ago, and look at Rich now. Stuck in a wheel-chair for the rest of his life. That coulda been me. After T-Bone ran away, Rich had run over and shielded my body from the bullets that West Coast fool had fired at me. I wonder if he regrets doing that shit now. I wonder if I would have done the same thing for him. One thing's for sure, I owe my life to that mothafucka, and for that, I love him.

"Hey, X. What time we gon' roll over to Black Tie tonight?" Rich asked me as Eyeisha pushed him up the ramp leading to the front porch of his rickety old house. From the outside the house looked like a piece of shit, but on the inside, it was pimped out. Pioneer stereo system, fifty-six-inch television, and a wet bar in the middle of the living room.

"I don't know, man. T-Bone said he gon' be there about nine."

"I didn't ask you nothing about T-Bone. I'm talking about me and you. T-Bone ain't nothing but a little scary punk. If we ever get onstage, he'll probably run off crying in the other direction."

I can't stand being in the middle of those two. They ain't gon' do nothing tonight but ignore each other or pass insults back and forth like little babies. How we gon' be a rap group if we can't even get along? If I didn't owe it to Rich, I'd drop both their asses and take my shit on the solo tip.

"Time to make some mo money," Rich said as his beeper sounded off. He pulled it from the pocket of his pants and checked the number. "Where'd you leave the cordless, Eyeisha?"

"It's in the bedroom. Want me to go get it?"

"Naw, I'll be right back after I go handle this business," he said and rolled himself into the house.

Aw, shit, here we go. Every time Rich turn his back, his bitch tries to work me over. That's one scandalous ho. If she only knew how stupid she looked, she'd give it up. I've tried to tell Rich about her in little ways, but he just don't catch on to nothing. One of these days I'm just gon' come right out and tell him that his woman's a tramp.

"Hey, X, you got a cigarette?" she said, switching her big butt across the front lawn toward me, knowing good and well I don't smoke.

"Naw, I ain't got no cigarette," I said and headed back past her toward the porch, until she caught me by the arm.

"Damn, you ain't gotta be so mean about it," she said, pulling me around to face her. "It's just that I needs me a Newport on a hot day like this." She ran her tongue over her top lip in a ridiculous effort to try to turn me on. "So what your fine ass wearing to the big, fancy party at Black Tie tonight?"

"I don't know, Eyeisha. I'm about to bone out and get ready," I said, trying to ease my way to the porch. "Where Rich put that DAT tape at?"

"It's right here, baby." She pointed at her oversized chest, and my stomach turned thinking of what her next move might be. I hope I don't have to tell this trick off and embarrass her today. "You want it?" she said, stepping closer to me.

"Look, girl, you better be glad I got some respect for my homeboy, or I'd . . ."

"Or you'd what, X? Take me home and stroke my body till I came all over your hand? You know you want it and I know that little white bitch you got can't do for you what I can. So stop playing around, you know how I feel about you."

I couldn't believe that skeezer. My homeboy, who she claims to love, is less than a hundred feet away and here she is trying to push up on me. Bitches. You can't trust 'em. "Look, you fat, stank, two-timin' . . ."

"Yo, X, I gotta go make a run," Rich said, wheeling himself out the front door. I guess he didn't hear or didn't want to hear what was going on between me and Eyeisha, 'cause all he did was roll down the ramp and throw a ring of keys at her. "I gotta go drop a stash off over in Century City, dude. Come on, Eyeisha, you driving."

"Where's the damn tape, man?" I asked.

"I got it right here in my pocket," he said, tapping the front of his pants leg.

Eyeisha looked at me and laughed, but at that moment, I didn't think shit was funny. "Just be back to pick me up at nine, dude. Late."

Rich was rollin' an Infiniti now, which made it easier for him to get in and out the car. Eyeisha helped him into the passenger side, then took his wheelchair and folded it up and put it in the trunk. She gave me a wink before getting in the car.

I walked over to my Impala that was parked across the far end of the lawn and squinted from the reflection that was bouncing off the Dayton rims I had polished earlier. Rich threw up the peace sign as they rolled off and Eyeisha blew me a kiss. Damn, I thought. After being that close to Eyeisha all day, Kelly's skinny ass was looking quite delicious right about now.

chapter three

business before pleasure

When Bobby Strong walked into a room, you knew you were in the presence of power. Everyone could feel it as he breezed down the corridor of Black Tie Records. He smiled his responses to the enthusiastic greetings he received from the receptionists and other executives as he made his way to his office suite.

"Afternoon, Bobby," his personal assistant said as he briefly stopped by her desk to pick up a file.

"Hey, Tish," he said, skimming through the papers as he walked into his office. Within seconds he was back at her desk. Embarrassment quivered his voice as he asked, "Have you seen this productivity report?"

"Yep. It's been a tough year, I guess," she said, trying to sound upbeat.

This has definitely *not* been my year, Bobby thought, as he flipped through the file once more.

"Don't worry. The next fiscal year is right around the corner. You'll do better, I'm sure. What's one bad year?" she said, handing him another file. "This one needs your signature, and I've put the sales and marketing reports on your desk, and—"

"What about Kirk Walker?" Bobby interrupted with a whisper and leaned down close to hear her answer. "Up or down?"

"What do you think?" she said, trying hard not to look him directly in the face.

Guess that means up, Bobby decided, and clenched his teeth.

"Don't even sweat him," Tish continued, still whispering. "He can't touch you. Everyone around here knows you're still *the* man," she said, anxiously tapping her pen against the desk. "So Kirk's had a few good months. You've had a few good years."

Bobby thought about it for a moment, then cracked a smile. She always knew the right thing to say to keep him motivated, but this time he wasn't buying it. He knew he'd been slacking up lately, and seeing the report only confirmed that notion. But Tish, the ever-faithful employee, wouldn't let him get down on himself.

"So what four of the acts Kirk is handling are up for American Music Awards. It's all beginner's luck. And so what the Calendar section did a big writeup on him. He's still nowhere near your league."

"I know, I know," Bobby said half-heartedly, but he wasn't convinced. He glanced at the clock on the wall and quickly tried to change the subject. "What are you still doing here?"

"I can't leave you like this, boss. All you're going to do is take that file and brood over it. But it's just one year. I know you can turn this around."

"I know, Tish, but I gave you the afternoon off. So go, I insist—I'll be fine."

"Are you sure?"

"See you at the party."

"Okay," she agreed hesitantly and began straightening up her desk. "Tell Sheryl to wear her dancing shoes. It's her turn to lead us in the Electric Slide."

"Did she call?" he asked hopefully.

"Nope," Tish said, locking her desk. "See ya later," she called over her shoulder as she headed down the hall.

"Oh, by the way. Did the boss call?" he yelled after her.

"No," she yelled back, then turned to look at him. "Sorry."

Damn, Bobby thought as he turned to enter his office. Mr. Timbers hadn't returned any of his calls all week. He must have seen this report, Bobby figured, and threw it down on top of the bar in the corner of the room. As he poured himself a shot of vodka, he could feel a headache creeping on. He rubbed his temples, then let out a deep sigh and took a sip of his drink. He moved over to his desk and sat his drink down next to the

Executive of the Year plaque Mr. Timbers had presented him with at last year's party. He wondered if he'd be getting any kind of recognition at all at tonight's affair. He quickly decided the answer was a definite hell no, but he hoped Tish would at least pick up an assistant's award. He knew that was a far-off hope as well. Assistants are only as good as their bosses, or at least that's the pretense Mr. Timbers always stood by.

He cradled his drink in his hand and thought back to last year's ceremony when Mr. Timbers presented him with the award for the fourth year in a row. That was the first time that Mr. Timbers admitted publicly that Bobby would someday replace him and take over the company. They stood before the crowded room much like father and son. Bobby remembered being so proud that night, but most of all he was amazed. Mr. Timbers often hinted privately to Bobby that he wanted him to be the new president of Black Tie Records, and it was no secret that he had been grooming Bobby for the position for years. But when Mr. Timbers handed Bobby that award and told everyone to "meet the next president of Black Tie Records," Bobby thought he was going to faint. Before that night it had just been their little secret. Now everyone else knew too.

Bobby felt so powerful standing in front of all those people. People who wished they were in his shoes. It had been obvious to everyone that Bobby was definitely the man. In fact they all looked upon him as a sort of teacher's pet. The exec that could do no wrong. The boy wonder. And he was all of those things. . . . Until this year—when everything began to fall apart.

"Knock, knock," a voice purred from the doorway.

Startled, Bobby jumped to his feet, almost spilling his drink, before he even recognized who was speaking to him. And when he did, he wished there was some kind of button underneath his desk that he could push to make her go away.

"Glad to see me?" Marilyn's voice echoed as she walked to his desk and leaned closer. She wore an ultra-tight spandex dress that would normally make any man stand up and take notice, but to Bobby it was just the same old thing.

In the position he was in, pretty young girls were at his beck and call day and night. He couldn't bring himself to count the number of times some woman wearing next to nothing would approach him with a tape and offer him all kinds of pleasures on the off chance that maybe, just maybe, he could make her a star. It was a part of the business. But Mr. Timbers had warned him early on that the gratification wasn't worth the sacrifice.

As he looked at Marilyn, trying so hard to ingratiate herself to him, he thought of his wife and how beautiful he expected her to look when he got home to her. He'd never cheated on her in the past, and he wasn't about to start now.

"So how'd you like it?" Marilyn asked, unaware that her come-ons were having little effect on Bobby.

"Like what?"

"The demo tape I gave you last week. Didn't you even listen to it?" she asked, obviously put off by the fact that her plan was not moving as smoothly as she'd expected.

Damn, he thought, feeling himself backed into a corner. He had indeed listened to the tape, at least as much of it as he could stand. It didn't take him long to conclude that she was just another wanna-be. "No," he lied, hoping she'd get fed up with his lack of enthusiasm and leave—forever.

But Marilyn was very persistent. "You promised you'd listen to it, Bobby," she said, lifting herself on top of his desk and crossing her long legs.

Bobby knew what he had promised and he didn't need her nagging to remind him. In fact he didn't need this at all. He had other problems, bigger problems. He grabbed the back of his neck and rotated his head from side to side.

"Here, let me get that," Marilyn insisted. She hopped down from the desk and strolled to the back of Bobby's chair and laid her hands on his shoulders. "Ooh, so much tension," she said, massaging her fingers into his flesh.

Bobby's first reaction was to show her to the door, but he couldn't deny it—the woman had the magic touch. She loosened his tie and gently lulled his head backward. "Now close your eyes and relax," she coaxed.

When he did, the only pictures that filled his mind were those of his two daughters, Tiffany and Brittany. He often thought of their smiling faces when he was completely relaxed and free from distractions. He'd do just about anything for those two girls, and although he never spent as much time with them as he would like, he always made sure they had everything they even thought about wanting. Tiffany was a senior in high school and the light of her father's eyes. He had just spent over three thousand dollars on a prom dress he had had made especially for her by Amy Price, one of the hottest designers in L.A., who specialized in elegant dresses with a touch of African flair. Tiffany had been so excited and appreciative when he presented her with the gown that he forked over another two thousand for a limo and a professional photographer to follow her and her date around for the evening and capture all the festivities on videotape. He wished he had been home that night to see his oldest daughter off on the most important evening of her young life, but a last-minute business trip to Atlanta took precedence. It was an absence he would always regret, but these days business always came first.

Brittany was his little angel and she could do no wrong in Bobby's eyes. He doted on her as if she were a little doll. Her clothing allowance was almost as much as her mother's, which Sheryl always complained about. "A nine-year-old doesn't need that many clothes, Bobby," she always reminded him. Deep down he knew that was true. He just wanted to make sure his girls knew their daddy loved them. That's something that Bobby never had time to truly find out as a child. By the age of ten, he was already a grown man.

Bobby was born and raised in Tyler, Texas, where life was peaceful, days were long, and nights were longer. It was a simple life, an ideal life—until the day his mother and father died. Their bodies were found on the back porch of their country house the day before Bobby's tenth birthday. The police labeled the deaths a murder-suicide, which didn't surprise Bobby. He had listened to enough of their late-night arguments and fist-fights to know that one of them would eventually wind up dead. He was just glad they died together. That way he wouldn't be left with the survivor.

Bobby was sent to stay with his grandmother after his parents' deaths, and for the longest time, almost four years, he never spoke a word. Everybody thought he was crazy and took pity on the little boy who had experienced too much living to be so young. He would sit in his room for hours at night, listening to music and crying lonely tears for what he had lost. The only time he seemed a little happy was on Saturday afternoons, when *Soul Train* came on television. For an hour he would sit in the front room of his grandmother's house, bobbing his head and trying to imitate the fancy footwork of all the dancers.

One Saturday when he could finally take it no more, much to his surprise and his grandmother's as well, he found himself speaking again. He stood up in the middle of the front room, in complete awe of Don Cornelius's perfectly coiffed Afro, and said, "We wish you love, peace, and souuul!" From then on, he was back to normal, although his grandmother thought it strange for a kid Bobby's age to stay in the house all day and night doing nothing but spinning 45s on that old record player he kept in his room.

It was natural to Bobby, though. He had been a lover of music ever since the first day he saw his mother standing in the front row of the choir at the neighborhood church. She sang almost as if in a trance about God and laying burdens down and bridges and troubled waters. He couldn't stand gospel music anymore, though. It reminded him too much of what he'd lost—a mother, a father, stability. Still, he liked the way all the hot rhythm-and-blues acts added a certain gospel flavor to their sound.

He always knew he wanted to be a music star just like the ones he saw on television, and he'd practice his dance moves for hours each day. His bed would be the stage and the floor was a sprawling audience. With his imaginary mic in hand, he'd jump from the bed to his knees while the imaginary girls went wild, grabbing their cheeks as tears of awe rolled down their faces. It was a classic James Brown moment.

There were only two things holding him back from being the world's next superstar. Number one, Bobby couldn't sing, and two, Bobby didn't *know* he couldn't sing. As a matter of fact, it wasn't until the senior class talent show at his high school that he found out he might never have what it takes to win a Grammy.

In the weeks prior to the talent show, he practiced his routine day and night. His grandmother even bought him a nice new suit for the occasion—light blue, with a sharp ruffled collar down the middle. He definitely had the clothes.

"You sound so sweet," his grandmother would tell him. "Now do that move I like," she'd say, clapping her hands with excitement. And there Bobby would go, sliding across the kitchen floor on his knees, gripping his imaginary mic as his grandmother watched on with pride. He definitely had the moves.

The talent show was on a Friday after school and before it began, all the contestants gathered backstage to anxiously await their turn to perform. Bobby stood alone in a corner, silently moving his lips and rehearsing his moves over and over again in his head. Everyone else was grouped together near the curtain so they could get a good peek at the audience and the person onstage. There were six acts altogether and Bobby was the last scheduled to appear. Act one was an awful a cappella rendition of a gospel song, which Bobby ignored. Act two was a tap dancer, but he got booed off the stage when the audience noticed he was wearing sneakers instead of tap shoes. Acts three and four were too scared to go on after they saw the way the audience responded to the tap dancer, and act five, though brave enough to take the stage, threw up halfway through her poetry reading.

Bobby was up next. He hadn't paid much attention to the acts that went before him, but when he reached center stage he could feel the tension in the audience. "Go 'head on, baby," he heard his grandmother scream from the corner of the auditorium. He nodded in the direction of her voice, then turned his back to the audience and waited for his cue. He listened for the first beat of the music, all the while silently preparing himself. *Just relax, relax, relax.* When the beat came he gave himself a countdown . . . *And five, six, seven, eight—turn to the crowd, kick and pause. And two, three, four—shimmy to the side and front and back. And six, seven, eight—run—and slide—and knees, and, six, seven, eight.* The crowd was going crazy at this point. The guys were clapping, the girls were cheering. *And wiggle up, and pause, and wait for beat and . . . SING! . . .*

Grandmother treated him to an ice cream sundae that evening, but Bobby didn't even touch it.

"Don't you mind them ignorant kids, you hear me? What they know about good singing?" she insisted as she stood at the kitchen sink and prepared a bucket of dishwater. Bobby sat silently at the table, reliving the humiliation of being booed off the stage. He definitely had the moves, he thought—*But what did I have to go opening my mouth to sing for?*

"That's all right, baby," his grandmother continued. "You sounded good to me."

"Nothing I do ever turns out right," Bobby said, wiping tears from his eyes and waiting for his grandmother to further console him. "Nothing ever, ever, turns out right for me," he repeated and waited for her response. "I mean I'm a good singer, right? You think so, don't you, Grand? Grand?"

"Hmm, what?" she said, turning around to him. "Did you say something, baby?" she asked, turning up her hearing aid.

"No. Nothing, Grand."

Bobby went to his room and put on a James Brown 45, then lay across his bed. "The only person who thinks I can sing is Grand, and she can't even hear straight," he said and rolled over on his back. He stared up at the ceiling, devastated that his dream of becoming a singer had turned into a nightmare. His first instinct was to block out the world like he'd done after his parents died, but something deep down inside told him his music days were not over.

Grand stayed up all night worrying about her grandson. She thought for sure he was having a relapse and that he would take to silence again. But her fears were put to rest the next afternoon when he came into the front room and turned on *Soul Train.* She watched as he glided across the floor along with the dancers on the screen, and tears came to her eyes as he sang off-key along with the Four Tops. "That's right, baby," she said, swaying with him. "You just keep on doing your thang and one day you're gonna make it."

Bobby's love of music continued to grow, though he finally resigned himself to the fact that he simply was not musically inclined. But what he lacked in talent he made up for in musical savvy. Bobby listened to all types of music, everything from Muddy Waters to Ike and Tina Turner, and when he heard a song for the first time, he could tell instantly if it was going to be a chart buster or a flop. His intuition never failed him.

By the time he started his first semester at Tyler Junior College, he knew he wanted to be on the business end of the music industry, but he didn't know how to get his dream off the ground. The tiny town where he lived had no radio station, and all the music was transmitted from Dallas–Fort Worth or Houston, which made radio reception in the area dismal. Needless to say, there were no record companies where he could apply for internships, and the only local DJ that played good music operated out of a little shack off the turnpike where no one under twenty-one was allowed entrance.

Still, he didn't give up his dream. He knew he had to leave Tyler if he ever wanted to make it in the business, but he had neither the money nor the courage to make such a drastic change in his life.

Later that year, Tyler Junior College held its annual scholarship conference for students who wanted to continue their education after two years. Bobby attended, thinking he'd apply to nearby Texas Southern University, but instead he came across the opportunity of a lifetime. A representative from the University of Southern California was there promoting the school and life in the big city, and Bobby fell for the idea like a speed bump in the middle of a hallway. That was the opportunity he'd been waiting for. What better place to get started in the music industry than L.A.? At the time USC was making a big push to get minority students on its enrollment list, and the representative assured Bobby that his GPA and academic history were up to par with the university's standards. All that was left to do was to fill out the application and turn it in.

And that's exactly what he did. He'd finally found a way to make his dream come true, but still he was afraid. What if he did get accepted? He'd have to move all the way to California. Alone. What about Grand? Who would take care of her if he moved all the way to California? Who would take care of him?

It didn't take Bobby long to find out the answers to his questions. Grand died of a stroke the following summer and there he was, barely twenty years old, with no family, no money, no job, no nothing. Once again his life had fallen apart.

The funeral was a small event put on by some of the members of the local church who took pity on him and decided to chip in a few dollars and give his grandmother a proper burial. But that was of no consequence to Bobby. He was alone. Again. And this time there was no one around to save him.

A week later, he received his acceptance letter from USC. Until then Bobby had thought his life was over, but suddenly, almost miraculously, he'd been given another chance. It was as if Grand was looking down on him and smiling. As he read the letter all he could hear were his grandmother's words: "You just keep doing your thang and one day you're gonna make it."

With the one hundred and fifty dollars his grandmother had left to him in a shoe box underneath her bed, Bobby was on his way out west. Though he never returned to Tyler, he refused to ever sell his grandmother's house. He couldn't bring himself to close the door on the last relative and friend he had in the world.

It was a typical beautiful day when he arrived in Los Angeles, and the moment he stepped foot off the bus, he knew it was his kind of place. The sun shone every day, even in winter, he had heard. It was like an open field of opportunity and no place was better, he thought, for breaking into the music business. His first week in town, he applied for general relief so he could get food stamps to tide him over until his financial aid went through, and in the meantime, he slept at the Greyhound bus terminal until he was assigned a dorm room on campus.

Bobby majored in business administration and took a few classes in marketing his first year at USC, none of which seemed to be preparing him for a career in the music industry. But just when he had begun to wonder if he had made the right choice by coming to L.A., he met Sheryl.

Sheryl had that California born-and-bred look, mixed with the old-fashioned southern politeness that he had grown accustomed to. She wasn't rich or uppity like most of the black students that had been lucky enough to make it to USC, and best of all, she had goals, a dream of becoming an attorney and making something of herself. He hadn't found that in the other girls he met at all the fraternity parties and nightclubs around Los Angeles. He jumped at the chance to be with her, which wasn't too complicated considering he had all the attributes and personality that any girl in her right mind could ever dream of wanting. Not to mention his tall, dark, and lovely features that made him the talk of the campus among both the black and white sororities.

Sheryl was the first girl Bobby loved. The first he'd ever been with, so when she turned up pregnant less than a year after they met, he knew instantly that he had to marry her—and he did. Two months after saying "I do," he became the father of a baby girl, and for the first time he realized that his life was moving too fast, but he couldn't put on the brakes. He not only had a wife to provide for but a newborn as well. It wasn't exactly the way he had expected his life to turn out in California, but he knew he had a responsibility to his family, and besides, for the first time in his life he was truly happy. The only thing left for him to do was drop out of school and get a job.

His first job was at Mack's Shack, a small restaurant that had only been in business a little over a year. It was the only soul food kitchen around, so it was always packed. On Fish Fridays the line for a table would lead all the way out the front door and around the corner. The hole-in-the-wall steadily grew in popularity and soon began attracting all sorts of black professionals and business people in search of a good southern-cooked meal.

Mitch Timbers, the president of Black Tie Records, was a faithful patron on Fish Fridays and often came in ordering fifty pounds of fried catfish with all the fixings to be sent over to his Century City office for his employees. "Black people are more productive on a full stomach," he'd say. Bobby knew he was his kind of man.

"Say, Mr. Timbers," Bobby said one Friday as he took his order. It had taken two months for Bobby to conjure up the nerve to actually talk to the man. He had seen his face in several articles he'd read over the years about the music industry and had even sent him his résumé while he was at USC. He couldn't believe that he was actually about to have a conversation with him, but he knew it was now or never. "I don't want to take up too much of your time, but I was just wondering. What's a brother gotta do to get a foot in the door at Black Tie Records?"

Mr. Timbers was taken aback by Bobby's straightforwardness. He had been coming in for months and never before had Bobby said much more to him than "May I take your order?" and "Have a nice day." Still, he could tell Bobby had a higher goal than waiting tables at a little hole-in-the-wall like Mack's Shack for the rest of his life. "Why you asking, son?

You know something about the business, or you just interested because you think it's an easy way to get rich?"

"No, no, Mr. Timbers. That's not what I'm about at all." To be true, he definitely needed the money but what he was interested in most was making something of himself. He hadn't come all the way from Texas to go home smelling like fish and grease every night. "Just give me a few minutes, Mr. Timbers. Let me explain."

Bobby sat and talked to Mr. Timbers for over an hour. He explained his goals, his life, and rattled off the usual clichés about how much of a hard worker he was and how he wanted to be associated with a fine organization such as Black Tie Records. But what impressed Mr. Timbers the most was that Bobby had actually done his homework. He knew the ins and outs of Black Tie Records and even offered some suggestions that could possibly change the whole scope of the company and make it even more successful.

Mr. Timbers knew all this talk was just that—talk. Still, he had to give Bobby credit for his confidence and ambition, and since he could see that Bobby was genuinely interested in the business, he gave him a chance. He hired him on as an intern, doing no more than answering phones and sorting mail, and vowed to fire him at the drop of a hat if he was ever late or did anything to compromise the success of the business.

Bobby didn't let him down. He quickly advanced from phones and mail to working in the artist-and-repertoire department, where he first earned the respect of Mr. Timbers. His uncanny ability to spot new and unique talent and artists astounded even the senior A&R reps and soon got him promoted to the department's VP position, where he single-handedly discovered over seven new acts that eventually went on to become major moneymakers for Black Tie Records.

The word around Black Tie was that Bobby was a boy wonder. And this did not go unnoticed by Mr. Timbers, who eventually took Bobby under his wing with plans of grooming him into one of the major company players. Bobby's accomplishments were not overlooked by his colleagues either, some of whom took offense at his rapid climb up the success ladder.

But none of the jealousy could stop Bobby. Within five years, a short time considering Bobby had no formal training in the music industry, Mr. Timbers advanced him to the Promotions department, and inside of another year and a half, Bobby was sitting pretty in his own private office in Century City as Vice President of Promotions.

Aside from Mr. Timbers himself and a few lawyers, Bobby Strong was the most important executive at Black Tie Records. He was the man calling the shots. He made all the critical decisions that could make or break an artist and their music. He decided which acts ended up on the company's priority list, which records would be advertised, and which artists would get that all-important company endorsement that could push them over the top and on to *Billboard*'s charts. For that reason everyone bowed down to him. Everyone from artists and musicians to his colleagues and the company lawyers. It didn't hurt that he was a personal friend of Mr. Timbers, who allowed him the right to run his department in whatever way he saw fit. And Bobby took full advantage of his status within the company. He was fair and tactful, yet he ruled with a firm hand, which earned him much respect from his colleagues. Whenever Bobby introduced a new or daring idea, everyone would fight among themselves for the opportunity to work with him. They all knew that everything he touched turned to gold, but they also knew that he expected the best effort from his team. You either went along with his program, or got the hell out of Dodge, because Bobby was not one to put up with incompetence. It was very rare for Bobby to have to take a hard stance, but he did what he had to do to keep his department on track. One word from his lips to Mr. Timbers' ears could have a person's office cleared out within an hour.

Bobby had been holding his position as second in command for the past ten years and was the sole reason Black Tie Records had become the foremost arena for black music in the United States and around the world. Because of Bobby, the company was able to branch out into new fields in addition to its long held reputation as a rhythm-and-blues haven. He helped cultivate black opera singers and brought to the musical forefront several long forgotten blues acts and helped them get their due attention, not to mention the royalty money some of them had been scammed out of by other companies. His major accomplishment and the most lucrative was his concentration on cultivating a slew of rap groups who proved to be the wave of the future and brought millions of dollars into the company.

Mr. Timbers had been leery of Bobby's idea to promote rap in the beginning. He thought the rap craze was just a fad that would eventually fade, but much to his surprise, he found rap music was here to stay. Bobby had known that for years and although he wasn't crazy about all the controversy the music brought with it, he promoted it with a vengeance.

When Bobby received the Executive of the Year Award last year, he knew it was due to the inroads he had made in the rap field. Mr. Timbers praised him for his vision and ability to spot the changing trends in the industry, and with that award, Bobby gained the confidence to delve even deeper into rap music. Over the past three years, he had been observing the changes in the rap field. The music was getting harder, the artists more street-oriented. It was the beginning of the gangsta rap craze, a genre that Bobby had promised Mr. Timbers the company would not get involved in, though it was getting harder for Bobby to resist. Though he and Mr. Timbers had several long discussions on the topic, he couldn't convince Mr. Timbers of the lucrativeness of gangsta rap. But it was selling like mad and Bobby wanted a piece of the pie. Since Mr. Timbers had praised his keen foresight and ability to predict changes in music in the past, Bobby thought it would make good business sense to give the go-ahead to a new gangsta rapper named Toby-T, whom he had had his eye on ever since he first considered entering the gangsta rap genre. By the time Mr. Timbers had gotten wind of this new rapper, his album was about to be released in stores.

Needless to say, Mr. Timbers was furious that Bobby had broken his promise and he let him know just that. Bobby would never forget the way Mr. Timbers stormed through his office when he found out about Toby-T. He'd never seen his boss so angry, nor had his anger ever been directed at him.

"You dare go behind my back after I specifically told you I didn't want to have anything to do with this gangsta rap business?" he had said. "Rap is one thing, but this gangsta rap is totally different. Our kids don't need any more negative influences than what they've already got! Gangsta rap is an image I refuse to have this company linked with."

"I know what you said, sir. But what's done is done," Bobby said, nonchalantly. "The record will be out in less than a week," he explained. "Have I ever been wrong in the past?"

"Have you forgotten who you work for?" Mr. Timbers asked, furious.

"No sir, but I'm telling you. This venture, like all the others, will simply add another platinum record to the walls of Black Tie. Trust me."

Bobby's arrogance only enraged Mr. Timbers more. "It damn well better," Mr. Timbers added, not knowing how to handle all the fury that was brewing inside him. "I'd hate to think what will happen to you if it doesn't."

A week later, it became evident that Bobby's confidence wasn't enough to make Toby-T a success. His strategy backfired on him and sent Black Tie Records into a seemingly unstoppable nosedive. Toby-T, to whom he'd allotted much time and promotional dollars, wound up in jail facing a rape conviction for allegedly attacking one of his female background dancers, an allegation that eventually led to five years' imprisonment. The incident was coined the Toby Tragedy, and was on the cover of every paper and trade magazine in the industry. It cost Black Tie Records hundreds of thousands of dollars in canceled advertisements and concerts, not to mention public embarrassment—something Mr. Timbers found more deplorable than anything else.

The media dragged the incident on for months and it became apparent that the incident was one Bobby would never be able to live down and certainly one Mr. Timbers would never forget. To this day, he still found himself trying to bounce back and regain the confidence of Mr. Timbers and his rightful status in the company. That one slipup, Bobby's only slipup, turned his world upside-down. No longer was he considered an icon of success to the younger executives who once looked up to him. He was now more symbolic of sloppiness. A monumental fuck-up on the highest level.

And to make matters worse, a new breed of young execs was pouring into the company. If the Toby Tragedy had taken place five years ago it may not have been such a fatal blow. Back then Bobby was all Black Tie Records had. Now, it seemed that everything he did was overshadowed. There always seemed to be some bright new kid with a better idea, a more lucrative contract, or an inside scoop. It had been hard for Bobby to compete with the new breed of talented business people pushing their way to the top positions at Black Tie. In a word, he was stagnated, and for Bobby Strong, stagnation was just one step before death.

There was only one way for him to pull himself out of the rut he found himself in, and that was to show Mr. Timbers and everyone else that he still had what it took. He needed a new idea, a brilliant idea, one that would jump-start his career again. It amazed him how a single mistake and a few unproductive months could almost completely wipe out his accomplishments at Black Tie Records. He was no longer the boy wonder or Mr. Timbers' prodigy, and unless he took action now, he was on his way out.

Marilyn gave Bobby one last squeeze on his shoulders, then walked over to the office door and turned the lock. "You still have my demo tape, don't you?" she cooed.

Talk about a one-track mind. If she only knew how utterly terrible she sounded on that tape, she'd realize the mootness of that point and go on with her life, he thought, trying to block out her presence and concentrate on what he needed to do to regain control of his career.

What he needed was someone with raw, untapped talent, he decided, passing Marilyn to get to his entertainment console. He flipped on the radio as Whitney Houston roared from the speakers that were strategically placed around the office to produce the best overall sound. That's what I need, he thought, snapping his fingers. That's what Black Tie needs—another Whitney, a Michael Jackson even. A megastar. Black Tie Records was the number-one producer of black music, but none of the acts was huge like, say, a Barbra Streisand. And aside from a few popular personalities, none of the acts generated a substantial cross-over audience or could fill a stadium overseas. The company dealt mainly with top-of-the-line R&B and rap artists who gained it all sorts of notoriety in the black communities across America, but a megastar could send the company over the top.

Just one, Bobby thought, hardly paying attention to Marilyn as she rambled on about her tape. Just one all-star sensation who had enough grit to please the black audience and enough charisma to pull in the white audience. If he could make that happen he would once again be back on top.

Bobby sat down on the oversized leather chair behind his desk, staring blankly out the window as his mind went to work on turning his idea into a reality.

"Bobby," Marilyn cooed. "Whatcha thinking about, baby?"

Bobby didn't answer. He was too engrossed by the ticking of his brain.

"Are you thinking about me?" she asked, swaying in front of him.

Bobby still didn't answer. His mind was cluttered, trying to figure out who he could cultivate his plan around. It had to be a woman, he thought. Someone with model looks and an all-American style, but someone who could sing—really sing. None of the artists on the priority list had those qualities. If they had, they'd already be megastars. No, Bobby wanted someone new. Someone he could mold and groom in the exact way he wanted. Someone who hadn't already been tainted by the industry. He needed young blood.

Just as his mental wheels began to spin, the phone rang. Mechanically, he reached for it and said, "Strong here."

"Bobby?" Sheryl said on the other end of the line.

"Hey, babe," he said and shot Marilyn a stifling look.

"Brittany's coming down with the flu. I don't think I'll be able to make it to the party tonight."

"Is my angel okay?" he asked, more concerned with his daughter than with the thought of having to go solo to the party that evening.

"She's all right. Just a little vomiting, that's all. When are you going to be home? I need to talk to you before you go out tonight. It's very important," she said sternly.

More bitching, Bobby figured. Before he'd left home that morning they were already at each other's throats. Something about toothpaste and leaving the toilet seat up, he remembered. He'd hoped she would have long forgotten about that by now, but apparently she hadn't. Sheryl could be pretty stubborn when she wanted to.

"I'll be on my way in about thirty minutes. No, make it an hour," he said, feeling tension once again creeping over his body.

Sheryl started to add something, but he quickly hung up the receiver. He didn't want to argue anymore. Maybe a dozen roses would do her some good, he decided, and made a mental note to pick up some on the way home. But he knew that wouldn't change things. Ever since he had started having trouble at work this year, their relationship had suffered. He had become so wrapped up in his own problems that he didn't have the time or energy to connect with his wife. He kept telling himself things would get better, but he knew that wouldn't be true until he got his professional life in order. In the meantime, Sheryl just stood by and waited. He knew she had been suffering, but there was nothing he could do. Feeling helpless, Bobby picked up the phone, dialed, listened for the beep, then entered a phone number. He could feel the tension in his neck mounting again as he hung up the receiver and waited.

Marilyn knew she was being ignored and didn't like it one bit. In a last-ditch effort to grab his attention, she stood herself in the middle of the room and began to undress, as if she were in her own private boudoir.

"What the fuck," Bobby questioned just as the phone rang again. He picked it up, keeping his eyes glued to Marilyn's exhibition.

"You got some stuff for me?" he asked, only slightly distracted by Marilyn's striptease. "Good, drop it by. I'll wait for you in the parking lot in about thirty minutes," he said and hung up again.

By then, Marilyn was directly before him, wearing nothing more than a pair of high-heeled pumps. "You like?"

"No, and you need to get out of here," he said, racing around his desk to retrieve the dress she had left lying in the middle of the floor. "I'm already taken," he said and tossed her dress across his desk.

"I don't mind sharing," Marilyn said, yanking the dress from the air.

"Yeah, well, my wife's greedy."

"But I was just getting to the good part."

"No, you were just about to struggle back into that dress, unlock the door, and forget about what just happened here." Bobby opened his briefcase and piled in a stack of papers, then looked back up at Marilyn, who was standing stiffly behind his desk. "Please, Marilyn. I'm just not that type of man."

"Every man is that type of man," she said, twisting her body from side to side until the dress was back on. She snatched up her purse from the sofa table and huffed off toward the door. "Are you going to listen to my tape, or not?"

"Cross my heart," he said and watched her disappear behind the door.

After she left, Bobby grabbed his jacket and tie and threw them over his shoulder in a rush. If Sheryl wanted to talk to him he had to prepare himself first. He hurried out of his office and put on his tie and jacket while he waited for the elevator to arrive. When he reached the parking lot, he walked over to his Range Rover, got in, then sat in silence sucking on a piece of chocolate candy he had taken from his pocket. A blue Infiniti pulled up next to him shortly after, and he rolled down his window and handed over two hundred dollars to the man on the passenger's side. He took the plastic bag the man offered and rolled his window back up. This ought to be enough to help me handle whatever bullshit Sheryl is about to throw in my face, he thought, and started the engine. Suddenly it hit him as he pulled out of his parking space. Is this the type of man I am?

chapter four

the schmooze

"Girl, I thought we'd never get here tonight," Dakota said to me as we pulled into the parking lot of Black Tie Records. The street out front was Avenue of the Stars and I scanned it, trying to catch a glimpse of some famous people, but came up empty. Avenue of the Stars is such a boring street, so undeserving of its name. Dakota and I were both a little nervous. Me, because all my hopes and dreams seemed so untouchable, like a cookie jar Daddy stuck on top of the refrigerator—too far for me to reach. Dakota was nervous just because that's the way she always gets when faced with the temptation of a room full of rich, successful, single or unhappily married men. She'd have no trouble turning a few heads in that red palazzo suit she had on. I figured she must have put a cellophane on her hair earlier because it was shining brighter than those diamond studs she had in her ears. I was royally upset with my hair. It was sitting on top of my head like a helmet. I had been so nervous getting dressed that I started sweating like a pig and it only takes two drops of moisture to turn my nappy hair into a bouffant.

"Where's the tape, Jazz?" she asked for what seemed like the hundredth time that night. Finally, I just reached inside my purse, took it out, and tossed it in her lap. I knew she wouldn't be satisfied until she had it in her hot little hand. That way she could be in control.

I was in my form-fitting black velvet dress that I had hidden in

Dakota's closet since I bought it two months ago. I hid all my tight, low-cut party dresses that I'd buy when I caught them on sale at the store over at Dakota's house. I'd wait till they went on sale as low as they would go, then snatch them up and apply my employee's discount, which was another 20 percent off, and walk out of the store with a hundred-dollar dress for a mere forty dollars. But I could never take them home. Who knew when Daddy would go rummaging through my closet? I sure didn't.

"Guess who called me earlier?" Dakota asked, turning off the engine and lighting up a Newport.

"Who?" I said, rolling my window down and hoping the stench of that cigarette wouldn't linger in my dress. I wasn't about to walk up to some producer or artist's representative smelling like an ashtray. A singer who smokes? They'd laugh in my face.

"Craig Johnson," she said and looked at me with a smile on her face like she knew some deep dark secret.

"My Craig?" I said, then thought how stupid that question sounded since I hadn't even seen or heard from him in over a year.

"Yes, honey. *Your* Craig, and he's gonna be in the house tonight," she said and started dancing in her seat. "Craig's in the house. I said Craig's in the house."

"Humph," I grunted, thinking of the last time I had seen him. He picked me up from school, looking as good as he wanted to look, and took me to a coffeehouse on Westwood Boulevard. Craig looked as handsome as ever, but I didn't let him know that. He thought he looked good enough for the both of us, and anyway, I was a little p.o.'d at him because he hadn't called me in over three weeks. I guess I shouldn't have been too mad. I mean, it wasn't like he was my man or anything. We'd known each other for eight years but the most we had ever done was go out—maybe a dozen times. And we'd kissed a few times too; just good night pecks though, nothing serious. Still, Craig was the man of my dreams. Dakota said I should make the first move, tear off his clothes, and tackle him one night out of the blue. "If you see what you want, pounce on it. Hell, that's what I do, honey."

But that wasn't my style. I have to admit, Daddy raised me right and I wasn't in the practice of being so aggressive. If Craig wanted me, he'd have to make the first move, and the second, and the third, then maybe I'd give him a little piece. Still, I must confess, I was most anxious to find out if the fling I had with Boston when I was twenty-one was as good as it was gonna get.

That afternoon at the coffeehouse, I realized why he had never tried anything with me. At first I thought he was still hung up on our age difference, but after a while I started to think the boy was gay or something. I mean, I'm not conceited or anything, but whenever Craig and I went out on a date, I made sure I was looking good. I knew he loved my red hair, so whenever I saw him, which was only once in a blue moon, I'd pay to get it done. That was quite a feat for me because I had been doing my own hair ever since I was ten. Shoot, why should I pay some slow, gossip-talking, soap opera–watching, mad woman with a hot comb, when I can do just as good a job in the comfort of my own kitchen? And most beauticians wear extensions anyway. I don't know, maybe it's just me, but I'm not paying anybody to fix my hair if they have to hide their own coif behind a weave. But for Craig, I'd break down and get my hair done professionally. I catered to that angel's every desire. I also made it a point never to curse around him. That's a bad habit I picked up from Dakota with her filthy mouth and it was a hard one to break. I couldn't just quit cold turkey though, so ever since I decided to stop, I've been making up my own set of curse words. Sometimes I get carried away and slip in a fuck or a shit here and there. Heck, sometimes the only word that can truly express the way you feel is profane, but I made sure Craig never heard me slip up.

"I don't know where these young, beautiful girls get these filthy mouths," he said to me once. "Yeah, it's a fu—I mean, it's a gosh darn shame, isn't it?" I answered.

But after what he told me that afternoon in the coffeehouse, I don't think there was one curse word I left unsaid. He had the nerve to tell me he had gotten engaged. Engaged! For a second there, I had actually tried to remember when he had gotten down on his knees and proposed to me, then I remembered that he never had.

I played it cool at first and asked him who the lucky girl was. It was some female officer named Maurine he worked with and had been dating for the past eight years—the same time he had been dating me.

"She's really nice. I bet you'd even like her," he said, with his eyes looking like they were gonna pop out of his head.

"Like her?" I said and felt my neck start to twist and turn uncontrollably. "Fuck her and fuck you too, Craig." I never felt so humiliated in all my life. Here was the man I loved, the man I told the Almighty Himself that I was going to marry, telling me he was about to marry someone else. Sure, we'd only been out a few times, but they were special times. Craig was the only guy who I could hold a decent conversation with, without having to stop and explain everything I said. Even the guys in my classes at college couldn't talk on world events or recite verses from Nikki Giovanni or e. e. cummings, and half of them didn't even know what Kwanzaa was, or if you asked them, thought it was some sort of African headdress.

"You asshole!" I screamed so loudly that the man behind the cash register turned and looked in our direction. "You're getting married to some tramp that you've been dating at the same time you've been dating me? Oh, that's good, Craig. Real classic. And you sit here and tell me this shit like I'm supposed to give you a pat on the back? Well, you better think again. So tell me, Craig, if you're so in love, then why are you with me?"

"Look, Jazmine. I thought we were friends. You're acting like we had some hot, heavy romance or something. I'm here with you because I wanted to share my good news with you personally. Now I wish I had never come."

"Well, I wish you had never come too, Craig," I said, on the verge of crying. He acted like I was just some love-struck kid—young, dumb, and full of cum. Hadn't he ever wanted me the way I'd wanted him? Hadn't he ever dreamed about me late at night and wondered how I'd feel lying next to him? Hadn't he ever prayed to God that I'd be the one he'd spend the rest of his life with? From the look on his face, I guessed not. I got up from the table, feeling the urge to somehow regain my pride. "You thought we were just friends, huh? Well, I don't need any stupid, arrogant, jackass friends like you, mister," I said and walked away. I knew I sounded stupid, but that was the best line I could come up with at the time. Besides, my heart had just been split in two, and although I tried like hell, I couldn't keep the tears from falling.

The guy behind the cash register stared at me as I walked toward the exit, wiping my eyes with the back of my hand. I stopped at the counter in front of him and grabbed two handfuls of napkins. "What the fuck are you looking at?" I said, and wiped the tears that had begun to roll down to my chin. "Mind your own flipping business," I added, and threw a wad of damp napkins in his face. I walked out feeling much better after that, until I saw Craig's Mustang parked at the curb and realized that I'd never be sitting in the passenger's seat again.

"**Put** out that damn cigarette, Dakota. I've got a career to start tonight."

"Don't you wanna know what Craig said?"

"No, I don't want to know what that mickey-fickey said. I don't even want to think about him tonight. And if I see him, I'm turning and walking in the other direction and you better do the same."

Dakota and I had a pact like that. If one of us was mad at somebody the other had to be mad too. It was sort of like our sisterly responsibility to each other. Two bitches are always better than one, especially when we join forces against the opposite species. I wasn't about to let Craig get to me. I had too much at stake to let myself get all distracted on things that had nothing to do with my ultimate purpose, which was to network. "Network, network, network," I said to myself as I got out of the car. Dakota pressed down the wrinkles in her jacket, then shot me a look I knew would be coming. It's that same look she always shoots me when she knows I'm nervous or upset. That "Go on girl, I got your back" look. Dakota always knew how to calm me down.

We walked through the humongous glass doors and were greeted by a gray-haired woman, sitting behind a black linen–covered table. I gazed around the lobby area as she checked our names off the guest list. The directory next to the elevator diagrammed the layout of the building. The executive offices were on the fifth through seventh floors. The president's office was located on the fifteenth, and in between, the directory showed the layout of the sales, production, A&R, and public relations departments. I was impressed. And furthermore, I felt in my heart that I would one day get to roam all floors of the building—and it wouldn't be on a guided tour either.

Dakota and I were escorted down a long corridor that supported all sorts of gold plaques, records, and medals. Our escort opened another pair of double doors that led to the ballroom and bid us a good evening. We stood inside in a state of amazement as the doors closed behind us. The place looked fantastic. The room was decked out in huge gold-and-silver glittered ribbons with black trimming. There were four full-service bars and at least fifty-some-odd tables all set up with black flowered center-pieces, black plates, and gold goblets. The DJ's booth stood in the far corner of the room behind a circular dance floor, and a stage with a mic and podium on it was next to that. The room was filled with beautiful people. Important, established-looking people. People who looked like they'd been places, seen things, done things.

"Girrrl, look at all the brothers," Dakota said, fanning herself with her hand. "And all this food. If my belly didn't promise to poof out after one mouthful, I'd get me a plate. Come on, let's go get us a drink and be cute."

We walked over to the bar and waited for the bartender to notice us. He closed the cash register and wiped his hands over the black vest he wore, then rattled off a sentence so fast Dakota and I had to look at each other to make sure the other was just as confused.

"No, honey. I don't speak Spanish," Dakota said, shaking a stiff finger back and forth in front of his face. "You in America now—get with it or quit it." Dakota leaned over the counter to get a better listen at his jumbled speech. After breaking the word Kamikaze down into its tiniest syllables and repeating it four or five times, she finally just ordered two waters. That was fine with me because I was in no mood for drinking. I was too overwhelmed by my surroundings. I'd never seen any place look so pretty. Not even Bullock's looked this good and that was saying a lot, because we hooked that store up, especially during Christmastime.

Dakota ran a hand over her hair, tightened her lips, and I knew Miss Militant was about to get started. "Why they got so many Mexicans working in here? You'd think a black establishment would have black people working for them, you know. Look at all of 'em, running around in uniforms and serving people. What? Black folks don't need jobs no more?"

Please don't start that Malcolm X crap tonight, I thought. I mean, I knew where she was coming from, but I just couldn't get into it right then.

Her attention was quickly diverted as soon as some fine gentleman in a navy suit and tie passed by. "Oop, baby's vibes are calling me," she said and slid off behind him toward the dance floor.

There were so many familiar faces in the crowd. Several people I'd seen on BET and on the covers of magazines, but I couldn't spot any of the Black Tie executives I'd seen pictured in the trade papers. Where was the president of A&R, the sales director, a producer—heck, anybody who I could give my tape to? Every single person I saw *looked* famous, although I knew most of them weren't. Most looked happy, but some, the real famous people, looked bored or distracted. Then there were the ones who were trying to be the center of attention. Laughing louder than anyone else at jokes that probably weren't one bit funny, or tossing their hair back from side to side and trying to look overly sexy. That's how I could always tell the stars from the wanna-bes. The stars just chilled like it was no big thing, the wanna-bes were always trying to get somebody to look at them.

I decided to mingle through the crowd a bit and see who I could see, but as soon as I took a step, I heard a deep, familiar voice call from behind me.

"Excuse me, miss."

It was Craig. I turned around to find him decked out in tails and a matching kente cloth cummerbund and tie. He looked like he had just stepped off one of the displays in the men's department down at the store. "Good evening, Craig," I said, trying to play it off like all his gorgeousness wasn't affecting me in the slightest. "You're looking pretty dapper tonight."

"Yeah, it's all a front though. I'm really working, but with all the people wandering around here, it's hard not to get distracted. But anyway, you look marvelous," he said in his best Billy Crystal impersonation.

How corny, I thought. And where's Mrs. Johnson? I wanted to ask, but decided to leave the subject of his wife alone. I didn't want to do anything to upset myself or lose my focus. But of course he had to go there.

"Missed you at the wedding," he said, sizing me up and trying to detect my mood. But I wasn't falling for it. I guess married life had been treating him well because he looked content enough. Then again Craig was a police officer, master of the straight face. "Look, I had been meaning to call you lately, but I wasn't sure if we were still friends. The last time we talked, if you can call it talking, you were . . . well, you were pretty upset."

Darn right I was upset, you broke my heart, you bastard. "Yeah, I know. But I'm over all that now. Let's let bygones be bygones." I offered him my hand.

Craig must have been in a good mood because instead of shaking my hand, he lifted it up to his lips and applied them. I felt like melting to the floor, then quickly checked myself. Craig was a married man now and totally off-limits. "So what's been going on?" I asked, hoping he'd break down and cry and tell me he was miserable and that he and his wife were getting a divorce.

"Just working mainly. Nothing new. Oh, Maurine and I just got back from Canada last week. That's a beautiful place. So peaceful and serene. . . ."

On and on and on, he kept on! Craig was pushing it. I mean, I was happy that he was happy, but I damn sure didn't need a step-by-step rundown of his blissful life with his new bride. My heart began to hurt. I knew this would happen if I ran into him. I knew it. Part of me wanted to slap the shit out of him. Another part of me wanted to grab him and kiss him, something I should have done more often when we were together. But I was younger then. I didn't know what was up on anything back in the day.

He finally stopped babbling about Maurine and said he had to get back to work. "Can I call you sometime? I've been thinking about going back to school for my master's. Don't ask me why, but this law enforcement shit ain't all it's cracked up to be."

"Sure, Craig. You can give me a call," I said, feeling myself wanting him like never before, but realizing that our time had passed.

"Your pops still be trippin'?" he asked and broke out laughing. "He's not still snatching the phone out your hand and hanging it up, is he? I mean, you are a full-fledged grown-up now, right?"

"Forget you, Craig," I said and couldn't help breaking out a smile. "You know the routine, just call before ten o'clock."

He bent down and gave me a soft, sincere hug. I hated it. I wanted him to hug me like a lover, not like a friend. "I'll talk to you later, sweetheart," he said and walked off toward the double doors, pulling out a walkie-talkie from his back pocket.

I watched him walk until he disappeared behind the doors, then tried to pull myself back to reality. It didn't work. I had only been at the party for thirty minutes, but I was ready to go.

. . .

Damn. Who's baby with the red hair and how can a brother like me get a piece of that? Baby sho-nuff popping in that velvet dress, but I bet she got a man. When they looking that good, they gots to have a man. I ought to go on over there and push up on her right now, 'cause ain't shit happening over this way with T-Bone and Rich. Them mothafuckas is too predictable, and just like I thought, they at each other's throats again.

I should just drop them fools like Kelly told me when I stopped by her place to get ready for tonight, but what the fuck does that bitch know anyway? She gon' tell me I should get rid of Rich and T and break out on my own and be a solo act. I knew she was trying to encourage me and give me confidence and shit, but that really pissed me off. It's the way she said it, like Rich and T wasn't nobody, like they was dirt and holding me back or something. I had to check her silly ass. "Don't be talking about my peoples like they don't mean nothing. You ain't no better than them just 'cause your daddy done bought you this condo and that BMW you rollin' in," I told her.

Then of course she started crying and carrying on, but I didn't care. I just went in her bedroom and got dressed. Hell, she knows how I feel about my boys. They the only real family I got. But white people don't understand that shit. Kelly never did understand me. White people are all alike, always trying to divide blacks in whatever way they can—or at least that's what I convinced myself Kelly was trying to do.

When I walked out the bedroom, she was still sitting on the couch crying. I didn't pay her no 'tention. I just grabbed her keys off the coffee table and headed for the door. Since I was gonna be cruising up in Century City, I decided to take her Beemer. Them fancy folks wouldn't understand if I rolled up in the baby blue '64, sitting on Daytons, with the Blaupunkt system bumpin'. Before I could slide her keys into my pocket she was whining again. "Please don't go. Aren't you even going to have dinner?" she asked, getting off the couch and following me toward the door.

I just looked at her, shook my head, and wondered what the hell she saw in me. I didn't have nothing to offer her but some good sex. I couldn't understand why someone would put up with a man who wasn't doing nothing for them. But the more I dogged Kelly, the harder she fought to save the relationship. Bitches. Too busy trying to please everybody else but themselves.

Now I could kick myself for not listening to Kelly earlier. I have to admit, she made a very good point about my jackass homeboys 'cause every time I look over at T-Bone and Rich, I wanna strangle them. Those two ain't nothing but a couple of kids. We had to sneak in the party through the side door, just in case they had metal detectors at the front entrance. For now rapping is just a part-time thing, but gangsta-ism is a twenty-four/seven job and we never leave home without our straps. But ever since we been in here them fools been acting like pussies. One pussy on my left, one pussy on my right, and I'm caught in the middle like a tuna fish sandwich.

When I got over to Rich's house to pick him up, T was waiting for me outside talking about he thought it would be better for all of us to roll up to the party together. If I had known then what I know now, I would have told him to go on without us, but instead we just went on in the house and kicked it while Rich, with his slow ass, was getting ready. When he finally rolled himself out to the front room, he was carrying a bottle of J.D. in one hand and holding the bullets for his .38 in the other.

"Time to get faded, my brothers," he said and took a long swig before passing the bottle to T-Bone. Then he took out two cigars from the pocket on his plaid shirt and stuck one in his mouth. The other he carefully peeled apart and let the cigar tobacco fall out onto the table, then filled it up with weed and rolled it back together. Rich always knew how to make a good blunt and he always filled it with the best weed he could find. None of that weak-ass sess. The real deal—Indica—the shit that get you faded.

T-Bone finally passed me the J.D., what was left of it, then lit up the blunt that Rich had just made. It didn't take that fool but two minutes before he started acting ignorant. Whenever Bone gets a bit of liquor in him he start thinking he Martin Lawrence or Eddie Murphy, or somebody. I have to admit, he is funny, but tonight he took that shit too far. Him and Rich started bagging on each other's moms and I just sat back laughing like I was at the Def Jam Comedy Show.

"Yo momma so fat, she sat on a nickel and squeezed out five pennies," T-Bone said, laughing as he blew out a cloud of smoke.

I was rollin' so hard I almost choked and Rich just sat in his chair looking stupid, but eventually he had to laugh a little 'cause Bone was funny as hell.

"Yo momma so black," Rich retaliated after thinking long and hard, "she so black, if you stick her between two buildings, she look like an alley."

Oh, I was rollin'. I had to give Rich a high five on that one, and T-Bone was laughing so hard you would have thought he was the one who told the joke. Then that fool got a little carried away. "Yo momma so stupid, she smoked so much cocaine till the bitch couldn't even remember her name," he said and broke out laughing. Me and Rich sat in silence.

I couldn't believe that nigga. He knew good and well Rich's moms died off that stuff. I looked at that fool like he was crazy, and Rich, I don't know if it was the weed or what, but I swear I thought I saw smoke coming out that brother's ears.

"What the fuck you say about my moms?" Rich said, staring at Bone like he was gonna pimp-slap that fool. I swear if Rich hadn't been in that damn wheelchair he would have got up and stomped the shit out of T-Bone. "I said what the fuck you say about my momma, nigga?" Rich started loading his .38. "Oh, that shit's funny to you, right? Well, I ain't even gonna get started on your crazy-ass momma, and how that bitch be rollin' down Western on skates and pushing that damn shoppin' cart."

It was on after that. T-Bone got off the couch and charged over toward Rich, and if I hadn't got in between them two all hell woulda broke loose. I grabbed Rich's hand before he could close the barrel on the gun and snatched it away. Then I turned toward T-Bone, who was trying to get around me to Rich, and pushed him backward until we both fell on the couch.

"Naw, fuck that shit. Let that nigga go. He don't want none of me with his scary punk-ass," Rich said. But I knew if I didn't hold Bone back I would of been taking one of them fools to the hospital. The ironic part is that it probably would have been T-Bone.

T-Bone almost looked like he was gon' cry, but I thought to myself, that's what that fool get. He never knew when to quit. He could dish out a whole bunch of shit, but when it comes back at him he can't handle it. It took me damn near thirty minutes to get them to settle down and by that time I was completely pissed off. Needless to say, it was a quiet ride to Century City, and we been up in this party for over an hour and them fools still haven't said a word to each other.

We been standing over here next to this bar for what seems like forever. This ain't what we came here for. We came here to get discovered, make some contacts, dish off this DAT tape we worked our asses off on. I can't believe this shit. I should leave these fools and go home to Kelly right now, but that would be even worse. Anyway, I don't want to hear no more of her whining.

I sat my empty Heineken bottle down on the bar counter and scratched my head. What I should do is go check out that honey with the red hair. She look like she all by herself. No, what she looks is damn good in that black dress, and a brother like me is curious to see what a sister like that got on her mind—and everywhere else.

"Yo, I'll check y'all later," I said to Rich and T-Bone, but they didn't even look in my direction as I walked off. They just kept on downing Coronas with their mouths poked out like a couple of babies.

I walked over to Little Miss Redhead like a man on a mission. I guess I musta startled her or something 'cause she nearly jumped out her skin when I tapped her on the shoulder. "Damn, girl," I said, checking her out from head to toe and liking every inch of what I saw. "Why you standing over here all by yourself? You waiting on your man or something?"

She looked at me like I was crazy and I could tell she didn't really want to talk, but that was too bad. She was gonna have to put up with me for a few minutes at least 'cause I wasn't about to turn around and walk away like I was some kinda punk. But I knew right away that I had to play it cool. Baby was fine as wine, but she wasn't no fool. She acted like she had some sense and I liked that, so I decided to play her by the book. "So what's your name?" I asked and stepped back so she wouldn't smell all the liquor I had on my breath.

"Jazmine," she said quickly, looking around like she had somewhere to go.

"Hold up. I ain't gonna bite you," I said and gave her a nice, big smile—my gentleman act. "I just saw you over here looking all lonely, and decided you were just too beautiful to be roaming around this party alone. All these people look cool, but there's a lot of crazy people up in here tonight. I ought to know, I'm one of 'em." I cracked a sly grin and she finally eased up a bit and let out a laugh. Damn, baby looked good when she laughed.

"So are you going to tell me your name or should I just call you Mr.

Dahmer, or better yet, Mr. Manson?" she said, laughing. I knew I had her hooked.

"Xavier Honor, but all my peoples call me X-Man."

"Xavier," she said, letting every syllable roll off her lips. "That's a nice name. Were you named after Saint Xavier?"

"Of course," I said blankly, not knowing who the hell she was talking about. The only other Xavier I knew was Xavier McDaniels from the Boston Celtics, and I know she wasn't talking about him. "So you enjoying yourself so far?"

"Well, to tell the truth, I'm ready to go home, and if I ever find my man-hungry girlfriend I'll be on my way," she said, smoothing out her dress. Damn. Sisters with red hair are just too sexy.

"Yeah, I could tell. This don't seem like your type of party."

"And what's that supposed to mean?" she asked and put her hands on her hips like she had just been offended. Go on, girl, get mad, I thought. I like it when my woman gets mad—so sexy.

"I mean you look like the quiet, shy type," I said and paused a minute and thought. Yeah, the quiet ones are always the best in bed, and with a body like she was holding down, a brother like me could get sprung real fast. "You know, you look like you got better things to do than hang out at parties."

"Well, I don't know if they're better things, but yes, I do have a life, and right now I'm wondering how on earth I'm going to be able to get up for school in the morning."

"Oh, so you're in school?" And brains too, I thought. "Where?"

"UCLA. I'm working on my master's. I need to get it over with so I can get on with my life, get a real job instead of this part-time madness."

And she works on top of that. Damn, baby does really got it going on. She had me thinking of a way to impress her now. But what the hell could I boast about? I ain't got no job, didn't even graduate from high school. Hell, the car I'm rollin' tonight ain't even mine. "Well, uh, I'm trying to do the rap thing, you know," I said and stroked my goatee with pride like I already had a contract and a fat wad of money in my pocket. "Yeah, me and my boys trying to hook up a little somethin'-somethin' with a producer, you know. Hook up a phat track and—Boom!—I'll be on my way."

"Oh really," she said and laughed.

Now what did I say that was so funny?

"Well, I gotta go find my friend now, but it was nice talking to you, Xavier. See ya."

What? Excuse me? What the fuck did I say? What? See, that's what's wrong with sisters. They can't wait for shit. Telling her I was on my way to *becoming* a rapper wasn't good enough. I shoulda told her I was already signed to a label and was working in the studio right now. Sisters. Can't never give a brother a chance.

I guess she caught up with her friend 'cause I saw her standing next to some chick in a red outfit that had it going on just as much as she did. Naw, couldn't nobody look as good as her with that red hair. She was all that. Baby was too fine and if I didn't do something quick, she'd be gone and all I'd be left with was a room fulla women walking around looking like hos and two stupid-ass friends who, the last time I looked back at them, were arguing like an old married couple. I thought about walking over to her and asking her for a dance, but then I saw that microphone sitting on that empty stage and had a better idea.

I made my way across the hot, crowded dance floor and had to push some fat, sweaty bitch who was taking up enough room for about four or five people out the way. I walked on to the stage just as the DJ was about to put on one of them slow jams. I grabbed the mic, cleared my throat, and started free-styling, letting out rhymes I didn't even know I had in me. By the time the crowd stopped dancing and started looking up at me, I was, as they say in basketball, unconscious. I stayed up there on the mic for what seemed like a lifetime, but was actually only about ten minutes or so. By the time I was finished the crowd was jumping up and down, pumping their fists in the air and calling out my name. "Go, X-Man, go, X-Man, go, X-man!"

All I gotta say is, if this is what fame is all about—I gots to get me a piece.

. . .

Bobby arrived at the Black Tie ballroom close to midnight, wearing the same suit he had on earlier, which was now wrinkled and rumpled in all the wrong places. He knew Mr. Timbers and the rest of the company executives were already upstairs in the private banquet hall in the midst of the presentation ceremony. He also knew he was late, but made no effort to rush upstairs. He was not so inclined to witness Mr. Timbers present someone else with the Executive of the Year Award, and definitely not in a hurry to sit and watch everyone's mocking eyes turn on him, laughing. They would be so happy to see his commanding star come tumbling down.

He decided to take his time and mingle through the crowd. He stopped at the bar and ordered a double shot of tequila and gulped it back at once, before roaming through the sea of anxious, hungry faces. Faces that turned toward him and called, "Good evening, Mr. Strong," "Happy to see you, sir," or whispered, "Hey, isn't that Bobby Strong?"

His body was present, but his mind was lingering all over the place and he couldn't get ahold of it. He was coming down from his high and his body was shrieking for more, but this was not the time nor the place. He had already finished off the two grams he had purchased earlier, but that had not been enough. A quarter used to be an adequate amount to get him through the night and thoroughly high, but that was months ago, when he first started dabbling in cocaine. Until then, he just messed around with uppers, weed, and occasionally a bit of heroin if he was having an especially bad day. He couldn't remember how his habit escalated to its current state, could not pinpoint the day he became a serious user, nor did it matter much to him. Coke was a new one for Bobby, but he had gotten to know it well. Now it seemed to him that a quarter wasn't even enough to keep him going for more than a couple hours, and it definitely hadn't been enough to prepare him for Sheryl's bomb.

When he had gotten home, she was waiting for him in the foyer. She didn't so much as pause for him to put his briefcase down before she hit him with the news. "I want a divorce, Bobby," she said directly, and walked away. He was so stoned at the time that the information didn't sink in. She might as well have told him that she had cleaned the house or bought him a new tie. He chuckled behind her back as she walked away and thought she surely must be crazy. He followed her through the foyer to the great room waiting for her to suddenly break out into laughter and tell him this was all a big joke, but Sheryl didn't say a word. He stood in the doorway and took a deep breath. He didn't know what he was in for, but he sensed something was different. Something in the way Sheryl held her head sternly above her shoulders let Bobby know that she was definitely serious. "So, how are my daughters?" he asked, helplessly trying to change the subject.

"Bobby!" Sheryl shouted and turned to face him. "Did you hear what I just said? I want out, Bobby. O, U, T!"

Her anger caught him off guard, but he tried not to show it. "Look, baby. We'll deal with this later." He forced her into a tight bear hug that Sheryl quickly avoided. "Why don't you just call the sitter and we can be on our way to the party?" he continued, trying to regain control of the situation.

"Don't even try it, Bobby," she said, slapping his hand away each time he reached for her. "The girls and I are out of here."

"Uh-huh. And where are you going, Sheryl?" he asked, fully expecting a response. "Where are you going?" He paused and held out his arms, waiting for an answer. When none came, he knew he had won. "That's what I thought. You and my daughters aren't going anywhere."

"You don't care about us. We're just a part of this illusion you've built. The perfect job, the perfect family, the perfect house. Bullshit. Maybe your childhood and family life were less than perfect, but you can't compensate for that by trying to make us into something we're not."

"You don't know a damn thing about the way I grew up. You had everything," Bobby spit out and turned away, wondering where the hell all this was coming from.

"Oh, get real. My family had to struggle their asses off for everything they had."

"Who gives a damn about what they *had*? They were there for you. A mother, a father. Who cares about anything else?"

"That's right, Bobby. Who cares about what they had or what *you* have? This house, these clothes—who cares? What this family needs is *you*. Here. That's why I thought we got married, so we could be a family."

"See, you don't understand me at all," he said, throwing his hands up. "I work my ass off for this family. My job is my life, but you, you want somebody to sit at home with you and hold your hand all day. And what would happen if I did that, Sheryl? I'll tell you. For one thing you wouldn't be riding around in that Benz station wagon, and you sure as hell wouldn't be sporting those damn Chanel slippers."

"It's not about *things*, Bobby."

"I'm doing the best I can, damn it," he said, grabbing her arm. "What the fuck have you done for me lately?"

"Let me go," Sheryl said, trying to yank free. "I said let me go!"

Bobby had no idea he had been holding on to her so tightly. He looked into her eyes but he could hear no words. The only thing he understood was the terrified look on her face.

"Get your goddamn hands off me!" Sheryl screamed at the top of her lungs. She stood frozen in the middle of the floor and glared at Bobby. Suddenly she let out a piercing primal scream that both shocked and confused him. Was she having a nervous breakdown? He clutched the arm of the couch, not sure whether to run away or go to her rescue. Should he slap her or try to calm her down? He anxiously awaited her next move, noticing that she was just as shocked as he when she put her shaking hand to her face in disbelief. Cautiously, she cleared her throat and began to speak softly. "The girls and I are leaving."

Bobby looked at her as she stood trembling in front of the lit fireplace. He could feel she meant every word she said. "Look, Sheryl," he began, matter-of-factly. "I don't know what's gotten into me, but hey, if you need to go away and be by yourself for a while that's fine with me. But the girls should stay here."

"Don't you dare pretend you give a damn about those girls," Sheryl said, trying to stay under control. "You only care about one thing," she said and stormed out of the room.

Bobby's mind was completely blown. When he left that morning they were fighting over who left the cap off the toothpaste. How does a simple hygiene problem turn to divorce in the course of a day? He fell on to the couch. He cupped his hands over his eyes, hoping against all hope that this was some kind of hallucination. He thought about going after her to at least find out *why*. Where was all this divorce talk coming from? She could at least tell me why. Is that too much to ask? He relaxed into the cushions of the couch and tried to calm his racing heart, but soon came the clicking of Sheryl's heels toward the room again.

"There," she said and threw a plastic bag down on Bobby's face. "That's what you care about. Not me, and certainly not our children."

"What the fuck?" Bobby shouted, grabbing for the bag as it rolled down his chest. He picked it up and looked closely at the contents of white powder. Damn, he thought to himself—busted.

"You know where I found that, Bobby? In the game room," she said, unable to hold back her tears. "In the game room!"

He looked up at her in disbelief. *When?* He retraced his actions in his mind.

"There it was, lying on top of the pinball machine. Do you know how many fucking times a day Tiff and Britt go in there to play that damn game? What if they had picked it up?" She threw her hands up in wonderment. "What—what if Brittany found it and mistook it for candy? What the hell are you doing to us?"

Bobby sat up straight on the couch, gripping the plastic bag in his hand. For the first time he felt out of control. He had always been so careful to hide his habit, especially after the time Sheryl had almost caught him getting high underneath the gazebo a few months ago. He promised himself then that he would stop, but now he didn't know how to stop. He quickly flashed on an imaginary scene and pictured his youngest daughter lying on the game room floor with white powder covering her lips. . . . What am I doing to us?

Sheryl knelt down in front of Bobby and pleaded. "I saw all the signs, but I didn't want to believe it. How long has this been going on?"

"I swear I'll stop. Please," he pleaded and tried to pull her to him, but she resisted.

"I don't know, Bobby. I just don't know," she said, fighting back tears. "I've stayed with you this long because I believe in you. But you see that bag in your hand?" She placed her hand over his. "I can't compete with this. An affair, I could handle. I can compete with any woman, but drugs—I don't have a weapon against that."

"No," Bobby said firmly. "No. I'm for real. I'll uh, I'll go to one of those rehab centers." He looked around as if the answers to his problems were somewhere in that room. "I'll uh, uh, I'll get back on track. I just need a little time. My work has been—"

"Your work?" Sheryl interrupted. "Don't try to blame this on your work. Not only are you putting your life on the line, but now you're compromising your daughters. It's not right, Bobby. It's just not right."

"*Mommy*," Brittany's little voice called from upstairs. "Mommy, I don't feel so hot."

Sheryl's eyes focused on Bobby as she stood up before him. "Here I come, sweetie," she said, wiping tears from her face.

"You know I'd never do anything to hurt my girls. You know that."

"I don't know anything anymore," she said and headed for the staircase. "All I know is you need help. And you're not going to find it in that bag, at that job, or anywhere else."

Bobby watched her as she ran up the stairs and disappeared into the darkness. How did I get to this point? he silently asked himself, eyeing the bag he held in his hand. "I'll change," he said and stuffed the bag into his pocket. He took one last look around the house and realized he needed to get out of there.

He drove around his neighborhood for hours, circling block after block, with no particular goal in mind other than to get away. Until then, he had forgotten how much he truly loved his wife. When he first met Sheryl, he knew from that moment on that he'd never be alone again. She had always been there for him, even when he didn't have a dime to his name. Now she wanted a divorce, and for the first time she actually sounded like she meant it. When they first married, he never dreamed it would come to this. That once again he would find himself alone. "I'll change, I'll change," he kept mumbling to himself, but the more he said the words, the more he felt unsure if he could actually do it. Change, he thought, putting a finger to his temple. What exactly does that mean? He was a successful man. What was there to change about that? The more he thought, the more his temples pounded, reminding him of the cocaine he had consumed earlier. He was coming down from his high, and the usual headache that plagued him when he sobered up seemed more intense than ever.

He picked up speed, hoping the faster he drove the quicker he could escape the nightmare his life was turning into. As he aimlessly drove, he marveled at the elegant houses he passed, all with electronic security gates and long pathways that curved across their lawns and led to the main houses. He was a long way from the dirt roads of Tyler, Texas, and his was the only black family in the vicinity. Bobby knew his colleagues had started referring to him as a sellout after he purchased his Brentwood home. They'd never tell him to his face though—none of them were that bold. He knew that was what they thought, but as far as he was concerned, they could think whatever their feeble minds allowed. He was proud to be out of the ghetto and away from the dirt roads, and made no effort to apologize for his status. He had dreamt about living in a large, expensive house his whole life, and more importantly, he had made his dream a reality. He loved being able to provide a secure life for his family, but now he realized that security meant more than money and a nice house. For his family to be secure they needed a loving father and husband.

It was after eleven o'clock when he finally made it to the party. The last thing he wanted to do was socialize, but he was even more afraid to go back home and face Sheryl. "I'll just give her some time," he mumbled to himself, before finding the courage to enter the party.

By the time he rose from the bar stool where he had been downing a slew of shots and mixed drinks, Bobby felt somewhat better. He tried to forget about Sheryl and concentrate on his next move for the future, a move that would put him back on top at Black Tie Records. He firmly believed that once everything was back to normal at work, his life and marriage would straighten out as well. He pondered the possibility of finding a potential star as he surveyed the room, looking for someone who might fit the bill. These affairs were always overcrowded with tramps and losers, no one of any caliber or depth, he thought. He asked the bartender for another shot and searched his pockets for a chocolate candy. Bobby always kept his pockets full of chocolate mints, Kisses, or M&M's. He rolled the chocolate around in his mouth until he spotted his secretary.

"Are you okay?" Tish asked, taken aback by Bobby's demeanor.

"Couldn't be better," he said, grinning and turning introspective. "What could be better, huh? I've gotten all the way to forty years of age to decide to start fucking up. Boy, I'll tell ya, Tish, life is just gggreat."

"Uh, okay," Tish replied, not knowing what to make of Bobby's sudden insight. "Look, everybody's been asking for you. I'm telling you, if one more person grabs my arm and asks me where the hell you are, I'm gonna slap the shit out of 'em."

"Hey," Bobby laughed and grabbed her arm. "Where am I?"

Tish didn't think that was too funny, but went along with it anyway. "You've got to get upstairs. *Now.*"

"Yeah, I know," he said and turned instantly somber.

"What's wrong, boss?"

"Nothing, nothing," he forced through a smile. "I'm on my way."

When he finally slid through the door of the private banquet hall, Mr. Timbers had just finished congratulating Kirk Walker for his valiant efforts that landed him this year's Executive of the Year Award. Bobby sat in the back of the room hoping no one would turn around and notice him, especially not Mr. Timbers.

Mr. Timbers went on to say how proud he was of management's endeavors, even in the light of the unsavory events of the past year. Bobby knew what he was talking about and slid down in his seat to make sure no one would catch his presence.

"It's been a long year, as you know. Too long for my sixty-year-old body," Mr. Timbers said from behind the podium.

Someone in the front of the room shouted out, "You're still the best, Mr. Timbers—still the best." And to that everyone applauded.

Ass-kisser, Bobby thought.

"That may be so," Mr. Timbers continued, "but I've seen Black Tie Records through many years. With your help, this company has grown and prospered beyond anything I could have hoped for. But now it's time for me to step down. Yes. The time has come for me to move to the background, take it easy in my latter days."

What was he getting at? Move to the background? Latter days? Spit it out, Bobby wanted to yell.

"I'm retiring."

No one said a word and most stared at him like they could not believe what the man had just said. Bobby sure couldn't.

"But before I retire, someone, one of you worthy people sitting in this room tonight, must take my place. All of you have the capability, but there can only be one president. I have made no decisions yet, but soon—very soon—one of you will be taking over." Mr. Timbers gave his customary, elegant bow and stepped down from the stage and walked toward a door at the side of the room, oblivious to his awestruck audience. "Good night, everyone. Enjoy the rest of your evening," he said, before closing the door behind him.

As soon as he was gone the room lit up with murmurs. Bobby surveyed the faces in the room, everyone clamoring over the news they had just heard. He saw Kirk Walker sitting silently with a mesmerized grin on his face, like he had just been given the key to the city. Surely he doesn't think he's going to be the next man in charge, Bobby thought. Oh, certainly not, if Bobby had anything to do with it. The presidency rightfully belonged to him and everybody in the room should know that.

Bobby's eyes met Kirk's for an instant as he walked to the back exit. No wet-behind-the-ears buppie is going to take this job away from me, he thought as he walked out the door and down the stairway. By then Bobby was completely sober and greatly agitated. He moved quickly through the crowd until he was stopped dead in his tracks by some bumbling young man dressed like he had just been released from prison. Another wanna-be rapper. He hurried to the rest room. He paced across the linoleum for half an hour, not knowing what to do with himself. This couldn't possibly be happening to me, he thought. He'd worked too hard to get where he was, and now, not only was he losing the only woman he ever loved, but the one man he'd looked up to was suddenly taking sides with the enemy. Surely Bobby knew he wouldn't be receiving the Executive of the Year Award, but for Kirk Walker to receive it, the one man he felt could challenge him for the presidency, was a back-breaker.

He slammed his hand against the hard porcelain sink and soon regretted that outburst as he rubbed the back of his throbbing knuckles. Without thinking, he stuck his hand in his pocket and retrieved the plastic bag Sheryl had thrown at him earlier. His moves were automatic . . . Finger—bag—nose—inhale. Finger—bag—nose—inhale . . .

When he left the rest room his desperation was replaced with renewed faith. His mind was racing a mile a minute as he silently plotted his next move, because now, more than ever, he needed a major coup. A business move that would make everyone at Black Tie stand up and take notice. His brain was working overtime trying to figure out how he could make his mark and give Mr. Timbers a reason to name him as his successor. He kept coming back to a singer. That's what he needed. A megastar talent; someone he could cultivate into a crossover success.

His thought process was broken up by a show-stopping young girl in a red suit. She looked intent as she approached him, like she had an important job to do.

"Remember me?" she said, stopping directly in front of him and running a hand over her short hair. He couldn't place the face. He'd met so many young, pretty girls, all of whom wanted something from him—a recording contract, money, fame. This one looked appealing, though, so he decided to let her stay and talk.

"Yeah, you look familiar but I can't recall your name," he said, feeling his high completely now and eyeing her petite, shapely frame.

"Dakota," she said and posed as if that small gesture would spark his memory. "You know, River and Earth's daughter."

No, he didn't know, but decided to play along. "Oh yes, how could I forget such a lovely face. What can I do for you?"

"Oh, nothing, Mr. Strong. I thought I would just come over and say hello."

Yeah right, he thought. They all want something. He never met a woman who didn't want *something*, and he could tell this one was no different. Just another Marilyn, but he didn't mind, as he thought back on the afternoon and what Marilyn had been willing to do for him. How far was this one willing to go to get what she wanted?

"Well, actually, Bobby . . . can I call you Bobby?"

Hmm, at least she's bold. "Sure, you can call me anything you like," he said, feeling especially chummy.

"I was wondering if I could have a moment of your time. Before you say no, I know you probably don't want to talk about business at a time like this, but if you just give me a minute I'm sure you won't be disappointed."

"For you, I've got all the time in the world," he said, taking her hand. He noticed she seemed a little apprehensive, but that would soon wear off. "I know a place where we can talk privately. It's a little too noisy in here. Follow me."

Bobby led her out of the main ballroom and down a long corridor to a secluded conference room filled with large, leather swiveling chairs that sat around a long oval table in the middle of the floor. The walls held paintings of legendary singers—Billie Holiday, Sarah Vaughan, and Jimi Hendrix. Bobby paid no attention to the pictures. He was too busy viewing the portrait standing right in front of him.

"Now. Tell me what's on your mind," Bobby said, running his eyes up and down her body. "I know what's on mine."

"Okay. I know you probably get bombarded with proposals and tapes every day. But I have a tape that will blow you away. Okay. You probably hear that every day too, but this is for real. I know a good voice when I hear one and if you just listen to this tape, I'm sure—"

"So you're a singer, are you?"

"No, no, not me. My friend. Her name is Jazmine Deems and she can sing like I don't know what. I mean she puts them all to shame," she said, whipping out a cassette from her red purse. "Okay, Bobby. I know the business. My parents have been in it for a long time, and I'm telling you this girl can *sang*!"

"Oh, is that right?" he said, walking closer to her. "But what can you do?"

"Excuse me?"

Bobby could tell she wasn't quite catching on, but he figured it was part of her game. She had gotten him all the way to this room and bent his ear about some singer who was probably no better than the rest of the wannabes he listened to day in and day out. And now she was going to repay the favor.

"Tell me, Dakota. Just how much are you willing to give up for your friend?" he whispered, slipping the tape into his jacket pocket. He briefly closed his eyes as the room seemed to lighten and darken all at once. When he reopened them, everything seemed blurred, but he continued talking, hoping the sound of his voice would keep him focused. "You know it will take a lot of my time to listen to that tape, and since you say you know about the business, then I think you should know what I mean."

Bobby didn't wait for her to answer. He grabbed her by the waist and hovered above her, amused by the bewildered look on her young, sweet face. He slipped his hand between her blazer and fumbled around until he found what he was looking for—a hard, delicate nipple. She tried to pull back, but Bobby held on to her like a vise. He pulled her to the floor, forcing her legs to bend, then slid down her pants as she squirmed beneath him. He smiled at her aggressiveness before locking his mouth over hers so tightly that he could barely breathe. He wanted her to keep moving. His hands were all over her and he could tell she was enjoying it. "Oh, Sheryl," he whispered, so sure. "I love you so much, Sheryl."

Suddenly—out of nowhere—a tiny fist with the force of a mallet landed on the side of his face. "What the fuck?" he said, startled. "What are you doing?"

"What am *I* doing?" she said, scooting as far away from him as she could. She pulled her pants back to her waist and clasped her jacket closed with her hand. Her body shook as she stared at Bobby in horror and tried to catch her breath.

"I thought—you wanted—" he stuttered, noticing the tears on her cheeks. *Oh my God.* "No, wait, I'm sorry. I thought—"

"You thought wrong, motherfucker," she said and scurried up to race for the door. "This woman ain't for free," she said and slammed the door behind her, leaving Bobby in a stupor in the middle of the floor.

"Oh, shit," he whispered into the silence of the room.

He stumbled out the main entrance to the parking lot and got in his car. He rested his head on the steering wheel and simply sat, wishing the entire night would delete itself from his memory. For some reason he couldn't help remembering what his boss had told him last year after he presented him with the Executive of the Year Award. Mr. Timbers had pulled him to the side and placed a fatherly arm around his shoulder. "Some day this company is going to be yours, you know," Mr. Timbers had said with tears in his eyes. "Just remember—this business corrupts. The more you get, the more you want, the more you expect. It fills you up. You just get fatter and fatter until one day—you burst," he said as Bobby listened on intently. "Stay lean," Mr. Timbers said and patted Bobby's chest. "You gotta stay lean to keep the pockets green."

Bobby turned on the radio to drown out his thoughts. He flipped from station to station, but nothing seemed to be able to push his thoughts away. Blindly, he searched in his jacket pocket for a piece of chocolate. What he came out with was the tape, and since he couldn't find anything he liked on the radio, he put it in.

What he heard astonished him. It was the most balanced, unique falsetto he'd ever heard. A deep, mournful voice that had just the right thickness and pull to make it stand out from all the rest of the nonsense he heard day in and day out. He listened to all three songs on the tape in strict silence. This was it. This was the fucking one he'd been waiting for!

He popped the tape out and read the label, which had a phone number and the name Jazmine Deems written on it. "Oh, baby, baby, baby!" he shouted, putting it back in the stereo and pushing the rewind button. "You are the one!"

chapter five

flip the script

I feel like crap. I'm not going to school and I'm calling in sick to work. Forget it. I'm tired of doing things for other people. Working for other people, going to college because Daddy wants me to. What about what I want? No, today I'm going to stay in this room, sit on this bed, and cry. That's what I'm going to do for me. Me, me, me. And why not?

If I could, I'd quit all this crying, but I can't. Last night was such a letdown, but I should have known it was gonna turn out like that. It was a stupid idea anyway. I don't know why I thought I could just walk into that party, hand my tape to someone, and get a recording contract just like that. Nothing ever goes the way I want it to. Nothing. I mean, am I a bad person or something? What was the point in getting my hopes all up? What was the point in getting a demo tape together? What was the point in lying to Daddy? Can somebody please tell me that? If this is some kind of joke, God, then call me stupid, because I just don't get the punch line. All I ask is for a little happiness and to fulfill my dreams. I mean, I know I'm a good singer. At least I'm better than most of those people I hear on the radio, with those tired songs where you hear more bass and synthesized drums than the singer's real voice. So how is it that they can get a record contract and I can't? What do they have that I don't have—more tits and ass? What's a person gotta do to get a break? I mean, really!

And Craig. I hate that asshole. I mean, who does he think he is, talking to me and looking all good and stuff? I hate him. And what's pissing me off even more is that I think I still love him. Damn, damn, damn! What is wrong with me? Am I the dumbest person on this earth or what? You'd think I'd have a little pride, a little self-respect. But here I am, still yearning and lusting after a man who made it clear—I think marrying someone else makes it crystal clear—that he doesn't want me.

I must be some kind of freak or something to even still be thinking about the man. I mean, when we were dating, if you can call a few lunches dating, I never wanted him this much. What is it about married men that makes them so appealing? You'd think that a married man would be a turn-off to single women. But *nooo*. Dakota says it's because married men are more relaxed, more self-assured, more happy. Craig sure seemed happy, and I know I should be glad for him or be jumping up and down because he's found someone to share the rest of his life with, but I'm not. I thought I would be the one. I thought he'd be coming home from a long day at work to me, have children with me, take *me* to Canada. I hate Craig. I think I hate men period, or at least I'm getting really tired of them. No, what it is, is that I'm getting really tired of the stupid ones. There's only two types of men who approach me. The dumb ones or the dumber ones. The ones who don't have a thing going for them and approach me because they think they have nothing to lose. Or the ones who have everything going for them and approach me because they think they can have any woman they want. I hate those kind the most. They walk around with their suits and briefcases like every woman they see wants them, and when they finally come and talk to you, all they do is brag about what they have, what they had, and what they're going to get. They're so arrogant that they make *you* arrogant, and by the time they finally shut up and give you a chance to talk, you end up lying about stuff you *don't* have or things that you've never done, just so you can feel as important as they make themselves out to be.

The ones that don't have anything going for them are just as bad. Those are the kind that bother you when you're on your way to work or somewhere else important, just so they can drop some tired line on you, like "You sho looking mighty tasty," or "If you were a piece of candy I'd suck on you all night." You can tell these kind right off the bat, because they usually begin their line with "Say, baby," or "Damn, baby . . . where you goin'?" "To my job, where you would be going if you had one," I wanna tell them. Sometimes I wanna ask them, "Do I really look that desperate or that hard up that I'd get with a man who obviously has no job or else he'd be in it, no manners because if he did he'd be using them, and no brains because if he had any he wouldn't be so downright, utterly stupid?"

I didn't have these problems with Craig. Craig knew how to treat me right, and if I had any sense, or if God would stop playing these nasty little tricks on me, I'd be Mrs. Johnson right now. I wish I could call Craig, just like I used to before he got married. I'd ask him to a movie, or pick him up and take him for a drive, or play dumb and ask him to help me with a math analysis question which I already know the answer to, or just talk—plain, old shoot the flipping breeze. But I can't. Besides, anything I had to say to him should have been said a long time ago when he was single. I'm not about to call him up now and risk causing any confusion in his marriage. What's right is right and I know I wouldn't want any ex-girlfriend, if you can call me an ex-girlfriend, or ex-whatever, calling up my house and asking to speak to my man.

What I should do is call Dakota, but I think she's in one of her moods. She didn't say one word to me last night when she drove me home. I didn't say anything to her either, but at least I had a reason. I was mad because I didn't find anybody to listen to my tape. She didn't have an excuse. In many ways she's just like Daddy. Controlling, never satisfied, and downright mean sometimes. I know what her problem was last night though. She was probably mad because she didn't find anyone to take back to her place and screw. It's seldom that Dakota leaves a party without a man on her arm, so she's probably pissed off that she had to go home alone. That's good for her though. I tell her all the time that she needs to stop worrying about where her next piece of dick is coming from and just take some time to be by herself. But she usually tells me to shut the hell up because if I ever got me a good piece I'd probably want it every night too . . . and every morning . . . and afternoon.

No, what I need to do is just turn on the radio, relax, and try to forget about last night. Try to forget that Craig is married and will never be mine, and try to forget that I might never get a chance to make it as a singer. That's a lot of forgetting for one day, but I'm gonna try. Relax, Jazz, just relax.

I hadn't even started to unwind when the phone started ringing. "Hello."

A woman's voice asked if I was Jazmine Deems, then asked if I would hold while her boss, Bobby Strong, picked up the line.

The name rang a bell, but I couldn't exactly remember where I'd heard it. When the man picked up the line his voice was deep and imposing, just like Craig's, and for a second I thought it was him playing a joke. He had said he'd be giving me a call before he left last night, but Craig usually greets me with "Hi, sweetheart," or at least he used to before he got married. Then I thought it could be that other guy I ran into last night, but I remembered that I hadn't given him my number, and besides his name was—oh, I couldn't remember his name, and besides his voice was not this commanding.

"Miss Deems, I'm sure my secretary told you who I am, so let's get down to business."

"Wait a minute. She told me your name, but I still don't know who you are. Should I?"

"I'll say you should, Miss Deems, because I'm about to make you an offer that I'm certain you won't refuse."

Oh no, not another telemarketer trying to sell me some crap that I don't want, don't need, or if I did want or need it, don't have the money for, or if I did have the money for would just go out and buy it instead of waiting around for someone to call and sell it to me. "What is it?" I said, purposely trying to sound agitated so maybe he'd make this short, so I could tell him whatever he was selling I didn't want and maybe, just maybe if I was lucky, get back to my rest and relaxation and forgetting.

"Ah ha, I see you're straightforward. I like that, Miss Deems. I like that. Let me start off by saying this, I'm Bobby Strong of Black Tie Records, and if possible I'd like to meet with you this afternoon to discuss your future here at Black Tie."

"What?"

"I have an opening in my schedule at four o'clock, and by the way, your friend Colorado was right, your voice is impeccable."

Then it started to hit me like a cast iron skillet on the top of my head. "Is this the same Bobby Strong that I've read about in *Music Muse*?"

"Yes, dear. Is this the same Jazmine Deems whose voice I heard on tape last night and knocked me out?"

"Oh my God! Okay, okay, okay. I can't believe this! You want to meet with me?"

"Yes, dear. At my office. It's on the seventh floor of the building you were in last night. Be here at four o'clock sharp."

"Of course, four o'clock. Thank you, Mr. Strong. I will be there."

"Don't thank me. Thank your friend Colorado."

I wanted to tell him her name was Dakota, but flip it, if he wanted to call her Colorado, let him. Heck, he could call her Alaska if he wanted to. I thanked him again and hung up the phone. I couldn't keep myself contained. I thought I was gonna burst out of my skin I was so excited. But most of all I was confused, because Dakota hadn't said a word to me about this. And here I was crying and worrying because I thought I had blown it, and that girl had already come through for me.

I tried to call her house, but her line was busy. I swear, I love that girl to death, but sometimes I think she's still living in the seventies. Now how many people in this world don't have call waiting? Her and maybe about two other people, but they don't count because they're probably living in some shack in the middle of the desert with no indoor plumbing either. Well, I couldn't just sit in my room, I was too jumpy to stay in one place. So I decided to go over to her house and tell her the good news in person. Besides, I had to be at Mr. Strong's office at four and all my cute clothes were in her closet.

I quickly got dressed, throwing on an old pair of Levi 501s and a sweater, grabbed my purse, and headed for the door. But I wasn't quick enough because before I could get my hand on the bedroom door, Daddy opened it up and stood in the doorway glaring at me like I had I just stolen the last cookie from the cupboard. He shocked the devil out of me because I thought he'd be at church, getting it ready for the second night of the revival. I was so elated that I walked up to him and gave him a big kiss, something that I rarely do because most of the time he's getting on my nerves. I almost told him I loved him, another thing that I rarely do, mostly because he never tells me, but then I thought that that would be too conspicuous. He'd probably ask me why I was so happy, and although I was dying to tell someone the good news, I wasn't quite ready to tell him that I might be on my way to becoming a singer just yet. Besides, he'd have a million and one questions for me, and if he'd start asking, I'd have to tell him I lied about last night. I wasn't about to tell Mr. Holier Than Thou that little secret. He was asleep when I crept in last night so I didn't have to explain my whereabouts then and I'm sure not going to give myself away now.

After I kissed him, he just kept on staring at me and I knew something was wrong. What had he gone peeking through my room and uncovered this time? "What's wrong, Daddy?" I asked and waited for him to tell me he found my birth control pills or my Naughty by Nature CD or a letter I had written to Craig and hidden in a book instead of giving it to him.

"You are a sinful, heathenish, wretched liar," he said, calmly, turning me to ice. He looked through me like I was made of glass. "Do I look stupid to you, girl? Do I look like I was just born yesterday? Like I don't know nothing about nothing? Huh! Answer me when I'm talking to you, girl."

"Daddy, I don't know what you're talking about. Why don't you just calm down?" I said, feeling about two years old and like I was about to get a whipping or something.

"Don't you tell me to calm down, missy. Why don't you just tell me where you were last night, you little liar."

Woo, was that all? I knew this would be coming since I knew he would make it home before me last night. I already had my lie figured out. "Daddy, I had to run to the university library. I needed a book to help me prepare for my test. That's all." *Ta-da.*

"You are an evil, lying wench. If I were you, I'd fall on my knees and pray that the good Lord don't strike you down for telling such trash. I know where you were, Jazmine. I just got back from church and Miss Ola told me her son Oliver saw you at a party last night. I liked to fell out from the shock and embarrassment of what she told me. My daughter, at some whorish night spot, drinking, dancing, dressed like a hooker in some tight, show-everything dress. *My* daughter. Girl, you ought to be shamed."

"Oh Daddy, please."

"Don't you 'Oh Daddy, please' me. I raised you right. Like a decent Christian. And what do you do? Run around and shame me in front of the whole congregation. You need Jesus, girl," he said and closed his eyes and started speaking in tongues or whatever they call that blabbering, mumbling mess.

I had just about enough. I was grown, no matter what Daddy thought. And I was tired of sneaking around, hiding shit, trying to be a decent little Christian girl. Yes, I am Christian, but that don't mean I have to stay locked up in the house like a hermit every night. Even Jesus Christ Himself went to a party every now and then, I'm sure, and even if He didn't, too bad—I'm not Him. "Just stop it, Daddy. I don't want to hear it anymore. I'm sick of this shit. Sick and tired."

"Girl, don't you dare curse in the Lord's house."

"Don't you tell me what the fuck I can and cannot do, damn it! You treat me like I'm a child. Like I don't have a mind of my own. Well I do!" I turned my back to him so he wouldn't see me cry, then turned to him again. I was too scared and he was too angry for me to take my eyes off him. "All I did was go out to a little party. What's so bad about that, huh? You act like I was out all night whoring in the streets. Nothing I do is ever good enough for you. And I'm sick of it, Daddy! What is it? Do you think I'm going to go out one night and never come back? Do you think I'm Momma?"

"No," he said and backed up a couple of steps, thrown off by my mention of Momma. "I don't care about you leaving me, if that's what you want to do. Your momma was a devil on earth. That's why she's dead. So if you want to take her route—go right ahead."

"Fuck you."

"Girl, you ain't too grown to get knocked upside your head. Who do you think you're talking to? This is still my house and as long as you're living under my roof, you're going to do as I say. Period!"

"Well then, you know what, Daddy? I won't be living under your roof anymore," I said and squeezed past him through the doorway.

"And just where do you think you're going? Lord have mercy on this child. She knows not what she does, dear Lord. Oh help me, Jesus, help me. Jazmine, don't you dare walk out that door, girl!"

I opened the door and stood there for a split second, then kept right on walking. I didn't know what it was, but at that moment I felt I could take on the world. At first I felt spirit-like, like the force of God was within me. But that couldn't be possible, because the way I had just cursed out Daddy, I knew God wouldn't be too thrilled to do me any favors anytime soon.

I had calmed down a bit by the time I made it to Dakota's apartment, or at least I had put my fight with Daddy out of my mind. Though I couldn't help thinking that maybe I shouldn't have been so hateful toward him. I mean, he is still my daddy, and although he has a tough way of showing it, he loves me. He doesn't want what happened to Momma to happen to me. I was glad I hadn't told him about my singing. That would only give him more reason to compare me to Momma.

Dakota answered the door in a pair of men's boxer shorts and a long T-shirt, looking like she had just gotten out of bed although it was already after one o'clock. She was tired and out of it, as though she had been through a rough night. "What's up, Jazz? Come on in. You want some coffee?"

No, I didn't want any coffee, it was the middle of the day, but she fixed me a cup anyway and added Amaretto-flavored creamer. She sat the cup on the coffee table in front of me and I started smiling from ear to ear and I knew she could sense that I had something to tell her, but she didn't look as excited as she usually does whenever she's about to get a juicy bit of gossip. I figured she was still pissed because she didn't get none last night and decided to drop my good news on her right away so she'd cheer up.

"Guess who just called me?" I said, still smiling like a Cheshire cat. I didn't wait for her to ask who because I was just too dang excited. "Bobby Strong from Black Tie Records!" I said and stomped my feet on her thick bronze carpet. "Girl, why didn't you tell me you gave him my tape last night? I liked to died when he told me he wanted to see me today."

"He actually called you?" she said, like she didn't believe what I had just told her.

"Yes, girl, and he wants to see me at his office at four o'clock."

"In his office? I'm going with you."

"No, no. I gotta do this by myself."

"Jazz, you don't know what this man's all about. He could be a mass murderer or a rapist or something, and I swear, sometimes you're just a little bit too naive when it comes to things like this."

Well, needless to say, I wasn't in the mood for that type of talk. I had just finished telling Daddy that I was capable of running my own life, now I had to sit here and defend myself against Dakota. She can be just like Daddy sometimes. "Look, Dakota, I'm gonna tell you like this. I am grown. I don't need anybody holding my hand and following behind me making sure I do things right. I can handle this one. Trust me, I know what I'm doing."

I guess I must have hurt her feelings because she got really quiet. I thought she'd be happy for me, that she'd start acting silly and say something like, "Go, Jazmine, it's your birthday." But she just sat there on the couch looking like someone had just stolen her best friend. But I was so elated that I just kept right on talking. "Come on, girl, you gotta help me pick out something cute to wear," I said, walking into her bedroom.

"You ought to wear something conservative. Something that doesn't show too much."

Now she was sounding just like Daddy, or at least nothing like the Dakota I knew. "Girl, please. I want the man to see everything he's gonna get. He already knows I can sing, now he needs to know that I can look good on the cover of a CD. That's all that really matters these days anyway. Most of the singers out there can't really sing. All they can do is dance and look good in spandex."

"Are you sure you don't want me to go with you? I could wait in the car," she said, pulling out a white cotton button-up blouse from her closet.

"I'm sure, Dakota. You might as well put that blouse down, because I'm wearing something low-cut today. What's wrong with you, anyway?"

"Nothing. I'm just trying to look out for you, girl," she said and sat down on her bed.

But I could tell she had something else on her mind and I wished she'd just spit it out, because she was starting to get on my nerves with all this goody-goody mess.

"Just be careful, Jazz. I know you want to make a good impression, but you gotta look out for yourself. I'm telling you, some people in this business are complete assholes. They're only looking out for themselves and they'll use you in whatever way they can to get what they want. I should know. River and Earth have told me stories about people in this business that would make your head spin."

"That's every business, D. Heck, that's men in general. They all want something from you and will use any shady means they know how to get it. You taught me that a long time ago."

"I know. I just hope you heard me."

I tried to change the subject because all this talk was killing my buzz. "Did you see Craig last night?" I asked, pulling out a pink strapless number that I had caught on sale at Bullock's. "He was looking good, as usual."

"I bet he was," she said and gave me a look that said, "You damn fool, you should've jumped on that piece when you had the chance."

I knew she was right.

"But don't even sweat it, honey. Men ain't nothing but a headache. They take you and use you and before you know it, it's all over. You've lost all control."

Oh no. This did not sound like Dakota, but I was tired of trying to guess what was wrong with her, and whatever it was I knew she'd eventually get over it. She always had in the past. But she was on a roll now, and once Dakota gets started on something, it's hard to get her to shut up.

"Men are just assholes, honey. They think they can do anything to you and get away with it. Especially the ones who have a little power or think they have something you want or something that they can do for you that no one else can do. You just have to protect yourself, girl. I know I am from now on. I ain't about to just let a man take any- and everything he wants from me like I'm just some piece of meat and get nothing in return. Fuck that shit. I'm tired of these motherfuckers. The next time I get a man that motherfucker's comin' out the pocket. I'm tired of these men taking control of me like I don't have a say-so in the matter. I'm tired of these fools who start out wining and dining you, buying you everything plus two more like they living large and in charge, then after they get a little coochie it's like, 'Can I borrow some money, baby.' "

"I know what you mean, girl. First it's a ten, then a twenty. Next thing you know he wants to borrow your car," I said, knowing full well the type of man she was describing, although I never had to deal with one personally.

"I know, and to top it off the motherfucker will drive your car and bring it back on E. I hate that shit. Matter a fact, I ain't dating no more men who don't have a car, period. Some men running around here, damn near thirty years old and ain't never had no car. Thirty years old and still getting their bus pass renewed. Thirty years old and still gotta have somebody drop their ass off everywhere. Fuck that. My next man has to have it together. If he ain't got no dollars, he ain't got no sense. And if he thinks he's coming up in here running things, that's gonna cost him even more. Oh yes. You gotta pay the cost to be the boss."

Dakota always had problems with men using her and running over her, but that's because she makes it too easy for them. They say one nice thing to her and the next thing you know they're in her bed. I told her about that stupid mess before. Imagine that. Me teaching her something about men.

"Jazz, I don't know why these men think they can run your life. You sleep with them once and all of a sudden they gotta know where you're going, who you're going with, what time you're gonna be back. They come over your house and just take over everything. Changing your radio station, flipping your television from channel to channel, stretching their sloppy ass all out across your couch. And they always hungry. They walk through your door talking about, 'Whatchoo got to eat?' Now I ask you, if the motherfucker was so damn hungry, why didn't he stop his lazy ass at the Taco Bell? It's right on the corner. Hell, there's a Taco Bell or a Subway or a Mickey Dee's on every damn corner. You know why they don't do that? Because the motherfuckers ain't got no money! They wanna come up in my kitchen pulling out drawers, opening canisters—justa looking—looking everywhere. Then they stop at the refrigerator and hold it open for damn near forever, scratching themselves and sticking their big-ass heads all the way in there as if there's something way in the back hiding that they can't see. Hell no. The next time I give it up it's gonna be different. I'm gonna find me a man who doesn't mind spending a few extra dollars to make his woman feel special."

"I hear you, girl," I said, understanding her point, but trying to figure out why she was going on and on about it. Whoever pissed her off must have done a damn good job, because I had never heard Dakota talk about men like this.

"That's right. I need a man who won't pop up over my house with his hand out, but with takeout—for two. We need men who respect our space, who treat us like the queens we are, men with a little bit of money and a car. And while I'm on the subject, he might as well be tall, clean-cut, well dressed, and smart. I just want a man who's already got it together before I get him. I'm tired of connecting the dots."

"I know what you mean. They always say at school: 'If your project's not complete, then don't turn it in.'" I walked over to the mirror and looked at myself for the first time that day. I looked ragged and my hair was sticking out all over the place and now it was almost two-thirty and I needed to start getting myself together. "Girl, do something with my hair," I told Dakota, but she was still sitting on the bed seething. She was really pissed and I can't blame her, and though I didn't know exactly what happened to put her in this mood, I was sort of glad for her. Maybe now she would see that you just can't go giving it away to any fool who winks his eye at you. At twenty-seven years old, it's about time she realized that. She deserves better than what she's been getting lately. I mean she's smart, maybe not in the book sense of the word, but she knows how to carry her own. She got that administrative assistant job she's been working at ever since she graduated from high school without any type of prior experience, so she's no dummy. Well actually, I figured she must have screwed her boss to get the position, but still Dakota knows about the way things work. Take this apartment, for instance. Talk about plush and laid out. When she first looked at this place the manager was asking nine hundred and fifty dollars a month for it, but she talked that idiot down to seven hundred. Well, she probably gave him a piece too, but still, I have to admit, the girl knows how to get what she wants.

I decided to tackle my hair myself. I pinned it up in a bun with some bobby pins in the back and left out a few curls to frame my face in the front. I decided to take D's advice and dress down a bit, so I put on a pair of Liz Claiborne slacks and a blue silk shirt and dressed it up with some gold jewelry and a gold chain belt. I did up my face with that new Cover Girl makeup made for black people that comes in shades like honey and cappuccino and mocha. It's about time they made something just for us so we don't have to go around looking beige and peach and buttery.

By the time I finished, Dakota was sitting in the living room listening to Aretha Franklin's "Respect." When she looked up and saw me she was pleased. "Now that's good, real smart. You look classy, like you got something to offer besides a big butt and a smile. By the way, what did Daddy say about all this?"

"Girl, we got so caught up on all that other stuff that I forgot to tell you."

"Well, sit on down and spill it. I know that mickey-fickey probably had something negative to say."

"I didn't even get around to telling him, girl. He came in all pissed off because somebody down at the church told him they saw me out last night. And of course, he acted like I was some sort of demon child for going out to a *party*. Girl, he acted a fool. But I tell you, you would have been so proud of me, Dakota. I told him I wasn't taking his shit no more. I told him I was old enough to make my own decisions and that he was not gonna run my life anymore."

"No you didn't, girl! What did he say?"

"He gave me the old line about following his rules in his house and shit. And I swear, girl. I don't know what the hell got into me, but I told him he could keep his little funky rules because I wasn't going to be living in his house no more."

"Shut up, girl. You didn't."

"Yes I did. I don't know where I got the strength to tell him that, but I just couldn't stop myself. I don't know. I'll call him later on and apologize, I guess."

"No you won't. Girl, it's about time you stood up to him. Shit, you twenty-six fucking years old. It don't make no sense for him to treat you like you in diapers. I don't care how much money he's paying for your education. He has too much control over you."

I knew Dakota was telling me the truth, but I couldn't help feeling sorry for Daddy. I mean, I was his baby. It had been just me and him for so many years that I didn't know how I could make it without him. True enough, he treated me like crap sometimes, but I know it's just because I'm his only child and he cares about me. Although he won't admit it, he needs me. Probably more than I need him, especially since Momma is gone.

"Honey, look around this apartment," Dakota said, rising up from the couch and throwing her arm out like she was one of the models on *The*

Price Is Right. "There's more than enough room here for you. I still haven't turned that second bedroom into a computer room, so you go right ahead and take it. I been telling you ever since we graduated high school that you needed to get out from under his wing. So don't go second-guessing yourself. You did the right thing, honey. You too damn old for somebody to be telling you what to do and watching over your every move."

"But D, I don't make near enough money at Bullock's to help you out on rent. I got credit card bills up the ass, and that piece of shit I got parked outside takes up half my check anyway."

"Shut up, girl. Ain't nobody worrying about money right now. So you just get your shit together and bring it right on over here. Besides, have you forgotten your appointment today? Shoot, you might be about to make enough money to buy your own pad. *If* this Bobby Strong character is really interested in your singing and not just out to get another piece of ass."

"You sure, girl? I mean, I don't wanna cramp your style. I know how much you like your privacy."

"Did you hear what I told you earlier? There ain't gonna be no more men running in and out this apartment every night. I mean that shit."

I couldn't be sure if she was for real about that, because ever since I've known Dakota, she's been on the prowl. But she was right about one thing. I shouldn't go back to Daddy's. "Girl, I gotta get outta here or I'm gonna be late."

"I'm serious, Jazz. Pack up your things and bring them over here," she said, following me to the door. "And one more thing," she said, grabbing my arm and pulling me around to face her. "Watch your back today. Play it cool and definitely don't sign your name to a damn thing before you talk it over with a lawyer. I'm telling you, girl it's some shady motherfuckers in this business. Now you be careful, honey. And give me a damn hug, damn it."

I did, but before I could tell her how grateful I was to her for giving my tape to Mr. Strong, she told me to get off of her and get on out the door. "You got business to tend to, honey. And remember, watch your back."

I left her apartment and got in my car. I put on "I'm Lost Without You" by BeBe and CeCe and sped off toward Century City. I needed to relax myself. So much had gone on in a matter of hours that it didn't seem real.

I needed to have a talk with God, but I knew He was probably still mad at me for the way I treated Daddy. So I just listened to BeBe and tried to get focused. I couldn't believe I was on my way to meet with a record company executive. I couldn't believe that I could be on the verge of making my dreams come true. What I could believe was that I was scared as hell. Here I was about to deal with a man who knew everything about the business, and I knew nothing. I wished I had some type of representation; a manager or an agent or somebody who could do my talking for me. But I figured if anybody was going to make this happen it was going to be me. I felt powerful in a way. Like I held the key to my future, and all that was left for me to do was put it in the lock. Another part of me was scared and all at once I wished I had let Dakota come with me. She'd know how to handle this situation. She'd say the right thing, do the right thing, and she wasn't above using her feminine wiles to get what she wanted. I decided right then and there that I was going to be more like Dakota. Not the part of her who'll do anything for a piece of dick, but the part of her that will do whatever it takes to get what she wanted. I knew I had it in me—that was evident from the way I handled Daddy earlier. But now the script had been flipped and I didn't know my next line. One thing was for sure, though—I was gonna keep practicing until I got it right.

chapter six

break 'em off some

Good shit happens, but it always happens best when you just chill and flow with it. The thought had crossed my mind many times that I could possibly get signed to Black Tie Records, but I didn't know that shit would happen this soon. Now here I am. Me, Xavier Honor. All the way up in the mothafuckin' house. And look at this place—pimped out! Gold records all over the walls, leather seats and glass and marble everywhere you turn. It looks more like a palace than a record company. Man, I'm glad I went on ahead and put on a good pair of pants and a nice shirt. I'd be looking real stupid up in here in a pair of jeans. But of course I had to throw on my baseball cap with the marijuana plant on the front—just so I could let these mothafuckas know I'm still down.

Life is crazy, man. I mean, there I was on the mic, trying to impress a girl. Then the next thing I know the whole crowd is jumping and shouting out my name and carrying on. And after I'm finished and get off the stage, I get rushed by this A&R man and he's all questioning me and shit about my experience and whether I'm represented or have a contract. And when I tell him I don't, he goes pulling me by the arm up the stairs to some private party and introduces me to Kirk Walker and—bing, bop, bam!—here I am about to meet with him and my lawyer about signing a contract. This is too crazy.

The first thing I did this morning was to call up Larry and give him the rundown on everything and ask that fool to represent me. Larry's cool and he knows all that technical shit that only confuses a brother like me. Besides, Larry been down with me ever since he helped me beat that bullshit charge the pigs tried to stick me and Rich with a few years back. We was down at the airport, just chillin' and minding our own business. We had just gotten off a flight from our vacation spot—East St. Louis. Back in St. Louis, an ounce of coke go for about fourteen hundred dollars. In L.A. we could only get about half that price for an ounce. So needless to say, me and Rich was some frequent-flying mothafuckas. But I swear, you can't tell Rich a damn thing. I told that nigga as plain as day: "Don't tape the fuckin' money to your body. Just put the shit in the suitcase 'cause the dogs ain't gon' be sniffing for money—they sniffing for blow." But no. That mothafucka was so scared the suitcase was gon' accidentally fly open or get lost in another state or some stupid shit like that and he'd lose all the money he had made on vacation. So like a dumb mothafucka, he secretly tape the money to his body—about six thousand dollars' worth—and thought he was just gon' pass on through the airport like O.J. Simpson in a wheel-chair. Now of course the pigs ain't stupid. They be sweating niggas in the airport like it ain't shit. We thinking we done made our little trip, got our money, and made it safely back home, right? Fuck that. We was in line waiting to pick up our luggage when about eight security pigs surrounded us and escorted us to a private room. They was talking about they was just checking us out on one of their random searches of the airport. Bullshit. They ended up making Rich roll through one of them metal detectors and sure enough, the mothafucka started beeping. The alarm had sounded when we was trying to leave St. Louis too, but he had convinced them backward-ass fags that it was just going off because of his wheelchair. Well, these Southern California pigs wasn't falling for the okie-doke. I had tried to tell that fool over and over: "Money got *lead* in it. Lead, moth-afucka. Just like jewelry and coins and shit. Of course it's gon' set off the metal detector." But did that fool listen to me? Hell naw. That's why we ended up in jail until Larry could finally fix up the shit and get us out. I don't know how he did it. All I know is that he used some type of defense about Rich was wrongfully searched, and he threw in some shit about him being handicapped and—ding, dong, doink!—we was out and back on the streets. Minus the vacation money them pigs *accidentally* lost during the search. All I know is Larry is one hell of an attorney, and that's one nigga I want by my side.

He needs to hurry up and get here though, 'cause I need to go over that mess about contracts we were talking about earlier. He told me to think long and hard about what kind of contract I wanted to sign. At first I was thinking about a master lease deal 'cause that way I'd get more money on royalties. But then I decided I wanted to go with the production contract 'cause that way I can keep total control of my music. The only thing is that I don't know if they'll let a newcomer have that type of deal. But fuck it. I'm so nervous right now I'll probably jump at the first offer they make me 'cause one way or another I'm gon' get my record made. I can't go out like no sucka. Not now. Not after I done fucked off my relationships with everybody.

Last night, after I got finished meeting with Mr. Walker and came back downstairs, T-Bone and Rich went off on me. They started popping all this bullshit about me leaving them out and trying to steal the show and shit. If you ask me, they was just jealous 'cause I rocked the house, but still, I told them fools I hadn't planned none of it. Hell, all I was trying to do was impress a bitch. But they thought I was lying, so they just went on and on. Like all their talk was gon' change what happened. Then Bone asked me what had gone on upstairs and I shoulda kept my damn mouth closed, but I just started blurting out everything. I told them about how they liked my style and that they said the lyrics were dope and that they wanted to meet with me the next day. He asked if they wanted him and Rich to be there, and I couldn't lie to the brother and get his hopes all up, so I just told him straight out—they wanted to sign me up by myself. And what did I do that for, 'cause that mothafucka nutted up on me, big-time. I told that fool that I tried to get them in on the deal too, but he just kept going off and calling me a busta and causing a scene. Then that fool tried to step up in my face, and I don't care who it is, don't nobody walk up on me like that. Punks that step up, get beat down. Period. I was just about to swing on that fool when security came over and dragged his stupid-ass outta there.

Rich didn't say nothing, but he kept on staring at me. I didn't know if he was mad or if he was just too drunk to do anything else. Then again it ain't too much that brother can do from that wheelchair. All he did was pull out his portable phone and call Eyeisha to come pick him up. I don't know how T-Bone got home, but if I see that punk I'ma fuck him up. When I went out to the car to go home, somebody had keyed it all the way around the sides and it smelled like piss. I know it couldn't have been nobody but Bone's stupid-ass, and he bet' not let me catch up with him. Damn, I sure was glad I didn't drive my '64. Kelly would just have to get her car fixed up herself. Or better yet, have her daddy buy her a new one altogether.

Anyway, I don't know why them two fools is mad at me. It ain't my fault that I got noticed last night, and besides, the three of us together woulda never worked out. So fuck it. Let them fools sit and cry about it like idiots. I ain't trying to hear all that. A brother like me is headed for the big time and I don't need no extra baggage weighing me down.

By the time I got to Kelly's pad last night, I was pissed off pass the point of return. I had just been offered the biggest opportunity of my life and everybody was trippin' out on me. I parked her car out on the street and went in and tried my best to be cool. But for some reason, the sight of her, sitting there waiting on me, ready to please like some lost little puppy, just pissed me off even more.

"T-Bone called and told me what happened tonight," she said, but I didn't even look in her direction.

"He sounded really upset and he said that you should watch your back from now on because he's looking for you. What went on between you two? I thought you said you'd never break up with your friends."

I knew what the fuck I had said and I didn't need her reminding me. "So you were right, okay? I broke up with them fools. You happy now? Isn't this what you wanted?" She started to look like she was gon' cry, so I left the room. That bitch cry about everything, like every uncomfortable situation is the end of the fucking world.

I went into the bedroom and closed the door. If nobody was gon' be happy for me, then I'd just be happy for my damn self. I sat down on the floor and turned on Nintendo, but Mario and Luigi were kicking my ass so I turned it off and started thinking about my future. It was weird to have a future to think about. Usually I'm just living from day to day. I get up, bone Kelly, get dressed, and go hang with the homies. But that's all about to change. Now I got a purpose, something more to look forward to than just the same old bullshit day in and day out. I gotta think about writing some new lyrics, hookin' up some funky beats, lawyers, managers, contracts, tours, image.

If I know one thing, it's how important image is in the business. People like the bad guys, though most of 'em won't admit it. But they do. It's like Pacino in *Scarface*. When that fool got killed in the end my feelings got hurt. He was a hard mothafucka and people liked him. That's how I wanna be. The kid from the streets, making it in the big world of music. But if I really wanna make it, I'm gon' have to get rid of that whining white chick in the other room. She's bad for my image. Black people hate it when they see a brother in the limelight with a white girl on his arm, especially if he's a rapper. Rappers are supposed to be the blackest entertainers in the business. I mean, blackness is a big part of their image. That's why that white boy Vanilla Ice got dissed big-time. That boy tried to act like he was from the streets, but when everybody found out he wasn't, the black community dropped that fool like a hot potato. I gotta give it to him though. That one song he had was the bomb, but you can't be white and be a rapper these days, and you sho can't be a brother with a white girl-friend. Sisters would go crazy. They go crazy when they see *any* brother with a white girl on his arm.

Kelly's been getting on my nerves anyway. This ain't my scene no more. It was cool for a minute, but when you break it down, there ain't nothing a white girl can offer a black man. Our worlds are too different. All she know about is BMWs, diamonds, and health spas. Me, I'm straight outta South-Central, the ghetto, the hood, the streets. The two just don't mix. She musta heard me thinking or picked up my vibes, 'cause the next thing I knew, she was walking into the room talking about, "We need to talk."

I wasn't in the mood for none of her shit, so I just came right on out and told her. "There ain't nothing to talk about 'cause I'm leaving." She started crying, but what else is new. I started packing up my shit in a brown paper bag. Then, she started getting stupid, talking about if I leave she was gon' kill herself. I told her to go right ahead 'cause I didn't give a fuck. That suicide shit don't work on me. I'm past that. I've seen niggas dying in the streets, so shit like that just don't affect me. In fact, if she had slit her wrists right then and there, I probably woulda just stood there and watched her die. Hell, white people been standing by watching black folks die for years, so what difference would it make?

She kept crying and acting crazy, but my mind was set. I had my career to think about and Kelly just couldn't go along for the ride. I picked up my two paper bags, the keys to my Impala, and hit the door. I didn't even think about where I was going until I got down to my car and realized that I didn't have anywhere to go. I thought about just kicking it in my car for the night, then I thought I should go back up and ask Kelly to loan me some money for a hotel. Then I thought that she was probably stupid enough to do it and I just got disgusted all over again, thinking about how dumb she was.

Then I said, fuck it. T-Bone was an asshole, but Rich, we had been through too much shit for him to trip out on me. No matter what, Rich had always been there for me and I knew if I could just talk to the brother, tell him I hadn't planned for things to turn out like this, that he'd understand and everything would be cool. Or at least he'd let me borrow his couch for the night. So, I headed back down the 405 toward the hood. When I got to his pad, I didn't see the Infiniti outside, so I figured he must be over Eyeisha's house. I drove around the corner to her crib and sure enough, his car was parked across the lawn. I shoulda known something was up when that bitch came to the door in her panties and a T-shirt, but stupid-ass me didn't pick up on it.

"Hi, X," she said, looking as trampy as I'd ever seen her.

"Yo, where's Rich? He in here? Yo, Rich, I need to talk you, man," I said, sliding through the door and trying my best not to accidentally touch her.

"He ain't here. I dropped him off at home already."

"A'ight, cool. I'll go back over there then."

"No you won't," she said, closing the door behind her. "Rich say you bet' not show your face around here no more. He mad as hell and he even talking about taking you out. And with that gun collection he got over there, you know he more than capable of doing just that."

Damn. I couldn't believe it. I had to sit down on that note. Rich and I had been too close for him to trip out on some shit like that. He ought to know I'd take care of his ass if I ever hit the big time. And anyway, that fool wasn't really into rapping in the first place. He was already a superstar in the hood. Everybody knew Rich: the hard-ass mothafucka in the wheelchair. He was a celebrity. And besides, he was just using the group as a front to stash the money he made off his dope sales so the feds wouldn't start asking questions. He had money stashed in all sorts of businesses around the hood. "It always feels good to give back to the community," he'd say. Rap didn't mean nothing to Rich. He had everything he could ever want already. Celebrity status, money, a home, a nice car. I couldn't believe he was threatening my life over some bullshit like this. Damn. I was already starting to see what they mean when they talk about the high price of fame 'cause at that point I didn't feel like I had a friend in the world.

Then I was shocked back to reality when Eyeisha's fat-ass starting getting all up in my face. Her big-ass had the nerve to have on a thong. A thong. I couldn't believe it.

"Why you looking so sad, X? Fuck Rich, he ain't shit no way. As a matter of fact, I'm 'bout to break up with his ugly, crippled ass. That mothafucka can't even get his dick hard no more."

Then she really started trippin'. She started dancing around and strippin' right there in front of me. I thought I was watching some bad porno flick, only her fat-ass pussy was in 3-D and all up in my face. Now I know she's a nasty, stank, trifling ho, but I don't know man alive that when some pussy staring him in the face gon' look the other way. Not me and especially not after I just broke up with Kelly and didn't know when I might be getting my next piece. And definitely not after Rich, who I thought was my homeboy, done straight threatened my life—shiiit. Pussy is pussy, and besides I heard that bitch was nasty as hell—just like I like 'em.

We fucked on her hard-ass mattress on the floor of her bedroom for about four hours and if it hadn't been for her face, that weave, them long-ass fingernails, and that fish smell, I mighta enjoyed it. It was wild though and I gotta admit, that bitch know how to suck some dick. Bitches that you don't care about are the best ones to fuck when your ass is horny 'cause you do whatever you want to and don't care about what they gon' say. Well I went acrobatic on that ho. I had her legs stretched out every which and way and no matter what I did she was wanting more. After about three hours, I had enough, but she just kept on begging so I went on and gave her another hour 'cause to tell the truth, the way I was feeling that night I thought that would be the last piece of pussy I saw.

I fucked up big-time though when I fell asleep. When I woke up the next morning that bitch was still wrapped around me, sleeping and snoring. As Kelly would say, I was grossed out to the max. I slid Eyeisha off of me and grabbed my drawls and put them on. I was buttoning up my pants at the door when she walked up butt-naked behind me talkin' about, "You leaving already? Why don't you stay for breakfast? I'll cook you up some grits and bacon and squeeze you some orange juice."

"Is you crazy?" I said, looking around for my keys. "I'm bouts to raise up outta here, and don't be getting no ideas about this happening again, 'cause it ain't."

"Come on, X. I know you liked it and I damn sho know my stuff is better than that white trash you been sticking it to for the past few months."

"Naw, naw. This was a one-time thing. I gots ta break you off, girl."

When she started crying, I thought I was gon' lose my fucking mind. Now I know I ain't no Don Juan and shit, but these girls be acting like they gon' fall out and die when a piece of dick get ready to walk out their door. Then she started talking crazy and saying she was gon' tell Rich and shit, but at that point I really didn't give a fuck. Rich wasn't my homeboy no more and since I didn't have any plans on coming around this neighborhood no more, I didn't give a damn if she told him or not. So I said fuck it and walked out the door. I drove straight to a phone booth and called up Larry. I wasn't thinking about them fools. They was part of the past and I was moving on.

It was five minutes to four and Larry hadn't even shown his face yet and I was getting more and more nervous as the seconds ticked away. I still couldn't even believe I was at Black Tie Records or that I had actually got up on that mic and got discovered at that party. And it was all because I was trying to impress that redhead. Well, I may not have gotten the girl, but I sho-nuff got what I wanted. I was sweating and I thought if Larry didn't hurry up, I was gon' start nuttin' up. What I needed to do was get up and walk around 'cause I was gon' go crazy sitting in that chair.

When I got up to stretch my legs, a fine young honey walked through the lobby and took a seat across from me. At first I thought I was seeing double 'cause this honey looked just like that redhead from last night. I stared and stared until she finally looked over at me and sure enough it was her. I didn't know what was going on and I never been too swift on the notion of God and all that religion mess, but somebody up there was hooking up my life in all the right ways. She looked nervous, like she was getting ready for a blind date or something, and she didn't even recognize me. So I took off my cap and kept staring, but she still just kept on sitting there like I was invisible. Then I got up and walked across the room and plopped down right next to her. She was gon' recognize me if it was the last thing she ever did.

I cleared my throat and started smiling until she looked up. "What's up you?" I said, remembering that she was that sophisticated type and that I had to do things just right. "You following me or something? If you are, I don't mind. Just let me know and I'll slow down so you can keep up."

She started smiling and flashing her teeth, but still the girl looked like she was scared to death. "I'm sorry, but I don't remember your name," she said, and for a second I felt my manhood shrink up a little bit.

"Oh, you don't remember Saint Xavier?" I said, still not knowing who the fuck that was.

"Oh yes, Xavier. How are you doing? Or should I say *what* are you doing here?"

Damn, a brother can't be chilling in a corporate office? What? Do I look like scum or something? "Well, I could be asking you the same thing, Little Miss Redhead." Then I thought this would be a good opportunity to try and impress her again so I laid my purpose on her. "Well you know, look like I'm gon' finally sign a contract and cut a record for these people. Yeah, they been after me for a while, so I decided to go on ahead and give in. Didn't you catch my act last night? Woo, I set that place off—if I do say so myself."

"Yeah, I heard you."

I stroked my goatee and tried to act like I had been performing all my life. "Yeah, you know how it is. I got on up there, threw down one of my raps, drove the crowd crazy. You know, the usual. Now they want me to sign a contract, so here I am." I could tell she was impressed and I gave myself an invisible pat on the back. I was scoring points with the honey already.

"What a coinky-dink," she said and started giggling. Damn, baby is fine. "That's what I'm here to do too. This is too much. This really is a small world."

She had her hair all pinned up and sexy-looking, and although her clothes were ordinary today, she still looked like some exotic queen. But for some reason though, the fact that she was there to sign a contract didn't sit right with me. She seemed like the type to be a lawyer or a teacher. You know, one of them sexy teachers, who after class is out, lets down her hair and takes off her glasses and unbuttons her shirt and pulls her skirt up, and. . . . Oh shit, I need to quit. "Damn, this really is a trip. So you're a singer, huh."

"Well, I certainly don't look like one of those female rappers, do I?"

"No, I have to say you don't," I said and picked apart her body with my eyes, piece by scrumptious piece. "So you meeting with Kirk?"

"No, my appointment's with Bobby Strong," she said. I don't care too much for that Strong mothafucka. On my way to meet Kirk last night I accidentally bumped into that fool, and since I was in dignified surroundings, I grabbed him by the arm and apologized. But that mothafucka just jerked away from me and kept on walking. If we had been in the streets I would of fucked him up for disrespecting me like that. Not to mention the fact that he stepped on my tennis shoes. Many a nigga have been beat down for committing that crime. I was glad she wasn't meeting with Kirk though. I mean, she was fine and all, but I didn't want to have no competition with her. She'll stick with Bobby and I'll stick with Kirk and if my day keeps going the way it has, we'll be sticking it to each other later on.

"So what you sing, Jazmine? Jazz?" I broke out laughing 'cause I thought it was funny, but I guess she had heard that line before 'cause she didn't even whimper.

"Well, I guess I'm pretty much an R&B singer. But I draw on influences from all types of music," she said, uncrossing and recrossing her fine legs.

She was obviously a classy lady. I could tell by the way she talked and carried herself, and I really wanted to ask her out, but I couldn't tell if she was interested in me or if she was just talkin' to me to be talkin'. Women have a bad habit of doing that shit. If a man don't think you fine or at least think he can get some from you, he won't give your ass a second look. But women, they'll sit and talk to anybody, and that shit gets downright confusing 'cause a brother can't tell if he should make a move or not. And ain't nothing worse than asking a woman out and she gives you a look like, "Nigga, please. I was talking to your ass to be nice." But fuck it, Little Miss Redhead had it goin' on too strong for a brother like me to let her pass up without giving it a shot. "So uh, you got a man?" I knew I shouldn't have said that the minute it walked out my mouth 'cause she looked at me like "Excuse me?" and that's exactly what she ended up saying, so I tried to straighten up and come correct. "I mean, you know. I'm just asking. A brother can ask, right? But uh, you know. Seeing as how we're gon' be coworkers in a sense. That is, if everything goes all right here today, I thought we could maybe get together sometime and uh, you know, do whatever it is two young, single people do when they get together."

"You're funny," she said and started laughing again, but I couldn't find anything funny about what I just said. I was throwing out my best drama and she was laughing in my face. Sisters.

"Well, here's my number. Actually it's my best friend's number but I'm probably going to move in with her sometime this week," she said, taking out a pen and paper and writing out her name and number in the most beautiful handwriting I've ever seen. She gave me the paper, then took out another and asked me for my number. I gave her the number to my pager and she wrote it down and stuck the paper in her purse.

Then the receptionist called her name and said, "Mr. Strong is ready to see you now." I could tell she was getting all tensed up again.

"Don't worry about it, baby. You'll be a'ight," I said as she got up and walked toward the reception desk. I don't think she even heard me, but I must admit, I impressed myself. I sounded like, almost sincere. Now that was some scary shit.

I watched her walk through the door and I almost felt sad. Me? Feeling sad 'cause a bitch, I mean a young lady, was leaving me? Something's definitely goin' on here. Something I don't have control of. I sat there shaking my head from side to side, trying to stop the theme from *The Twilight Zone* from playing in my mind. The way I was feeling was so new to me—new and odd. But hey, I'm the X-Man, I can handle this. Right?

chapter seven

mind blowing

Bobby sat behind his desk, watching the CD cover he had placed in front of him spin around. He was bored out of his mind and could find no better way of passing the time than flicking the side of a CD cover and watching as it swiveled around upon his desk. He shifted his body in his seat and clasped his dark hands in front of him and tried to keep them from shaking. He couldn't tell if his body was going through a minor withdrawal syndrome or if he was just reeling from how drastically his life seemed to be changing. He knew he didn't have much time before his four o'clock appointment with the singer he was hoping would help him regain control of his career. Still, he took his time, watching the CD twist before him, and when it stopped, he flicked it again and watched as his mind drifted back to the previous evening and tried to make sense of what now seemed a crazed nightmare.

He cringed when he remembered the way he had stumbled through the house after he returned from the party. He made a beeline to the great room and quickly retrieved a full bottle of scotch and opened it in the darkness. He drank heartily, barely flinching as the liquid stung through his throat. He knew his high had maxed out and all he could do was wait for the ultimate relief when his body would overtake his mind and he'd pass out. He'd only been this high once before that he could remember, and that had been the night the media got ahold of the Toby-T story. He didn't remember much about that night except that when he passed out, it was the most at peace he'd ever been. As he took another gulp from the bottle, he felt himself becoming anxious. He couldn't wait to pass out, to slip into the peace of nothingness.

He had held the bottle against his temple and shut his eyes in a futile attempt to forget the girl in the red suit and what he had almost done to her—what he *had* done to her. Had he really touched her that way? Did he actually force her to the ground and climb on top of her? His aching jaw confirmed his transgressions, and he quickly tilted the bottle to his mouth. What is happening to me? In eighteen years, he hadn't touched any other woman except Sheryl, yet today he had come close to pure disaster twice. He squeezed his eyes together tightly, trying to fight away the horrible things his mind was telling him his body had done.

"Sheryl," he mumbled underneath his breath, feeling the need for her presence. He needed to hear her say everything was going to be okay, but most of all he needed to confess. He needed to come clean. It was the only way, he thought. He had to make her understand that this was not him, that this was not what he wanted. Not for him, her, and especially not for their children. "Sheryl," he yelled through the darkness and lifted the bottle to his lips until the last drop came trickling on his tongue. "Sheryl!" he shouted and stumbled toward the stairs.

"Oops," he whispered and let out a soft giggle when he tripped over the first step. "Sher—uh—shit!" he said louder, this time falling midway through his climb. He slowly stood and held on to the rail, then cautiously proceeded to the top. "Ssh," he whispered, holding a finger to his mouth as he passed Tiffany and Brittany's rooms. He tiptoed further and entered his bedroom, closing the door behind him.

"Sheryl," he called as he flipped on the lights and squinted from the glare, but there was no answer. The room was empty. Panic pumped through his veins as he called her name again and ran to the master bath. To his surprise, her side of the double sink was completely cleared away. Had she really left him? he wondered, while the room spun around him. She can't be gone. He tripped over the bath rug as he rushed out. In a flash he was down the stairs and in the kitchen, but there was no Sheryl. He fled to the game room. Empty. Exhausted, he tried one last place, the maid's quarter.

Sheryl jumped when Bobby opened the door and stumbled through. She sat in the window seat, glaring in his direction, her stare intensifying as it became clear to her that he was under the influence.

As he stared back he could see her repulsed look as he got closer and closer. He couldn't believe it, but what he saw on her face was fear and that confused him. After all these years she should know I'd never hurt her. She should know I'd do anything for her.

Carefully, he reached out for her, but instead of falling into his embrace, Sheryl was repelled, squeezing her body as close as she could against the window.

"What do you want, Bobby?"

"To talk, Sheryl. I know we can make this right," he said with the shyness of a schoolboy. "I'll be good from now on."

"There's nothing left to say."

There was plenty left to say, Bobby thought. So much he needed to tell her. He desperately wanted her forgiveness, but most of all he wanted her to understand. He reached for her again, but Sheryl wasn't having it.

"I'm serious this time," she said, refusing to let him close to her.

But Bobby needed her desperately. He held out his arms, but when she brushed him off, he grabbed her, roughly, and pulled her up to his chest. He closed his eyes and enjoyed having her near.

Sheryl squirmed, pressing her hand against his stomach. "Get off of me," she pleaded, but Bobby was oblivious to everything except his desire to have her close to him. He held her tighter as he felt his way up and down her body.

"Stop!" she screamed, shaking his hands off of her. She stepped as far away from him as she could and looked him dead in the eyes. "It's over," she screamed louder, trying to break through Bobby's intoxication.

Bobby smiled through his confusion and reached out to caress her face, only to have his hand slapped away. Instantly something seemed to click in Bobby's head. Sheryl could see the change and it frightened her. He suddenly seemed strangely in control of the situation and there was nothing she could do.

"You're not leaving me alone, Sheryl," he stated directly. "You cannot leave me."

Sheryl trembled as Bobby stared at her. Her body tightened when he touched her again. "I love you," he mumbled and grabbed her tightly, dotting sloppy kisses all over her face. She could smell the alcohol on his breath as he brought his lips to her mouth.

"No!" she yelled and pushed his face away with both hands. But Bobby just kept going. She slapped the side of his face and pushed him back. "Don't touch me!"

Bobby grabbed his jaw, stunned, and looked at her with glazed-over eyes. Sheryl tried to back away, but there was nowhere else to move. Reflexively, Bobby swung out at her. He knocked her away from him so hard that she went tumbling backward into the curve of the window seat and her head bobbled against the glass.

"Bobby, please," she said in total shock, and straightened up. But Bobby didn't seem to hear her. She cried when he slapped her head against the window again. "Hey, look . . . Everything's fine," she tried to reason and smiled out of fright, only she couldn't get through to him. She tried to calm him down between blows to the face. "Wait a minute, Bobby. Just tell me what to do. I'll do it. Please," she pleaded before he knocked her off the seat and to her knees. "Whatchoo want, Bobby?"

He stood above her rubbing the back of his aching hand as Sheryl groveled at his feet. As he stared down at her through glazed eyes he thought about her question. "*Whatchoo want? Whatchoo want?*" The answer was easy to find. "I want my life back."

Swiftly, he pulled her up and pinned her against the wall, then smothered her face with his mouth. Her body shivered against him, but he was only aware of his passion for her. It was uncontrollable, but his desire was not returned. Sheryl's arms hung stiffly by her sides as Bobby's mouth pressed hard against hers. Unconsciously, in one swift grip and tug, he tore the silk shirt she wore from her body. If it hadn't been for Sheryl's shriek, he wouldn't have noticed what he had done. He could feel Sheryl's body completely now as he glided his hands around her.

Suddenly Bobby stopped. He licked his lips and tasted blood. Confused, he put his finger to his mouth and wiped the blood away. He looked at Sheryl and for the first time he recognized her face. It was bruised. Her lips were red with blood. Suddenly he was aware of what he had done. He froze in front of Sheryl, stiffly watching her as she trembled. "*Oh my God,*" he said aloud and stepped backward. Shame washed over his body as he eased away from her like a frightened child, watching her naked vision as he backed his way toward the door. When he reached the doorway he turned around and stopped dead. His oldest daughter, Tiffany, stood watching him, tears streaming down her cheeks. He opened his mouth to speak, but no words were available. All he could do was stare into her eyes and wonder how long she'd been standing there.

"It's okay," Sheryl called from behind Bobby. "Go on back to your room, Tiff," she said, trying to cover her naked body with her arms.

Tiffany did not budge. She just stood there oblivious to everything except Bobby.

He looked back at Sheryl, then cautiously moved past his daughter almost as if he expected her to lash out at him as he passed. He stopped in the middle of the hallway, wanting to turn back around and face his daughter. He wanted her to know that the man she saw was not her daddy. Her daddy was a good man, he wanted to tell her, but he couldn't bring himself to turn around. Full of shame, he turned the corner and bolted up the stairs to his room.

When he got there he went straight to his jewelry box, but all that was there were chains and watches and rings. Next, he checked the drawers of his nightstand, though he knew nothing was there either. There had to be some. Somewhere in this damn house. He threw open the door of his closet and started checking the pockets of every pair of pants, shirt, and jacket he had in there. He didn't stop searching until every piece of clothing he owned was in a pile in the middle of the room. Still, there were no drugs to be found. Not in the house. Not around his children. He climbed into bed exhausted. He'd have to get through the night alone.

The intercom on his desk buzzed out and startled Bobby back into the present.

"What's up, Tish?"

"Mr. Timbers is on his way down to see you."

"Now?"

"Yep."

Tension shot over Bobby's face and worry filled his mind. Mr. Timbers hadn't returned any of his calls all week, yet suddenly he was on his way to see him. He couldn't help feeling betrayed by his boss, especially after last night's awards ceremony. He felt as if he was slowly but surely being pushed aside. Out with the old, in with the new.

When Mr. Timbers burst through his office door, Bobby went into a frenzy. He stood up, cleared his throat, straightened his tie, and pushed the CD he'd been playing with to the corner of his desk. "Mr. Timbers. What a surprise, sir. I hadn't been expecting you," he said, extending his hand.

"Sit down, son. No need for formalities. I just stopped by for a little, shall we say—*rap*," Mr. Timbers said, waving a hand at Bobby to be seated, while he remained standing.

Bobby nervously sat down and clasped his shaking hands together tightly. Though he had wanted to speak to his boss all week, now he could find nothing to say to him.

After a couple minutes of dishing salutations and pleasantries at his boss, Bobby began to relax and decided his boss's mood showed no signs of agitation. He watched the gray-haired man standing before him and for the first time he noticed how old his boss looked. He was in excellent physical condition, better than Bobby had ever been, and he admired him for that. But looking at Mr. Timbers' eyes, he could tell the old man's time was up. He could see why he was ready to retire. Better now, he thought, before his body and spirit caught up with the worn-out look that showed through his face. Bobby wished he had a mirror handy so he could take a look at himself. Although he was twenty years Mr. Timbers' junior, he wondered if his eyes were beginning to show signs of expiration like the man he'd envied for so many years. Bobby always figured that if he wanted to be successful, he should follow the ways of successful people, and since Mr. Timbers had always been everything he wanted to be, he tried to mimic his style, mannerisms, even the way he walked, talked, and dealt with people. As he studied his boss, he recognized that he had become pretty good at the follow-the-leader game because what he saw before him was an exact mirror image of himself.

Since Mr. Timbers seemed in good spirits, Bobby offered him a shot of bourbon, but Mr. Timbers refused. "No, no, son. I've got to keep my conscience clean. I'm knocking off early today and taking the missus up the coast to Santa Barbara. It's our fortieth anniversary, you know," he said and finally sat down in one of the two chairs across from Bobby. His mood seemed to instantly change. He didn't speak for what seemed to Bobby to be an eternity. Then he leaned forward in his seat. "What the hell is going on with you?"

Bobby realized he had let himself get too comfortable and caught up in his boss's seemingly pleasant conversation. He sat up straight in his seat, not knowing exactly what his boss was getting at, or how to answer the overloaded question. "I'm not sure what you mean. Nothing's going on with me."

"I know better than that, Bobby," he said and clutched Bobby's eyes with his. "I may be old, but I ain't no fool. You're slipping. I don't know why, but you're slipping."

Bobby shifted in his seat, hoping Mr. Timbers would stop staring at him with those eyes that looked like they could crush glass. Bobby was trapped and he felt like screaming "Let me go." But there was nothing he could do. Mr. Timbers had always commanded the full attention of his public with his cold-as-ice glare, and like everyone else, Bobby was not immune to it. He listened to as much of Mr. Timbers' speech as he could manage. He couldn't concentrate on anything when he was nervous. Bobby didn't know where the conversation was leading, but he felt an overwhelming urge to remind Mr. Timbers of his accomplishments at Black Tie. When he first started, the company was generating a revenue of only a couple million dollars a year. Now the company was pulling in that amount by the month, due in large part to the new talent Bobby had hauled in. Surely, Mr. Timbers hadn't forgotten about that minor miracle, he thought. In his mind, he was the only logical choice to fill the boss's shoes. No one else had the years of experience that he did and no one, not even Kirk Walker, had the track record that he'd been able to establish in such a short period of time.

"There's nothing that I'd like better than to see you take over this company after I'm gone. But I've got to tell you, Bobby. You've got some strong competition from Kirk Walker," he said matter-of-factly. "He's a fast-paced player. And his promo plans for new talent in the short time he's been here have been outstanding."

Bobby's face twitched as he thought back to a time when Mr. Timbers had said the exact same thing about him. He removed the lid from the silver candy dish that sat on his desk and grabbed a handful of Reese's Pieces and slowly guided them into his mouth, one by one.

"Living with the success that I have," Mr. Timbers continued, "has made me, shall we say, hypersensitive to failure. This company was my baby from the beginning, and I must make absolutely certain that when I walk out these doors for the last time, this company will be left in capable hands."

"What are you saying? Do you doubt my ability to lead this company?" Bobby muttered through a full mouth of candy. "I know you took a big chance on me eighteen years ago, but I think I have more than proven my ability to run this company."

"Have you?" Mr. Timbers asked. His eyes were almost squinting now, but never once did he ease his stare off Bobby. "Seems to me you've forgotten what this company is all about. We're built on heart," he exclaimed, pounding his chest. "We may not be a billion-dollar company like Sony or RCA, but we got something they don't know about. We got heart. That's why we've been in the game for so long. But I don't know, Bobby . . . Your actions over the past year . . ." He stopped, trying to ward off the emotion that had begun to creep over his face. He shook his head pitifully. "Where's your heart, Bobby?"

Bobby let out a hard sigh, knowing Mr. Timbers was yet again referring to the Toby Tragedy. He was so tired of defending himself against it that he found himself almost shouting. "So that's what all the uncertainty is about? My God, that was one mistake. One—in seventeen years of giving you nothing less than my best." Bobby paused for a moment and tried to lower his voice. "All right, I made a mistake. A big one. But you're kidding yourself if you think Kirk won't eventually do the same. I am the one, the rightful one to take over this company. I've put in my time and for the most part have given you nothing but success after success. Isn't that worth something?"

"That depends on what kind of success you're talking about," Mr. Timbers said heatedly. "It's about more than money here at Black Tie. It's about hard work, dedication, being responsible to the community, giving the people what they want, not just what sells. Sure, we could sit around all day snorting coke up our noses and fucking our secretaries across our desks," he said, wailing his hands in exasperation. "You and I know there are a lot of people in the business who do just that. But we don't. We can't afford to. We gotta stay one up on the competition at all times. And anyone in this company who can't fall in line with my vision of the way this company should be run gets his walking papers."

Bobby sat still as a stone, wishing Mr. Timbers would stop talking. He couldn't take the guilt. Why was he saying all this? Why now? Did he know more than he let on? "What—what's all this drugs and screwing-around shit about? You—you know me better than that, Mr. T."

"I hope I do," he said and leaned back in his seat, examining Bobby. "I'm going to tell you like this because I love you like you were my own flesh and blood," Mr. Timbers continued. "Don't get caught up in a bunch of bullshit that you can't get yourself out of. You're smarter than that. You've got a wife and two kids who need you. This company needs you. But I'm going to tell you straight out because that's the kind of man I am, if I had to make my decision today, you wouldn't be the man I'd choose to lead this company. I need a reason *not* to give the job to Kirk Walker. You haven't given me one."

Bobby couldn't say a word. All he could do was watch his mentor and hope. Hope that it wasn't too late.

Mr. Timbers stood straight up from his seat, gave his head a quick turn to the left so that the bones in his neck cracked, then smiled down at Bobby, his mood and intensity completely changed. He had said all he had come to say. "Boy, I can't wait to get home to the missus," he said, heading for the door. "She always gets horny when I take her out of town." He slowly grabbed the door handle, then turned back around. "I don't run my business like the others. We're a family here at Black Tie. Don't forget that."

Bobby aimlessly tried to busy himself after Mr. Timbers left, but it didn't work. No matter what he did, he still couldn't get him off his mind. He didn't know what to do with all the feelings that were rumbling through his body. Mr. Timbers had given him a lot to think about. Too much. Bobby instinctively searched through his jacket pocket for a form of relief. He retrieved a single white rock, smelled it, and placed it atop the CD cover that sat in the corner of his desk. He stared at it like it was a work of art, then tapped the side of the cover and watched the CD and cocaine spin around in front of him. He examined the white rock from every angle and he hated himself for wanting it so much. What was it about this stuff? he thought, watching it as if his life depended on it. He beat his desk as if it were a drum, trying to distract himself from the sin that sat before him. His willpower won out, as he pushed his chair back and swiveled around to gaze out the window.

Mr. Timbers has always been big on long speeches, Bobby thought. Long, boring speeches that could usually be summed up in a single sentence. The moral of Mr. Timbers' oration: "Give me a reason not to give the position to Kirk Walker." That was it, plain and simple. At first, he was put out because he felt he had proven himself enough over the years and was upset that Mr. Timbers still wanted more confirmation. But after he thought on it for a while, things became clearer. Signing that awful rapper last year had been a major mistake. The PR department was still warding off bad press over it. And Mr. Timbers, being the media-savvy and image-obsessed man that he is, was more shocked by the incident than anyone. "I fucked up," Bobby whispered to himself. "The idea that Mr. Timbers still considers me a major contender in this thing shows that I do have a fighting chance for the position. He wants to give me that job," he said louder to himself. "Now all I have to do is prove that I can still stomp with the big dogs.

"The only problem is that Kirk Walker will also be trying to prove that he can play, which is why I've got to do something big, something impressive, something that can send this company on its way to the billion-dollar mark. Something that will overshadow any of Kirk's feeble attempts to overwhelm Mr. Timbers and run off with the presidency of Black Tie Records." Bobby didn't notice he was talking aloud until he found himself struggling with the pronunciation of his words. He rocked back in his seat and took a deep breath. He didn't know whether to be overwhelmed because he was definitely in the running to take over Black Tie Records or whether to be pissed off because after all his years of hard work, he was still no closer to the top position than Kirk Walker, a man who hadn't been with the company for more than four years. At least Mr. Timbers laid all the cards out. Now all he had to do was do what he did best—seize the moment.

He turned back to his desk and eyed the white rock, then searched through his desk for a razor to chop it up. Mr. Timbers' visit was more than a business pep talk, he thought as he cut into the rock. It was more like a wake-up call—a call back to life. To snort or not to snort? He laughed as he finished cutting the cocaine and forming several white lines. His eyes watered at that moment and he realized that this was no laughing matter. Not to snort, he concluded and pushed the cocaine way from him.

An hour later, he still could not bring his mind to the present. He still dissected his talk with Mr. Timbers and the question that at first seemed so silly but now remained imprinted on his brain. "What the hell is going on with you?" Mr. Timbers had asked the question so sternly that Bobby thought he was going to follow through with the answer. He felt like picking up the phone and ringing Mr. Timbers' office to find out if he did have any insight on what it could be that was making him lose his touch, but he knew the reason was sitting right in front of him on top of the CD cover.

Bobby reached for the phone, hesitantly, but couldn't bring himself to pick it up. He wanted to call Sheryl, but what could he possibly say to her? He wondered what she was thinking. He wondered if it was really over.

The intercom on his desk buzzed out once again.

"Yes, Tish."

"Your four o'clock's waiting."

"Send her in," Bobby said, stashing the CD and cocaine in his desk and wiping powder traces with the sleeve of his shirt. He blew his nose and stood up to greet his guest as she walked in the room. When the door opened, he was still trying to clear his mind of the memories, but just one look at the vision before him was enough to jolt his mind back to the present. She was beautiful. It took every ounce of restraint in him not to call her Sheryl. It was like he had been taken back eighteen years. Except for the red hair, she was the spitting image of his college wife. Everything from her skin color and freckles to her petite frame and the way she meekly stuck her head around the edge of the door before fully entering the room. He couldn't figure out if the resemblance was good or bad, but he knew one thing: she was the one.

"Hello, Mr. Strong. I'm Jazmine Deems," she said and extended her hand.

Bobby folded his arms across his chest, not noticing her polite gesture, then shook his head. This girl could change my life, he thought, and finally noticed her hand. He took it softly and shook it in silence as his eyes crept down to the desk drawer where his cocaine hid. Did he really need it? he thought, almost dazed. Of course not, he assured himself. Not when the presidency was so close at hand and there was so much reason to live. He released Jazmine's hand and took a step back, examining the potential gold mine he was sure would earn Mr. Timbers' respect.

"Yes, indeed," he said and flashed a smile. "You are definitely the one."

chapter eight

niggaz 4 life

Life is a beautiful bitch with a big butt and I love her. Up until now, all that life has allowed me to be was a gangsta. That's the door that was opened for me and that's the job I took. But now shit is flowing out legit and for once in my fucked-up life, I actually feel like an insider. Like life has more to offer me than a .38, a forty-ounce, and a joint.

The meeting with me, Larry, and Kirk Walker took less than an hour, and—flip, flop, flam!—I got a record contract. This is like some kinda dream. Now I know what it feels like to be one of them game-show contestants, like on *The Price Is Right* and shit. I feel like I just won a *fabulous* new sports car or one of them wicker bedroom sets or at least one of them refrigerator-freezers Bob be giving away like they're the world's greatest gift.

Kirk's a stupid mothafucka though. He try to act all high-priced and shit, but if you ask me the boy's in over his black head. He may be all educated and what not, which is cool—you know a brother needs some edjumakashen and shit—but that fool don't know nothing about the streets. He was talking all this ying-yang about the responsibility of rappers, and being a role model through music, and all that kinda mess. Telling me how black rap artists have a responsibility to teach and educate younger black men about their heritage and shit.

Please.

I'm not trying to hear all that. I know what black people want from rappers, and ain't nothing no suited-up black nerd like Kirk can tell me about what folks want to hear in the streets. I felt like asking that fool when was the last time he hung out on Crenshaw, with the top down, with ten other brothers lined up behind him and all of them got their Kenwood, Alpine, or Blaupunkt systems thumping out bass so loud that people two blocks away can hear. And they ain't thumping no role-model music. None of that *Fresh Prince of Bel-Air* shit. They blasting Too Short, NWA, and Tupac. Straight gangsta music—music of the streets.

I played it cool though and sat there and listened to Kirk's boring-ass speech. Larry had already warned me to just keep my mouth shut and go with the program. So I just did a lot of shaking my head, and Yes-siring and No-siring and "Hey, that sounds terrific" bullshit. I really felt like lighting up a joint, throwing my feet up on his desk, and asking him when was the last time he had a good piece of pussy, 'cause that nigga was too fucking uptight. What is it about the corporate scene that turns brothers into little dark-skin clones of the white man? I bet that brother can't even dance no more. And I swear, if I had closed my eyes while he was talking, I would have bet my last dollar that I was listening to some blond, blue-eyed rich boy.

But I don't care how that fool sound as long as I get my record made and get my black ass paid. I don't get no advance money till I turn out a finished product, and to tell the truth, I really don't give a fuck 'cause Larry is kicking me down, big-time. I decided to go on ahead and let that fool act as my agent too, 'cause that's one nigga who's on the ball. He already set me up in this new apartment in West L.A. and gave me some spending change, and tomorrow we gon' go pick me out a new wardrobe so I'll look legit when I go into the studio and meet all the rest of them fools down at Black Tie. I just hope I can get along with all these white people he got me living next to in this building. I would have preferred to live in Ladera Heights or somewhere up in the Dons, close to some black folks, but I didn't say one goddamn word about it when he gave me them keys; the rent ain't coming outta my pockets.

All I have to do now is get in the studio and throw down my rhymes—and plippity, plop, ping!—nothing but dollars. I know one thing though. Something must be going on at that company 'cause everybody I saw up there was running around like somebody was holding a match under they ass. Kirk said he wanted a completed recording in two months. Two months. That's pretty quick, but I didn't complain. A brother like me need strict deadlines or else I get distracted on all sorts of other things I ain't got no business getting into. And two months ain't no problem anyway, 'cause I got three whole spiral notebooks full of lyrics and at least four DATs' worth of beats and samples and remixed music to set my rhymes to. T-Bone hooked most of the music up, but I don't give a fuck. I'm still using 'em. Fuck that yellow nigga. Most of the shit was my idea in the first place, plus I'm sure this new producer Larry talking about hooking me up with knows about that eight-note law. Shit, all he gotta do is change the beat before every eighth note and as far as the law is concerned it's a different song.

I would get started on reworking some of that music right now, but like I say, a brother like me is easily distracted and right about now, all l can think about is Little Miss Redhead. Now that's the type of chick that makes me nervous. She ain't like all the hoochies in the hood. She made of much better stuff than that. I bet she ain't never seen the inside of a swap meet. In fact she look like the Sascha of London type, not one of them Payless Shoe Source bitches. I checked out her nails too. Proper. None of that Lee Press-On shit, just her own natural length and they was painted white on the tips too. Now that's classy. She kinda make me think she *too* classy—for me, that is. Shit, I may be on my way to hitting the big time now, but all I really am is just a street nigga. Not that I'm ashamed of who I am, 'cause I ain't. There's plenty of other broke, uneducated by conventional standards, former gang bangers, former dope dealers, Indo-smokin', forty drinkin', '64-drivin' brothers out there in the hood who ain't ashamed of what they are either. All me or anybody else out there need is a fucking break. It pisses me off when people talk about folks from the hood like they ain't shit. Well it's easy for somebody who ain't never been to the ghetto to sit and talk about us like we ought to have our heads hanging low or something. But if them same people had come from where I come from, they wouldn't be so quick to pass judgment. Now I'll admit, it's some downright ignorant shit going on in the hood, and I've been a part of some scandalous shit myself, but people gotta look at the whole picture before they open their mouths talking about, "Why them black folk act so crazy?" Hell, we all know the answer to that million-dollar question.

First of all, what the fuck is a father? Didn't nobody have daddies where I come from. They say all you gotta do is look across your dinner table to find a role model. Yeah, right. When I looked across the table all I saw was a wall, or if I think real hard I can still remember seeing my moms before she died. But I'm a man. What can I learn from a woman but how to paint my fingernails and douche?

And number two. What the fuck is a good school? I mean a *good* school. One where there ain't forty nappy-head kids in one classroom and where three kids don't have to share one textbook. And I ain't talkin' about no school that you gotta take a bus over the mountains, through the woods, around the bend, and over the river to get to. Fuck that integration shit anyway. All black folks was saying when they voted for desegregation and busing was that they were too dumb to educate their own children in their own neighborhoods. So they said, "Hey! Since our black schools ain't shit, let's make our kids get up at the crack of fucking dawn and bus they little black asses out to the Valley so the white man can teach 'em, 'cause us, we just too damn stupid to take care of our own."

And number three. If you ain't had no real role model and you ain't had no real education, how the hell you supposed to get a fucking job? And I mean a real job, not no "Hi, may I take your order?" kinda job. I'm talking about a suit, tie, and briefcase job. I mean, what's *really* going on? Can a brother get a break, or what? Hell no he can't get no break. Not today. Not in this society. Not in this lifetime.

But all that's about to change for me. And all I got to say is thank God for rap. And white folks, though most of 'em hate the shit, ought to be thanking God for rap too. It's one thing to sit down and write lyrics about killing police and hating white folks and it's another thing to actually go out and do it. And a whole lot of brothers would be out there killing up white folks if they didn't have an outlet like rap music where they could vent their anger. I know I would. If I hadn't been so busy the last three years trying to write music and shit, I woulda been right out there in the streets, robbing and car-jacking stupid white people. But instead, I been sitting my black ass down—like I'm gon' do right now—and getting busy on my music.

I'm feeling romantic, so I think I'll write something slow and smooth. A sexy rap that people can put on when they in the bump-and-grind mood, like I am right about now. As a matter of fact, what I should do is give Little Miss Redhead a call. I wonder what she doing right now, besides looking good. This would be a good time to call, too. I could play like I was just trying to see how her meeting went at Black Tie. I could put on a real worried voice and say something like "Did everything go all right?" or "I was concerned about you, you looked so nervous earlier." Naw, fuck that. I can't believe I'm actually sitting here getting all tripped about calling up a bitch, I mean, a young lady. See. I can't even talk bad about this girl. I'm acting pussy-whipped already, and I ain't even got none from her—yet. Damn. If I didn't know any better, I'd think I was in love or something . . . Hell no! Not the X-Man.

In a couple hours, I had finished writing three songs. I was like a maniac with that pen—totally unconscious. When my pager started vibrating, the first person I thought of was Little Miss Redhead. Girls always love to page a nigga. It's their subtle way of making the first move. Only it's not really a first move 'cause you have to call they asses back. So if things don't work out right they can always say, "Why you call me in the first place?" I took the pager off my hip and checked the number. "Damn," I said to myself, pissed off 'cause it wasn't Jazmine's number. I knew it the second I looked down at my pager 'cause I had already memorized her number in my head. I shoulda known she was going to be the type to play hard to get, but at that time I wasn't down for no love games. I had too much other stuff on my mind to be getting all mixed up over some girl who was probably just another airhead in disguise anyway.

I looked down at my pager again and recognized the number. It was Rich's. Now what that nigga doing calling me? From what his bitch told me, I was on that fool's shit list. I sat my pager down on the table and picked my pen back up and started writing, but it was too late to get back into it. That page had got me all distracted. Then I started thinking. Niggas. You think somebody's your homie, your ace, your boy, and just like that—crank, cronk, capoof!—they turn into your enemy. I couldn't believe it when Eyeisha told me he was out for my ass. Rich had been like a brother to me for so long that I thought nothing could ever break us up. Ever since we was little snot-nosed kids, we been hanging out together— tougher than leather. For the past thirteen years I been kicking it with that nigga practically every day, except for that time he was in jail. He got locked up back in '88 for some stupid shit that even Larry couldn't get him out of. I actually felt sorry for that nigga, but mostly I felt sorry for myself 'cause I was alone.

For two whole years that nigga was locked up for assault with a deadly weapon. I can still remember Bone and Rich begging me to go cruising with them that night it happened, but at the time I was all sprung over some bitch and was more concerned about digging into her than hanging out with the fellas.

It was the year after Rich had got shot for me and he was just getting used to life in a wheelchair, though he fought the process every inch of the way. For him, getting in and out of the car was like this major deal and shit. T-Bone was driving, but of course that punk nigga didn't lift a finger to help Rich. It was always me lifting him up and carrying him like a baby, making sure he didn't hit his head on the roof of the car as I loaded him in. I told Rich to be careful. "Don't take no shorts," I said as they drove off. You would think being paralyzed would have slowed that nigga down. I know it slowed me way down. But like always, Rich couldn't be told a mothafuckin' thing. He didn't have any other choice but to quit bangin' though. It wasn't too much combat he could do in that chair. He could point a gun, but if one was pointing back at him, what could he do? Run? He sho couldn't hide. It ain't too many trees I know of big enough to hide a wheelchair behind. But just as soon as he stopped bangin', he started slangin'. I can't tell which lifestyle is worse. They both can get yo ass shot up and ain't neither one no better than the other when it comes down to it, except with slangin' yo ass get paid.

But anyway, them two mothafuckas was trying to get me to roll with them to drop off a sale over there off Imperial, but I wasn't havin' it. I was too busy trying to get me some pussy. They rolled out without me and I be damn if less than twenty minutes later I didn't hear police sirens blazing up the street. I was just about to get in my car and go over my bitch's house when I saw the long line of black-and-whites filling the streets. I didn't know where they were going at the time, but I knew wherever they ended up, Rich and T-Bone would be nearby. Something told me to follow those police cars and no sooner had I thought it than I was actually in my car, doing eighty-five miles a hour, trying to keep up. They bent the corner on at Imperial and Link Street and I was right behind them. The middle of Link was filled with people. Niggas walking around with their pants sagging, talking about, "This is Link Street, Blood. Cross Street killa, deuce times fo da set." More niggas were sitting on the curb drinking forties and taking in the action. Women were standing around with pink rollers in their heads and babies on their hips. All of them were crying, or shaking their heads, or saying "Why? Why?" And still there were more niggas.

I parked my car behind the last police car and got out, not even stopping to take notice that I was in enemy territory. I was too concerned about my boys, though I still had no concrete evidence that they were even involved. Nobody fucked with me though. I guess they chilled out 'cause the police were there, not to mention I lifted my jacket every now and then so them fools could see the handle of my piece sticking out my pants. I made my way through the crowd and halfway, I got my first sign that my instincts were correct: T-Bone's '85 El Camino. There was no other like it in the hood. It was money green with gold flakes, sitting on polished Lorinzers. I eased my way closer to the heart of the confusion and there the two knuckleheads were. Rich's wheelchair was knocked on its side and he was laying face down on the sidewalk with his wrists cuffed behind his back. T was right next to him, same position, only his ankles were tied up with rope. "What the fuck is up?" I asked out loud to anyone who would listen. Nobody answered me though. They had never seen my face so they knew I wasn't down with their set. To them I was just another enemy—a busta. Finally I went up to one of the police officers and asked him what was up.

"So you know these niggers?" he asked, pointing at them with a smirk on his face. "Better be glad you weren't with them, boy. They'll be locked up for life for pulling a stunt like this," he said and walked away.

Thanks a whole fucking lot for the info, I thought, feeling no more enlightened as to what went on than before I spoke to him. Nobody else would talk to me and I got so frustrated that I started cussing, just standing there in the middle of the street with my hands on my hips and cussing. What the hell else could I do? I guess Rich recognized my voice 'cause he raised his head from the ground and looked up at me. It looked like his eyes were gon' roll up out of his head, he was straining so hard to look at me. Then he gave me a jerk of the head and I knew that meant I should get the fuck up out of there. I don't know if Bone saw me or not. He just lied there, staring at the ground, looking like he'd just seen a ghost. I went back to my car and boned out. Them pussy Link Streets waited until I got to the end of the street before they started throwing bottles and rocks at the back of my car. I didn't go back and say nothing to 'em though. A brother like me know when he outnumbered, and furthermore, I ain't stupid. I didn't even bother going home. I called up Larry and told him to meet me at the Seventy-seventh Street Station. We waited for them to haul Rich and T-Bone in, and when they finally let me in to see Rich, I could tell by the look on his face that he knew he was gon' do time. It wasn't a look of shame or misfortune. It was a look of pride. Like jail was the last frontier—more fertile ground to be conquered. I don't know how a simple drug sale got turned into attempted murder, but that's the charge him and T-Bone were facing. Rich told me that they had gone over to Link Street to look for some nigga that had paged him to buy some rocks. When they got to the house where he was supposed to make the sale, the people inside the house started firing on him. It was a setup. He and Bone had to fire back in self-defense, but somehow or other, the story got switched around that Bone and Rich had gone over there to do a drive-by. At any rate, them fools got cold busted. Rich was actually sentenced to four years, but only served two due to overcrowding. T-Bone ended up with only a year, of which he served seven months. I figured that punk probably sold Rich out to the police, but at the time didn't nobody sweat him about it. We was all too busy trying to find a way to keep Rich from being locked up at all. But it didn't work. That fool had to do the time, two years, surrounded by nothing but men. I felt bad for my homie. I wrote him all the time, visited him every weekend, and sent him money for candy bars and cigarettes and shit. But I could never imagine how it musta felt for him to be locked up. No freedom, no pussy, not even a good In-N-Out burger. It was a sad case, but it only made us that much closer, 'cause as it turned out, I was the only one of his friends to keep in touch with him. There's two times in the life of a gangsta when you really find out who your friends are: at funerals and when somebody goes to jail. Your real friends stick by you and support you. People who just say they your friend ain't nowhere to be found. When Rich needed something I sent it to him right away 'cause I knew nobody else would. Not even that ho Eyeisha who called herself his woman. Everybody was talking about they ain't have no money or they didn't have time. Yeah right. I told Rich we needed to get us some more white friends 'cause they always got money. Ask a nigga for some change and all you get is excuses: "I gotta pay my rent" or "I gots to pay bills." But if you ask that same nigga to go to Vegas or to the racetrack, he'd be right on your heels.

I learned a lot while Rich was locked up. Probably more than he learned from the whole situation. I learned that I wasn't gon' end up in jail. I didn't have time for the gang life. Slangin' and bangin' just didn't appeal to me no more. Especially since I had firsthand proof of where you could end up for getting caught up in that shit. That's when I really started getting into rap. I needed a diversion to keep me off the streets. I was one of the lucky ones. For most niggas, it takes one of their homies getting killed for them to realize that bangin' ain't the way. But for a lot of them, the death of a homie only makes them more determined to stay loyal to the set. The set becomes their security. See, for me, I had my rap. Most other niggas ain't got shit. You can't change the way you living your life if you ain't got nothing to change into.

M y pager went off again. I put down my pen and turned on the television. *Martin* was on, but I couldn't even get into it 'cause I was still trying to figure out why Rich was trying to get in touch with me. I thought maybe he was paging me so I could call him back and he could curse me out since he was too fucked up last night to do it. Then I thought that maybe Eyeisha had told him what happened between us. That would really piss him off. But I didn't let myself get all tensed up over the shit. In fact I straight picked up the phone and dialed that nigga's number. I had been waiting for the longest to tell that stupid mothafucka about that tramp he'd been with for the longest. And anyway he couldn't do nothing to me now 'cause he didn't know my phone number or where I lived no more. So I said fuck it. If he wanted a showdown he was gon' get one.

He answered the phone in the same stupid way he always did, "Who dis?"

"Who you think it is?" I said in my hardest gangsta growl.

"What's up, X?"

"What you mean, what the fuck is up? What you fuckin' page me for, nigga?"

"Oh, you rollin' so tough now that you don't have time for your boy no more?"

"Man, what the fuck you talking about?"

"Nothing, man. Damn. Can't a nigga just call to see how you doing? How things go down at Black Tie today?"

I paused for a minute and tried to figure out what was going on. Rich didn't sound like a man bent on revenge like I thought he would. I had expected him to be mad as hell, yelling and screaming about me boning his girlfriend or at least threatening to kick my ass 'cause I dumped him and Bone at the party. But he was cool and that caught me off guard.

"So did they offer you a contract, or what?"

"Uh, yeah. I signed the contract a few hours ago. No! Wait a minute. What the fuck is up witchoo?"

"Chill out, man. What the fuck is up *witchoo?*"

"Eyeisha told me you was out for blood where I was concerned, nigga. She said you was talking about taking me out. Blowing my head off and shit."

"Ah, man, you know how I be talkin'. I don't even remember half the shit I said last night, I was so fucked up. I ain't sweating that shit, man. You know you my boy. I'm happy for you. And anyway, you know I wasn't all into that rap shit in the first place. I was just doing it 'cause you was doing it. You the real rapper. I likes to make my money in other ways, know what I'm saying."

Damn I felt low. There I was thinking that fool was out to get me and all he had been doin' was talkin' a bunch of ying-yang. I should of known my homie would always be in my corner. We were niggaz for life. Then all at once, it hit me—I straight fucked my homeboy's girl. How stupid am I?

"Yo man, I love you like a brother, you know. So I'll keep doing my thing and you go on ahead and do your rap thing. Just promise you won't get too famous and forget about me."

Ah, damn! I really felt bad then. I had never heard Rich sound so sincere. If I hadn't been thinking how much of a dog I had been for sleeping with his girl, I probably would have choked up and cried. But instead all his mushy talk was just making me feel more and more guilty. So I got off the phone with him.

"Yo, X," Rich called out before I put my receiver down.

"Huh?"

"I'm proud of you. Later."

He had to go add that last sentimental line, didn't he? Now I had done a lot of wicked shit in my lifetime, like robbing, lying, cheating, jacking, I even shot some fool in the arm once. But nothing, nothing had ever made me feel so guilty than talking to Rich and listening to him give me props and all the while I had betrayed him. Betrayal. That's some serious shit to a brother like me. Where I come from you never betray your homeboy. That's like the unspoken motto of the hood. If your boy get busted by the cops and you know everything that happened, you bet' not open your mouth. Even if you see somebody you don't know doing something scandalous, you don't butt in. You mind your own business and let the chips fall where they have to. But you definitely don't betray nobody, 'cause payback for betrayal is a mothafucka.

I sat there in front of the television thinking how I was gon' get myself out of this situation. If Eyeisha was to say anything to Rich it would be all over. Bitches like her like to start shit, and I knew it would only be a matter of time before she opened her big mouth to Rich about what had happened. I didn't know if I should call Rich back up and tell him straight out what happened or what. I could say something like: "Yo, Rich. It was an accident. She was there, I was there—and bing, boop, bip—it just happened." But I knew that wouldn't work. Then I thought about calling Eyeisha and threatening her not to say anything, but she probably would just use the situation to get even further between me and Rich. She been on my tip every since she started going out with Rich. Always grinding up against me, winking when Rich wasn't looking and all that kinda shit. Now she was right where she wanted to be. In the middle. She was holding all the cards and all I could do was sit back and hope she wouldn't say nothing. Damn I hate being in this position, but I wasn't about to back away from me and Rich's friendship. I need that nigga. He's the only family I got.

I started feeling really bad and like always when I start feeling bad I wanted to have sex. Sex is the ultimate cure-all for me. Whenever I'm feeling low or depressed a good piece of ass can always put things back in perspective. I could have called up Kelly, but she would just be another headache. She never could distinguish between a fuck and real love, and if I went over there looking for a good screw she'd think I was trying to get back with her. And that's never gon' happen. So I decided to go on ahead and call Jazmine, but as soon as I thought of her I didn't feel like having sex anymore. Not that baby wasn't fine, 'cause she was, and I was sure she knew how to work that body of hers. But she wasn't the kind of girl you could meet one day and screw the next. She had more class about her than that. Still I wanted to call her. I needed something to do to get my mind off my situation.

It was after one o'clock when I finally stopped trying to think of what I was gon' say and picked up the phone and called her. Nobody answered the first four or five times. At about one-thirty, some other female finally picked up the phone and said Jazmine wasn't in. Now where the hell could she be at damn near two o'clock in the morning? She ain't the nightlife type of girl. I called a couple more times after that, but when her friend picked up the phone, I hung up. Fuck it, I decided. All this shit was giving me a headache instead of a hard-on. I was going to bed, by myself— what I should have done last night.

chapter nine

butterflies

I was so anxious and nervous by the time I got back to Dakota's apartment that I was sweating underneath my arms and I had to pee so bad I was squenching my legs together so tight that I could barely stand up straight. When she opened the door for me, I shot right past her and into the bathroom. I didn't even bother to close the door behind me before I pushed down my pants and let it out. Dakota came up right behind me and stood in the bathroom doorway, looking just as eager as I was. "So spit it out. What happened?" she asked. The smile on my face was enough to let her know that something indeed had happened, but when I started to open my mouth and tell her, I realized that I had to do more than just pee.

"Give me a minute, girl," I said and kicked the door halfway shut with my foot. She couldn't wait for me to finish my business, so she started blurting out questions through the crack in the door.

"Is it on or what?" she said, now yelling because she had walked back into the living room to turn off the television.

"Yes, girl. It's on!" I shouted back. "I'm so keyed up I don't know what to do."

"So what the hell were you guys doing all day? It's after three in the morning. I know you guys weren't talking for that long. It ain't that much conversation in the world."

"Okay, let me give you the rundown. When I got there, I was nervous as hell and when his secretary called me into the office I thought I was going to throw up. But Bobby Strong is cool, girl."

"Yeah, I bet he is."

"Shut up and stop interrupting me," I said and paused for a minute. It's hard to talk and do the number two at the same time. "Okay," I continued. "First he told me that he loved my demo tape and that he thought that I could be a real asset to Black Tie Records and all that other bullshit people say to try to make you relax, you know. Then he started getting to the nitty-gritty, girl. The way he was talking, you would have thought that I was already famous because he started telling me all these plans he had for me and what he wanted me to do. He was talking like I had already signed a contract and everything."

"What he *wants* you to do? What did he mean by that?"

"Would you be quiet so I can tell you? Okay. He was talking so fast that I was sort of getting confused."

"See, I knew I should have gone with you. Those music execs are always trying to double-talk new artists and get them confused. That shifty motherfu—"

I let out a big sigh and cut her off. "D, are you gonna let me finish or what?" I got off the toilet and cleaned myself up and felt 100 percent better. Then I went over to the sink and washed my hands. "Okay. So he was going on and on and finally I just cut him off and said hey, it sounds like you're really interested in my talent, so are you making me an offer or what? Then he came right on out and said, 'Hell yeah, I'm making you an offer,' and I thought I was gonna die right then and there, girl. Then he asked me if I had representation and I didn't know what to say so I just said yeah. Then I told him you were working as my agent and manager." I held my breath and waited to see what she was going to say because I hadn't even asked her if she would do it yet. She busted through the door and just looked at me as if to say, "You did what?" I smiled back hoping she wouldn't be too mad.

"And what did he say to that?"

"Nothing," I said, still smiling and trying to figure out her response. "You *will* act as my representation, won't you?"

She walked away from the door and back to the living room, so I followed her and sat down on the couch. "I mean, I know I didn't ask you earlier, but come on, D, you know the business and it's not like you have to give up your job or anything. All you have to do is advise me on certain things, make sure I don't mess up. This is scary enough as it is, and I don't want somebody I don't know working with me. I want someone I can trust."

She didn't really look pissed off about it, but still, I know how Dakota hates it when other people volunteer her services without asking.

"I guess it will be all right. But you know I don't have any type of training in being someone's manager or agent. But . . . I'm sure River and Earth can give me some pointers on what to do. Just don't think that I have all the answers. All I can tell you is what I *think* is right."

"Good. So you'll do it."

"Yeah, I guess," she said and finally cracked a smile.

"Okay. Now shut up so I can tell you the rest."

As I told her the rest of my story, I was struck by how unbelievable everything seemed. It had been one of those whirlwind days, like the ones you see on television where everything happens all at once, but nothing is really changed. I had sat in Bobby Strong's office for nearly two hours listening to all the big plans he had for me. It was as though he was in a race against time because he was talking so fast and making decisions and telling me this and that. At first I thought it was all a hoax because I couldn't believe that he had that much faith in my ability. He hadn't even heard me sing live yet and already he was talking about arranging studio time for me, what producers he wanted to work on my project, and asking me when I could get started on the first song. He seemed like a nice guy. A little presumptuous, yes, but still nice. I guess when you are at the top of your profession, presumption and conceit become a part of your personality. But I really felt like I could trust him and that he had my best interests at heart. Besides, when it's all said and done, he's the one who's going to be left looking stupid if my career is a flop. So I guess that's why he took so much time with me today. I didn't even have a minute to go to the bathroom because after we finished in his office he took me down to a studio in Redondo Beach and introduced me to a producer and let me hang out and watch a recording session. The producer's name was Mack and he introduced me to all the equipment as if they were living and breathing human beings. "You need to get to know all this stuff because you'll be working with it day in and day out," he said, making me feel as if I should go up to the keyboard and give it a hug. Bobby just stood back watching me for the most part until he asked me to go into this insulated, sound-proof booth and stand behind the microphone. I was literally shaking when I went inside there. He motioned for me to put on the headphones, and when I did I could hear his voice loud and clear.

"I just want to hear your voice. Sing whatever you want. Just take your time," he said.

I noticed he was staring at me, but I was already so uncomfortable that I let it go.

It took me a long time to start, but I couldn't help it. He had put me on the spot and although I knew I could pull it off, I was scared my voice was going to crack, as jittery as I was and all.

"Just take your time, dear," he said, trying to console me. "I don't care what you sing. Relax."

I just stood there for a few more minutes until I could calm myself enough to speak without my upper lip shaking. Then I just closed my eyes and started belting out a song that I had written the week before:

Victory is not mine
Every time you say, you're goin' away.
I can't put handcuffs on you
To make you stay.
I can't run to the door
And block your way.
Don't tell me it's over.
Don't say it's all right.
Just leave how you came, baby.
Why don't you just say good-bye.
'Cause I've been
Tossing and turning all night.
You say it's wrong, I say it's right.
There's gotta be more to my life.
But baby you just won't do right.
So I
Give up the fight, I give up the fight.

I ain't gonna battle with you
I-I-I ain't gonna throw down with you.
No I
Victory is not mine. Oh not this time.

When I finally opened my eyes, Mack and Bobby were looking at each other like they'd just seen a ghost. And that just made me all the more scared. Then finally Bobby spoke to me through the headphones. "Come on out, dear."

I took off the headphones in slow motion and prepared myself for the letdown, but when I walked back into the engineer's room both of them just stared at me like I was some sort of untouchable alien. "Where on God's green earth did you get a voice like that?" Mack finally said. "And where did you study your delivery? It's amazing."

"So you liked it," I said, still unwilling to believe that I hadn't just made a fool of myself and sung my way right out of a recording contract.

"Dear, it's only a matter of time before that voice lands you on *Billboard*'s top-ten list. And I'm serious about that. I listen to singers every day, and nothing I've heard has been anywhere near what you've just displayed. Listen, dear," Bobby said, walking over to me and putting his arm around my shoulder. "Make no mistake about it. You are headed for the big time. It's as plain and simple as that."

Bobby insisted that we get started on setting the song I had just sung to music, and he insisted that we start immediately, while my creative juices were in full swing. He didn't want to waste any time. He left me there with Mack while he went back to his office and arranged for one of the company's lawyers to start drafting a contract for me. Before I could even finish saying good-bye to Bobby, Mack was at his keyboard pounding out a melody. "Let me hear that first line again," he said. When I sung it for him again he hummed along with me. I sang the song all the way through, while he dabbled with different notes on the keyboard, and by the time I was finished, he had memorized the whole song. He played with different melodies for about a half hour while I just sat and watched, amazed by his obvious talent and ear for music. Then he asked me to go back in the booth and take it from the top. And this time when I put on the headphones I felt self-assured. He started playing an introduction and I started humming to the melody, then he gave me a nod of his head to begin the first verse. It was like magic. The music fit right with the lyrics and instinctively I knew where to soften or tighten my voice. By the end of that first run-through I was feeling like I had been in the music business all my life. I guess you could say I was in heaven, because I was so relaxed and uninhibited that the lyrics just flowed off my lips like little butterflies.

By the time Bobby came back to the studio it was after midnight and he was joined by a harsh-looking lady with hair that was bleached blond on the tips and black as charcoal at the roots. If she hadn't been wearing an expensive business suit, much like one I had sold at Bullock's last week, I would have thought she was a hooker. "So this is our next big star," she said, taking my hand in a firm grip. "I'm Monica Savidge."

"Yes, Jazmine," Bobby interrupted in his usual bold manner. "Monica's one of Black Tie's leading lawyers and I got her to draw up a contract for you. Now of course, there's no pressure. You can look it over, have your lawyer look it over, but I'm sure you'll find everything to your liking."

Monica handed me a document that looked like an eight-and-a-half-by-eleven dictionary. "If you have any questions, just have your lawyer give me a call and we'll work it out."

Bobby butted in again, and put his hand on my waist. "We need to move quickly on this, Jazmine. Tomorrow evening, I want to have an A&R representative meet with you here, and listen to some of the songs you've written and help you choose material for your first album."

My first album. I couldn't believe it. I almost wanted to ask him to pinch me to make sure I wasn't dreaming.

"Now how'd you like working with Mack? Did you like this studio? Because money's no problem, we can change studios, producers, engineers, whatever—you just say the word."

"No. Mack is fine, the studio's fine, really. I'm just so excited to even be here. I don't know what to say."

"Don't say anything. Just keep singing, dear," he said, staring at me again.

I had gotten so wrapped up in relaying my story to Dakota that I didn't notice when she took out the contract I had left in a heap by the door when I came breezing in earlier. She had also taken out a Yellow Pages directory and was going through the contract page by page, marking the margins with little red circles and question marks as she went along. Then she put down the contract and started thumbing through the phone directory. "Who are you about to call?" I asked.

"Well, you need a lawyer. A good lawyer to muddle through this big-ass piece of work here."

"D, it's damn near four in the morning."

"Oh, you're right," she said and threw down the Yellow Pages and picked up the cordless phone and dialed.

"River? Were you sleep? Good. Jazz needs a lawyer, like yesterday."

She stayed on the phone with her daddy for a good thirty minutes and I got changed into one of her old, oversized T-shirts. Then I remembered my daddy. I hadn't thought about him all day long, and I know he must have been worrying about me. He was probably up right now, sitting by the door, waiting for me to come in so he could have another chance to be-little me. I thought about calling him when Dakota got off the phone, then decided to wait till morning and prayed that by then he would have calmed down. I had actually thought about going home earlier, but I had no idea that I was going to spend so much time at the recording studio. By eleven o'clock, I knew I dared not walk in his house. He'd only use my coming in late as another excuse to prove I was some type of whore put on this earth to challenge his ever-increasing faith. Besides I had told him that I wasn't ever coming back, and if I went back on that promise, he'd rule my life forever.

When I went back into the living room, Dakota was still going over the contract with her red pen. "Girl, aren't you tired yet? I'll take the couch, so you go on ahead and get some rest," I said.

"No, girl. I've got business to tend to. I'm your manager-slash-agent, re-member? And my first job is to make sure that you don't get weighed down with all these business technicalities. All you have to do is concen-trate on making music. River gave me the name of a lawyer and I'm gonna call him first thing in the morning." Dakota sounded like she was a lawyer herself. It was four in the morning and she was talking about work. I al-most forgot she was my best friend there for a second.

"Oh yeah. I'll be going down to the studio with you tomorrow. I need to meet this producer and make sure he's on the ball. And you said there's gonna be an A&R rep there, right? Good, I need to meet him . . . or her . . .

or whoever, too. And by the way. I *will* be taking twenty percent off the top," she said, laughing. "This is a business, baby. A *business*."

"Twenty percent?" I said, cracking a smile. "Don't I get the special homegirl rate?"

"For you—fifteen percent."

"Ten."

"Twelve and a half."

"Deal."

She walked over to me and gave me a hug. "I'm so proud of you, Jazz. I knew you could do it. Now get off of me," she said, pushing me away. She picked up the contract and headed to her bedroom.

I hardly slept at all. I guess I was still too excited. I woke up after only four hours of sleep at eight-thirty, but I had so much energy that I turned on the VCR and stuck in one of Dakota's aerobic dance tapes. Then I decided I wasn't that perky after all and strolled into the kitchen and started a pot of coffee. I opened Dakota's refrigerator and all she had in there was an opened can of Dr. Pepper, a half-eaten bagel, and about six different varieties of flavored coffee creamer. I picked up the French vanilla, then decided to try out the hazelnut and waited for the coffee to finish brewing. I decided to make iced coffee instead, and opened the freezer to get some cubes. There were six different frozen boxes of Weight Watchers and Lean Cuisine entrees and four ice trays, but they were all empty. I closed the freezer and took out a coffee cup, then heard Dakota's voice coming from her room. She was already on the phone with the lawyer setting up an appointment for the three of us. I took another cup out and filled it up and since I didn't know what kind of cream she was in the mood for, I grabbed all six of them in my arms, put the coffee cups one on top of the other, and tried to balance everything all the way to her room. When I got there she was off the phone and I sat everything down on her nightstand except my cup and plopped myself down on the foot of her bed.

"Three o'clock, and his name is Mr. Booker," she said, still sounding like a lawyer or doctor or some other executive type. "Now listen. You've got to start making some decisions, like now—right this minute. First of all, what are you going to do about school?"

Damn. I hadn't even thought ahead that far. "I don't know. Can't I still finish out the semester? I mean, it's my last semester anyway," I said and took a sip of coffee and vowed never to use hazelnut creamer again.

"Well, it's all up to you, but since you have just a couple more months, I think it wise to just juggle the two for a while. Now, I'll call up Bullock's and tell them you're resigning and pick up your last check for you."

"Girl, I can't quit my job. I barely got a pot to piss in as it is. I need that paycheck, however little it may be."

"Didn't you read your contract at all? Oh, I'm so glad you put me in charge of the business end of this," she said and pointed to a paragraph she had circled and put four stars next to. "Read that."

I read, while she continued jabbering away. "They're offering you an advance of seventy-five thousand dollars plus recording expenses, girl. These people ain't fucking around. Now of course you can't just go blowing away money because before you get paid any more, they have to recoup all the expenses they paid out to get the record made. But still, fuck Bullock's. Pretty soon, you'll be able to buy your own clothing store."

"Girl, shut your mouth," I said and busted out laughing, trying to hide how totally freaked out I was about how fast and how much my life was changing. I closed my eyes for a second and silently thanked God for Dakota. If I didn't have her to stand by me now, I'd be a basket case. I kept skimming through the contract, but my mind wasn't really into it. I just kept thinking how Dakota had always been there for me and I wondered if she knew how much I appreciated her. She had once said that she would do anything for me. She was pissy drunk at the time, but I guess she meant it because as always, she's right there, looking out for me and making sure I don't stumble along the way.

"Now," she said, falling back into her executive routine. "Your daddy. Have you told him yet?"

"No, I haven't even spoken to him since yesterday."

"And?"

"And what? I mean, I guess I have to face up to him sooner or later. Hopefully later."

"So you're going to stay here, right?"

I didn't answer her because I wasn't sure what the hell I was gonna do. I really and truly wanted to stay with Daddy, but I knew I couldn't deal with him looking over my shoulder all the time, and if I told him about my record contract, he'd have a fit and start comparing me to Momma. I looked at Dakota and I could see she was getting impatient with me, so I made up my mind right then and there and told her I would stay with her.

"Good! It's time to move forward. No looking back. You need to stay focused on your goal. You're in it to win it, Jazz. No looking back, no regrets."

"You ought to consider going on tour as one of those motivational speakers," I told her and started laughing, but she didn't. Dakota was on a roll.

"No, I'm serious. After we finish at Mr. Booker's office, we're going to get your stuff from his house and move it over here. Then we need to stop by Levitz or somewhere and get you a bed, because I know that mickey-fickey ain't gonna let you take yours. And while we're at it, we might as well get a dresser and mirror and whatever else you need to make yourself comfortable here because you ain't going back to that old house."

"All right, D. Damn. I get the picture. Just as long as we can stop by the grocery store while we're out. You don't have a thing to eat in that kitchen."

"Puleeze, Jazz. You know I ain't into that housewife mess. If I can't pop it into the microwave or boil it, I don't eat it."

I got up and went into the kitchen to pour us another cup of coffee and came back. This time I added cinnamon spice creamer and it tasted much better. I started going through her closet looking for something to wear and pulled out about six different outfits. The first one I decided on was a linen pants outfit, but Dakota said she had planned on wearing that, so I picked out a high-waisted skirt with a matching top and blazer. I slid on the skirt to make sure it fit.

"Oh yeah, who's Xavier?" she asked, looking at me slyly.

"He called already? Dang, I just gave him the number yesterday."

"Does he look as good as he sounds?"

"He's all right. I met him at the party the other night. He's supposed to be signing up with Black Tie Records, too."

"He can sing?"

"He's a rapper."

"A rapper? I know you not about to get mixed up with one of them women-hating, macho, hand-on-penis rappers."

"He's not like that. He's cool, and he's funny as hell. You know I like a man with a sense of humor," I said and walked into the bathroom and closed the door. I didn't feel like talking to her about him. I didn't even know if I really liked him or not. And anyway, I wasn't hardly ready for a relationship. Dakota never liked rappers much. She's really a feminist at heart and anybody who doesn't respect women gets a big fat zero in her book. I know what she means though. Most rappers talk about females like all we're here for is to worship them and suck their dicks, which most of them talk about and hold on to like it could pass for money. I must admit, I like some of the music. Even some of the music that talks bad about women. I figure it's mostly just talk anyway. If a woman knows her own self-worth there isn't too much anybody can say, least of all some un-educated rapper, to make her feel less about herself. And I figure it like this, most gangsta rappers come from the ghetto and all they know are hard, conniving women of the streets—dope addicts, prostitutes, gangsta girls. Not to say that all girls in the ghetto are like that—I mean I'm from South-Central myself and I'm definitely not like that. But I think their views are based on the small, isolated world they live in. I don't know, I like rap, and if you push away all the expletives there's a whole lot of truth in what's being said. Besides, you can't fault a man—or a woman for that matter—for trying to raise a dollar. Rap is where the money's at.

I thought about paging Xavier, but decided to wait until after I got home later. He is kind of cute and he makes me laugh and his body ain't too bad either. I guess he's worth a chance. If he respects me. If he's think-ing he's gonna bed me down or that I'm gonna be dancing poolside in a bikini like those tramps in rap videos he can forget it. I could kill Spike Lee for starting that disgusting bikini dancing crap. Nobody had even thought about doing that in their videos until he came out with that "Doin' the butt" madness. But hey, if Xavier treats me right, I don't give a damn if he's a rapper or a ditch digger. It's been too long since I had some-body in my life.

For some reason I started thinking of Billy Dee Williams and Diana Ross in *Mahogany,* or was that *Lady Sings the Blues?* "Success is nothing without someone to share it with." Or was that "Life is nothing without someone by your side"? Oh, forget it. That retarded guy said it best any-way. "Life is like a box of chocolates. You never know what you're biting into. . . ." Or something like that.

chapter ten

making beautiful
music together

■ met this *fine*-ass honey this morning just outside my apartment. I was
coming back from jogging—you know a brother's gotta stay in shape if he
gonna be all up on television and on rap videos, and shit. Not to mention I
had to go to bed alone last night with a rock-hard dick; I need some kind
of outlet for all my pent-up frustrations. But anyway, I was walking into
the building and what do I see but this luscious pack of red bones, in a pair
of Daisy Dukes and a tank top. She was bending over, picking up a skinny
white puppy who took one look at me and nutted up. The puppy looked
sickly, but it was barking like a pit bull, and when it scrambled out of her
arms and came running up to me, my first instinct was to stomp the little
bastard. Then baby yelled out, "Muffin, *Muffin*, get over here, you silly
dog!" It may be hard to believe, but I'm scared to death of dogs, even little
ant-sized dogs like that one, so I backed up against the wall and felt
around for my gun, which was noticeably absent. I couldn't believe I had
slipped up enough to leave the house without my gat, so I started to panic.
Then baby came over and scooped the little fucker up and tried to calm it
down. Laughing, she introduced herself as Janet. I felt like a punk,
strapped against the wall and shaking over that little dog, so I felt I better
try to redeem myself. "Damn, baby. I hope your dog don't get all that
barking from you," I said, straightening myself up so she would know I
was still in control of things.

"No, I don't bark, I just bite," she said and held out her hand for me to shake. "You must be new around here. I haven't seen too many of *us* in this complex."

I told her I had just moved in yesterday, and since I knew the next question was gonna be "What kinda work do you do?"—it always is with sisters—I went on ahead and told her I was a rapper and that I was about to start working on my album. Ah ya. Got her.

She looked at me and smiled with what seemed to be about a thousand teeth, then invited me to come down to her apartment for a cup of tea. I don't drink tea, but I ain't one to pass up no invitation to a fine woman's apartment, so I followed her inside. She was making this too easy for me.

Her apartment was laid out in pink and white, with all kinds of pictures of black people on the walls, crystal knickknacks on the table, and in the corner, there was this Oriental-looking table with a sculpted Buddha sitting on top. I wasn't much for the religion thing myself, but still I was curious why she had Buddha up there and not Jesus Christ. I didn't know black people worshipped anybody other than Jesus. Religion wasn't on my mind though 'cause baby was looking too good in them cut-off shorts to be thinking about stuff like that. It had been two whole days since I had me a piece and my mind was filled with scheming on how to get from the dinette table to her bedroom without looking conspicuous.

She brought out two cups of tea and sat them on the table and took a seat across from me. "It's so good to see a young brother, making it the right way. Besides me and you, it's only about two other black couples in this building."

Couples? Was she referring to us—me and her? I liked her style so I decided to cut to the chase. "What's a beautiful sister like you doing living in this big-ass apartment all by yourself? Don't you need a man around to protect you?"

A frown replaced her big Kool-Aid smile and I knew I had said the wrong thing. "First of all, I don't need a man to protect me, I can take care of myself. Secondly, I don't live alone. I have a roommate."

Damn. She didn't tell me she had a man. I felt instantly uncomfortable and gulped down my tea so I could get the hell out of Dodge. I knew if I had a fine-looking woman like her, I'd have to kick somebody's ass if I came home and found another man in the house with her.

"Trudy! We got company!" she yelled, as the tooth-filled smile eased back on to her face. I felt relieved when she called a woman's name and held off on downing the last sip of my tea. This movie wasn't over. Not just yet.

Trudy came out of the bathroom with nothing but a towel wrapped around her. I felt myself kick up 'cause this was just too much. *Two* fine-ass women, neither with rings on their fingers—I was in heaven. I slumped back in my chair, examining the two and trying to figure out which one I was gonna make mine.

"Trudy," Janet said, showing millions of teeth, "this is Xavier. He's our new neighbor."

My attention focused on the roommate. Mostly because the thought of what was underneath that towel had me getting a hard-on. Besides, I was looking toward the future, and Janet could kill a nigga with all them teeth she had stuck in her mouth.

Trudy walked over to me and shook my hand. I was all ready to throw some drama at her like, "Damn, baby, you working that towel," but before I could get my line straight in my head, she walked over to Janet, grabbed her head, and kissed her dead on the mouth. "How's my baby this morning?" she cooed and added another kiss on her neck.

I guess they could tell I was sickened by the whole sight 'cause I immediately drank up, slammed the cup back down on the table, and raised the fuck up out of there. I actually had to hold my stomach on the way back to my apartment. That kind of scene usually got me aroused when I saw it on X-rated movies. But seeing that shit up close and in person had me illin'. I don't understand why two females would want to bump donuts anyway. Not when they had a willing and able man right in front of their faces. All that loveliness was just going to waste.

After I got back inside my empty walls, I kicked up all over again. I guess it was because I kept thinking about Janet and Trudy and what I knew they were probably doing. I went over to the table and opened up my lyric book and tried to get the thought of them out of my mind. Then I decided to give Jazmine one more shot. If that girl wasn't home I wasn't ever calling again. I had too much other shit to do besides ringing her line every fifteen minutes.

I dialed her number for what I thought was the last time, and when her friend picked up the phone, I almost hung up again. But since I had told myself that this was it and I had nothing to lose, I asked if Jazmine was in and for the first time she said "Yes."

. . .

I was in no particular mood to talk on the phone when Dakota came in my room and handed me the cordless. It was almost midday and I had yet to get out from under the covers. Moving the last of my things from Daddy's house had been more than an ordeal. He made a complete ass out of himself when Dakota and I showed up to get my stuff. We were lugging things from the house to Dakota's car as Daddy stood out on the sidewalk cursing, and calling Jesus, and shouting at the top of his lungs. We ignored him for the most part, but Dakota, with her big mouth, ended up getting in a shouting match with him, until Daddy blocked her out and started speaking in tongues. I felt like a soldier going off to war. I'd go in, grab an armful of clothes, march them out to the car past Daddy, then head straight back to the house to get another load, trying my best not to even look at him while he followed behind me, screaming and crying, "Lord help this child. She's a sinner."

I made the mistake of telling him that I had signed a contract with Black Tie Records to become a singer and that I was going to go live with Dakota since it was apparent that he would never give me enough freedom to live my life like I wanted to. The first thing out of his mouth was that he wanted me to pay back all the money he had spent on my tuition at UCLA. I didn't give a damn about that. I owed it to him anyway. Then he started rattling off sums that he wanted me to pay him for living in his house, eating his food, using his electricity, water—basically for being born. I knew there was no sense in standing out in the middle of the street arguing with him so I just scribbled Dakota's number on a piece of paper and handed it to him and told him to call me when he felt like talking to me rationally. That only incensed him more and by the time D and I had finished loading up the car, he was down on his knees in the front lawn, still crying, cursing me, and calling the Lord. Then he asked a question that I'd never heard him ask before. "What would your mother say?"

I just looked at him, shook my head, and got in the car. Before I closed the door, I looked back at him and said, "I don't know what Momma would say. I never had a chance to meet her."

I couldn't sleep all night. I thought for sure God was gonna strike me down in a bolt of lightning if I closed my eyes. I finally drifted off about seven in the morning for a couple of hours. And ever since I awoke I'd just been lying here, trying not to think about Daddy—Momma either, for that matter.

When Dakota handed me the phone I gave her a look that asked "Who the hell is it?"

"It's not Pops," she said and gave me a sly smile.

I adjusted the antenna and gave a shallow "Hello."

"Damn. What's a brother gotta do to get in touch with you?"

I knew it had to be Xavier. No one else had that ragged voice and dotted every sentence, damn near every other word, with slang.

"Did your roommate tell you I called?"

"Yes, about a hundred times," I said, laughing, hoping he could tell that I was impressed not irritated by his persistence.

"Well, I don't know about a hundred times, but yeah, I was tracking you down, baby. So did everything go all right when you met Mr. Strong? You looked as nervous as I don't know what."

"Yes, it did, as a matter of fact. We signed the contract yesterday and now I'm officially on my way. Thankyouverymuch."

"Well excuse me, Little Miss Redhead, but I also signed my contract yesterday and now I'm on my way too. Thank*you*verymuch."

"Get out of here. This world is too small! Congratulations. So you'll be working with Kirk, right?"

"That's right. And I guess we'll be running into each other a lot from now on, huh."

"I guess so."

"Well, uh, you know . . . I'm gonna get right to the point 'cause I know if I let you off the phone it'll be another fifty years before I track you down again, so . . . Look here. Why don't I swoop on over there and take you out. You know, nothing serious, just lunch or whatever—a sammich, a piece of fruit, a cold drink of water. Whatever you want."

"A sammich?" I said and almost choked on my laughter.

"Yeah, a sammich. You know. A couple pieces of bread with some meat in the middle. A sammich! And if you're really good, I'll buy you a box of Goobers for dessert."

Well, how could I resist such a delightful meal? "Sure. But I think I'll pass on the sammich. I know this great African restaurant on Sepulveda. How about that?"

He agreed and I gave him my address and we got off the phone. Suddenly, I felt energy and got out of the bed. I floated to the kitchen and poured a cup of coffee, black. All those damn creamers were making me nauseous.

"Don Juan sure did wake your ass up," Dakota said, sitting down at the dinette table.

I shot her a look as if to say "Don't start with me." But it was no use, she was already well on her way.

"So you guys going out or what?"

"Yes, Dakota."

"He's probably gonna take you to some ghetto rib joint over in the *hood*."

"No, as a matter of fact, he's taking me to Red Sea's. Thankyouverymuch." That changed her tune.

"Girl, bring me some of that selssi back. And make sure they make it extra spicy."

"I ain't bringing your mean ass nothing back."

"Forget you then. You guys probably won't make it past the appetizers before he tries to get you back to his bed anyway. I can't believe you're falling for this rap guy in the first place. They ain't about shit but grabbing their dicks," she said and broke into rhyme. "I know a girl name Jazz. Goin' out with a rapper. He wined her then he dined and for dessert he attacked her."

"Fuck you, D," I said, thinking how utterly stupid she sounded. "He's not like that. And besides, we're just going to get something to eat. I'm not about to marry him," I said and shoved her out of the way while she danced around like she was one of the *In Living Color* fly girls. "Did I tell you he got signed to Black Tie yesterday?"

"Good for him," she said and clapped her hands. "But just because he's got a contract don't mean he any different from the rest of these thuggish rappers. You can take a nigga out the hood, but you can't take the hood out of the nigga."

"Fuck off, D," I said and put my coffee cup in the sink. Her negativity was bringing me down and I was hardly in the mood to listen to another lecture from anybody. I went to my room and picked out a nice linen outfit to wear, then put it back and took out a pair of baggy jeans and a T-shirt and put that on instead. I went to the bathroom and combed my hair, but decided to put on a baseball cap, which I turned to the back. I took a long look at myself in the mirror, then pulled off the hat and the rest of my clothes. What the hell was I doing? Xavier was the rapper, not me, and I wasn't going to dress down because of that. That would be an insult. Besides, he had shown me nothing but kindness and until he portrayed something different I was going to treat him like any other man I would go out with. I changed into the linen outfit, curled my hair and applied my makeup, and made a mental note to stop by the mall and pick up another tube of Forever Red by Flori Roberts.

I didn't know quite what to expect when Xavier buzzed the intercom. But I relaxed and decided to go with the flow. Whatever will be, will be. I just hoped he wouldn't make me regret this.

He rang the doorbell a minute later, and I had to sprint to the door to beat Dakota to it. "Step off," I told her and gave her the old evil eye.

"Yuk, you already sound like a rapper's girlfriend," she said.

I opened the door and was pleasantly surprised to find him appropriately dressed in a pair of Levi's Dockers, a colorful silk shirt, and a nice pair of black suede shoes. Ha! I glanced at Dakota. No tennis shoes, no jeans hanging off his ass, and no baseball cap. Great!

I introduced him to Dakota and we left before she had a chance to give him the third degree. I was taken aback when we got downstairs to his car. It looked clean, had a nice paint job, and I could tell the rims were expensive. Still, it looked sort of thuggish and I prayed it didn't have hydraulics and that we wouldn't be riding down the street bouncing up and down with music blasting from a fifty-inch woofer in the trunk.

I could tell he was watching his p's and q's when he opened the passenger door for me, and since he was being so polite and gentlemanly, I decided to let the look of the car pass. Besides, it's probably worth more than that piece of crap I drive around in. I was even more impressed because we didn't have to listen to a bunch of loud rap songs on the way to the restaurant. Instead he slid in a tape of Loose Ends, *Zagora.* I was glad to see he had some taste in music.

We made idle conversation on the way to Red Sea's, mostly about the music business and what each of us had planned for our upcoming projects. We both agreed that there was something strange going on at Black Tie, but neither of us could actually put our finger on the reason everything seemed so rushed at the company. Then again, neither of us cared, as long as we got our projects completed.

By the time we entered the restaurant, I felt somewhat secure. He hadn't grabbed his crotch or called me a bitch or otherwise threatened my life, so I was thrilled. We were seated in a booth and the waiter placed a Jabena in front of us and filled two clay cups with coffee before he whisked off to serve another table.

I could tell Xavier didn't know exactly what was going on, but he played it off by burying his head in his menu. "Is this your first time at an African restaurant?"

"Who me? No," he said and kept his eyes glued to the menu. I knew that was a little white lie if I ever heard one, so I took the liberty of ordering for the both of us. When the waiter came to take our order, I said, "Xavier, you should really try the hot goregored. It's filet of beef and red peppers. That's if you can handle a little spice."

"I like it hot and spicy," he said, looking at me with that cool smile.

"I'll have the vegetarian shuro. And you might as well bring the water over now because he's gonna need it," I said to the waiter.

It took forever for them to prepare our meal, but it always does because they make everything from scratch after you order it. But it gave us time to talk, and it gave me time to realize that Dakota was all wrong about Xavier. He may be from the streets, but he's as smart as a whip and I thought if he made me laugh one more time, my stomach was gonna crack wide open.

"Did I tell you you look good enough to eat?" he said, smiling from ear to ear. "Matter of fact, if they don't hurry up with the food, I might have to go on ahead and pour some hot sauce over you and take a bite."

I chuckled. For some reason I wasn't turned off by what was obviously just another pick-up line. I hated it when other men said that kind of stuff to me, but coming from Xavier, it sounded cute instead of belligerent. Besides, I was hungry as hell myself.

"So tell me, Xavier."

"Oh, you can call me X."

"Anyway, *Xavier* . . . What made you want to get into rap?"

"'Cause I can't sing," he said and broke out into Luther Vandross's "A House Is Not a Home." " '*Ooooh a chair is not a house*' . . . See what I mean?"

"Yeah, I see what you mean," I said and chuckled a bit more. Boy, did I see what he meant.

"Why don't you sing a little somethin'-somethin'. You're the singer."

"I'm not gonna sing right here in this restaurant."

"Come on, Little Miss Redhead. Blow a song for me."

"My name is Jazmine."

"Anyway, *Little Miss Redhead* . . . Come on. You be Gladys Knight and I'll be your Pip. '*Leaving, leaving on the midnight train.*' "

"No thank you. And if you sing one more time, I'm gonna jump on the next train and leave you sitting right here."

"Okay, okay. So tell me. Is your man treating you right?"

"What man?"

"Ah, please. I know a fine sister like you gots to have a man lurking around somewhere. Looking like you do? Shiiit, you probably got about four or five men."

It was another pick-up line, but I could tell he didn't think so. This was just his way of saying he was interested in me, so I let it slide. "Whether I have a man or not, I'm here with you, so change the subject."

"Oh, you got some fire in you to match that red hair, I see. So what do you do? Sit at home all by yourself, singing into the bathroom mirror?"

If only he knew how true that was. "No, I go out every now and then, but I don't hang out in the streets like most people. I'd rather stay home, watch videos, play cards, you know, that type of thing."

"Yeah, I know what you mean. I'm trying to do more of that myself these days. Ain't nothing out in the streets but knuckleheads and bad influences."

I could tell he knew what he was talking about and that made me curious. "So where are you from?"

"Born and raised in South-Central."

"So am I."

"Yeah, but I bet your South-Central was different than mine. I'm gonna tell you like this, 'cause it ain't no need in me lying. I played the streets, the gang life, slangin' and bangin'. But when you get past twenty-five, that shit gets tired. And to tell the truth, if I wasn't rappin', I don't know where I'd be. Probably behind bars, or working some bullshit job at Mickey Dee's, or worse. Probably still hanging out in the streets, robbing and stealing and fighting fools 'cause they had on the wrong color. But, hey, I consider myself one of the lucky ones. I got a little bit of talent, so I said I better use it and—bing, bap, bang!—I got hooked up with Black Tie."

"So you're down with the gangsta life?"

"Well, I didn't say that. Gangsta life sells records. People are curious about shit they don't know, so I'm just gonna use it to my advantage now."

Well, I sure was curious about it, but I wasn't sure exactly what he meant. "So you mean you're gonna be another one of those rappers who talk about killing up people, dissing the police, and calling women 'bitches.' "

"No, I'm just gonna speak the truth. I'm gonna tell about the streets. In the hood, the reality is that niggas be killing each other. Police are a bunch of faggots, and a bitch is a bitch."

"What! I'm from the hood too, remember? And I don't consider myself a bitch, Xavier."

"See, there you go. It's like I said. We come from two different South-Centrals. What part are you from?"

"My daddy and I lived on Baring Cross."

"Uh-huh, you was right in the heart of my hood. Cross Street territory. But let me guess. Y'all lived off Cross Street and Eightieth, right?"

"Yeah."

"In a house probably, right?"

"Yes, but it's still South-Central, and every night I went to sleep with the sound of gunfire. But that don't mean—"

"Hold on now, Little Miss Redhead. Let me make my point. You had a father—and I know I don't have to tell you how scarce fathers are in the hood. But anyway, you had a house. You went to school. UCLA, if I remember right." He paused. "See, a nigga like me didn't have all that shit. All I had was my gang. That was my reality. And where I come from, if someone threatened the gang, or should I say, my family, they got their ass taken out. I bet you never had to ride around in your car worried if the police were gonna pull you over—for no fucking reason whatsoever—and make you lay down in the middle of the street with a gun pointed at the back of your head. Did you? And as far as the women go—they're just as scandalous as the men. They go around fucking anything that moves, getting pregnant just so they can collect welfare or get some money out of a nigga for an abortion they never intend to have. Now that's a bitch. Plain and simple. That's the real."

"Well, if that's the real then I've been living some type of fantasy. But I get your point. We come from two different South-Centrals. Fine. What I don't understand is why black people have to air our dirty laundry out in public. White people have these same problems, but you don't hear Madonna or Sting coming out on their records talking about all the white people they know in their lives who aren't living right. So why do we have to do it?"

The waiter came back with our meals before Xavier could answer that question and I was glad, because the conversation was getting a little too deep for a first date. I didn't agree with everything he said, but I gave him credit for speaking his mind. I was relieved that he was able to hold a decent conversation. Unlike most of the men I ran into, he had something to say—unorthodox as it was, but still, he had something to say.

We both ate like scavengers, wolfing down mouthful after mouthful, only breaking momentarily to wash it all down with water. Xavier had four glasses, I had three, and when it was all over, my mouth burned for thirty minutes. I did a lot of shaking my head yes and no, so I wouldn't scare him away with my breath before the Tic Tac I secretly put in my mouth had time to work. I couldn't believe how comfortable I felt with him. It was as though I had grown up with him all my life. But I like to died when he gestured toward my face to let me know I had something hanging out of my nose. And of course he couldn't just let it go at that. He had to go on and on about it.

"What is it?" I asked, grabbing my nose with my napkin.

"I don't know, baby, but it's green and slimy. Guess it's a booger."

"Shut up, Xavier."

"I mean really, Red. You're cute and all, but could you please tell your little friends to stay in the house while we're eating?" he said, laughing.

"Shut up, Xavier. I'm embarrassed enough as it is." I know my face was turning as red as my hair, but he just kept right on talking about it and snickering at me.

"I mean, I'm just saying. Do those things just swing out at any time they want, or is it just when you're out on a date?" He almost fell out of his seat, he was laughing so hard. And after I thoroughly dabbed at my nose fifteen or twenty times, I had to laugh out loud myself. I was embarrassed as hell, but I was liking his style. Call me a sucker for a punch line, because I was falling hard for this guy.

"So what's next?" he asked, gazing at me, still grinning. For the first time I noticed how pretty his teeth were. They were all lined up like a picket fence in his mouth and I figured he probably never had a cavity. I'm a sucker for nice teeth, too.

"Next?" I asked, stalling for time. I didn't want the date to end, but I didn't want to seem too anxious to be with him either.

"Yeah, I figured we could go up to the Universal Cineplex, miniature golf, bowling . . ."

"Bowling? You like to bowl?"

"Hell yeah, baby girl. I don't know, it's something about that big black ball, rolling down the lane at top speed, knocking those red-neck white pins to kingdom come."

"Oh shut up, Xavier. How about we rent some videos, get a pint of Häagen-Dazs and take them back to your place? You do have a VCR, don't you?"

"Uh, no, Miss Ma'am. I's justa po country boy. I's don't know nothin' 'bout dem der fancy, doo-hickey VCRs." He paused and then laughed. "Yeah, girl. I got a VCR. These are the nineties."

Someone needs to tell Dakota that. She's got that high-tech apartment, but if you ask her about a VCR, call waiting, an answering machine, fax, computer, or a self-cleaning oven, she'll look at you like you're asking her about the space shuttle. The only something that girl cares about is that damn cordless phone and the microwave. But I already made up my mind. I'm going shopping for an answering machine and I'm getting call waiting and star 69 installed on that phone. Dakota may still be floating around in that hippie world her parents created, but a girl like me goes into shock without modern technology. But all this shopping is going to have to wait till tomorrow, because like Dakota always says, "Baby's vibes are calling me." And as far as I'm concerned, Xavier's call is one that I don't want to miss.

. . .

When a mothafucka is on a roll, I mean a mothafucka is on a *roll*. When I thought about taking Little Miss Redhead out, I thought the most I'd be able to do was slide my arm around her in the car. You know, digging the scene with a gangsta lean. But when baby said she wanted to get some movies and go back to my crib, I kicked up into full gear. But just as soon as I rose, I had to calm my black ass back down. I had gotten this far with Jazmine and I wasn't gon' fuck it up by trying to take advantage of her. Hell no! I'm gonna switch it up on her. This time I'm gonna be the one playing hard to get. It's gonna test every testosterone pore in my body, but I'm gonna do it. I ain't doing nothing to blow it with Little Miss Redhead.

I don't know what it is and to tell the truth I probably don't want to find out, but it's something about Jazmine that's got me feenin'. She got my eyes wide open and when I think about her, I get to twitching and jerking. Just like them damn crackheads I used to sell to. Jazz got me on a natural high though, and if I just chill and let her take the lead, I'll be in with her. In other words I'm gonna act like a little punk. Oprah say women like all that sensitive shit, so if Jazz wants sensitive, then that's what she's gonna get. I'll be anything for Little Miss Redhead.

The video store was crowded and hot and I thought I was gonna have to knock this one dude out. That fool knew he saw me about to pick up that *Scarface* tape and he gonna run over and snatch it up. And that was the last copy. I was about to get all up in that fool's ass, till Jazmine came around the corner. I couldn't let her see me like that, so I just gave that fool the peace sign and went on about my business.

Since *Scarface* was gone, which is what I really wanted to see, even though I'd seen it damn near fifty times, I decided to pick out one of them sappy love stories. I thought about my vow to be a punk for the night and figured I might as well go all the way and cry on her ass. She'll really think I'm the sensitive type if I break out in tears. But all the good love stories were already checked out. So then I strolled on down to the B section and looked for Eddie Murphy's *Boomerang*. At least it's a romantic comedy, but it was all gone too. By then I was pissed off, so I asked one of the inventory people if they had some extra copies in the back. The guy told me they only ordered three copies of *Boomerang* for the whole store and I said, "What! But y'all got damn near thirty copies of *Beethoven* on the shelf." He gave me some bullshit about they only order copies based on the consumer graphics of the neighborhood the store is in. But I know all that fool was really trying to say was, "Y'all black folks take y'all's asses on down to the ghetto video store if you want movies with niggers in 'em."

I finally gave up and let Jazmine finish the movie picking. At first I thought she was gonna come up with some whacked feminine shit like *Beauty and the Beast* or *Steel Magnolias*, but she did a'ight. She picked out *Sparkle* and *Lady Sings the Blues*. She stood behind me in the line to pay for the movies and it surprised the shit out of me when she gave me a little slap on the ass. She tried to say I had some lint on the back of my pants, but I know she was just trying to get in a little sneak feel. Women like my "black ground" and I know my butt was probably looking too good for her to resist rubbing on it.

I had tried to resist grabbing her ass all night long and I got my first really good view of it when she walked ahead of me into the mini-mart we stopped at to pick up some ice cream. She insisted on paying for the Häagen-Dazs, but I had to be even more insistent. "I got you, baby. You don't gotta pay for nothing when you with the X-Man," I told her. The ice cream was four dollars, but I pulled out a C note to pay for it, even though I had plenty of fives in my wallet. Women also like big spenders, I heard Oprah say one day. I realized that I had forgotten to get some beer and asked Jazmine to pick me out some while I was waiting for the change. She strolled back up to the counter with some damn Coors Light. Coors Light? Naw, baby I needs me a forty, I thought, but didn't say anything. Whatever Little Miss Redhead wants, she gets.

When we got back to my place, she walked through the door and started checking everything out. She was impressed. I know she was. She probably thought a nigga like me was living in the hood in some broken-down section-eight apartment with no lights and a bathroom in the hall-way. No, no. Not the X-Man. Black leather, black lacquer, and remote controls for everything from the stereo to the light switches. She made herself right at home and sat down on the couch and did what I usually do—picked up the remote. I put the Häagen-Dazs and beer in the freezer 'cause not only did she get the wrong kind, she got the hot ones from a stack on the floor. But I decided not to drink any anyway. I didn't want to fuck around and get drunk on her. That would blow my punk role.

"So which one do you want to start with?" I said, holding up the videos in front of her face.

"*Sparkle*," she said with a big, cheesy smile.

"Then *Sparkle* it is, Red."

"My name is Jazmine."

"Anyway, Red," I said and put the tape in. I took a seat on the opposite end of the leather sofa and sunk myself into the cushion. She looked at me, smiling from ear to ear.

"Would you mind getting the ice cream?" she said just as I was getting comfortably uncomfortable.

No problem, I thought, and raised up. "And two spoons," she added when I walked into the kitchen.

I came back and handed her the ice cream and the spoons and sat back down at the other end. "Aren't you gonna help me eat this?"

I could think of something else I'd like to eat, I thought, but I was glad she asked 'cause it gave me a reason to slide down and get closer to her. The punk role was working already.

I couldn't concentrate on the movie sitting that close to her, but she was getting a kick out of it. She sang all the songs and when "Giving Him Something He Can Feel" came on, she got up and did the little dance right along with Irene Cara and those other two girls. I wished she would sit down 'cause she was turning me all the way on and I felt myself kicking up—in a hard way. I had seen *Sparkle* a couple times before, but I never noticed it was such a long movie and I could barely stand it sitting there, right up under her, smelling her perfume and trying to cross my legs in every which way so she couldn't see how excited I was. When it was over

I got up and put in the next movie and she got up to use the bathroom. When I went back to the sofa I sat down on the opposite corner. I couldn't take the pressure of being so close to her without touching her for another two and a half hours. But when she came back, she sat down right next to me and I thought I was gonna explode from all the tension I had built up.

"In case I forget, I just wanna tell you I had a great time," she said, looking me dead in the face and smiling that beautiful smile. I couldn't even say anything, 'cause if I did it would have been something stupid like, "Wanna see the bedroom?" but Jazmine just kept on looking at me and flashing those teeth.

"I didn't know you were such a gentleman, Xavier."

I ain't, I wanted to say, and wished she'd shut the hell up before I did something really stupid like grab her by her fiery red hair, lean her head back, and kiss her.

"I thought you were gonna be all aggressive and vulgar and disrespectful. But you proved me wrong," she said.

"Naw, baby. That ain't me. I know how to treat a good thing when I see it. I leave all the vulgar stuff for people who deserve it."

"Well, I just want to make one thing clear. I may be from South-Central, but I'm not like one of those bitches you were talking about earlier, and I don't stand for any kind of disrespect."

"I know that."

"Well, I'm just making sure, because I like you. And if you plan on taking me out again, I expect to be treated like a lady at all times."

I shrugged my shoulders and chuckled. What kind of guy did she think I was? "I know that, Jazmine."

"Good."

I thought that was the end of that discussion, but Jazmine just kept on staring at me like she was trying to figure out something. I turned my attention back to the television, 'cause if I looked at her any longer, I thought I'd start twitching. She was making it too hard to be a punk. Then she went and did the wrong thing. She brushed her hand over my head and kissed me softly on the cheek. Now what did she go and do that for? I tried so hard to focus in on Diana and Billy Dee, but then I felt another pair of lips on my ear and it was all over after that. I turned my head to face her again, but had to look away. *Come on, X, be strong. Don't blow it.* She had my face between her hands now, and her lips were running all over my face and like I always say, a brother's gotta do what a brother's gotta do, so I leaned in and kissed her on the mouth. That's all I planned to do, but baby just kept on going. Before I knew it, I was on top of her and the leather sofa was making all kinds of squeaky, romantic noises and I just couldn't stop. And to tell the truth, I don't think she wanted me to stop. But I had to check myself. I had already broken my vow of punktitude and I knew if I didn't quit right then, that would be all she wrote. I stole one final last kiss and sat back up. She sat up with me and continued her longing stare as if she didn't quite know what kind of creature she was sitting next to. That's when she got up and pulled me by my hand. She led me to the bedroom like it was her own apartment and by that time I was so kicked up that I didn't even try to hold back. Something in my head told me this was the right thing to do, so if I was gonna do it, I was gonna do it right. I wasn't taking her back home until I showed her how a real man makes love.

I was gentle at first. Oprah said women like a man who takes his time. I savored every bit of her body, tickled all the right places, and since I was on a roll, I decided to break that myth that black men don't go down below the belly button. It was hard to break away from her belly button though. It was so cute 'cause she was an outie. And when I finally went lower, all hell broke loose. She got to shaking and moaning and grabbing my head, and thank God I didn't have any hair up there 'cause the way she was acting, she probably would have pulled it all out. She came with a force, like it was her first time or something and I knew then that I had done my job well. But then I remembered, I was supposed to be playing the sensitive role. I figured, since I hadn't even expected to get this far, that I might as well quit while I was ahead. I worked my way back up to her mouth and she kissed me long and hard, expecting me to finish it off by going inside her. I didn't. It took every ounce of restraint that I had in me, but I didn't. I rolled over beside her and she rolled on top of me and I held her like that until she rested her head on my chest and fell asleep.

I couldn't close my eyes. Partly because I still had a hard-on bigger than Mount Everest, and partly because I couldn't believe how right this felt. If I didn't know myself any better, I'd say I'd fallen in love. But then again, what do I know about love? Not a damn thing. For all I know this feeling could be heartburn. I'd had a bad case of gas ever since we left that African restaurant. But then another thought popped into my head. This definitely had to be love, 'cause if it wasn't, why was I suddenly feeling like a true punk? It wasn't an act anymore. Jazmine made me softer. So soft that my body felt like a sponge and all I could do was lay there and soak her up.

I heard the VCR in the other room tick off and I wondered if this movie, me and Jazz's movie, would end so soon. Well, if I have anything to do with it, we'll be sneaking into another feature.

chapter eleven

competition

"Ah, *ah, ah, ah, ah, ah. Caught up in the rapture of love. Nothing else could compare."* It was only seven o'clock in the morning, but I had Anita moaning full blast on the stereo as I sang with her around the apartment. All thoughts were focused on Xavier and the wonderful night we had, and I could feel myself getting giddy. I've been this way ever since I started going out with Xavier. It's been over a month now and I can't believe how well it's been going. It's like some kind of fairy tale, one I hope will never end. I guess this is what they call lovesick. I don't really know, but whatever it is, I got it bad with a capital BAD. I kissed the shit out of him when he brought me back home last night. It was like one of those kisses you give someone at the airport before they go off on a long trip. After I did it, I felt sort of embarrassed. I was trying to let him know that I liked him and wanted to see him again, but when he drove off I was left feeling desperate. It worked out though because he called me as soon as he got back to his place. We didn't even talk about anything, just held the phone up to our ears and listened to each other breathe until we fell asleep. When I woke up I was still cradling the cordless. I called him back at six-thirty this morning, but his line was busy. I could imagine him still lying in his bed with the phone hugged against his neck.

I didn't hear Dakota when she creeped out of her bedroom. When I finally recognized her she was staring at me like I was crazy. I guess I did look stupid, standing in the middle of the kitchen doing nothing but grinning. She eyed me as she walked over to the stereo and turned down Anita, then walked back to the kitchen and stopped in front of me. She squinted her eyes at me and said, "Y'all fucked," and started preparing coffee.

I didn't respond. Mostly because it was none of her business whether we did or didn't, but also because she was absolutely right.

"You don't have to say anything, I can tell," she said, taking out a carton of Kahlúa creamer from the refrigerator. "As a matter of fact, I don't even want to hear the details. I bet it was disgusting anyway."

"For your information, we had a very nice evening. Xavier was the perfect gentleman. Now let's change the subject before you kill my buzz."

"You can do so much better."

"Oh, really? What's better? Craig?"

"Craig is a very nice man. You should have rushed him when you had the chance."

I put my hand up in front of her face and she changed the subject real quick.

"Anyway," she said, taking a seat at the dinette table, "while you were out romancing the stone yesterday, your agent-slash-manager was working her ass off," she said, forming imaginary quotations with her fingers.

"Thanks again for helping me out," I said, walking over to give her a hug. She brushed me away with her hand and motioned for me to sit down across from her. "So what did you do?"

"Went to brunch with River and Earth."

"I thought you said you were working your ass off."

"I was, honey. I was getting all the latest gossip," she said, getting up and walking back to the kitchen to pour a cup of coffee. "Now check this out," she said, straddling her seat again. "Black Tie Records is in the middle of a major shake-up, honey."

"As in earthquake?" I said, laughing, and banging the table with the palm of my hand. Dakota didn't join in. Ms. Executive was all business now.

"Shut up and listen," she said, adjusting herself in her seat. "Now peep this. River told me that Mr. Timbers—"

"Who's that?"

"The president of Black Tie Records, dingy. Where you been? I swear sometimes I think your hair color should be blond instead of red," she said, frowning. "Anyway, Mr. Timbers just announced his retirement and word has it that he's looking for someone to take over the company after he's gone. Are you still with me?"

I nodded, obediently.

"Now, Earth said she heard there's only two people being considered for the job and that's Kirk Walker *and* . . . ," she said, waiting for me to add the other name. She sucked her teeth with disgust when I couldn't figure out who the other person was. Then a lightbulb went on inside my head.

"Bobby Strong," I said, with a burst of energy.

"Very good. Do I need to explain who he is too?"

"No, smart-ass, and I know who Kirk Walker is too. That's the guy Xavier's working with."

"So I heard," she said, sipping her coffee. "Looks like you and your new man are going to be in stiff competition."

"Now how do you figure that?"

"Don't you get it? If Kirk and Bobby are going head up, then you and Xavier are going head up too. It's you and Bobby against Kirk and Xavier, and the winning team gets control of Black Tie Records. River says everybody in the business is talking about it. I'm thinking about starting up a pool and taking bets. This is going to be interesting."

"Hmm," I moaned, getting up from the table.

"What's that 'hmm' for?" Dakota asked, eyeing me.

"I don't know if I'm gonna like this whole competition thing. I mean what happens to the loser?"

"The loser makes like Casper, honey."

"Well, all I know is that Xavier is good for me and I'm not going to do anything to compromise our relationship."

"Compr—compromise your relationship?" she said, almost choking on her coffee. "Y'all only been going out for a month," she said, snapping her fingers. "So don't even trip. Your career is more important than any man will ever be."

"Look who's talking."

"Yeah, you better look who's talking, because I'm your agent-slash-manager," she said. "And I say you're gonna do whatever those people down at BTR tell you to do if it's gonna make you some money."

I poured myself a cup of coffee and set it to the side. If Dakota knew the kind of night I spent with Xavier she wouldn't be talking about career first, I thought, having a flashback of his bedroom. I know she's right, but I think she's making too much out of it. If Bobby's looking for some kind of big-time promotion, then that's between him and Kirk. All I'm getting paid to do is sing, not back-stab, not scheme, and certainly not hurt my man. *My man.* That's the first time I've ever referred to anyone as my man. *My man, my man.*

"I said, it's your man," Dakota yelled, holding the cordless in her hand as if it were going to break her wrist. I reached for it, but she let it go before I got a grip on it. She laughed as it fell to the floor and disconnected, but I was getting pissed off.

"Don't make me have to hurt you up in here," I said, rolling my eyes.

"Ooo. Did your boyfriend teach you that? I'm so scared," she said and walked away snickering.

The phone rang again and I answered.

"Why you hang up?" Xavier asked.

"No, I dropped the phone."

"I mean last night."

"I didn't. I just woke up and the phone was dead."

"Oh shit. I hope that ain't no omen."

"It's not," I said and prayed silently for a split second. "So what are you doing today?"

"Kickin' it witchoo."

"Who says?"

"I says."

"Are you asking me or telling me?"

"Put it like this. I'm on my way. Bye."

He said it so fast that I thought he was going to hang up, but I didn't hear a click.

"Aren't you going to say bye?" he said, surprising me. "Don't tell me you're like them people on TV who just hang up when they finish a sentence without saying bye."

"No," I said. "I hate that, it's so rude."

"Well then say bye."

"You're on your way right now?"

"Yeah."

I hung up the phone in his face. It was a joke and I expected him to call right back, but he didn't and when I called him, there was no answer. Thank God the apartment intercom rang thirty minutes later. It was my man. I quickly buzzed him in and when he got to the door he was holding two take-out bags from The Boulevard Soul Kitchen.

"Hi," he said.

"Bye," I replied.

.   .   .

Bobby worked with a passion as though every minute he spent in his office added an extra hour to his life. He loved being busy again, his life having purpose. Until recently, he'd forgotten that, but Jazmine bought it all back for him. Since the day she walked into his office he had been working overtime on how best to cultivate her image and make her into the superstar he intended her to be. Planning Jazmine's career had become the most important thing in his life, especially now that Sheryl had divorced him.

He pushed aside the publicity photos of Jazmine he'd been going over and picked up a framed picture of Sheryl and his daughters that sat on his desk. He fought back tears as he looked into their smiling faces, then quickly put the photo inside his desk drawer. The divorce had taken place so quickly that he hadn't had a chance to grieve and he wasn't going to start now. He was afraid that if he let himself truly grieve for what he had lost he would never be able to overcome the devastation. So he accepted it and moved on. His job was the only thing he had going for him these days and he immersed himself in it in an effort to keep his mind off the loss of his family. But today it wasn't so easy for him to forget.

He cradled his head in his hands and tried to make sense of what had happened to his life. Last month he was a married father. Today, a bachelor. The more he thought over what had happened the more unbelievable it seemed.

Originally, Sheryl had asked Bobby to move out of the house for a couple of weeks. She said she needed some time to be by herself, to sort things out—space. Though he didn't like the idea of being away from his family, Bobby agreed to go along with it anyway. He wanted to show Sheryl that he was willing to do whatever it would take to salvage their marriage and earn her trust again. But what had started out as a brief separation turned into something far worse. Less than a week after he left the house, he was served with divorce papers at his hotel. The minute he read through the papers, he picked up the phone and called Sheryl, but there was no answer. Anxious and confused, he hopped in his car and drove to the house to wait for her return, but when he got to the front door he found the lock had been changed. Furious, he stormed around to the side entrance, then to the back, only to find that his key no longer fit any of the locks.

Stunned and unable to find the logic in what was going on, he returned to the front of the house, sat down on the front steps, and waited. Three hours passed before he returned to his car. He phoned his hotel for messages, but there were none. So he sat. And he waited.

It was after ten o'clock the next morning when he finally left the house and headed for his office. He slouched down the hallway toward his suite, ignoring everyone and their greetings until he reached his assistant's desk. Hesitantly he looked at her, and without saying a word she handed him a piece of paper. It read: "B—I've taken the girls out of town for a few weeks until we can get this situation settled. Hope you understand. It's better we make a clean break from each other. I'll be in touch—S."

Even more confused than he had been before, he flipped the paper over, wondering where the rest of it could be. Was this all there was to it? After eighteen years of marriage? Bam! Just like that? He crumpled the note in his fist and headed back down the hallway, ignoring Tish as she called out behind him. The next thing he remembered was waking up in his hotel room, face down in his own vomit, a bottle of vodka beneath his leg, a syringe still sticking out from his arm.

The divorce had been quick and easy—if divorces can ever be considered easy. Sheryl hadn't wanted anything from him except basic child support for the kids and a modest alimony to support her while she went back to college. When her lawyer told Bobby that Sheryl would be permanently moving the kids away from L.A., he thought he would lose his mind. Taking his girls away was Sheryl's final blow, the ultimate sucker punch. He considered seeking full custody of the kids at one point, but his lawyer advised him against that novel idea. Of course, he was a successful businessman and loved his precious girls dearly, but the odds are always stacked against fathers when it comes to gaining custody of their children, his lawyer advised him. Plus, there was that pesky problem that Sheryl knew about the drugs. He knew he couldn't be the type of father his girls needed. It takes more than love and adoration to be a father these days, not to mention the fact that he was always out of town or at some promotional shindig or meeting with clients—anywhere but at home.

The last time he saw his family was the day after the divorce had become final. Sheryl brought the girls back to L.A. to pack up the rest of their belongings before they headed back to North Carolina where she had purchased a new home. He hadn't spoken to his girls since they had left and as he walked up the front lawn, he tried to figure out exactly what he would say to them. He didn't know what Sheryl had told them or if they even understood what was going on. But how could they understand? he thought, as he made his way to the front door. He barely understood himself.

He felt strange knocking on the door of his own house, and when Sheryl finally answered he felt even more out of place. Neither of them could look the other in the eye and the tension was unbearable. Finally Bobby spoke. " I want to see my girls," he told her, looking around the almost empty house.

"They're upstairs," she responded, trying to hide the awkwardness in her voice.

Quickly, he climbed the stairs to Tiffany's room and found her on the floor amid countless boxes she had been packing for their departure. She was on the phone, obviously talking to a male friend and telling him she would miss him and that she would write him every day. She looked beautiful, but he could tell by the look in her eyes that she was falling apart at the seams. "It's Daddy, my angel," he called to her from the doorway. She turned to look up at him, then quickly got off the phone.

"I've gotta go, Anthony. I have company," she said, looking down at the floor. "Call me back in about ten minutes, this won't take long." She hung up and went back to throwing things in boxes. She didn't even look at Bobby again until he walked over and sat down on the floor beside her.

"You're getting all packed up, I see."

She didn't answer.

"I hope you're going to write *me* every day too."

She got up and walked into her closet, which was as big as another room, and started pulling clothes off hangers.

"You know, I'm going to miss you, angel," he said, shouting so she could hear him inside the closet. She didn't respond.

"Angel, don't do this to Daddy. I love you. You know I love you."

She came back to the opening of her closet. Tears were piercing her eyes, but she didn't speak. All Bobby could do was break down and cry right there on the floor. No more words needed to be spoken. There was nothing more to say. Tiffany stood watching as her father cowered on the floor in tears until Brittany came bustling through the room. She ran over to her father and gave him a tight bear hug.

"Hi, Daddy," she yelled, though she was right in his face. She had always been the loving one, too young to know what an idiot her father really was. "We're going on a long trip. Wanna come?"

"No, sweet muffin. Daddy can't go this time."

"But you never go anywhere with us anymore. Why you move away, huh?"

"Well, sugar head, Daddy and Mommy can't live together anymore. So you won't be seeing me much for a while," he said, trying in vain to stop his tears. "But I'll always be with you, no matter where you are." He held her close to him until she started to squirm.

"Okay, Daddy," she said and placed a sloppy, wet kiss on his cheek. "Want some ice cream?"

"No," Tiffany interrupted. "Daddy doesn't want ice cream, Brittany. But I do," she said, still standing firmly in the closet doorway. "Why don't you go get us some?"

Obediently, Brittany ran out of the room calling for cook. There was silence for what seemed like an hour, but had only been a few minutes.

Then Tiffany finally spoke. "I know I'm grown up now, and I should be able to think like an adult, but Daddy, I don't understand this. I never knew you and Mom were having problems. Then all of sudden you're gone. Where's the logic? Where does this fit into the nice, comfortable world you said I would always have?"

"It doesn't fit, dear. Sometimes things just go astray, but I want you to know the problems that your mother and I have are ours. This doesn't affect my relationship with you at all."

"But it does affect us, Daddy. For so long I've been Daddy's precious little girl. Now what am I supposed to be? I don't know how to act anymore. You didn't teach me enough to handle this, Daddy. So, now you tell me. What am I supposed to do?"

"You're supposed to keep on keeping on," Bobby said, kicking a box out of his way and standing up. "Remember that Gladys Knight and the Pips song we used to listen to when you were little? What did she say?"

She thought for a second then said, "I really got to use my imagination."

"That's right. What else?"

"To think of good reasons to keep on keeping on."

The tears came pouring down her face and Bobby's too. They both understood. The subject was closed.

When he returned downstairs to leave, he found Sheryl waiting for him. They silently walked outside together, barely touching, like old high school friends. When they finally spoke, they looked straight ahead, both of them unwilling to face the other.

"So, is everything going well for you?" Sheryl asked.

"Uh-huh."

"Oh, uh, did the girls show you the picture of our new house?"

"Yeah."

"It's a wonderful neighborhood. I've already enrolled Britt into private school and Tiff just got accepted into UNC. She's all excited about trying out for the cheerleading squad," she said, pausing for Bobby to respond, but he just kept walking to his car. "If she makes it, I was thinking you could come out during basketball season. We should all be settled in by then and uh, I know how much you like basketball."

"Cut the bullshit, Sheryl," Bobby said and stopped in his tracks. "How can you stand there talking about basketball after what you've done to me?"

"What I've done to you? What about what you've done to me and the kids?"

"You know what? I knew you'd say some shit like that. What have I done for you and the kids? I'll tell you what I've done for you and the kids. I provided for you guys for eighteen fucking years. That's what I've done for you and the kids. I made a way out of no way for you and this is how you repay me? I was always good to you, Sheryl. Always."

"No, Bobby. You were a drug addict and you were abusive."

"Abusive? One time, Sheryl, one time."

"And just exactly how many times do I have to get my ass kicked by my husband before I get a divorce? Huh? Twice? Ten? Fifty?" Bobby had never seen her so angry before. "Did you ever go to that rehab center?" she asked, as if she already knew the answer.

"I don't have a problem," Bobby said, defensively.

Sheryl shook her head in disgust. "Do you think I'm stupid?" she asked, closing the distance between them. "Do you?" she asked again and reached inside his jacket pocket.

"What the fuck?" Bobby shouted, trying to restrain her, but Sheryl just kept right on searching. She grabbed his belt buckle to hold on to him as she stuffed her hands into his pants pockets.

"Do I look stupid?" she continued to ask, reaching around to his back pocket. She retrieved a small piece of aluminum foil and pulled it away while Bobby reached out, trying to stop her. She turned her back to block him and unraveled the foil to find a single white rock. She looked at him again in disgust. "So you don't have a problem?" she asked and threw the foil and cocaine to the ground.

Bobby watched it fall, then looked away in embarrassment.

"If you don't have a problem, why don't you get in your car and leave? Right now," she said, standing before him with authority.

Bobby stood there stiffly, unable to feel his body. He wished he could make himself disappear or that Sheryl would go back into the house and leave him to his embarrassment. But she stood there eyeing him, waiting for him to make a move. Finally, he turned toward his car then stopped. He felt disgust for himself, but he couldn't help it. He turned back around and picked up the cocaine from the ground and put it back in his pocket.

Sheryl began to cry and as much as he wanted to comfort her he couldn't bring himself to do it. How could he comfort someone else when it was he who needed the comfort?

"Tell the girls to call me," he said before getting in his car and driving off.

That was the last time he'd seen Sheryl and his children. The last day he felt complete.

Bobby was forced back into the present when he felt a teardrop roll down his chin. He wiped his eyes, trying desperately to force the past out of his memory. He opened a pack of chocolate-covered almonds and tried to refocus on his work, but there was too much noise coming from outside his doorway. He recognized one of the voices as Kirk Walker's and quickly went to the door to make his presence known. As he put his hand on the doorknob, he heard the voice of Mr. Timbers and decided to wait. He listened as Kirk boasted about a new rapper he had signed named X-Man. "Well, his real name is Xavier Honor, sir. And I tell you, he's definitely got what it takes. You'd love this guy."

He sounded so sure of himself, Bobby thought, but he's got to be out of his mind if he thinks all this ass-kissing is going to land him the presidency. The more Kirk spoke, the more Bobby's confidence rose. It was as if every word out of his mouth was giving Bobby strength. He wanted so badly to prove he was better than him, that he hadn't lost his touch.

He finally opened the door and went out to greet the two men. He nodded to Kirk and shook Mr. Timbers' hand, then took a step back and crossed his arms. Everything about Kirk pissed him off. From the curly way he wore his hair to the silly smirk that tainted his face. He wanted so much to tell him what a piece of shit he thought he was. Instead he simply stuck out his chest and rocked backward on his heels. Kirk was too little a man for Bobby to worry about.

"So nice to see you, Mr. Timbers," he said, purposely turning so he wouldn't have to look at Kirk's wimpy face.

"Yes, yes. Just got back from vacation and I tell you—"

"Excuse me, Mr. Timbers," Kirk interrupted. "I don't mean to cut you short, sir, but I know you're a busy man. How about we finish this conversation in my office?"

"Um, excuse *me,*" Bobby said, turning to Kirk. "It's impolite to interrupt grown folks' conversations," Bobby said, laughing. He was pleased when Mr. Timbers joined in too.

"You mean old folks, don't you, Bobby?" Mr. Timbers said, slapping him on the back.

"Actually I meant *experienced* folks," he said, pausing to look at the stupid expression on Kirk's face.

"Look you two," Mr. Timbers said, backing toward the elevator. "I'm meeting with A and R in about two minutes. It was nice talking to you both and I'm sure I'll have a detailed outlined of your new projects on my desk by, oh, let's say noon. I hear a lot happened while I was away," he said, stepping through the double doors.

"I'll get that right to you," Bobby said.

"I sent mine up this morning, sir," Kirk added.

"Well then, you gentlemen have a productive day. And uh, Bob, stop by the office later. I'm ordering some catfish from Mack's Shack this evening," Mr. Timbers said before the doors closed.

Bobby turned toward Kirk and smiled. He still had Mr. Timbers right where he wanted him—on his side. "Ever had lunch with the boss?" he asked Kirk, who stood staring at him in rage.

"You interrupted a very important discussion, you know."

"Oh no," Bobby said, placing a hand over his mouth. "Still collecting money for the yearly candy drive, young buck?"

"We'll see who's talking trash when I'm sitting in my office on the fifteenth floor."

"Look here, boy scout. You wouldn't know the first thing about running this company. You haven't put in your time. You have neither the experience nor the drive to take over this company. And furthermore," Bobby said, walking closer to Kirk, "you are not me." He turned to walk back to his office. "I advise you to tread back over to the shallow end of the pool, son," Bobby said, standing in his doorway. He took one final look at Kirk's pitiful face before entering. "You better ask somebody," he said and slammed his door.

"Now, back to business," Bobby said to himself as he strolled back to his desk. He sat down and dialed Jazmine's number. He didn't know why he was calling, other than to make sure his ticket to the presidency was still intact. She answered the phone laughing, and he was glad she was in good spirits.

"Strong here, Jazmine," he said, leaning back into his chair.

"Hello, Mr. Strong. So nice to hear from you," she said, stifling a giggle.

"Just making sure you're all right. Wouldn't want anything to happen to my superstar."

"Of course I'm all right. Why wouldn't I be?"

"Sounds like you're having a good time." He tightened his grip on the receiver when he heard the sound of a male voice in the background. "Having a party?"

"Oh no," she said, chuckling.

"Sounds like a party to me."

"No, that's just Xavier."

"As in the X-Man?"

"That's right. You've probably seen him around. He's signed at Black Tie, too."

"Uh-huh." Bobby paused and wondered why the hell Xavier would be at her apartment. Didn't she know she was consorting with the enemy?

"Mr. Strong? Are you still there?"

"I've set up another recording session for you tomorrow and I expect you to be there, nine o'clock sharp. This is not a party. This is a business."

"Of course, Mr. Str—"

"Of course," he said and replaced the receiver.

He was seething as he got up to pour himself a drink from the bar. He had no idea Jazmine knew Xavier, but he was sure he didn't like the whole situation. Just what type of relationship do they have together? he wondered and downed a shot of gin. He poured himself another shot and tried to figure out why he was so upset. There was no way to explain himself to himself, but he was jealous. He gulped down the drink, then reached inside the mini-refrigerator and pulled out a peanut container. He hated peanuts. They were too cheap. He'd rather have cashews or almonds. He opened the container and pulled out a tightly wrapped plastic bag. These ain't peanuts, he thought, eyeing two white pebbles.

And they sure as hell ain't cheap.

. . .

I was too busy nibbling Jazmine's neck to notice she had hung up the phone. I worked my way to her lips and noticed she wasn't as into it as she was before the phone call. I pulled back and checked her out. "Was that your man?"

"Please, Xavier," she said and got up from the couch.

Women. They change moods like a pair of shoes. One minute they chillin', the next they all emotional about something.

"That was Bobby Strong. Want something to drink?"

I can't stand that fool, I thought, enjoying the view as she bent over and took two wine coolers from the refrigerator. I hadn't had one of those since junior high. "What he want?"

"Nothing."

"Then what he call for?"

She handed me the cooler and sat down next to me. "I don't know why he called. He's a trip sometimes."

"Ah, naw. That mothafucka be trippin'," I said, about to get pissed off. I never did like that fool, so I was ready to hear anything that would give me an excuse to go fuck that nigga up.

"Calm down, babe," she said and handed her bottle to me. I opened it for her and gave it back, feeling like a real man. Women need men for shit like opening bottles and taking out the garbage. And for Jazmine, I'm happy to help out in any way I can, especially when I get rewarded with one of those "gotta have ya" looks she just gave me. "You know we're supposed to be in some sort of weird competition."

"What you mean?"

"Dakota told me that Mr. Timbers—"

"Yeah, Mr. T . . . I met that fool the other day. I like that old nigga."

"Yeah, I hear he's nice. But anyway, Dakota said he's retiring."

"Shiiit. If I had his dollars, I'd keep my black ass at home too."

"Listen, babe. She says Bobby and Kirk are both trying to get his job."

She paused like I was supposed to draw some kind of conclusion, but all I could concentrate on were her lips.

"You see what I'm saying?"

"Ah, I'm sorry girl," I said, snapping out of the daze she put me under. "Break it down for me."

"Well you noticed how everything seems rushed at Black Tie, right? You said Kirk wanted a finished recording from you in two months, right?"

"Right, right. Now break it down a little further."

"It's like we're their final exam projects. It's like whoever sells the most records gets an A. And the man behind the A project gets to take over the company. Understand?"

"So you're saying it all boils down to me and you. Whoever sells the most records is the winner."

"I guess so," she said, eyeing me for my reaction.

There wasn't no need in me trying to play cool 'cause I was pissed off. The last thing I wanted to do was get into competition with my girl. I opened my cooler and downed half of it in one gulp.

"You're not mad are you?"

"Hell no. Why should I be mad?" I said, strangling my bottle. I was mad as hell.

"Good, because the way I see it, it can only be a competition if we make it a competition. Just because Bobby and Kirk are at each other's throats doesn't mean we have to be."

The hell it doesn't, I thought to myself and finished off the rest of my drink. "I'm cool with this."

She sat her bottle on the table and turned to look me in the face. "I mean, let's say I end up selling more records than you. That doesn't mean I'm the winner and you lose."

Shiiit.

"I mean, you're not one of those insecure men who have to be the bread-winner to feel like a real man, are you?"

She just has to keep going with this. I said I was cool with it, but she just gotta keep going. And what makes her think she's going to be the one to sell the most records?

"I mean, I hate men like that. Just because a woman makes more money or sells more records, or whatever the case may be, men always seem to get insecure. It's like their manhood is threatened. Hell, you'd think black men would be used to that by now. Black women have been the family breadwinners and supporters for the longest."

Oh she had gone far enough. "What the hell is that supposed to mean?"

"Nothing. I'm just saying, if you look at most black families, the woman is usually making the most money. The man is either not there at all, or working some blue-collar job because he was too lazy to go to college so he could get something better out of life. Then the man gets all mad when his woman starts beating him out. It's a shame," she said, getting up to turn on the stereo. "I'm glad you're not that type of man though."

"Ah, hell naw. Come sit your ass right back down."

"What's wrong with you?"

"So you're saying a black man can't handle it when his woman is more successful. You're saying black men get stuck with low-paying jobs 'cause they too lazy. Fuck that shit. Black men get low-paying jobs 'cause of this racist-ass society that's too threatened by us to give us a chance. They too scared that if they give us a shot, we'll end up ruling thangs and taking over."

"Oh please, Xavier. You think racism doesn't exist for the black woman? Hell, we have two strikes against us—our skin *and* our vagina. Still, we do what it takes to get over."

"You're really trippin'. A black woman can get a job over a black man any day, 'cause whitie not scared of women. But when it comes to us men, they suddenly get threatened. And when they finally do give one of us a job, they do they best to find some reason to tear us down. Look at Clarence Thomas. Look at uh, uh, shit, uh, Mike Tyson."

"Mike Tyson? He ought to be up under the jail."

"Shiiit. They didn't fuck with that Kennedy boy."

"Look, Xavier, I didn't mean for this conversation to go to this level."

"Too bad, girl. You done started somethin' now. And what about—"

"Hold it, Xavier. This doesn't have anything to do with you and me."

I got up from the couch and walked into the kitchen. I had gotten so riled up that I couldn't sit still. But she was right. What did all this have to do with me and her? I didn't know what I was doing in the kitchen, but I didn't want to look like a fool so I opened the refrigerator and took out another wine cooler. I couldn't believe we were arguing. Kelly and I never argued like this, but then again, Kelly usually just went along with whatever I said. I wasn't used to somebody talking back to me, but I liked it. When I walked back into the living room, Jazmine was smiling. "Don't be smilin' at me," I said and went back to the couch. She gave me a nudge with her knee and I knew everything was cool.

"Look, babe. Let's get back to the subject. We like each other, right?"

I'm in love, I wanted to say, but instead just nodded my head.

"All I'm saying is that we shouldn't let anything that happens at Black Tie mess us up. Okay."

"I'm down with that."

"Oh, you're down with that."

"I'm down."

"Good. Now give your schnookie-bookie some sugar," she said, puckering up and rubbing against me. Women. They always know how to get what they want. It's amazing what a carefully placed tongue will do to a nigga after his blood pressure been up. I sank back into the couch and enjoyed the fireworks. How could there ever be any competition between us? With a tongue like hers, she'd win every time.

chapter twelve

what's *really* goin' on

Ah yeah. My man Kirk has got it made, I thought to myself as I slid behind his desk and plopped down in his leather chair. A brother like me
could get real use this big-ass office. I know some homies of mine whose
whole apartment could fit inside this office. Kirk has definitely got it going
on and I bet his pockets stay fat too. I know he pulling in at least six figures
a year. A brother like me ain't never seen that kind of money in my whole
lifetime. But I ain't here to kick back and wonder about what kind of life
Kirk is living. I'm here to get some answers. I played cool when Jazz was
telling me about all this competition madness, but I need to know the real.
I wanna know the real deal about what's gonna happen if that punk Bobby
Strong takes over this company. I've worked too hard to get where I am
today to let that fool mess it up. Yeah, I know Jazz say she down for me
and everything, but the truth of the matter is, she don't have no control
over it. Whether she likes it or not we are in competition.

I guess if the truth must be known, I am kind of nervous about the
whole situation. Jazmine can sing her ass off and it's only a matter of time
before she blows the roof off the charts. As for me, I just don't know. I've
been working hard, real hard, but I don't know if it's enough. All I really
need to know is what's up with all this mess so I can prepare myself, but I
can't get any answers until Kirk skips his happy ass back into this office.
His secretary, Mary, said he would be back from lunch thirty minutes ago,

but I been kicking it in his office for damn near an hour and that fool still ain't back yet. "Yo Mary. Mary. What's up with these three-hour lunches your boss be taking?" I yelled out the door.

"When you start signing my paychecks, I'll start answering your questions," Kirk said, appearing out of nowhere.

"Well, it's about time you got back, homeboy. We gots some bi'ness to take care of."

"Is that right?"

"Hell yeah, so just put your briefcase down and relax. I got some questions for you, my man."

"Um, my seat," Kirk said, patiently waiting for me to get up.

"Oh yeah. Be my guest," I said and raised up. He slowly sat down and started rearranging all the things on the desk that I had moved around while I was waiting for him. "Sorry about the mess, but I had to keep myself busy. Where were you anyway?"

"Well, if you must know, I was meeting with your producers. They told me some good things about you, Xavier, but we'll get into that later. What's this surprise visit all about?"

"Check it, K-Dog. What's all this mess about you and Bobby Strong going head up for the presidency of this company, and why was I the last to find out?" I asked and sat myself on top of his desk.

"Is that all this is about?" he said, opening his briefcase and sorting through a bunch of files. "It's nothing to get bent out of shape about. Mr. Timbers is retiring and it looks like the only two men capable of taking his place are yours truly and of course Bobby Strong, but there are a few others in the running as well."

"Naw, man. I heard the shit was a little thicker than what you're making it out to be."

"And who are you getting your information from?"

"Don't worry about all that, a'ight. I heard it was a strict competition between you and Bobby or more specifically me and Jazmine Deems."

"Is that what you heard?" he asked, looking up from his files.

"That's what I heard, homie. So what up with that?"

"Okay," he said, finally closing his briefcase. "It's true. You are a big part of the equation. That's why I've been pushing you so hard. It is imperative that you put out the kind of music that will sell—big-time. We've got to make a killing on your debut."

"Ah man! What is this? I ain't trying to hear all this competition madness. All I wanna do is be true to my music and true to the streets. Now you tell me I'm in the middle of all this political business. Man, I just ain't trying to hear that."

"Music is a business, Xavier. You need to understand that first and foremost. Getting on the stage and rapping and having fun is only a small part of the picture. That's why I met with your producers today, and from what they tell me we're pretty much on our way. But there are a few things we need to get clear."

"And what's that?" I asked, feeling myself get defensive.

"Your producers say you have a natural flow to your music, but I already knew that. That's why I signed you on," he said with pride. He got up from his desk and turned to face the window. He paused before he continued. "You can't keep coming up with the same old shit," he said, shocking the hell out of me. I had never heard Kirk talk like that before. He was usually so straitlaced and reserved, but now I was beginning to get a taste of the raw Kirk. I knew he had it in him 'cause there's no way he could have gotten to the position he was in without being tough.

"Look," he continued. "I don't know if you heard about what went down with that rapper we had signed last year by the name of Toby-T."

"Yeah," I interrupted. "Me and that brother used to hang back in the day, but that was before he got all big-time."

"Then you know how his career ended. He's locked up and this company is still paying the price for being associated with him."

"Yeah, I knew that brother was headed for the pen. He loved the street life too much. Even after his single was released, he was still hanging in the hood on the street corner, trying to prove to everybody that he was still down for his set. I think he used to run with one of them gangs on the Eastside."

"Yeah, well that gang mentality led him to rape a girl and now he's doing time. This company can't afford another fiasco like that. Which is why you have to do something different. Look at Snoop Doggy Dogg. That man is a genius in rap. Now he's indicted on a murder charge. Look at uh, uh, Tupac Shakur. Not only an excellent rapper, but an accomplished actor. And look at him now, doing time on a rape-and-assault conviction. This is bullshit. All this *gangsta* rap has got to go. "

"What?" I said, jumping down off his desk. "That's what I do best. That's what I'm about."

"I don't give a damn what you are about. That's not what this company is about. Mr. Timbers built this company to serve the community. We don't do business the way other billion-dollar companies do. Those kids out there who buy our music are a part of our family, and we've got to do something to lift them up, not tear them down."

"Ah man, puleeze," I said and sucked my teeth. "Gangsta rap is what they want to hear. I told you before, I ain't down with that white-boy rap. That shit don't make money."

"I'm not for the white-boy rap either. But I sure as hell don't want to put anything out there that's only going to sink us further in the hole. Those kids out there in the streets see rappers on videos talking about stealing and cursing and all that other mess and think it's okay to do it themselves. They idolize what they see on TV. The more we put it out there, the more they think it's okay."

"Man, you talking about saving the world."

"I'm talking about selling records and staying on top in this company. Do you know who was responsible for the Toby-T fiasco? Bobby Strong. He's never fully recovered. That's why I'm in the running for the presidency and that's why I was named Executive of the Year."

"Because Bobby Strong is slipping."

"Because Bobby Strong forgot what this company is all about. Mr. Timbers wants more than just someone to take over the everyday business. He wants someone who falls in line with his vision of what this company is all about. I took a big chance on you when I decided to promote another rapper, especially after what happened with Toby-T, but if we can prove to Mr. Timbers that we intend to do something positive with rap music, my road to the presidency will be set in stone, as well as your spot as this company's premier rapper."

"So that's what this is all about. You. Fuck what I want to do. It's all about getting you that office on the fifteenth floor."

"It's about doing what's right, damn it," he said.

I guess he was starting to get impatient with me, but I didn't give a fuck. He was turning the tables on me. When he signed me to this company, he knew what I was about. Now he was trying to tell me that what I am isn't good enough.

"Naw, man. Fuck this shit."

"Ah, trouble in paradise," a voice interrupted from behind me. I turned around to find Bobby Strong looming in the doorway. He folded his arms across his chest and stared at Kirk and me like we were second-class citizens. "I didn't mean to barge in on your discussion, but I couldn't help but hear, as loud as you two were talking," he said, easing his way into the room. "Now what is wrong, boys? Can't see eye to eye?"

"Xavier," Kirk said, sitting back down behind his desk. "Have you met Mr. Strong?"

Before I could answer, Bobby took over the conversation.

"So this is the X-Man, huh? I've heard so much about you. You're another one of those gangsta rappers, right?"

"If that's what you want to call it, my man," I said, standing toe to toe with him. "And you're the man who's backing Jazmine Deems, right? She's my woman."

"Woo, your woman, huh. That's a cute way to put it," he said with a smirk. "Well, your *woman* and I have been working very closely. She's a wonderful singer, beautiful too. I hope you can keep up with her."

And just exactly what was that supposed to mean? I thought to myself as I sized him up and wondered if it would be easier to take him out with a left or a right hook. I didn't like nothing about him and I especially didn't like him working with Jazmine.

"So I guess you heard there are going to be some changes around here," he said, obviously sizing me up too. "That's right. The big boss is retiring and guess who's going to be running things," he said, rocking back and forth on his heels.

"Not you," Kirk broke in.

"Now come on, Kirkie boy," Bobby said. "You and I both know who's going to take over this company," he said, making his way back toward the doorway. "You know, I've been thinking. When I become president, I think I may do a little downsizing. You know, get rid of all the excess baggage, so to speak. So in other words, I guess what I'm trying to say is, you might as well start packing up your things now because when I'm president, you guys are history."

I looked at Kirk, waiting for him to say something, but all he did was look off into space. I couldn't believe it. How could he let this clown come in here and run over him like that? Kirk may be a punk, but I don't let nobody talk to me like that. "Look man. I don't give a fuck who you are, but—"

"Look yourself, tough guy, or X or whatever you go by. Isn't there a car you need to go steal?"

"Fuck you," I said and walked up in his face. Kirk bolted from behind his desk and ran over to stand between the two of us.

"I think it's time you left, Bobby."

"You know, for once you're right, Kirk," he said and walked into the hallway. "Oh yeah, Xavier. Tell your *woman* I'll see her later."

I left Kirk's office more pissed-off than ever. I intended to go straight home, but I ended up heading for Jazmine's. I figured I wouldn't tell her about my meeting with Kirk and Bobby. As far as she was concerned this competition between us was just a bunch of talk. Now I knew that it was reality and I didn't want to admit it, but when it comes down to it, Jazz has the upper hand. She's got her shit together and she knows where she's going with it. As for me, everything's up in the air. Kirk is trying to change me into something I'm not and don't want to be. Man, I tell you. If I knew it was gonna be all like this, I woulda stayed in the hood. At least it's safer there.

. . .

I had just finished my vocal exercises when I heard the doorbell ring. I grabbed a bottle of water from the kitchen and headed toward the door, wondering where on earth Dakota could have lost her keys this time. I opened the door and found Xavier standing in the hall with a solemn look on his face.

"Don't you even ask who is it before you open the door?" he asked, brushing by me to get inside.

"I thought you were Dakota," I said, detecting a bad mood.

"That's how folks get got," he said, as he walked to the couch and spread himself out over it. "I coulda been anybody, a burglar, a, a—"

"A man with an attitude," I said, cutting him off with a smile. "So what's this mood all about?"

"What mood?" he said and got even more comfortable, kicking off his shoes.

I sat down on the floor and decided to drop the subject. I looked up at him and wondered what was bothering him and if I should ask. He was so different from everyone else I had dated—well, all two of the other guys I dated—that at times I didn't know how to approach him. Before I could figure it out, I looked back up at him to find him sleeping like a baby. A big baby. His eyes were closed and he was breathing deeply. Suddenly the giant was gone.

I got up and went in my room so I wouldn't disturb him. I sat on the end of the bed and flipped on the television. I was barely watching the brunette lady in the pink suit. I had given up watching talk shows my first year of college when I found I was doing more talk-show hopping than homework. I was just about to turn the channel when the lady looked dead into the camera and asked, "Why do we fall in love with our exact opposites?" I looked over my shoulder, then back at the television. It was as if she was talking directly to me. I was just about to come up with an answer when I heard the front door open. I ran into the living room to find Dakota standing in front of the door, staring at Xavier. When she saw me, she put her hand on her hip and twisted her neck. "Uh, uh. This ain't no damn homeless shelter," she said, loud enough to stir Xavier. He turned over peacefully and continued sleeping.

"Keep your voice down," I said, grabbing her by the arm and leading her into my room.

"Don't he got a home of his own?" she said, once in my room.

"Shut up. He's just taking a nap. I think he's got an attitude," I said, standing in front of the television. "Dang, I missed the answer to the question."

"Is this the Vickey Varnell show?" she said, sucking her teeth. "Everybody and their momma's got a damn talk show now." She sat down on the bed and threw her bag on the floor. "So what's she talking about today?" she sighed.

I sat down next to her and nudged her over. "Why we fall in love with people who are different from us."

"Oh, you should be taking notes."

"Shut up," I said, trying hard to get back into the show. Another lady in a sweater and long skirt was on now. She was obviously some type of expert on the subject because she was answering all the questions.

"She don't know what she's talking about," Dakota said, frowning.

"You haven't even listened to what she's saying."

"I don't need to listen. There's only one reason why people get involved with their opposites and that's so they can feed off each other. Look at Sonny and Cher. He wanted her height, she wanted his money. It's simple."

"Yeah, right, Doctor D," I said, giggling.

"No, I'm serious. Look at Whitney Houston and Bobby Brown—the princess and the bad boy. One image balances out the other."

"It's not about image. They love each other."

"You've been reading too many issues of *Jet* magazine," she said and fell back on the bed. "Now as for you and that thing in there on the couch—I don't know what to say about that match made in hell."

"I'm getting tired of your funky comments about Xavier. You don't even know him."

"Well, excuse me," she said, propping herself up on her elbows. "Okay, let's see. You're sweet, a little naive at times, but smart, ambitious—he's probably never met anyone like you. See, you balance out the street in him. He's probably learning a lot from you."

"Yeah, he has mellowed out a bit since that night I met him at the party. I guess what I'm wondering is what I'm supposed to learn from him."

"I don't know," Dakota said, leaning her head back to think. "How to rob a bank?"

"Fuck you, D. Don't get me started," I warned her and got off the bed to turn the television down. "You know what he has that I want?"

"Besides a dick?"

"Don't get slapped, hear," I said, turning serious. "I want his strength. You know, he's so sure of himself. He can handle himself in any situation. I like that. I don't know how, but his strength seems to be rubbing off on me already," I said, tucking a strand of hair behind my head. "Take my singing, for instance. Before we got together, I'd be so nervous whenever I went to the studio. But just the other day he told me, 'Jazz, just put everything on ice and chill.' And you know what?"

"What?" she said, obviously bored with the conversation. I ignored her and kept right on talking.

"I did what he said. I chilled. And now when I walk in that studio, it's like walking into my own private mansion. For the first time I feel like I can do whatever the hell I want to do and hold my head up high. Seriously," I said, watching her get up from the bed. "I just put everything on ice. I don't worry about anything anymore. I'm not nervous, I just chill. You know what I'm saying?"

"Yeah, Jazz," she said, already at the door. "That was such a touching story, I think I'm going to cry," she said, faking tears. "Ghetto love is so special."

"Forget you," I said, rolling my eyes as she headed to her bedroom.

She closed the door behind her, but I didn't care if she wasn't interested. I went back into the living room where Xavier was still sleeping and knelt down in front of the couch and hovered over him, watching him breathe deeply. "Why are we together?" I whispered and brushed the side of his face. All I knew was that being with him made me feel whole. I finally felt like an independent, strong woman. I can't truly explain this new feeling, but I know that I didn't have it before I met him. I would hate to ever lose him, but I knew if I did that I could still make it on my own. That's what I've learned from him. How to stand by myself. When I was with my daddy, I was just a frightened little girl. Now I feel like I can stand. Tall. Alone. It didn't matter that Xavier was different from me, he was what I wanted. He brought out the best in me, I brought out the best in him. Without each other . . . Well, I thought, that's something I'll never have to worry about. I kissed the side of his face, but he didn't wake. That's all right, I thought to myself. Sleep on, baby, I can handle things on this side of dreamland.

chapter thirteen

understand this

Bobby rushed around his new home fluffing pillows and spraying air freshener as he waited for Jazmine to arrive. He was surprised at how easily she'd accepted his invitation to his home and hoped he wasn't reading too much into the situation. After all, it was a celebration, and they had good reason to be happy. Her debut single would be out the following week. He felt like a kid on the day he'd asked her over for dinner. Since Sheryl had left he hadn't even thought about being with another woman, but Jazmine was special. Jazmine made him feel needed. With Jazmine he didn't feel alone. Bobby had been lying to himself about the way he felt for Jazmine for quite some time, but he could no longer fake it. Whenever Jazmine was around he lit up. It was as if the part of himself that he had lost when his family broke up reappeared when she was around. He often daydreamed about ways to let her know what he really felt for her, but he could never seem to get the words out. He knew he was practically old enough to be her father, but that didn't matter either. The only thing that concerned him was that Jazmine was the only person that meant something in his life.

He straightened out the magazines on the coffee table for the third time, then rearranged the bouquet of flowers that sat next to them. Everything had to be perfect, he thought, as he stepped back to survey the room. All was well, but still he worried. He wanted so badly to tell

Jazmine his true feelings, but the thought of that kind of honesty frightened him.

He blew off his thoughts, then fumbled with the flowers again before heading to the kitchen. He opened the stove and checked on the dinner he'd ordered and had sent over earlier. Then he glanced at his watch only to find he had an hour to kill before Jazmine's arrival. Finally he calmed down long enough to have a seat on the couch. Exhausted, he leaned his head against the cushions and stared up into the empty space. Thirty-foot-high ceilings are supposed to be a mark of elegance, or at least that's what the interior designer had told him. He found nothing special about the changes that were made to the place. It still seemed too large and isolated, and whenever he spoke, his voice echoed through the condo as if he were standing in a tunnel. Still it was a good place for entertaining clients, with ninety-degree views of the city, a cook's kitchen, and three master-bedroom suites. At four thousand dollars a month it should have come with an indoor pool, a bowling alley, or at least a movie theater. But Bobby was a bachelor again, and with no family to fill the place up, all those extra amenities would only remind him of what he had lost.

So this is what life's all about after divorce, he thought. A humongous condo in the heart of the Wilshire district, a fire-engine red Audi Quattro to make him feel closer to thirty than forty, and a never-ending supply of white powder, booze, and whatever else he could get his doctor to prescribe for the *pain*. Of course, there was always Jazmine. That girl was a one-in-a-million catch, Bobby thought, so proud to be the one responsible for signing her to the label. "Take *that*, Kirk Walker. Are you listening, Mr. Timbers . . . *imbers* . . . *bers?*" He hated that damn echo. He stretched his legs out in front of him and clamped his hands together behind his head. He figured he should maybe try to get some business out of the way while he waited. He knew he had a ton of work to do, but judging by the way he felt, he wouldn't be getting to it any time soon. Jazmine's debut single would be out next week, which meant he needed to send out tip sheets to all the locals, schedule a performance for her, preferably at the House of Blues, and send out her posters and bios to record stores. But he couldn't find the energy to get started. He tried to convince himself that Jazmine's talent would do most of the promotion for her anyway, but he knew better than that. Even the most talented artist needs good promotion.

But Bobby had more important things on his agenda. He didn't know exactly what, but for a man having so few people in his life, he always felt busy. Most of his days were filled with keeping a close eye on Kirk, watching his moves, making sure he stayed one step ahead of him. That new rap kid Kirk's got on his roster won't measure up to anything, Bobby figured. The rap field was getting too congested. Everybody and their mother seemed to be making a rap record these days and from what Bobby had seen, that kid was just another in a long line of hip-hopping jive talkers. He doubted if the kid's debut would cause much of a stir in the industry, especially considering the fact that rap fans aren't the most loyal in the world. An R&B artist can make record after record because the fans stick with them. In rap, the fans usually run out and buy the first record, but the second and third albums never sell as well. Unless you're that Ice Sickle or Ice-Box guy or whatever that kid's name is, Bobby theorized. Whatever his name, he wasn't with Black Tie, so he didn't count. And at any rate, Bobby predicted, Kirk's going to turn out to be a loser.

All the dealings at Black Tie had wound up to be a double-edged sword for Bobby. On one hand, he was trying to stay ahead of the game, but on the other, he really didn't give a damn anymore if he took over the company. No. That's a lie. He wanted that position so bad he could smell it. He just wasn't as interested in it as he used to be. Taking over the company used to symbolize something. It was the ultimate badge of glory. Not just for Bobby, but for his girls. If he had that position, their futures would be set for generations to come. Now that they were gone, his heart was no longer in it. His days were spent longing for his precious girls. His nights spent longing for someone to fill up his bed.

He checked his watch again; he still had lots of time to kill. He couldn't figure out why he was so nervous, but he felt as if he were about to go out on his first date. Though he had promised himself he'd stay sober for the night, he couldn't shake the eerie feeling that crept over him. He hated that anxious, nervous feeling. It always made him feel so out of control, something Bobby couldn't afford to be tonight.

A one-liner wouldn't hurt, he reasoned with himself as he took out his stash from beneath the sofa. But just like with potato chips, he could never have just one, and he ended up inhaling four lines before he heard a knock at his front door.

He ducked his cocaine box back under the sofa before hurrying to the door. When he opened it he found his star, standing before him and looking amazingly beautiful. He couldn't tell if his heart was beating so fast because she had finally arrived or if it was the cocaine he'd just consumed. He put his hand to his chest and inhaled to relax. "Come on in," he said, trying to hide his discomfort.

"Well," she said and entered, looking Bobby up and down. "Nice suit. I feel so underdressed," she said and picked at her T-shirt.

"You look absolutely wonderful," he said, feeling relieved that his heart rate had begun to slow. He realized that he was staring at her when he noticed her beginning to blush. Embarrassed, he motioned for her to have a seat, then rushed to the kitchen to retrieve a bottle of Dom Pérignon and two champagne flutes. He expertly removed the cork and filled her glass, sneaking in glances at her along the way.

"This place is really nice," Jazmine said, breaking the silence. "I've never been to an apartment building that had valet parking and bell boys. And this view," she said, getting up to walk to the balcony. "It's beautiful," she gasped.

Slowly, Bobby walked up behind her. He stood nervously, not knowing what to do, then leaned over her and pointed west. "You can almost see Black Tie from here," he said, enjoying the smell of her perfume.

"That's right," she said, enthusiastically pointing with him. She turned around to find Bobby directly in front of her face. "Well, let's see the rest of the place."

He led her up the spiral staircase to the loft area, then up another flight of stairs to the sun deck. By this time he was feeling much more relaxed. His nervousness had been replaced by self-confidence. He draped his arm around her shoulder as they looked out over the city.

"Xavier would love this view," she said, with a far-off glance in her eyes.

The mere mention of his name made Bobby tighten, as he tried to hold back what he wanted to say. Didn't she know that she was too good for that thug? Xavier had been the one problem standing between him and Jazmine. For weeks he had sat back and watched as the two of them got closer and closer, but never had he expected it to go on for this long. He wished he could say something to make her understand that Xavier wasn't the man for her, but then he reconsidered. Actions speak louder than words, he thought to himself as he led her back down the stairs by the hand. When they reached the bottom, he politely pulled her hair back on one side and leaned down to speak in her ear. "Dinner's in the kitchen, sweetheart," he said and guided her in the right direction.

Bobby set the table and placed scented candles in the center as Jazmine stood to the side watching. Every time she tried to help, he stopped her and took over whatever she was doing. "We're celebrating you tonight," he said and pulled out a chair for her.

"I am so impressed," Jazmine said, her eyes wide and happy like a little girl about to cut into her birthday cake.

"Someday all this could be yours," he said watching the excitement in her eyes. He could barely touch his food. He was too busy eyeing Jazmine, making sure her water glass stayed full and that all the condiments were within her reach. He didn't want her to want for anything. He wanted to show her that he could be there for her. Could the X-Man do the same?

There were so many things he wanted to tell her, but he just didn't know how. He didn't know how she'd take it. He didn't want to come off as some old man out for a good time with a naive schoolgirl. He wanted her to know he was serious. That he would take care of her, that he could be whatever she wanted him to be. He passed her a clean napkin, then leaned back in his chair and stared across the table.

"I know we're here to celebrate the fact that my single is coming out next week," Jazmine said, as she stopped to take a sip of her water. "But I want you to know that none of this would have been possible without you."

"You're the one with the golden voice," Bobby said, humbly.

"Yes, but you're the one doing all the work. I know all the long hours it takes behind the scenes to get a record into the stores."

Bobby knew he hadn't quite lived up to that compliment yet, and resolved to get on the job first thing tomorrow.

"I mean, I appreciate the way you've been looking out for me. You're like a father to me, you know."

A *father*.

"I can't thank you enough, Bobby. And as a matter of fact Xavier and I are going to take *you* out to celebrate. How about next week?" she said, with a burst of energy.

Xavier? Every other word that comes out of her mouth is about *Xavier*.

"So what do you say?" she asked. "Bobby?" she questioned. "Did I say something wrong?"

Bobby thought his heart was going to stop as he sat stiffly, taking in her words. He tried to speak calmly. Still, Jazmine noted the change in his mood. "I don't really want to talk about Xavier."

"Is there a problem?" she asked, confused.

"No problem," he said and paused to weigh his words. "Well yes, actually, there is a problem."

"What is it?"

"You're young," he began, trying to fake a smile to put her at ease. "You've got a bright future ahead of you . . . I just don't think you ought to be getting too involved with someone like Xavier." He paused again and noticed the shock on her face and decided he needed to explain more. "You understand, don't you? You're a young, intelligent lady. You need more."

"More?"

"Yes, Jazmine, more," he said, getting up from the table. "I could give you so much more." He knelt down beside her chair and placed his hands over her knee. "I don't think you should see Xavier anymore."

Jazmine breathed deeply, trying to absorb what she'd just heard. She looked confused and uncomfortable, but she didn't move.

"I could make you so happy," he said, looking up into her innocent face. He moved her as close to him as he could, then did what he had been wanting to do all night long.

. . .

It's been a week since it happened and I still can't get that night out of my mind. It disturbed me so much that I can hardly concentrate on anything else.

Mack and I had spent all day putting the final touches on a remix version of my debut song, and I was physically worn to the bone. Mack was in his usual upbeat mood, but I wasn't feeling so good myself, which only made the whole session take even longer. I had to do the first verse over about twenty times before I got it right and finally Mack just called it a day. He could tell I wasn't into it.

"Why don't you just take the tape home and work on your delivery? I'll finish up here, and tomorrow we can pick up where we left off."

"Sure," I said, cleaning up the mess of papers and tapes I had sprawled out over the synthesizer. I was still tripping off of Bobby and what he had said to me that night at dinner. He was acting so strange and I could hardly believe my ears when he told me that I better stop seeing Xavier. I looked at him like he was a fool. Nobody had talked to me like that since Daddy, and even he knows his place now.

I had almost gotten up from the table and left, but then I thought that wouldn't be the best way to handle the situation. Technically, Bobby is my boss, and I owe him a great debt of gratitude for taking a chance on me and my music. Still, my relationship with him is on a professional level. Only. He has no right to tell me who I should or shouldn't date. Yet I sat and listened to his comments, which were more like demands, and it struck me that he might be a little jealous. I didn't know how to react. I thought about all the times I had caught him staring at me, all the polite arms around my shoulder, my waist, the hands that stroked across my face. But the thought had never occurred to me before that night that he could actually be interested in me. Not in *that* way. He had always been like a father figure to me. He was so concerned about my future and that I keep away from all the bad influences this business of music has embedded in it. Never had he let on that there might be more to all the personal attention he was giving me. Plus he knew I had been seeing Xavier for the past three months and he knew I was in love. Everybody knew that.

When he knelt down in front of me, I didn't know what to do. I'd never seen him like that before. He just stared at me helplessly like a little boy in love. Then he did something that totally blew my mind. The old fart grabbed my face and kissed me—dead on the mouth. Tongue and everything.

"What the hell are you doing?" I had said, pushing him off me.

"Just give me a chance, Jazmine."

"What the hell are you talking about?" I shouted and wiped my mouth.

For a minute there, I thought he was going to break down and cry, then he started laying all this heavy business on me about his divorce and how much he missed his kids, and suddenly the man who I had once thought of as the Rock of Gibraltar seemed like a puny, lost soul. It was weird, but at least it explained why he had taken this sudden interest in my love life. I didn't know what to do at that point. He just kept looking at me as if he expected something from me. But what could I do for him? He wasn't my man.

I didn't tell Xavier about what happened, although he was filled with questions about our celebration dinner. I didn't tell anyone, as a matter of fact, but the wnole incident is beginning to weigh on me. I thought it would be all over after that night. I thought my reactions made it clear that I wasn't interested, but Bobby doesn't seem to be getting the message. He called that night after dinner and said he was just making sure I was home, then hung up. Just like that. I could tell he was drunk, so I just let it slide. He was probably just hurt. I was sure he'd get over it. But ever since then my phone has been ringing off the hook. I've been getting late-night phone calls like that ever since that night, but when I pick up the phone, all I hear is breathing. I know for sure it's Bobby. The first couple times it happened I hung up the phone and dialed star 69, and sure enough, Bobby picked up the other line. I mean, I know he's hurt because of the divorce and his kids and all, and I do feel sorry for the man, but there is absolutely no way that I'm going to get involved in his mixed-up life. I'm not the one.

What I need to do is talk to somebody about this, but I just don't know how to put it. I know everybody's been tripping off of my moods lately, especially Dakota. That girl knows me like a book, but lately she's been so bogged down with work that I haven't had a decent chance to sit down and have a real bitch session with her.

I don't know what is going on with Bobby, but I sure as hell am going to find out.

I was in the kitchen making a wok full of vegetables and rice when Dakota came in looking as exhausted as I felt. She came into the kitchen and slammed her briefcase down on the counter and started blurting out every curse word known to man. Damn, I knew she was under a lot of stress, but this was ridiculous. She's been working so hard for me, planning, organizing, and whatever else it is that agents-slash-managers do. I never knew it was such a big responsibility and when she told me that she was quitting her job to work for me full-time, I learned a whole new respect for her dedication to me.

She was pacing back and forth, still cursing, so I just moved to the side and continued mixing my broccoli. She'd eventually calm down enough to tell me what was up.

"That motherfucking Bobby Strong," she said, gripping her hands against her waist. "I can't believe that asshole. Do you know what that stupid, idiot, piece of shit did? Or should I say, has not done? Don't answer that 'cause I'm about to tell you."

I hadn't planned on it.

"That motherfucker hasn't done one damn thing to prepare for your record's debut next week. Not one damn thing. No advertisements, no info to the trades, the fucking records haven't even been distributed to the stores. This shit is ridiculous."

I couldn't believe what she was saying. I thought everything was going just fine on the business end of things. I took out a bottle of Arrowhead from the refrigerator and listened in disbelief.

"Here I am thinking everything is good to go," she continued. "Then I call up *Music Muse* magazine to try and set up an interview for you, and they say they don't know a thing about you. What is this shit?"

Well, I had been waiting all week for a bitch session and I guess I was finally getting what I wanted. I shoved the bottle of water into Dakota's hand and told her to sit down at the dinette table. It was time to talk.

"I'm telling you, D. I don't know what the hell is going on with Bobby, but that man is beginning to scare the shit out of me. He's been calling me late at night, telling me who I should and shouldn't be dating. The man is fucking out of his mind."

Dakota didn't say anything, but I could tell she was livid. She looked like she was going to explode, and since she had already reached her boiling point I decided to tell her the whole truth.

"Remember last week when I went to his house for dinner?" She nodded her head. "Well, the mickey-fickey tried to make a move on me."

That was all it took. She was up again, pacing and cursing and shaking her head. "I knew it. I knew that motherfucker was no good. Damn it, shit, fucking . . ."

What did she mean, she knew it? And if she knew, why the hell didn't she let me in on it? "Just what exactly do you know, Dakota?"

"Nothing," she said weakly and sat back down. She put her head in her hands, and I knew there was something about that "nothing."

"What's going on, Dakota?"

She picked her head up and looked me directly in the eyes and I instantly began to hurt. "He tried to rape me."

"He what?"

She cried.

As militant and hell-bent on women's rights as Dakota is, I couldn't believe she didn't want to go to the police with this. She was adamant about it too. "It happened a long time ago, that night we went to the Executive of the Year party. There's nothing the police can do, and besides, nothing *really* happened," she said. "They won't believe me. I'm a far cry from a virgin."

Who gives a damn? I told her. I didn't care if she was a prostitute. If a man tries to force sex on you when you don't want him to, it's sexual assault. A crime. Period. I told her assholes like Bobby needed to be stopped. I didn't care how rich he was or how much influence he had in the community. He was dangerous, plain and simple. And if we didn't do anything about it, nothing would ever change. I never thought of Dakota as the type to run and hide from problems like this, but that's exactly what she was doing. She left the apartment after we argued about going to the police. It was now after midnight and I hadn't heard from her since. And as usual, I was at a loss for what to do.

It was twelve-thirty when the phone finally rang and I picked it up quickly, thinking it was her. It was Xavier.

"What up, baby?"

"Get over here. Now."

Fifteen minutes later, he arrived. And as frantic as I was over Dakota's leaving in the state she was in, all I could do was fall into his arms and be held.

"You a'ight?"

"I'm okay. I just need . . . I just . . ."

He knew what I needed. Or did he?

"You wanna talk, babe?" he said, pulling me over to the couch and sitting me down.

"I don't want . . ."

"Come on, tell me. What's the matter?"

"Damn, it Xavier! Can we just fuck?"

He was obviously taken by surprise and he looked a little confused. But I wasn't concerned about all that. I didn't want to be treated like a princess. I didn't want to communicate. I wanted to do it, to be taken away in ecstasy, for however long. Nothing else mattered.

I grabbed his hand and put it where I wanted it, and moved it back and forth. It was my turn. This was for me. I straddled him and took off my shirt, grabbed his head and guided it to my breasts. I felt myself getting moist all over and when I got tired of that position I pushed his head back, got up and pulled off my pants, then his, and climbed back on top of him. I didn't let him in until I was ready and when I did we both let out harsh gasps as I began moving and controlling the rhythm. But Xavier was enjoying this too much. Didn't he know this wasn't for him? Didn't he understand? This wasn't about what he wanted. It was all about me and every other women who had been fondled at the hands of men against their will.

I got up and stepped away from him, and the bewildered look on his face let me know that I was back in full control. He was aching for me, and I knew it. He wanted me to come back to him, but that wasn't going to happen.

I laid myself down on the floor and ran my hands up and down my body, then rested them in my hottest spot and drove myself to the ecstasy that I had been looking for.

When I was finished, I laid there looking at the ceiling and wondered how I was going to get up and go on about my business without looking like a complete idiot. I was embarrassed now. What had I been trying to prove? Just what did I think I was doing by performing this little scene? Standing up for women's rights, or simply making a fool out of myself?

When I finally looked up at Xavier, he was smiling. "Damn, baby. That was a good show. I always knew you had a little freak in you."

"Shut the fuck up, Xavier," I said, getting up and pulling back on my clothes. "I guess you enjoyed that, huh. Well, fuck you!"

Xavier didn't say a word and I was glad because I was about to let him know "What up."

"I'm tired of men thinking they're the ones in charge of a woman's pussy. This shit ain't yours. It's mine. And you're not the one who's going to be calling the shots on what I do with it."

I expected him to jump in and say something, but he didn't and that only pissed me off more. Well, let him sit there looking stupid. I had enough to say all by myself.

"All you men are dogs. Selfish dogs. You think more about that shit between your legs than you do women. Well, let me tell you one thing. This is one cat who's not gonna roll over and let you have your way with her. And if you don't like it, you can get the fuck out."

I knew it was only a matter of time before I pushed all of his buttons, but this was taking too long. He pulled up his pants, crossed his arms over his chest, and sat there watching me. Suddenly I felt embarrassed again. But I was going to win this fight.

"No, I tell you what. Get the fuck out right now," I said and walked over to the door.

He finally spoke, but it wasn't what I wanted to hear. Or was it? "I ain't going nowhere. Not until you stop acting like some maniac and tell me what the hell is wrong with you."

"I said get out. Now!" He didn't move, so stupidly I thought I could make him move. I walked over to the couch and pulled him by the arm, growing more and more angry when he wouldn't budge and hysterical when the tears that I had been fighting back came pouring down my face. He gave me a firm tug and pulled me to his chest. I struggled furiously, not because I didn't want to be held, but because now I felt like a damn fool, unworthy of being held.

He kept me in his arms tightly, stroking my back and soothing me. "I love you," he said, and after hearing that, there was no way I could stop crying, not even when I didn't have any tears left. I didn't want to explain, not yet. It felt too good being safe in his arms. "Please tell me what's wrong, Red," he said softly. I couldn't say a word, not just yet, not while it felt so good.

"Xavier," I said and looked at his lovely dark face. "Don't fuck me, make love to me. Please. Right now."

chapter fourteen

fat black lies

I was just about ready to go hunt Bobby Strong down and blow a hole in that mothafucka's head. I told Jazmine if he ever lays a hand on her to just give me a call and I'd be right there, pistol in hand. Fuck it. She thought I was talking crazy, but I was dead serious. It would probably destroy my career, but I wasn't about to let that fool do the same thing he did to Dakota to my baby. I don't care who he is. He had my baby all worried and frustrated and now she's talking about forgetting about her music career and going back to college. That would be a damn shame, 'cause that girl's got major talent, and I'm not just saying that 'cause she's my girl. She got that kind of voice that can make a nigga cry.

Before I left, Dakota finally came back. She didn't look upset, but I left anyway 'cause I knew they wanted to do some girl talking. I know Dakota doesn't like me very much, but I told her the same thing I told Jazz, if that nigga ever tries anything again, all she has to do is call me. I can round some of my boys up in a minute and be over there to kick Bobby's ass— just like that. And if it means having to go to jail, then fuck it. I know guys who have gone to jail for much less than this, and since this is my baby and her friend, it'll be worth it.

When I got in my car, I was gon' go straight home, but then I decided to stop by Rich's house. I wanted to let that fool know what was up just in case he got a call from me, telling him to break out the heavy artillery. And anyway, I hadn't seen him in almost a month. Between kicking it with Jazmine and putting the final touches on my album them fools at Black Tie been rushing me on, I haven't had time to get over to the hood. I'm sure I could have made time if I really wanted to, but I've been trying to keep my distance from all them fools. They're still my homies and every-thing, but it's just something about the streets that pulls me down, makes me want to prove something. What, I don't know. I guess it's just that old sense of trying to be hard. When I was younger that was a major thing. You had to be harder than the next guy. You had to prove that you were not to be fucked with, 'cause if someone sensed you were weak they'd sho-nuff try and take advantage of you. I don't feel that way now though. Being with Jazmine has made me see that there is a different way of life. "A real man doesn't have to gain respect by being hard," she said. "A real man demands respect just by his very essence." That shit was deep to me. And after I thought about it for a while, I realized she was right. What does respect have to do with how many fools you take out from a rival gang? What does respect have to do with how many dollars you make from selling cocaine, or how many pagers you have, or what kind of rims you got on your ride, or how many bitches you fuck a day? Not a damn thing. I didn't have any idea how backward my priorities were until I started listening to Jazz. Even my career was backward. The only reason I wanted to be a rapper was so I could show my homies back in the hood how down I was. I thought if I put out a hard record with a lot of cussing, dissing bitches, talking about how big my dick was, and uplifting street life, that everybody would know I was the man. Fuck that shit. My album ain't gon' be like that. My views about life in South-Central haven't changed all that much—girls still act like bitches, police are still punks, and so on and so forth, so I'm still gon' rap about that shit, but the only dif-ference now is that it's not going to be in a negative way. Those subjects are still in my music, but now when I rap about them, I do it to set an example of the way things should *not* be. I try to offer alternatives in my raps, on how things can be changed. It's not just about how things are in the streets anymore. It's about what we can do to change things in the streets. Need-less to say Kirk was happy as a fucking butterfly when I let him hear a few sample cuts. He's into all that positive shit, so of course the new scope of my record is right up his alley. It took me a long time to see what Jazmine meant about the way black people are always airing their dirty laundry out in public. Now that I've decided to change some things on my debut record, it's taking me even longer to get it finished on time. Kirk didn't sweat me about the time though. I'm way past my two-month deadline and I still got another three weeks' worth of work to do before I can hand over a concrete set of songs. But after Kirk heard a few samples of my work, all he said was, "Take your time. This one's in the bag."

When I pulled into Rich's driveway, I saw Eyeisha's car and almost decided to turn around and go on back home. I didn't have time to be hounded by her and I knew she would be dropping all kinds of hints about that night we spent together behind Rich's back. That still bugged the shit out of me. The fact that I hadn't told Rich about it only made it worse. But how could I tell that fool I slept with his girl? It wouldn't make any difference that I thought our friendship was over, or that I had had too much to drink, or that she had practically thrown herself at me. She was still his girl, however trifling she may be, and I knew he wouldn't understand, no matter what I said. But since I hadn't heard anything about it, I assumed that for once she had kept her mouth closed and that it would be our little secret—our nasty, stank secret. I knocked on the door, and who should answer but Eyeisha, looking as whorish as she wanted to look in a cat suit that was too damn tight on her big-ass. She looked fatter than ever, and she had the nerve to give me a hug—a big bear hug, and it seemed that she would never let go. "Rich! Look who's here," she called out before giving me a pat on the ass. "Get out here. It's X!"

Rich came rolling himself out in his wheelchair with a forty stuck between his legs. "What up, man?" he said, laughing. "Sit your ass down. What you drinking? I got some J.D., some Cisco, and you know I keeps the forty on tap. Eyeisha, go get X a forty."

She switched off into the kitchen and came back unscrewing the top off the bottle and before she gave it to me she leaned her head back and took a gulp. "Here you go, X," she said, smiling from here to eternity. I took it and sat it down on the table. I wasn't drinking nothing after her. Who knows where them lips been?

Rich told her to get out the room so me and him could talk, but before she left she winked at me and blew me a kiss right in front of Rich. But all Rich said was, "Stop flirting and go make me a sammich." Rich waited for her to leave the room before he started talking. "So what's been up, man? Your ass ain't been over here in so long, I damn near forgot what you looked like."

That was the truth. I had forgotten what he looked like too. When I first came in, I had expected him to walk out, like he always did when we were little, with that gangsta stroll. And when I saw him in that wheelchair, I realized that nothing ever changes in the hood. "Ah, man. I just been working like a dog. You know them fools got me on deadline at the studio, and since I had to make some last-minute changes, my shit ain't gon' be through for at least another month."

"So you straight on money. I can loan you some if you need it. My pockets are still fat, in case you forgot."

"Naw. Larry been kicking me down on funds until I start seeing some royalties coming in. The money's cool."

"So what about that honey you was telling me about the last time I talked to you? Y'all still kicking it?"

"Yeah, man. You ought to be hearing her shit on the radio pretty soon. I'm telling you it's dope! But if that fool she working for don't stop trippin', I'm gon' have to put a cap in his mothafuckin' ass."

"Aw, naw. What the fuck is up?" Rich's eyes got wide 'cause he knew I was about to drop some heavy shit on his ass.

"Man, that fool got a problem. He straight tried to rape Jazmine's girlfriend. At that Black Tie party we all went to. And I think he been trying stuff with Jazmine too, but she won't fess up to me. She know if I ever hear about that nigga getting out of line with her I'd have to kill that mothafucka."

"Are you for real? We ought to go find that mothafucka right now. Show that fool what happens to a nigga when they get to fucking around with the wrong people. Who is this fool anyway?"

"Bobby Strong."

"Bobby Strong?" he said and rolled closer to me. "I know that fool. Are you serious?"

"As a heart attack."

"He one of my biggest customers. That fool be paging me damn near four times a week so I can drop him off a stash. Never fails. We meet over there in the parking lot at Black Tie Records all the time. How do you think I got the invites for that party over there? I made him come up with something, 'cause I wanted to help you."

"Why didn't you tell me?"

"Tell you what? How was I suppose to know you knew that fool? Man, I sell to businessmen all over this damn city. Bobby Strong ain't no different than any of the rest of them poor rich boys I sell to."

"I always knew there was a reason why I didn't like that mothafucka."

"Man, I'm telling you. Just say the word and me and the boys will take his ass out!"

"If I don't get to that mothafucka first."

"Naw, X," Rich said seriously. "You can't be doing that shit. You got a future now, man. Don't be fucking it up by getting mixed up in some shit like this. If anything happens, let me handle it. I ain't got shit to lose anyway. But you, you been trying to get where you are now for the longest, and I'm proud of you, man. Now don't go fucking it up. Leave all the dirty shit for me to do."

I knew Rich was gon' say some shit like that. He's always trying to protect me. The way he talks, it's hard to believe that he's confined to a wheelchair for the rest of his life. But that wheelchair ain't never stopped that brother from running the streets. You don't need a good pair of legs when you got a gun. And Rich had plenty of those. "A'ight, man. Let's change the subject. Wheel your ass on over here and bring the dominoes. I ain't kicked your ass in some bones in a long time."

"Eyeisha, make that two sammiches," Rich yelled out. "X gon' need some nutrition after I whip his ass."

He laid out the dominoes on the table and shuffled them around and picked out his hand. I picked up mine and pushed the rest to the side. Eyeisha came out and put the food down on the table. I slid mine to the corner. I didn't know where her hands had been either. Rich beat the shit out of me for two rounds, but I redeemed myself and won the last game before he had to wheel himself into the bathroom and take a leak. When Eyeisha sat down at the table after he left, I felt like running in the bathroom behind him but he had already closed the door and would be in there for at least fifteen minutes. Even simple things like pissing were a chore for Rich from that chair.

"So what's been up?" Eyeisha asked, picking up my forty and taking a long swig.

"Nothing," I answered, feeling uncomfortable.

"Why you ain't been over to see me?"

"What?" I grimaced.

"I ain't forgot, X. That night we spent together was the bomb. I think about it everyday."

I wanted to tell her to shut up, but I didn't want to get her mad. Who knows what she might say to Rich if I pissed her off? She looked awful. Like she had gained another twenty pounds. She still had them long fingernails, and tonight she was wearing green contacts that made her look like a devil.

"Why don't you meet me around the corner at my place after you leave here? We could pick up right where we left off. You know you want to."

"Look, girl. I done told you before. That was a one-night thing. That ain't gon' happen no more so you might as well give it up."

That's not what she wanted to hear. She took another sip of the forty as her smile dwindled away. "So what you saying? I ain't good enough for you no more? You got some other girl or something? Well, let me tell you one thing. I ain't so easy to shake, X. You better learn that. Look at me. Don't I look different?"

Hell no. You still the same fat tramp you always were, I thought.

"These extra pounds I'm carrying around ain't from eating no damn Twinkies," she said and stood up so I could get a full view of her disgusting body. "All this weight is 'cause I'm carrying your baby."

Hold up, hold up! What did this skeezer just tell me?

"That's right, X. *Your* baby."

"Bitch, please. We had sex one time."

"We had sex all night long."

"So the fuck what. I don't know what kind of game you're trying to pull, but you might as well stop playing 'cause I ain't falling for the okie-doke. Not me, not now, not in this lifetime."

"Well, if it's not yours, then whose is it? It sho ain't Rich's 'cause that crippled mothafucka been shooting blanks since he got shot."

"Please, girl. It ain't gotta be Rich's neither. You probably been fucking everybody in the neighborhood anyway. Rich just too blind to see that."

"No, I ain't been fucking around, X. You're the only other person I had sex with."

"Well then, your big-ass probably ain't even pregnant. You just fat. And if you trying to get money out of me for an abortion, you can just forget that too. It ain't gon' happen."

"Nigga, I don't need your money. Rich is rolling big-time. I got all the money I need right here. You might as well face it, baby, you're gon' be a daddy," she said, pointing a long, orange finger in my face. "And no, I ain't having no abortion. I'm having your baby and you're gon' be with me. So get it together, Daddy-X."

I felt like swinging on that bitch. And if I was less of a man, I would have knocked her fat ass right to the floor. But then Rich opened the bathroom door and both of us got silent. I realized she didn't want Rich to know just as much I didn't. He'd probably kick her ass and kill me, if he knew what was going on behind his back.

I raised the fuck up out of there after that. I told Rich I had to get back over to Jazmine's and make sure she was all right. "A'ight, man. Remember, if you need me, just call. I'll take care of everything. I know you'd help me out if something happened to my girl," he said. I gave him a pound with my fist and jumped back into my car.

I felt sorry for Rich. Nothing had changed with him. He was still the same old thug, selling dope, rollin' with the gangsta life, and stuck with a stupid tramp like Eyeisha. I felt even sorrier for myself 'cause something inside me told me that Eyeisha was telling the truth. Damn. What the fuck am I gon' do now? I finally get myself on the right track. My career's taking off, I got a beautiful, smart girlfriend, I'm living in a decent community, got money in my pocket and more to come, and now this! If what Eyeisha said turned out to be true, how could I ever explain it to Jazmine? Since we've been together my life has been like a nonstop weekend at Magic Mountain. I never thought I would get a woman like Jazmine. A woman who's got things going in her life and who cares about me. Not because I'm X-Man, the gangsta or the rapper, but because I'm Xavier Honor, a man—period.

When I got back to Jazmine's and buzzed her on the intercom I felt sick to my stomach. I didn't know if I should come right out and tell her now, or wait and see if Eyeisha was really serious about keeping the baby. By the time I got to her door, I had decided to hold off on telling her. She already had enough to deal with, with Bobby Strong and Dakota. When she opened the door, my heart sank to my feet. It was four o'clock in the morning and it didn't look like she had gotten any sleep. "Dakota's okay now. She's in her room," she said, looking like she had been crying all night.

"How are you?" I asked and gave her a hug and felt her melt into me.

"I'm fine. I was hoping you'd come back. Now maybe I can get some sleep, if you lie down with me."

We walked to her room and undressed. When we got in bed, I held her close and her body was so cold that I had to pull the sheets all the way up to our necks. "I'm really sorry about earlier," she said, turning to me. I know I shouldn't have taken my frustrations out on you like that. You've always been a gentle lover to me. I just let that stuff with Bobby Strong get to me."

"I know, Red. Don't worry about it. Everything's gon' be a'ight." Then I thought back to that scene and I remembered I had told Jazmine I loved her. I had never said that to another person before. I also remembered that she didn't say anything back. It didn't bother me at the time, but now I was wondering if she felt for me as much as I felt for her. I was so confused about everything that had taken place that I needed to hear it from her. I had to be sure that this just wasn't a game for her, but I didn't know how to put my feelings into words. Call it ESP, I don't know, but it was like she was reading my mind.

"I love you too," she said and kissed me on my chest. "I love you so much it hurts, Xavier."

"Thank you," I said and instantly felt stupid. *Thank you?* What kind of response was that? She wasn't doing me a favor. Or was she? "I love you," I said. "I don't wanna do anything to hurt you. Ever. Remember that."

I held her until she fell asleep. Then I got out of bed and stood at the window. The sun was coming up and birds were chirping. It was nice outside. So nice that I felt like going for a jog. But if I had left that room, I don't think I would have ever come back. I probably would have run all the way to Africa if I could. But I couldn't leave. I was gon' stay and face the music—like a man. I just prayed that the music wouldn't stop before I had a chance to do my solo.

chapter fifteen

i'm tellin'

The volume on the stereo system could never be too loud for Bobby, especially when he was listening to Jazmine's voice. He blasted the sample copy of her debut so loud that it could be heard throughout the entire seventh floor of Black Tie Records. He blasted it as much for his own enjoyment as well as so others could hear the new talent that he had discovered. He turned up the volume even louder and listened as he found himself becoming nostalgic. He remembered how he used to hole up in his bedroom at his grandmother's house and blast his 45s all day and night. Music was his life back then. It was all he needed. Now things were different. He needed more. He thought he'd found it with Sheryl, but somehow he'd let her slip through his hands. But not this time. Not with Jazmine. This time it would be forever.

He was too involved with his thoughts to notice Kirk Walker when he walked into his office and turned the volume on the stereo down. He turned around when he heard the silence, and the sight of Kirk both angered and amused him. He hated the man, but the envy he saw on his face pleased him.

"So that's the new singer everybody's been buzzing about around here," Kirk said, sticking his hands deeply into his pockets.

Bobby deplored the sight of Kirk. He was short, too thin for a man, and his gestures and movements were a bit too feminine to fit Bobby's idea of what a man should be. He wanted to tell him to get the hell out of his office. Just who did this kid think he was, coming into his domain unannounced? But he let him stay. It was the perfect opportunity to boast about Jazmine. He was one up on him and he knew it. It was just a matter of time before he'd be the one sitting in Mr. Timbers' office—not Kirk. "Well, if it isn't the new boy wonder. So nice of you to barge in, son. Didn't your mommy ever tell you it's polite to knock before entering a room?"

"The door was wide open, Bob."

"That's Mr. Strong to you, son." Who the hell did this juvenile think he was to call him by his first name? Bob, of all things. Youngsters have no respect for their elders.

"I heard through the grapevine, this Jazmine girl is going to be the next Mariah Carey."

Bobby let the grin on his face confirm that remark.

"I also heard through the grapevine that you haven't done a thing to prepare for her release," he said.

"That's true, freshman. But I've been around many years. I, unlike some of us around here, know what I'm doing."

"That may be true, but a little bird dropped another bug in my ear. Seems as though Timbers got a whiff of this singer too. She impressed the hell out of him."

Again there was nothing more to say than what the grin and confident bow of his head expressed.

"Yeah," Kirk said, making himself at home in Bobby's office. He walked around to the desk and observed its neatness. "Old Timbers likes that Jazmine character. He figures she could make us tons of money. But." He paused as if in a dramatic play and held up a finger. "The old boss is not too impressed with the way you've been handling her career. No one outside of this company knows anything about her. Tsk, tsk." Kirk shook his head. "I was just saying to Mr. T the other day, it would be a shame to blow a talent like that just because of bad promotion." He shook his head more vigorously. "A damn shame."

If Bobby were to grab him by the collar and knock that smirk off his face, that would be a damn shame too, he thought. But he couldn't let on that he wasn't in control of the situation. Nothing Kirk had said had been news to Bobby. He knew he'd have to do some last-minute hustling to get the word out about Jazmine. And he'd do it, just as soon as he had the time. Just as soon as he could clear his head for long enough to concentrate.

Kirk picked up the photo of Bobby's ex-wife and kids from his desk. The picture seemed to amuse him. "They're a lovely bunch," he said and continued to shake his head. "I guess we all pay a price for our success," he said, putting the silver frame back down, "or lack of it."

"You know, Kirk," Bobby said, walking over to the slender man, "you're a stupid son of a bitch, and I use the phrase sparingly—your mother doesn't have a thing to do with this." Bobby's large frame hovered over Kirk and it gave him a feeling of victory. "Don't ever second-guess me. I've been in the game far too long to let a little bitch like you come in here and change the rules. You know what you need, Kirk?" he said, sinking away from him. "You need fear. That's what's wrong with your generation. You don't fear anything," he said and squinted his eyes from the headache he felt coming on. "Back in the day, we feared our parents. One false move and we got our asses smacked. Our parents had the fear of God. One false move and they'd be struck down. You, you think because you've grown up, gone to the Ivy League, and landed a job, that the world is your oyster. Bullshit. You better get scared, Kirk. You better get real scared."

Kirk cracked a smile and headed for the doorway. The sight of his head shaking in amusement made Bobby want to slap him on the neck. "Whatever you say," Kirk said, turning around before he left the room. "You're the man."

Indignant son of a bitch, Bobby thought, turning the volume up on the stereo again. He slammed his door before sitting down at his desk and stared off into space. He wasn't thinking about Kirk any longer. He'd made his point.

He spun his chair around to gaze out the window, shook his head, and closed his eyes tightly before slowly opening them again. He could have sworn he saw Jazmine hanging outside his window. His mind had been spacing out like that for the past week. He was sure there was a medical term for the hallucinations he'd been having, but he couldn't remember what it was. He laughed at the irony. Drugs will make you forgetful, he thought and turned his chair back around and continued to laugh. Drugs will definitely make you forgetful.

. . .

Xavier had left too soon, but it was already after twelve and he had to get down to the studio and work on his album. I wanted to go with him, but I couldn't leave Dakota. There was still too much to talk about; too many decisions to be made. What the hell am I supposed to do now? I wondered. I can't just go back and work with Bobby like nothing happened. Call me overly pessimistic, but I don't see how I can continue singing. This is all so much like a nightmare. Everything is shot to hell.

Hell. That's an ironic thought. Daddy said I'd go to hell for dishonoring him. "Singers are sluts," he said. "They all go to hell." Looks like Daddy's right again, because the way I feel right now, hell would almost be a welcome vacation. At least it would be, compared to facing Bobby again.

It took me almost an hour to get out of bed and make my way to the kitchen. Dakota was already there, sipping coffee and staring off into some unknown cosmos. I didn't know what to say to her. What could I say, besides something dumb like, "Everything's gonna be all right." I didn't have to say much, because as soon as she saw me, she began to do all the talking.

"Morning, girlfriend. Ready for another blissful day in the music business?" She laughed heartily, and I didn't know if she was being facetious or if she was simply in denial. "I've got our day all planned. First we'll go down to the studio. I called Mack and told him to expect us in an hour. Then we'll go over to *Music Muse*. I finally made contact with the managing editor, and she's willing to set up an interview with you and one of the reporters so we can get the word out about the album. Then—."

"Stop it, D. Just slow down. You don't actually expect me to keep working for Bobby, do you? He's slime."

"Jazz, there's one thing you've got to understand. Everybody's slime in the music industry. You're living in a world of movers and shakers. Sometimes you've just got to roll with the punches."

Was I talking to Dakota? Miss Feminist, USA? "Maybe you're living in denial, but I'm not. The fact is, this man almost raped you! That's not something you roll with. That's something you stand up against. What's wrong with you?"

"Not a damn thing's wrong with me, Jazmine. What's wrong with you? You're about to hit the big time, baby. What happened was between me and Bobby. Not you. And I'm not about to let you blow off your career over me. Just forget about it. I've lived with it this long and I haven't let it break me yet."

"Fuck that shit, D. I just can't go on like nothing's happened. What if he tries that shit with you again? What if he tries it with me? You've heard the phone ringing off the hook at all hours of the night. That's Bobby. I know it is. He's taking this too far. I may work for him, but I'm not his personal toy. And that man hasn't done shit to promote my debut. I'm not putting up with this. I'm not." I opened the refrigerator, not knowing what I was looking for, then closed it and paced the floor.

"Now you sound like your damn boyfriend. What are you gonna do? Go over to his office and blow his brains out? Or better yet, why don't you send Xavier down there to do a drive-by? He'd get a kick out of that, wouldn't he?"

"Fuck you, bitch."

"No, fuck you, Jazmine. I did what I did for *you*. That night at the party, all I was thinking about was how I could help you. What I could do to get your demo tape into the right hands. When Bobby threw me down on the floor, a part of me wanted to cut his heart out. The other part of me knew that I had to endure it. How else was I gonna get him to give you a shot?" She was shaking like crazy and her eyes were as red as rubies. "Do you think all these half-ass singers simply send their tapes to A&R people and get discovered just like that? Hell no! There's a price to pay for every damn thing you want in life. I paid the price for you, so don't go fucking it off because you want to be self-righteous. I worked too hard to get you where you're at today."

"So, in other words, you're saying you let him almost rape you for me? Bullshit, D. And by the way, kiss my ass." The tears that welled up in her eyes did nothing to justify the words she had spoken to me. How could she blame me for what Bobby did to her? I wasn't the one who nearly fucked her and I wasn't the stupid one who decided that that was the best way for me to break into the business. I was mad as hell at her, but I knew she was speaking out of pain. I went back to my room and got dressed. I threw on the first thing I laid my hand on in my closet, blue slacks and a black T shirt that read: "No justice, no peace" in bright red letters. I brushed my hair with my hands, grabbed my keys, and headed out the door, past Dakota, who was still sitting at the dinette table, zoned out. I didn't tell her where I was going. She wouldn't have heard me anyway. And besides, I didn't have time to explain. I had business to tend to.

In a half hour I was riding the elevator to the seventh floor of Black Tie Records. I was a woman on a mission, until I got to the second floor. By the third, my palms were getting sweaty and I realized I hadn't the slightest idea what I was going to say to Bobby. "I quit," didn't quite seem enough. "I quit, you asshole," sounded meaner, but still didn't seem enough to shake Bobby's world. What do you say to a jerk like that? "Eat pussy and die"? No. That would only make me look bad.

When the elevator stopped at the fourth floor, I felt an urge to get off and take the stairs back down to the first floor, but so many people got on that I couldn't move. I was trapped. I thought about what Xavier would do in a situation like this, but since I didn't have a gun I quickly dismissed that thought. Dakota would simply saunter in the office, walk over to Bobby, and slap his face, and it would be over. But I was not Dakota or Xavier, and neither of their tactics suited me. I could never handle anything like this by myself and that's why I always ended up taking whatever dirty scraps someone threw me. If I were in school, I'd probably raise my hand and ask the teacher to help me or go running to the principal's office. By the time I reached the seventh floor that idea didn't sound so bad. The elevator doors opened and I stood back and thought instead about going to see Mr. Timbers. No one ever went up to his office unless they had a very good reason and at that moment I was unsure just how good mine was. I had heard Mr. Timbers was a nice man, but I knew he didn't like dealing with people one on one and I probably wouldn't make it past his overprotective secretary anyway. Besides I could just see myself going in there, sucking my thumb and crying. "I no wanna work with Bobby no more." He'd think I was an immature schoolgirl. Which I really am at heart, but for business purposes, that image doesn't suit. Somehow, I had to find the strength to handle this.

I got off the elevator, took a deep breath, and headed for Bobby's door. I heard his secretary shout out some nonsense as I passed her, but I acted like I didn't hear a word she said. I heard the click of her heels behind me and sped up. When I opened the door, I immediately closed it and locked it behind me. I stared at Bobby, who looked at me like I was crazy as we both listened to his secretary's knocks behind the door. "No problem, I'll handle this," Bobby shouted out to her and pulled out a Kleenex to dab his nose. I stared at him as hard as I could, trying to figure out exactly what kind of man I was dealing with. He had once been so protective and concerned. Now I saw him in a different light. He was really no different than my father. They both needed control like chocoholics need M&M's, and everything they did for me was only to pull my strings in the direction they wanted me to go. They were the same man, only different bodies.

He gazed at me as if I were on display and I became self-conscious of my appearance. I folded my arms across my chest, but what I really wanted to do was cover my face. I didn't want him to see my eyes; they give me away every time.

"You look . . . lovely," he said and walked around to the front of his desk. "Nice shirt. Must be a black thang," he said and jokingly held up the peace sign. He was smiling as if I had stopped by for a tea party. Everything about him painted arrogance and I felt myself growing angrier.

"Just who do you think you are? Do you think you can just do anything, to anybody, anytime you damn well please?"

Confusion crossed his face and he looked at me with bewilderment. "What are you talking about?" he asked innocently, and motioned for me to take a seat. "Did I do something wrong?"

I didn't move and I didn't take my eyes off him. This character was slick. Too slick. But I wasn't falling for this concerned role he was playing. "I know what happened between you and Dakota. You're filthy," I said, putting my hands on my hips. "You disgust me. And you know what else? I quit."

"Jazmine, please," he said, almost whining. "I've no idea what you're talking about. Just tell me the problem and I promise I'll make it right."

"Just shut up," I yelled, so tired of this game he was playing.

"What is it?" he pleaded. "Is it the studio, you don't like the songs? Is it the remix? What?"

"Shut up!" I screamed. I wanted so badly to whack that innocent look off his face. "I know, Bobby. I know you tried to rape Dakota."

Bobby looked confused, but somewhere in that confusion was the knowledge that I was on to him. "She told you that?" he asked, trying to avoid my stare.

"You thought she wouldn't? You thought she'd just let this *slide*?"

He leaned against his desk and stared at the floor. I could tell he wanted to say something, but he stopped completely. I expected him to at least try to lie his way out of it, but when he clammed up I didn't know what to do. Finally he looked up from the floor. "Let me explain," he begged. "You don't understand. I didn't mean to—"

"You didn't mean to what? Get caught?"

He walked slowly in my direction and stared at me hard. "You don't understand. I'm not like that anymore." He paused for a moment and weighed his thoughts. "Nothing's been the same since I met you, Jazmine. The thought of you gets me through the day. When my wife and kids left town, I thought I'd die. Then I remembered you and suddenly, I had reason to keep going. I love you, Jazmine."

I stared at him in disbelief and my stomach turned so hard, I was sure I was going to throw up. That statement set everything clear for me. If nothing else, I was sure Bobby was losing his mind. He could tell I was disgusted by what he said, because his somber expression turned cold. The look on his face told me there was nothing more I could do. Whatever he had on his mind was set in stone.

"You're not quitting and that's all there is to it," he said very seriously.

"No. You can forget that. I'll die before I work with you again. You're not the president of this company and I'm not your personal property."

I reached behind me and unlocked the door. When I turned to leave, he closed in on me like darkness and shut the door with one hand and kept it there as I tugged to force it back open. He slowly leaned over my shoulder and whispered in my ear. His breath smelled of chocolate liqueur. "You are not going to leave me," he grunted. "You owe me, Jazmine. You owe me."

He lifted his hand and I hurried out without looking back. Bobby thought he had won that round, but little did he know I was on my way to the principal's office.

chapter sixteen

say what?

Bobby couldn't get Jazmine off his mind no matter how many times he paced the floor, or how many drinks he knocked back. Still he continued the ritual and poured himself another shot. He stirred it with his finger as he walked back and forth between his desk and the door.

What does she think of me now? he wondered and gulped down his drink. He sat down at his desk and drummed his fingers against his glass. "How many times am I going to fuck up?" he said aloud to himself.

He wondered where Jazmine had gone and if she was okay. He'd never meant to get so forceful with her earlier, but he couldn't help himself. He couldn't just let her quit. She had too much talent and had come too far to quit now. Besides, he needed her. Not for love, but for his career. He knew he was close to the presidency now and it was all because of Jazmine. Without her, his career would be over.

"I need to talk to you, Jazmine," he mumbled and reached for the phone, but as soon as he touched the receiver, the phone rang out, startling him. He closed his eyes for a brief second, hoping the caller would be Jazmine. Hoping he'd have another chance to explain things to her. He picked up the receiver and was startled again.

"I need you in my office," Mr. Timbers' voice boomed through the receiver. There was an urgency to his voice that Bobby couldn't understand, but Mr. Timbers hung up the phone before Bobby could ask why he wanted to see him. As he slowly rose from his seat, it suddenly hit him. Mr. Timbers had made his decision. He'd finally selected who he was going to turn the company over to.

He couldn't control his nervousness. This impromptu meeting could only mean that he had beat out Kirk, and the presidency of Black Tie Records was his. He ran a firm hand over his hair and wiped his nose with a handkerchief from his coat pocket. He took out a chocolate candy and put it on his tongue and smoothed it against the roof of his mouth. He could hardly keep himself contained. He practically jumped over his desk and ran to the elevator and pushed the up button. The elevator is always so slow, Bobby thought. When the company was officially his, he vowed to take them out and install escalators, but for now he couldn't stand the wait. He zipped down the hallway and up the stairs. He took two at a time until he reached the fifteenth floor. Walking down the corridor he smoothed his hair back and fumbled with his nose, then straightened his tie before entering Mr. Timbers' door. He walked straight up to the front of the desk, cleared his throat, and waited for the good news. Then out of the corner of his eye, he saw Jazmine. She was sitting on the sofa, staring at him with eyes as fiery as her hair.

Immediately, his mind went blank. What was she doing here? And what did she say to Mr. Timbers? He quickly looked back to his boss and this time he noticed the disturbed look on his face.

"You're fired," Mr. Timbers said, coldly.

"Now hold on, Mr. Timbers. Let's talk about this, sir," Bobby said, nervously picking at his tie.

"You are out of here," Mr. Timbers continued. "I don't know what kind of circus you think I'm running here, but you had better get a clue. If there's one thing everyone knows around here, it's that Black Tie is a family. Black *Ties*," he said, interlocking his fingers. "Your shabby business tactics are not welcome here, Mr. Strong. I rest assured that you will have your office cleaned out by tomorrow midday," he said, pausing to take a long look at Bobby.

"Wait a damn minute. What the hell is going on here? What did I do?"

"You know what you did, Bobby," Jazmine broke in. You... you, you..." She couldn't get the rest of the sentence out before she broke into tears.

Bobby looked at Jazmine in amazement. Is she responsible for this?

"Please leave now, Mr. Strong," Mr. Timbers said, as if he had never met Bobby before in his life. He rushed to Jazmine with a box of tissues and sat down next to her, putting a soft arm around her shoulder. "I tried to warn you, son," he said, with one last glimmer of pity in his eyes. "Too bad you wouldn't listen."

Bobby watched the two of them as he silently backed up toward the doorway, stunned. It's all over, he thought, and wondered why he almost felt relieved. As he stepped out the door, he stole one last glance at Jazmine, then closed the door behind him. He leaned against the wall, then bent over as if he'd just been kicked in the stomach. "It's all over," he whispered and took a deep breath. "It's all over and I don't even give a damn."

. . .

Mission accomplished, though not exactly in the manner that I had expected. I had wanted to handle Bobby all by myself. Take an affirmative stand for once in my life. But all that I ended up doing was running for help—again. Still, I felt relieved. I wouldn't have to work with Bobby anymore and I wouldn't have to put up with his constant advances and sexual overtures. And most of all I wouldn't have to look into his face, knowing what he had done to Dakota. If there's one thing I've learned, it's that I am a strong woman. I may not have gone to Bobby's office and kicked down the door, but I handled the situation just the same. I was proud of myself and the first person I wanted to tell was Xavier. After all, he's the reason why I feel so strong. Before I met Xavier, I would never have thought about confronting Bobby. I would have accepted the situation and reconciled myself to being miserable. Instead, I handled my bi'ness, I thought, and chuckled to myself. I'm even beginning to talk like Xavier. I decided I would page him the minute I walked in. I needed to see him if for nothing else than to be reassured that something in my life was constant. I couldn't believe how much I had grown to love him. I had seen a change in him recently. He seemed to have mellowed out. Not that he was a wimp, just that he was simpler now. Simpler in the fact that he didn't seem to be hung up on expressing his rugged side. He was coming full stride into his manhood and I could tell he enjoyed it.

When I pulled into the garage, I hoped Dakota would be home. I needed to talk to her, not only to let her know that Bobby was out of our lives, but to straighten things out with her. I had left her on bad terms earlier and I wanted her to know that I was still there for her. And in a sick way, I wanted her to know that I appreciated what she had done for me. I didn't want to thank her for almost getting raped, but I did want to thank her for caring enough about me to do what she did. The thought seemed stupid to me as I took the stairs up to our apartment, but I realized Dakota would understand what I meant, even if I couldn't put it in sensible terms. She was my best friend and I loved her. We'd get through this like we get through everything else—together.

I opened the door to find Craig, of all people, relaxing on the couch. He seemed as startled to see me as I was to see him. He sat up straight and awkward as I walked to the middle of the room. I hadn't seen him since the Black Tie party and although I wasn't holding on to any feelings for him anymore, I had to admit he looked good enough to eat.

"Long time, no see, stranger," I said and walked over to him and gave him a tight hug. He barely reached out for me, which was okay, but strange. I was only trying to be pleasant.

Dakota walked into the room wearing nothing but a T-shirt and looked at me like I like I had two heads. "You're back," she said, fidgeting with her hair.

"Yep, I'm back and I've got good news, but we'll talk about that later," I said, walking to her and giving her a firm hug, but receiving much the same response I got from Craig. I turned my attention back to him and smiled. "So what brings you by?" I said, having no idea that he knew where I lived or that Dakota and I were roommates.

"Just passing through," he replied and shot Dakota a strange look. It got uncomfortably quiet after that. The three of us just sort of looked at each other, but no one said a word. Then finally Dakota let out a big sigh and threw up her hands, the way she always did when she just didn't give a damn any longer. She walked over to the couch and sat right under Craig and put her hand on his thigh. The smile on my face turned to confusion and I took a step backward to assess the situation. Was this her way of telling me they were an item? And if so, for how long? And how did his wife fit into this equation? I didn't know whether to be mad or what.

Dakota and I had a strong rule about men. We vowed never to date the other one's ex-boyfriend—no matter what. Never. The both of them just sort of sat there and stared at me. I felt so embarrassed, like I was invading their privacy, so I excused myself and went to my room.

I couldn't sort all this out in my head quick enough. Dakota had said she wasn't seeing anyone. Craig was married. What the heck was going on? I sat down on the edge of my bed and tried to gather my thoughts. I didn't know what I was feeling, but feeling I definitely was. I wasn't upset in the sense that I felt like I had lost the love of my life. I was over Craig. Had been for quite a while now. Especially since he was married and showed no apparent interest in me. Still, I was pissed. I felt betrayed. Like Dakota should have gotten permission from me, before seeing him. I mean, we had a pact. Out of all the men in this world, why did she have to date one of my old flings? Did she think I could handle it or was this her way of punishing me because she felt I didn't appreciate her? I didn't know what to think, but I knew I had to get out of that apartment. I packed my old college backpack with a change of clothes and headed back into the front room. Craig seemed to be wiping tears from Dakota's eyes as I passed them on my way to the door. I didn't know if she was crying because she had told him what had happened with Bobby, or if it was because she knew she had upset me. I didn't care one way or the other. All I knew was that I had to get out of there and quick. It was all too weird for me. I needed to be where my heart belonged. With my man. The one who made me happy.

I drove like a bat out of hell to Xavier's place. I let myself in with the key he had given me and when I walked into his bedroom, he was on the phone asking Dakota if I had made it home yet. Finally someone who really cares about me. "I'm right here, baby," I said and gave him a hug, and this time the hug was returned, desperately. I put my bag on the dresser and fell down on top of him on the bed. "Looks like we're really coworkers now," I said and kissed him. He looked up at me with this goofy look of confusion on his face.

"What? What happened?" he asked, trying to push me off and sit up straight. I leaned down on him to keep him from moving.

"Bobby's fired."

"Say what?"

"That's right. I told Mr. Timbers what happened and he fired him on the spot."

"Go on, girl," he said, sitting up and looking at me like a proud father. "You got old B.S. sent to the unemployment line, huh. Cool. So now you can concentrate on your music."

"Yeah, that's what I meant when I said we're really coworkers now. I'm going to be working with Kirk."

"Say what?" he said, deeply.

"Timbers said he really liked my work and he didn't want my debut delayed because of Bobby, so he hooked me up with Kirk," I said and immediately sensed Xavier getting uneasy.

"So what happens to me? I just get knocked to the background now?"

"Xavier, please. My working with Kirk is not going to affect your project. It's not like he's going to drop you because I'm suddenly on the scene, and besides, Dakota's handling most of my business anyway. She had to when she found out Bobby wasn't doing shit." I hated having this conversation with him and I suddenly got pissed off. "Damn, Xavier. We've talked about this before. We are not in competition, okay?" I said and stood up. I was so mad. Everybody's always concerned about what they can get out of a situation. Whatever happened to the big picture? If one of us comes up, the other comes up too. It's not man against woman. It's us against them. I picked up my bag and headed for the door. "I'm going home."

"Hey, hey, hey," he said, standing up and grabbing me. I was so pissed that I started to cry. Too much bullshit had taken place and I just couldn't hold it in anymore.

"Look, babe. My bad, my bad," he said and held me tight. "I don't know why I'm trippin'. I just don't want anything to mess up what I've got going for me."

"And you think I'd do that?"

"No, no. I'm just trippin'."

"You don't have to be threatened by me, Xavier. You're already a success."

"I know and it's because of you."

"No, it's because of you. You are where you are today because you made it happen. You could be hanging out on the street corner selling rocks, but you're not. You made it happen for yourself."

"Is this some kinda pep talk?"

"No, it's the real."

"I'm not threatened by you, Jazmine. I just want you to be proud of me."

"I am proud of you," I said as we fell backward onto the bed.

"Staying the night?"

"Staying the night," I said and kissed him deeply. I stared down at him and thought how lucky I was to have found him. Yes, I said to myself. There must be a God.

the truth

What do you call it when you don't tell somebody something that you think will hurt them, only you know if they find out you've been hiding whatever it is you're not telling them, they'd be upset—break up with you, cry, never see you again? I laid in bed next to Jazmine thinking over that scenario all morning long. I mean, it's not like I'm really lying to her by not telling her about Eyeisha and the baby. I still don't trust that girl. She could be making the whole thing up. Ghetto bitches are like that. That's why I could never deal with them. They always talking about how scandalous the men are, but they need to take a look at themselves. They're just as bad as we are, only they get to hide behind all that feminine shit. Men—we fuck you over and it's like, hey, whatever, I'm a man, I'm supposed to do stupid shit. Women fuck you over and they get to feeling remorseful and start in on all that crying shit. Like tears can make up for whatever scandalous thing they did.

Rich falls for that every time. He gave Eyeisha a C-note one time, to go out and get her mother a birthday present. Come to find out, Mom's birthday had already passed and Eyeisha was using the money to get some other nigga a birthday gift. Now ain't that some shit? Scandalous if I ever seen scandalous. But did Rich break up with her? Hell naw, that stupid mothafucka didn't. Eyeisha pulled that crying routine, talking about she so sorry, and she'll never do it again. And Rich fell for it. Yeah, he knocked the shit out of her, but hell, he always doing that. But he didn't break up with her. Stupid, stupid, stupid.

Now if that situation had been reversed and a man had took his woman's money and spent it on another woman—oh, all hell woulda broke loose. It would be nothing a brother could say to get out of that. What he gonna do? Cry? Hell naw. He gonna stand up in the middle of the floor and say, "Yeah, I did it. Now what?" He's only being honest. You'd think his woman would recognize that and have pity on the poor, stupid mothafucka. But no. Women don't give brothers no kind of break.

It's stuff like that that makes me scared to tell Jazmine about Eyeisha. Especially a tough woman like Jazz. Women like her don't put up with as much bullshit as other girls do. You look at them the wrong way and your ass is history. But I've been lying here thinking like this: Jazmine can't get mad if I tell her what's going on. Number one, it ain't like I give a damn about Eyeisha or some stupid baby she's gonna have. The damn baby will probably be born with four eyes, two heads, and a tail, the way that girl be abusing her body. And that bitch think she slick, but I know what's really up. Rich always be complaining about how his supply be disappearing. I know that bitch be dipping into that cocaine. I ain't never seen her, but it ain't too hard to tell—she smoked out. But regardless of all that, Jazmine can't get mad 'cause all this happened before we met. It ain't like I been playing around on her. Me and Eyeisha was a one-night thing before me and Jazz even knew we liked each other, so how can she get mad over something like that? Easy. Women always getting mad over the stupidest shit.

Jazmine rolled over, rubbed her eyes, and looked up at me as if she could tell I was thinking about her. "How long you been up?" she asked, staring up at me with white gunk caught in the corners of her eyes. I didn't care. She still looked beautiful to me. I brushed my hand over her face, thinking, is there anything I wouldn't do for this lady? She kissed my wrists and drilled the answer to that question home for me: No.

She got up and walked to the bathroom and my eyes followed her all the way. Before I knew it, my body was right behind her. It's funny how stupid stuff like peeing can be so cute when you see someone you love doing it. Even gross shit like belching is cute when Jazmine does it. I stood in the doorway watching and I could have kicked myself for wasting my time on all those other women in my past. You never know what you're missing until the right woman comes along and shows you how things should really be. And once you see how it's done, you never wanna go back to the way things were.

"I'm hungry, baby," she said, pulling out a *Jet* magazine from a basket beside the toilet. I figured she was going to be there for a while so I closed the door and gave her some privacy. There are still some things that aren't cute no matter who's doing them.

"You want me to make you some pancakes and eggs?" I asked from behind the door.

"Got some Froot Loops?" she asked, straining.

I went into the kitchen and poured two bowls of cereal, but held off on adding the milk until Red finished up in the bathroom and joined me. She hugged me from behind and let her hands go where they pleased. "Don't start nothing you can't finish," I said, looking back at her over my shoulder.

She grabbed a bowl, poured the milk, took it to the table, and dug in. Jazmine was so easy to please. "I'm going to the studio with you today," she said as she filled her jaws with cereal.

"Are you asking me or telling me?"

"What do you think?"

I think I love you, I thought, but decided not to say it. It was too early in the morning to be getting all soft. I had to stay rugged, the whole day was ahead of me. "Well I guess you can go, but only 'cause I said you could go."

"Puleeze," she said and sucked her teeth. "You know who's running this relationship."

Yeah, you are, I thought. "Girl, you know I'm the man," I said, walking behind her chair. I leaned down and kissed her neck and she started to laugh so hard, milk came shooting out of her mouth all over the table. "Don't start nothing you can't finish," she said, twisting around to look me in the face.

"I never do," I whispered and took what she was offering me.

Another hour had passed before we made it downstairs to the car. It was a chillin' day, warm, but not too hot, so I decided to let the top down on the Impala. Jazmine pushed her sunglasses from her eyes up into her hair, then opened the glove compartment and searched for a tape. She took out an old Smokey Robinson tape and popped it in. I gave her a look and she knew what was coming next. Hydraulics time. I flipped the switch and the car began to go up and down in the front. Then I flipped another and we started bouncing from side to side. Jazmine looked at me and rolled her eyes and I knew it was time to turn the hydraulics off. I leaned over and gave her a kiss as Smokey began crooning, "*I love it when we're cruising together.*"

It was eleven-thirty when we reached the studio, and the engineer, Tony, and the producer, 8-Ball, were already there listening to what I had put on tape the day before. Jazmine sat behind us and every once in a while I'd turn around to see her grooving to the music. I knew my record would be a hit.

We had worked on three songs and perfected them by the time seven o'clock rolled around and we had one more to go. But something just wasn't hitting with that song. So 8-Ball suggested we just scrap it, but I wasn't doing that. That song was too close to my heart to let it go. I had written it one day when I was home by myself, thinking about Jazmine, which is something I find myself doing more and more these days. I was thinking how different I had become since I had met her and how my life had taken on a new twist. I was thinking about how so many other boys in the hood needed someone like Jazmine in their lives. Not necessarily as a girlfriend, but as someone they could bounce ideas about reality off of. Someone who they could talk to about any- and everything and someone who would check them when they start to slip up. The rap was called, "Because of You," and we were going round and round with the chorus of the song and no matter how we switched it up, it sounded like it was missing something. We had all but given up until Jazmine started humming in the background. All she was saying was, "Because of you," over and over again. It was so simple that it was brilliant, and when Tony had her sing it with the tape it sounded so good, all of us had to get up and jam to it. And 8-Ball didn't waste no time about it. He put both of us in the sound booth and had us lay down the track from the top. We were rocking the house. I would lay down the rap, then she'd jump in on the chorus and do a little scat and a riff and—wick, wop, wham!—we had a hit on our hands.

Tony played it back for us and we could tell it was the bomb. Then

Jazmine started up again with me, touching all the wrong but right places. I knew Tony and 8-Ball could see us, but I didn't give a damn. I leaned her against the wall and kissed her like there was no tomorrow.

Then suddenly the music stopped. I got in one last kiss before looking out at Tony and 8-Ball. They had their backs turned to us and they were talking to someone, but I couldn't see who it was. "Who is it?" Jazmine asked me, rubbing my back.

"I don't know," I said and grabbed her by the hand. "Let's get out of here. We'll finish up in the morning."

We walked out the booth just as the voices were getting louder. By the time we made it back to the engineering room, the voices were shouting and I had no idea what was going on. I opened the door for Jazmine and let her pass through, then stopped dead in my tracks. What the fuck was Eyeisha doing here?

"There that no-good mothafucka go. I knew his tired-ass was up in here. Oh and he got his bitch wit him." That girl was going off and looking just as crazy as she was sounding. She had on a pair of raggedy house slippers, a pair of old faded jeans that would have looked in style if her stomach hadn't been smooshing out over the belt loops. Long strands of hair were greased down around her temples and the rest of her hair was pulled back into a ponytail, but of course the tail wasn't her own. She musta bought it at the same place she bought that purple lipstick she had on. But regardless of how the bitch looked, she sounded like she was going out of her mind.

"What the fuck y'all looking at? Y'all thank y'all too good or somethin'? Everybody in here need to mind they fuckin' business, 'cept fo X— I got a bone ta pick witchoo." She pointed her long fingernail in my direction and I was so shocked to see this terrible-looking creature that I had forgotten all about Jazmine. I turned to look at her and she was watching me with a look on her face that said, "I know you got some explaining to do."

I bent down to tell her to go wait in the car while I handled this business, but before I could get a word out, Eyeisha was back at it again. Tony had to grab her by the arm 'cause she was looking like she was ready to lunge right at me and Jazmine.

"So this yo bitch, X? This the bad mamma jamma you been bragging about like her pussy made of gold? What the fuck you looking at, ho? I ought to kick yo ass fo messing wit my man."

At that moment I knew she was either headed for the insane asylum or high as a kite. Her man? "Bitch, please, a'ight? I don't know what the fuck you talkin' about, but you better chill on my girl. Don't be disrespecting my woman."

Jazmine was still staring back and forth between me and Eyeisha, trying to figure out what the hell was going on. It looked like she didn't know whether to be mad or break down and cry. Then she finally managed to say something and I could tell she was trying her best to keep it together. "Xavier," she said, holding up her hand in front of me like she was bracing herself against the air. "What is going on?" Her words were so careful, I knew she was confused. I wanted to reach out and hold her, or better yet, snap my fingers and make Eyeisha and this whole incident disappear, but my life has never been that easy.

"I'll tell you what's going on," Eyeisha said, breaking loose from Tony's grasp. "*Xavier* is the father of my baby." The pride she took in saying that made me want to slap the shit out of her, and if it wasn't for Jazz's stare, I woulda been on that bitch like white on rice.

Jazmine stared down at Eyeisha's round stomach, then at me. She didn't say a word, only bit down on her bottom lip. She was trying to keep it from shaking. She pushed me aside and snatched up her purse, then turned around and headed for the door.

"Wait a minute," I said and barely caught her by the sleeve of her blouse before she could get away. She snatched away from me and swung her arm around to freedom, just missing my head.

"Naw, bitch, you ain't gotta go nowhere," Eyeisha said, waddling past Jazmine to the door. "I'm on my way out. I just wanted to stop by here and let Mr. X know he bet' not forget about me and this baby. I'd hate to have to take his punk-ass to court. It would be a terrible experience for the baby."

Jazmine stared hard at Eyeisha and I knew that I'd better get between the two of them, 'cause Jazz looked like she was hot enough to snatch somebody's head off. I stood with my back to Jazmine and watched Eyeisha walk out the door, not 'cause I wanted to watch the disgusting sight in front of me, but 'cause I didn't want to turn around and face Jazmine's eyes.

Tony and 8-Ball walked out without saying anything. What could be said? I was cold busted. I knew it, they knew it, and worse of all Jazmine knew it. I started my sentence before I turned completely around. I wanted to get a jump on explaining what seemed to be inexplicable. "Jazmine, I know how this looks, but I—,"

"Don't say another word to me," she said, choosing her words as if each one had to fit perfectly. "A baby, Xavier? A baby?"

"Look, I don't even know if she's really pregnant. That bitch been after me for the longest and this is probably just another one of her scams."

"Why didn't you tell me?" Jazmine didn't seem to want to hear anything I had to say. It was like her mind was made up and she was just standing there asking questions to kill time.

"Tell you what? Do I have to tell you about every girl I've ever known, or just the ones I fucked?"

"No, Xavier. Why don't you start with the ones you haven't fucked? That ought to be a short list."

"Look. Let's not go there. The fact is, I was with Eyeisha only one time. And it was before me and you ever met."

"So what? She's still pregnant and you're still the father. You say she could be lying, but I haven't heard you deny it."

"You wouldn't believe me if I did deny it."

"You know what, Xavier? You're right. I wouldn't believe your black ass. It's the same ole, same ole. Black man see pussy, black man fuck pussy, black man go on about his business. It never changes. Then you have the conceit to stand up here talking about she was after you like you didn't have a damn thing to do with it. Bullshit. I'm sure nobody had to tie you down and take your drawls off and force you to have sex with her. You did it, now you're standing here looking stupid because your ass got caught up. Well, too bad, life's a bitch—and then you get a girl pregnant—then you die."

She walked right up to me like she was gonna knock the shit out of me. She started searching through my pockets and I didn't know what the fuck was going on. Then she found the car keys in my back pocket and pulled them out and headed for the door again. "Where you going?" I asked and ran up behind her.

"Away from your sorry, tired ass."

"Let's talk about this, Jazmine."

"Fuck talk," she said and looked at me like if I said one more word she was gonna swing her purse at me.

I didn't know what to say, but I couldn't let her go like that. "How am I supposed to get home?"

"I don't know, Xavier. Why don't you fly?" She walked quickly out the door and didn't even give me a second look. Part of me wanted to run after her and would have got down on my knees and begged her to stay. The other part of me knew that this was only the beginning of this tragedy. I'd better save my begging for when I really needed it.

· · ·

I didn't know where I was going, but I went. I had never driven the Impala before, but I knew I could handle it as long as I didn't mess around and hit one of those switches underneath the dash that controlled the hydraulics. When I sat behind the wheel, my feet could barely touch the pedals. I tried to move the seat up, but since the whole front section was connected, it was too heavy for me to do by myself. I caught a glimpse of Xavier watching me fumble with the seat from the doorway, so I finally gave up and left it like it was. I didn't want to look like I wasn't in control, at least not while he was watching.

Talk about a shock back to reality. You think you're riding high one day, then the next someone sticks a syringe in your balloon. If I had taken a second to analyze the whole situation I probably would have started crying and never stopped. So I just drove. Fast. Something in the back of my mind was nudging at me, "But you've lost Xavier." And every time I heard that voice, another would slap me in the face, "Who gives a fuck?" I didn't want to care but I did, but the faster I drove, the easier everything was to deal with. When I reached seventy-five miles per hour, it was either keep my mind on my problems or keep my mind on the road. After I ran the intersection at Manchester and Vermont, I decided I'd better watch where I was going. But I didn't slow down. It took only fifteen minutes for me to reach South-Central from Redondo Beach. It was strange how the scenery could change so dramatically in so short a period. I went from freshly paved streets and the smell of saltwater to dodging potholes and the stench of clutter. It didn't take long after that to figure out where I was going. It had been obvious from the start. Every time something went wrong there was only one place I thought to go. I had fought off the desire before, but this time my problem was too much for me to handle alone. I wanted my daddy.

I hooked a left on Baring Cross and slowed my pace enough to clear my head. I wondered if I really should do this. I hadn't seen him since I left to move in with Dakota. I had spoken to him only once. That conversation had lasted about two minutes and was filled mostly with dead air. Still, there was something in the silence that let me know I'd always have a home to return to. I parked the car in the driveway and searched my purse for my old set of keys as I walked to the door. By the time I reached the steps, Daddy had opened the door and looked out. He held it open for me until I reached him, gave me a nod with his head, and went back inside. It was hot in there. Daddy had been cooking and forgot to open the windows. It smelled delicious though, like pork chops and greens. I sat down on the couch and sunk halfway to the bottom. A spring was sticking me in the butt, but I didn't care. It felt good to be surrounded by all those cushions.

"Come fix you a plate," Daddy called from the kitchen.

I scrambled out of the couch and into the kitchen, where it was even hotter. I maneuvered in there like I'd never left. I brushed Daddy off and told him to sit down while I fixed his plate. The dishes were in the same place and so were the glasses and silverware, and of course, the Kool-Aid was right in the door of the refrigerator. The Kool-Aid always had its own separate shelf. I brought the food to the table and snatched a few napkins out of the plastic wrapper and set them on my lap. Daddy was watching me intently and I knew he was trying to see if I was going to bless my food or not. I did, quickly, then started filling my face. I made sure there was always a jawful of food in my mouth just in case Daddy felt like talking. That way I could just shake my head yes or no and wouldn't have to get into any of the reasons why I had decided to drop by out of the blue. Daddy didn't ask questions though. He ate. Heartily. When he was finished, he slumped back in his chair and patted his belly. "You still on that fruit and vegetable kick?" he asked.

"Sort of. But not as much as I used to."

Daddy shook his head and sipped his Kool-Aid.

"How's everybody at the church?"

"They fine. Everybody been asking about you. I told 'em you was making an album. I didn't tell them what kind, though. Them old cows would die if they knew you was making secular music." Daddy actually laughed at that. I'd never heard him joke about the people at church before. He got up from the table and moved our dishes to the sink and poured water on them. "So when am I gonna get to hear this album?"

"Well, we had a little problem with the guy I was working with. But now, I'm working with someone else, so it should be out soon."

"Is it any good?"

"I think so."

"Sound anything like your mother's?"

I paused before answering that question. It was so loaded. "It's better than Momma's." I fumbled with the napkin on my lap as Daddy turned around to look at me.

"I hope it is."

I knew we weren't talking about voice quality or music arrangement. We were comparing our lifestyles. I wished I still had my plate so I could stuff some food in my mouth and be unable to talk, but food couldn't save me now. Besides I was curious. "Daddy, please tell me what she was like."

"Just like you," he said, then took his eyes off me. Daddy never liked talking about Momma, especially not to me. It was like he was afraid that if he told me anything about her, I'd turn out just like her. Mostly I think he was scared of losing me like he lost her. Momma died just two weeks after I was born. Daddy hated her for that.

"You still miss her, don't you?" He didn't answer, but I knew he did. "And you're still angry."

He sat down across from me and braced himself to speak. "I'm not angry at her. I'm angry at what she did. It didn't have to be this way. She should still be here."

I felt the same way. Momma would still be here if it hadn't been for that damn force she had in her. A force that not even a husband or a newborn child could keep her from. Daddy had never actually sat down and told me the whole story about Momma's death and I knew he wouldn't get into it now. But I had put the pieces of the puzzle together in my head a long time ago. Momma had always wanted to be a singer, and no matter how sternly Daddy tried to stop her from pursuing her dream, she kept up the fight to live her life the way she wanted. Daddy wanted a family, Momma wanted fame. Why the two ever got married with such different views, I'll never know, but one thing's for sure, Daddy loved her. He thinks I don't know, but I've seen him take out an old eight-track rehearsal tape of hers every once in a while. I remember how upset he'd gotten when his old tape deck broke down. He tried for months to repair it, but he couldn't find any dealers with eight-track tape parts anymore. Ever since, he just takes out the tape and looks at it for a while, then puts it back in his drawer.

"I hope you're smarter than her," he said and fumbled with his hands.

I am smarter, I thought. Smart enough to know that drugs can't make me any more artistic than I already am. Smart enough not to get caught up in the *music lifestyle*. Smart enough to know the difference between right and wrong. Smarter than Billie Holiday, smarter than Janice Joplin, smarter than Jim and Jimi, and yes, smarter than Momma.

I reached across the table for Daddy's hands and held them for as long as he'd let me. Before he stood up, he lifted my hands to his face and kissed my palms. I felt closer to him than I ever had before.

We moved back into the front room and I sat down on the couch and sank in. I busied my eyes with everything in the room, from the knick-knacks on the coffee table to the pictures of Martin Luther King and Mahalia Jackson on the walls.

"Do you need to come back home to stay?" Daddy asked me and shocked me back to his presence. Why did he think I needed to move back home? Did my insecurities show that much?

"No, Daddy, I'm fine." He wasn't falling for that. He knew there was more, but I was grateful he didn't try to force it out of me. "I better go, Daddy. I've got to be at the studio first thing in the morning." Daddy didn't respond. He got up and walked to the doorway, and I picked up my purse and followed. Before I could say thank you, his arms were around me, filling me with a feeling I had missed so much since I had left. Security. There was nothing like it, I thought. The knowledge that everything is taken care of and all you have to do is relax into the moment. I figured that must be what heaven is like. I gave Daddy a kiss on the cheek and let myself out. The burden has been lifted, I thought, walking back to the car. But when I got inside, Xavier's essence pierced me and I was confused all over again. I didn't know exactly how to feel and at that moment I didn't want to feel. I took Hoover toward Slauson, this time driving more slowly. I was in no rush to get back home to find Dakota and Craig, sprawled out all over the couch, and I definitely wasn't going back to Xavier.

I turned on the radio but barely heard a thing. I can't remember what song was playing, but I know it sounded odd. And at that moment I began to feel odd. Like I had to shake something off of me. I drove for another block or two with this feeling until I came to a red light at Vermont and Exposition. I didn't see it coming. Didn't hear a sound. All I know is that the windows of the car were crashing in all around me. I slumped down and pressed the gas pedal to the floor. I didn't even look at the road until the car had moved through the intersection. Then I heard gun shots bouncing off the hood of the car. The whole car shook and fell down on one side and dragged the ground. I was afraid to look up but I knew I had to see where I was going. When I did, I saw a body hanging out of a car from across the street. His hand was still pumping the barrel of the gun. "This is T-Bone, mothafucka. Don't you ever forget who you fucking with. Cross Street gangsta Crip, fool. You know how we do it."

The last thing I remembered was the barrel of that gun pointing directly at my face.

chapter eighteen

seek and ye shall find

Bobby couldn't remember what day it was when he managed to lug himself off the stool at the Palmetto Bar. He couldn't remember how long he had been there or just how he had gotten there. All he knew was that his head was killing him and he had to go to the men's room. He barely made it into the stall before he started throwing up. He knelt down on the floor in front of the toilet and convulsed until it was all out, then got up and wiped his mouth with the back of his hand. He went to the sink to wash his face and when he looked in the mirror, he saw his nose was bleeding. He smeared the blood with his finger and held it underneath the stream of water. The sight of blood made his stomach cringe. He knew he had reached his limit; still, he wanted another hit. He fumbled through his pockets in search of the tiny Ziploc bag, but when he found it, it was empty. Now he was mad as well as sick. He turned the bag inside out and ran his tongue across it trying to pick up any traces of white powder that were left. He wasn't satisfied with the thought of having no cocaine. He stumbled out of the men's room and found a pay phone and paged his supplier. The phone rang less than a minute after he put it down. "I'm coming by to pick up a fix. You got some handy? Good. I'm on my way."

He made it outside and somehow found his car and got in. His whole body was screaming, but there was nothing he could do. This is all Timbers' fault, he thought, and started his car. He could barely keep his head up straight and as he drove, the car jerked from side to side and he hoped he wouldn't get pulled over. To be stopped by the cops before he had a chance to score some blow was the last thing he needed. He stopped at the intersection of Palms and Overland and snapped his head from side to side. What am I supposed to do now, he thought, and turned right on Sepulveda. He tried to figure everything out, but nothing seemed to make sense. It all must be some sick joke, he concluded, feeling a sudden spurt of confidence. He refused to worry himself about it. Mr. Timbers was no fool. He'd realize what a big mistake he'd made, and by the end of the day he'd be calling, begging Bobby to forgive him and come back to work. He'd have to give the presidency to Bobby now. After the big mistake he'd made in firing him, he'd have to do something pretty drastic to ensure that Bobby would come back to work for him. Timbers will come to his senses, Bobby thought. He was certain he'd be back at work tomorrow.

Still, Bobby needed something to take the pain away—an aspirin or some type of nerve deadener. He searched his pockets again, but all he came up with was a chocolate mint that he hurriedly stuck in his mouth. What he needed was Jazmine, he thought. She'd be able to take his sting away. The image of her played in his mind. He pictured her onstage accepting a Grammy. She would be in tears and the first person she'd thank would be Bobby Strong—the man she owed her career to. He wanted badly to see her. So bad that his body ached for her, but he wasn't really sure if it was for her or because he needed another fix. He knew for sure that if he could just see her, everything would be okay. If he could just have her close enough, all his pain would disappear. But even in his intoxicated state, he knew that would never happen. Jazmine wouldn't want him now. Nobody did. Not Sheryl, not his daughters, not Mr. Timbers, his mother, his father—and certainly not Jazmine.

. . .

I had been calling Jazmine's apartment every ten minutes, but Dakota kept saying she wasn't home. Finally, I just told Dakota what had happened. Well, I told her we had an argument and asked her if she would come pick me up from the studio. Dakota started to freak out then. She thought Jazmine might have done something really stupid like tried to kill herself or something, but I told her to just calm down. Jazmine wasn't crazy, although when she left here she was on the edge of losing it.

I stood outside the studio and waited for Dakota to pull up in her car. When I saw her coming down the street I ran up to the car and opened the passenger side door before she even had a chance to come to a complete stop. "What the hell did you do to her?" she yelled at me. I didn't want to get into it with her. I was too concerned about where Jazmine had disappeared to.

"Don't start, D, we gots to find Jazmine. Just drive the fucking car."

"I don't know where to go," she said, throwing up her hands.

"She ain't called you at all?"

"No, she hasn't called, idiot. Don't you think I would have said something by now? I left Craig at the apartment in case she tries to get in touch with me and I gave him your pager number to call as soon as she gets in."

"Who's Craig?"

"Shut the fuck up, Xavier," she said, turning her head away from me. "Just tell me where to go." When she turned back around she was crying, and I didn't know what that was all about, but then again, I didn't give a shit. I had to find my baby.

We decided to drive over to her father's house. It was the only place we thought she would go, but when we got to his house we didn't see my car anywhere around, so we just kept driving.

"If she was so upset, why did you let her go off by herself?" Dakota said, coming to a screeching halt at a stop sign.

"Would you shut up? I'm trying to think." I didn't know where to go after that and Craig, whoever that was, hadn't paged me, which meant Jazmine was still nowhere to be found. On a whim, I told Dakota to drive in the direction of Rich's house. I knew Jazmine wouldn't be over there, but at least I could put my head together with my homeboy and try to find out where my baby disappeared to.

When we turned on to Rich's street there were four police cars lined up in front of his house. I felt relieved when I didn't see my car anywhere around, but still I wanted to know what the fuck was going on.

"Where the hell you got me?" Dakota screamed.

"Just pull up behind that black-and-white," I said and put my hand on the door to get out. I stood up and walked across the lawn and saw Rich sitting in his wheelchair on the porch. He acted like he was gonna jump out his seat when he saw me walking up the steps.

"Damn, X. You a'ight? I thought yo ass would be laid up in some hospital, man."

"What the fuck you talking about?"

"Man, I thought you was dead, homeboy. They taking T-Bone's ass to jail right now. There he go, in the back of that black-and-white. You sure you a'ight?"

"Yeah, man. Just tell me what the fuck is going on."

"Where your car?"

"What?"

"Man, T-Bone rolled over here, talking mucho shit. He said he capped yo ass. Put ten or twelve bullets in your car. Said he took yo ass out over there on Exposition Boulevard. He came speeding through here talking about can he hide in my backyard. But it was over fo him. The cops showed up right after he did and beat that nigga to a pulp. They just finished up here. His ass is going to the pen fo sho."

"Where's Jazmine?"

"Where's who?"

"Jazmine, man. She was driving the car, not me."

"Your woman was in the car?"

"Yeah, man. Where the fuck is the phone?"

"Right here, brother. Use the portable."

I couldn't dial Jazmine's number fast enough. A man's voice picked up the other end. "Who dis?—I mean where's Jazmine?"

"It's Craig. Jazmine still hasn't made it home."

"She ain't even called yet?"

"Not a word. I checked with the police station, the hospitals—nothing."

"Damn," I shouted and hung up the phone. "Where the fuck is she?" I said and looked to Rich as if he had the answer. "The police don't know and she ain't at the hospital."

"Yo, man," Rich said, thinking hard. "You better check over there on Exposition. That's where T-Bone said it all happened."

T-Bone, I thought, and turned toward the police cars, but they were already filing out. I was mad as hell that I didn't get a chance to see T-Bone's face as they took him off to jail. That mothafucka better hope nothing happened to my baby, or I would make sure his ass got what was coming to him. I know a gang of niggas in the pen. All I have to do is say the word and that fool can be dealt with real quick.

I was just about to get back in the car and head over to Exposition, when a green Range Rover pulled up into the driveway. I wouldn't have paid it any attention if it hadn't swerved so much that it almost nipped the back of Dakota's car. Rich had a lot of people stopping by at all times of the day and night to buy a quick fix. I glanced inside the car to get a good look at the person I was about to throw up my middle finger at. It was Bobby Strong. I had been longing to fuck that nigga up ever since Jazmine told me what he had done to Dakota. I knew he was probably trying the same thing with Jazmine too. But I was in a rush to get to my baby. I knew she needed me. But it was too late. Dakota caught a glimpse of him from her rearview mirror and before I could stop her she was out the car and heading toward Bobby.

"This asshole probably did something to her," Dakota said, reaching out for the doorknob of Bobby's car. I tried to tell her that Jazmine was okay and that she was waiting for us back at the apartment, but I couldn't get the words out fast enough. Dakota opened his door and practically dragged Bobby's limp body out the car. I could tell he was already high off something 'cause Dakota was able to pull him with no effort. He was fucked and his lifeless body just rolled around on the ground as Dakota kicked at his ribs and chest.

"Get her before she kills him," Rich said, rolling down the ramp toward us. He was laughing, and I might have laughed too, the scene was funny as hell, but I was too ready to get home to my girlfriend. I grabbed Dakota by the arm and she jerked away from me and kept kicking Bobby. "How does it feel, Bobby? You ain't in control no more, are you?" she said, kicking away. I finally grabbed her from behind with both hands and dragged her back to the car. "We got to go find Jazz. Now!" I told her and put her sweaty body into the passenger's side. Before I could get around to the driver's side she had rolled the window down, stuck half her body out, and started cussing Bobby out again.

He managed to get back up to his feet. He grabbed his rib cage and fell against his car. "Hey, X-Man," he called to me, panting and out of breath. "You want a piece of me too?"

I didn't have time to respond. I had to get back to Jazmine. But if I could have responded, I would have walked right up to that fool and chin checked him to the curb. Don't nobody fuck with my peoples and get away with it. I don't give a fuck who they are. Or, in Bobby's case—were.

chapter nineteen

seeing the
light

When I saw that gun pointed at me I nearly fainted. All I really remember was the sound of the tires burning rubber as I blazed away. I don't know how I made it home, but I did. I hunched down in the seat and slammed my foot on the gas. I never even looked up to see where I was driving until I was far enough away that I couldn't hear the sound of bullets anymore. I never took my foot completely off the pedal until I got to my neighborhood. If I came to a red light, I'd ease up a little until the coast was clear, then speed right on through. Or if an intersection was too crowded, I'd hook a turn and keep going. My heart could've pounded right out of my chest and when I stopped the car around the corner from my apartment, I grabbed between my breasts as if I were trying to keep my heart on the inside of my body. I got out of the car and sat down on the sidewalk and tried to catch my breath. Why was all this shit happening to me? I mean, I'm a good person, I pray every day, every night. I try to be the best I can be . . . I just don't get this shit. "God?" I yelled at the top of my voice. "What the hell are you trying to do to me?"

I sat on the curb for close to an hour until I finally got up enough strength to get back into the car and drive the rest of the way home. It took forever to get up to the apartment, it seemed. I opened the front door widely before I stepped in. Craig ran up to me and grabbed me by the arm. "Where the hell have you been?" I wanted to tell him to get the fuck out of my home, but all I could do was try to make it to the couch before I passed out. "What happened? Are you okay? Everybody's been going crazy trying to find you. So are you okay? Talk to me."

Just get out of my face, I wanted to scream. I had been through hell and I didn't want to explain anything just yet, least of all to Craig. I looked around and waited for Dakota to come sauntering out, but no one else was there. "What are you doing here?"

"I stayed here to wait for you. Dakota is out with Xavier looking for you."

Yeah right, she's probably off fucking him, just like she did you. And knowing Xavier, he was enjoying every second of it. I wanted to go to my room and hide under my bed, but Craig just kept going with the questions. He wouldn't stop until he got the whole truth. "I almost got killed. Okay. That's what happened. That's where I've been. In a drive-by. Anything else you want to know?" Craig didn't know what to say or do after that. The idiot started feeling my forehead like I had a fever. I guess he was satisfied that I didn't have a nasty head cold because the next thing he did was pick up the cordless and call the police station.

"I need some guys over here ASAP. I want to report an attempted murder. . . ." He gave the person on the phone my address and hung up. "You okay? Let me get you some water," he said and dashed off to the kitchen. He came back and hovered over me with the glass and I just stared up at him and refused to take it. Who did he think he was fooling, with this concerned role he was playing? He wasn't concerned about me when he decided to get involved with Dakota. He wasn't concerned when he sat me down in that coffee shop and rocked my world by telling me he was getting married. Craig could inhale a fat bullet as far as I was concerned. I wasn't taking anything he offered, even if it was only water.

He sat the glass down in front of me on the coffee table and took a seat across from me. "You want to tell me what happened?"

"No, I don't. You can leave now," I said, finding the strength to hold my hand out toward the door.

"Look, I'm not leaving you like this. Not at least until someone gets here to take care of you."

"Someone like who? Dakota? Or better yet, Xavier? Fuck all of you. You all can choke on spit and die." The words nuzzled up in my head before I could get them out. I had to stop and take a deep breath. I didn't have the strength to say anything more.

I heard rumbling outside in the hallway and in a flash, Xavier and Dakota came busting through the door, looking like a pair of thieves who'd just pulled off a major jewelry heist. "Jazmine!" Dakota wailed and plopped down next to me on the couch. "My poor Jazmine," she said and grabbed my neck and gave me a stiff hug. I pulled away from her and got up. I shot Xavier a look that stopped him dead in his tracks. He knew he had better not come any closer to me, not while the memory of what had happened at the studio was still so fresh in my mind.

"You, you, and you," I said, pointing at each of them. "All of you can kiss my freckled ass. I don't need any of you," I said, wearily walking toward my room. I stood at the doorway to my room and turned around to face them. "With friends like you, I don't need enemies."

I heard the police when they came in, but I didn't go out into the front. I could barely sit up straight on my bed, let alone go out there and rehash the whole incident in front of strangers. All I could remember was the sound of the gunshots plastering that car and the sight of that light-skinned guy hanging out the other car with that gun pointed in my direction. Revenge showed all over his face. How the hell did I get mixed up in this shit? I had made it over twenty years living in South-Central without getting pulled down by gang life. I sat next to guys in high school who had killed their best friends, girls who had stabbed the fathers of their children, but I had made it through unscathed—until now. And why now? Why, when I'm on the verge of making my dreams come true, is this happening to me? My dream was becoming a nightmare and it was all because of Xavier. How could I be so stupid as to fall in love with a street thug like that? A guy who would get a girl pregnant then walk out on her. A guy who people hated so much that they would shoot up his car to try to kill him. This is what happens when you get involved with gangsters. I don't care how successful they get or how much money they rake in, they're still gangsters at heart. And they still can't shake the pull of the streets. I was so stupid to think Xavier would be any different. They're all the same. All out for number one, forget anybody else. It's all about them and how much money they can make for slanging cocaine or how much respect they can get from killing another brother or how much of a man they are if they get a girl pregnant. It's all a bunch of bullshit. But they're too stupid to see that. Xavier is the biggest fool of all, thinking he could change who he is by getting a record contract. Nothing's ever going to change for him. Ten years from now he'll be a has-been, back on the corner selling rocks, with that fat girl and bald-headed baby by his side, talking about, "Remember me? I used to be a rapper." His life is going to be a bunch of used to's. Starting with he used to have a girlfriend named Jazmine. I don't know who he thinks I am, but I want more out of life than being stuck with some low-life street punk who's never going to change and being a stepmother to some illegitimate baby. No. I'm not having it. I've come too far to blow it away now. The first thing I'm going to do is move out on my own. By that time my album should be in the stores and I'll be home free. Nothing's going to stop me now. I've made up my mind. If I'm going to do this, it's going to be on my own. No Xavier, no Dakota, no Daddy, no Bobby Strong. Just me. Making it by myself.

.   .   .

I stood outside Jazmine's bedroom door for the longest, thinking of what I could possibly say to make things better. But there was nothing I could say. Sorry wasn't enough. I had put her through hell. It wasn't enough to shock the shit out of her by telling her another girl was about to have my baby. No, I had to go and almost get her killed by letting her drive around in my car alone. If I could take it all back I would, but life ain't no David Copperfield show. You gotta live with the decisions you make. And I had to admit, I had made some fucked-up decisions in my life. But none so fucked up as what I had put Jazmine through. I had tried so hard to chill out. Change my stupid ways and live right. But them damn streets won't leave a nigga like me alone. They always creep up when you least expect it and drag you right back down into the gutter. I laid my head against her door, closed my eyes, and hoped she'd give me a chance to talk to her before she threw me out. I opened the door and found her sitting on the edge of her bed. She didn't even turn to look at me. "Get out, Xavier," she said with her back to me. I closed the door behind me and walked to the bed and sat down on the other end.

"I know you don't want to hear a word I have to say and I don't blame you. But just let me try to explain."

"Explain what, Xavier? Just what do you think you could possibly say that I want to hear?"

"I'm sorry."

"You're sorry?" she repeated, laughing. She laughed so hard she almost choked. "You know who I feel sorry for? That baby. That poor little baby who's going to have a father like you to look up to. A father that doesn't even want him. A father that's so deep in the streets that people want to see him dead."

"Jazmine, I can't even start to tell you how sorry I am about tonight. That nigga T-Bone ain't nothing but a jealous motha—"

"It's always somebody else, Xavier. It's never you. Because of you, I was almost killed tonight." She paused only to catch her breath. "What a wonderful father you're gonna make."

"What can I do? I didn't tell her to go and get pregnant."

She laughed heartily again. "So it's all her fault, huh? You didn't have anything to do with it. You're the victim, huh, Xavier? I almost wish one of those bullets would have caught me. At least then I'd be unconscious in a hospital somewhere and I wouldn't have to listen to your bullshit."

"Don't say that, Jazmine." Why was she saying that? I loved her, I didn't even want to think about what could have happened. I wanted to grab her and hold her and tell her everything would be all right. But I couldn't. I had already messed things up past the point of return. My head was hanging so low that I thought it was gonna drop off my neck. I couldn't help myself, I couldn't help Jazmine. And I couldn't stop the tears that were streaming out of my eyes.

"I want you to leave me alone," she said and finally turned to face me. She was unaffected by my tears, she didn't care about my pain. I guess hers was too great to notice mine.

"This isn't like you."

"Hmm. What's not like me?" She squinted her eyes at me. There was no fear in her face, no timidness, no shame. "You expect me to back down, Xavier? Give in? Take you back?" she said, shaking her head. "Not this time, X-Man. I'm strong now. You have yourself to thank for that."

I got up and walked out the room. I couldn't bring myself to close the door behind me as I left. I walked slowly back to the living room, hoping that at any minute she'd call out my name and ask me to come back. I slugged all the way to the front door, but she never made a sound. It was over. That much was obvious. But why it had to end like this, I'll never know.

chapter twenty

advanced ghettoize

"Come on in," Rich told Bobby as he rolled his wheelchair backward to make room for Bobby to step through the doorway.

"You got some stuff for me?" Bobby asked anxiously and took a seat on the couch.

"Yeah, I got some stuff for you," Rich said, wheeling himself toward Bobby. Out of nowhere, he pulled a gun and stuck it to Bobby's head. "Oh, I got somethin' fo yo ass a'ight."

"What the fuck?" Bobby yelled, leaning back into the cushions. "You crazy or something?"

"Naw, I ain't crazy, but you must be," Rich said, smiling. "I heard you was messing with my homeboy's girl and her friend," Rich said, cocking the gun against Bobby's head and holding up a bag of coke in front of his face. "You a good customer and all, but I'd hate to have to smoke yo ass for fucking with my peoples," he said, then wiped the smile off his face. "If my boy ever tell me about you fucking with his girl again, I swear I'll kill yo punk-ass myself."

Bobby hadn't heard everything Rich said. He was too scared and too busy eyeing the cocaine that was staring him in the face. Still he got the gist, and promised to stay away from Jazmine. It was only a promise, Bobby thought. He would have said anything to get his hands on that bag Rich held in front of him.

Finally, Rich put down the gun and threw the plastic bag at Bobby's face. Relieved, Bobby picked it up and opened it.

"Ain't you forgettin' somethin', fool?"

"Sorry," Bobby said and handed Rich a wad of money, then turned his attention back to the plastic bag.

Bobby was unaware of how much time had passed until Rich wheeled himself over to him and shook him by the arm. "You gonna have ta raise up outta here in a minute, my man," Rich said. "This ain't no mothafucking Holiday Inn."

"Just let me get one more hit," Bobby said and folded a piece of foil in half. He sat in the middle of Rich's living room and prepared his final fix. Rich had run out of coke and now Bobby was doing some heroin Rich had sold him for half price. He peeled the heroin off the tiny piece of paper Rich handed him and stuck it underneath the foil, then lit a match to it and sucked up the smoke. His head rolled round after the fog had seeped into his body, and all he could think of in his state was Jazmine and if she was okay. While Bobby got high, Rich told him about the big commotion that had gone on earlier, but Bobby's dazed mind could only remember bits and pieces. There was no mistaking the fact that Rich had said Jazmine had been caught in a case of mistaken identity and that she was nearly killed while driving Xavier's car. He had warned her to stay away from that thug. He was only trouble. Now, Bobby thought, she should see what he meant. She didn't need trouble like that. She needed a man who loved her and would take care of her. A man like Bobby Strong, he thought, trying to keep his head upright.

Bobby's vision started to blur, and he thought he was hallucinating when he saw a vision of what he thought was Jazmine walking through the door. He shook his head fiercely and focused. The vision he saw was definitely not Jazmine.

"What y'all doing up at this hour?" the woman said, and walked over to Rich and gave him a kiss on the mouth.

"Just handling my business," Rich said, and patted the woman's ass.

"Who's that?"

"A customer, baby."

"Well, what he doing over here this early?"

"It ain't never too early when you washed up like this dude."

Bobby's head warbled loosely. Who was he calling washed up? he thought, as the room began to spin.

"Git this smoka outta here," she said, looking down at him with a grimace on her face.

"I told you, man. You gots ta raise up," Rich yelled.

I'm going, Bobby thought he said. He also thought he had gotten up, but realized he hadn't moved when the woman started cursing at him.

"He leaving, baby damn. Calm down. Let me tell you what happened tonight. T-Bone gonna be doing some serious time. That fool tried to pull a drive-by on X."

"On X!" she shouted and grabbed her stomach. "No, he didn't kill my X!"

"What? *Your* X?"

"Uh, I mean, is X okay?"

"Yeah, he a'ight. He wasn't in the car. But what you getting so upset about? You act like X is yo man or somethin'."

"I ain't acting like he my man, Rich. I'm just concerned about him," she said, spinning her neck around on her shoulders.

"Well, I'm just saying. Yo ass wasn't even this concerned when my black ass got locked up before."

"Fuck you, Rich. You ain't X."

"So what's that supposed to mean?"

"Fuck it. You wanna know the truth?" she said, patting her big belly. "I'm pregnant and we all know you didn't have nothing to do with it." She put her hands on her hips and bent down in Rich's face. "This is X's baby."

Bobby couldn't take any more of the noise. His head had begun to pound again, and when he saw Rich slap the woman's face, he knew that was his cue to leave. He scrambled up to his knees and patted around the floor for his keys. The new morning sun hit his face hard when he stepped out onto the porch. He could still hear them arguing as he closed the door on his car. He fought to get the key in the ignition and when he finally started it up, he zoomed out like lightning. He had to see Jazmine himself and make sure she was okay. He was the only one who really cared about her, the only one who really loved her. And now, he had to show her just how much.

· · ·

Driving and drinking, drinking and driving. That's all I been doing since I left Jazmine's apartment. Don't wanna go home, fuck the studio, fuck it all. Everything's turned upside-down and I don't know how to get it back the right way. Every time I look at the bullet holes in the door or on the hood of the car, I think about Jazmine and the fact that she coulda almost died tonight. Because of me. I stopped at the liquor store and picked up three more forties, got back in my fucked-up car, and kept driving. It was strange but the longer I drove, the closer I kept getting to Rich's house. I guess it was only inevitable. I had been running to him when I had a problem for as long as I could remember. He always had a way of putting things in perspective for me and if that didn't work he always had a gun close by. Guns always come in handy when you dealing in the streets. I wasn't even thinking about Eyeisha no more. I figured I had time to deal with that situation for the rest of my life. I knew she wouldn't open her mouth to Rich just yet. That fool would go ballistic on her if she told him she was having my baby and besides, I thought she got a kick out of keeping it a secret. In a sick sort of way it made her feel closer to me. Like we shared a bond.

I opened another forty and made my way down Rich's block. If nothing else, I could just sit with him and think. About what, I didn't know. I was way past thinking about the situation. Thinking was something I shoulda done a long time ago, before I decided to get in bed with Eyeisha. By the time I pulled up into his driveway, I was so fucked up that I could barely stand. Part of the reason was that I was so damn drained. My body was worn to the bone and I basically just wanted to sit with my forty and zone out. I heard Rich ranting and raving before I made it to the door. That nigga was always talking loud about something, like the louder he spoke the more people would understand. I opened the door and that fool got as silent as a cockroach. I came in and sat my bottle down on the table. I slouched down on the couch and closed my eyes. Maybe Rich would be able to make me feel better. If not he'd at least get drunk with me and help me forget. I opened my eyes and looked at Rich. He was sitting in his chair in the middle of the floor just watching me and I couldn't figure out what that nigga was tripping off of. Then Eyeisha came switching into the room and when she saw me, she stopped and stared too. I didn't even have to ask questions, I knew the only thing that could have happened was that she must of opened her big mouth. Eyeisha moved back against the wall as if she was scared to be in the same room with me and Rich. I sat up straight on the couch and waited for somebody, anybody, to say something. I had thought this would be the hardest part when Rich found out, but I had been through so much already that all I wanted was for him to curse me out, throw things at me, and get it over with. Then at least everything would be out in the open and I could go home, lock myself in my apartment, and sink lower into the depression that was setting in. Rich still didn't say a word for the longest time. He just moved his eyes back and forth between me and Eyeisha. And I don't know what came over her, 'cause she just broke out crying like a baby and walked over to the table and picked up my forty and took a long swig.

"I don't care what you do, Rich," she said, cradling the bottle in her arms. "I'm having X's baby and that's final."

"Shut the fuck up, bitch. This ain't about you no more," he said and re-fixed his glare on me. "This is between us boys."

"Look, man," I said, talking carefully so he wouldn't get madder than what he already was. "I don't know what to say. It happened. It happened that night after the party. I thought our friendship was over. Eyeisha was pumping all sorts of madness in my head. Didn't nobody plan for this to happen, man."

Rich just shook his head and looked like he was thinking real hard about something. "Didn't I always look out for you, man?"

I didn't respond. I didn't know what to say.

"Didn't I?"

"Yeah."

"Didn't I always tell you I'd take care of you when you needed me?"

"Yeah."

"So why you do this to me? Why you stab me in the back like this?"

What was I supposed to say? I already told him I fucked up. What did he want to hear me say?

"Why, man? Why you go behind my back and take my girl?"

"I ain't your girl," Eyeisha jumped in. "You ain't about shit. What makes your crippled ass think I'd want to be with you for the rest of my life? What can you do for me in that wheelchair? You can't even get it up no more." She was leaning down and talking directly in Rich's face and all

I could figure was that she musta ate a giant bowl of Wheaties that morning 'cause she was acting like Superwoman.

Rich reached out and grabbed her by the neck with one hand, and I didn't know whether to jump in and stop him or just sit back and watch. Eyeisha deserved everything she got, but still she was a woman and I couldn't let her get beat down right in front of my face. I got up off the couch to stop them, but Rich pushed her back and pulled out a gun from between his legs. "What the fuck you gonna do, partner?" he said, pointing the gun at me. I backed up and concentrated on the barrel of the gun. Part of me wished he'd just pull the trigger, that way we could all be done with this mess. It would have been the perfect ending. I could picture myself moving backward like in *Scarface* when they pumped that fool full of lead at the end of that movie. What a dope way to go out.

When Eyeisha caught her balance she ran over to me. "You better not shoot him," she said, throwing her sweaty arms around me. I wanted to jerk her off of me, but I didn't want to move too suddenly and agitate Rich. I carefully pushed her away with one hand and calmly turned to Rich.

"Think about what you're doing, man. It ain't worth it. *I* ain't worth it."

"What the fuck do I got to lose? Look at me. Do I look like I give a damn about what happens to me? And I sho don't give a damn about neither one of y'all no more."

Eyeisha was crying and shaking against the wall. "Stop it, Rich," she kept screaming. I don't know what got into that girl, but out of the corner of my eye I could see her moving toward Rich. Before I could reach out to stop her, she lunged at the gun in Rich's hand and tried to twist it away from him. The gun went off and a bullet flew past my head and hit the wall behind me. Rich swung out with both hands and knocked Eyeisha backward against the big-screen television as the gun dropped to the floor and went off again. I quickly bent down and picked it up. Eyeisha slid down to the floor holding her stomach and convulsing. She was screaming at the top of her lungs. Rich wheeled himself over to her and I ran to stop him. I pulled his chair back and stood between the two of them. Eyeisha couldn't stop screaming. She was hunched over on the floor and blood was gushing out the back of her head.

"My stomach," Eyeisha screamed. "Something's wrong with my baby."

I bent down to help her up, but she couldn't move. "Call 911!" I shouted to Rich, but he didn't move one inch. I got up and found the portable and dialed it myself.

"That's what happens when you fuck with the wrong man," Rich said, hovering over her crumpled body. "You fucked with the wrong nigga this time, bitch."

I sat down with Eyeisha on the floor and waited for the paramedics, but they were taking forever and she couldn't stop yelling. It didn't help that Rich kept cussing at her and threatening her. He didn't say too much to me though and I couldn't figure out why. It was partly my fault too, but he didn't dwell on that. It was strange. It was almost like he didn't blame me at all. I wanted him to lash out at me too. I was feeling too good about myself and I wanted him to make me feel bad. But he didn't say a word to me. In a sick way I knew this had something to do with the gang. We had made a vow to stick together. We was family and nothing could tear us apart. That's what it meant to be in a gang. Once you were in, you were in for life. I looked at Rich with a mixture of disgust and admiration. At least he was loyal to something. Me, I wasn't shit.

I went to the hospital with Eyeisha. They kept her there all day after they found out she miscarried. I poked my head in the room a couple times, but she was knocked out. I looked at her limp body lying on that bed and thought, this is what I caused. I couldn't understand it. I had tried so hard to do things the right way, but the more I tried the more I kept fucking up. I fucked up her life, Rich's life, and worse of all, Jazmine's life. I wasn't fit for nothing. I'd never be anything more than a street hood. My music career seemed like a lost dream. What was the point in trying to make it out the hood? There was no way out. Once you were in, you were in, and nothing you did could change what you were. I wasn't shit. I knew it in my heart. I felt it in my pores. My movie was over. There'd be no sequel.

chapter twenty-one

amazing
grace

I stood in the mirror, brushing my hair, hoping I'd have the apartment to myself for at least another hour. I didn't know if I had done the right thing, but I felt as if a hundred pounds had been lifted off my head. I was tired of carrying burdens and I was at a time in my life that all I wanted was to be carefree. I didn't want to think about Daddy, Dakota, Bobby, or Xavier. I wanted to concentrate on me. And damn it, I deserved a little peace. I had gotten to the point where I felt capable for the first time. Capable of handling my career and capable of handling my life. And I could do it all on my own. Fuck everybody else. Family and friends are much too overrated. They only cause problems, or let you down, or add to problems that are already big enough. And that goes double for men. The only man I can count on is God, and I wouldn't be surprised if He turns out to be a She. I had totally lost my faith in men. What is it with them? I mean, I have yet to find one who's human and not hell-bent on controlling, lying, cheating, or otherwise being just plain stupid. From now on I'm putting the men in my life to a test. No one gets past stage one with me unless they first prove that they have some humility. I wanna see them cry. And not those fake-ass tears Xavier tried to pull on me earlier. No, I wanna see real tears. If a man can't cry then he can't have a heart. I used to think that if a man had a sense of humor that meant he had a heart, but now I see it takes more than a punch line to prove that a man is decent. I want to see more.

A tear, a sniffle—heck, anything to prove to me that he's more than just another macho dog on the prowl. And sex is a no-no for at least six months. You give a man your body and he thinks he's God. And oral sex is totally out of the question. Once they do that to you they know they've got you hooked. That's right, it's gonna take more than a slick tongue and a perfectly placed finger to impress me from now on.

I was so sure Xavier was the one to break the mold. How could I have been so ignorant? I figured just because he worshipped me that he would be good to me. But look at us now. All fucked up. I should have listened to Dakota when she told me not to get mixed up with him. I didn't want to believe that people couldn't change. Who cares, I thought, where a person comes from or how they lived their life until they met you? What does that have to do with how they're gonna treat you? But now I see. Xavier couldn't shake that ghetto mentality. I don't care how many records he sells, he'll still be nothing more than a ghetto bird. I think he likes it that way. How could he come in here and tell me that he was going to change? He had said that before and I sure as hell wasn't falling for it again. I don't care if that stupid girl had a miscarriage or not. So what? He was still the father of that baby, he still lied to me about it, and he still won't take responsibility for it. Who needs that? Next time, it'll be me who comes up pregnant and what then? He'll probably say it's not his. Black men never take responsibility for their kids. They just make 'em and move on.

And how dare he try to make me feel guilty by crying? Well, he was one tear too late. Just how stupid and gullible does he think I am? I hope he knows now that I'm nobody's fool.

What I need to do is focus on self. What does Jazmine want? That's an overloaded question if I ever heard one. I know what I need is to finally do things on my own. That's why the first chance I get, I'm moving into my own place. I saw some great locations listed in the paper and I'm making enough money now to move out. And that's exactly what I'm gonna do. I need solitude. A place where I can be alone and think. A place where I feel secure enough to be myself, where I can make my own decisions without anybody else butting their fat heads in. Besides, ever since Dakota started dating again, this place has gotten a little too crowded. I need my own space. Life pushes on.

What I don't understand is why it has to be like this. Why couldn't

Xavier be true? I thought for sure that we'd make it last. I knew I'd be better off without him, but I wondered if I had been too hard on him. I mean, yes he had gotten that girl pregnant. But that was before he had even met me. How could I fault him for something he didn't even have control over? I know why. Because he did have control over it. He could have put on a condom. He could have avoided all of this by keeping his zipper up. He made a bad choice, a stupid choice. But is it his fault that he's stupid? What kind of question is that? But really, is it his fault that he was born into a world that would ultimately control him? What if he had been born in Bel-Air? He probably wouldn't have made the same choices. I don't know if a person should be faulted for living under circumstances that are out of their control. "Damn it!" I screamed and threw the brush against the mirror. I'm confused again.

I felt myself wanting him and I couldn't throw off the feeling. All I know is that he tried. And in my book that's worth a whole hell of a lot. He tried to make a difference in his life. Most people don't do half as much as he did to better themselves. He had a dream, he worked hard at it, and if it wasn't for one stupid mistake he'd be right here. With me. I had an urge to go over to his apartment, but I thought it would be better to call first. I didn't know what to say though. "I'm sorry I told you to get the fuck out of my life. I was just playing." That wouldn't cut it. I knew I had hurt him. Hell, I told him he was no more than a common hood. I made him feel like dirt. Now I felt like dirt. Then I decided to just let him come back to me. If he really wanted to be with me, he'd realize that I was just distraught when I said all those things to him. I was confused and talking out the side of my neck. He should know that. Right?

I decided to take a shower and if he hadn't called by the time I got out, I'd switch to plan B and call him. But when I finished showering, the phone hadn't rung and although I wanted to hear his voice, I couldn't bring myself to pick up the phone. Then the intercom buzzed and I knew it was him. Plan A worked out just fine. I didn't even ask who it was, I felt in my heart it was my man. Something inside me said, don't ask questions, just buzz him up. And that's what I did. I wrapped a towel around me and went to the door. My man was back, and this time I wasn't letting him go.

. . .

That was easy, Bobby thought, swallowing the last of the Raisinets he had stuck in his mouth. She must have known it was him, since she buzzed open the gate so readily, he thought. He knew Jazmine had only been playing games up until now. She wanted him just as bad as he wanted her, and who could blame her? He was still Bobby Strong. No one could take that away from him.

He took the elevator up to the fifth floor and there she was. She looked so happy to see him, so glad that he had come back to her. He quickened his steps as he got closer to the door and when she tried to close it, he became amused. Another one of her games, he thought. And how sexy. He leaned on the door with all his weight until it flung back against the wall and he was in. He smiled at her and took out a handkerchief from his pocket. He wiped his nose and threw it on the floor. "Jazmine, Jazmine. Still playing hard to get, huh? That's cute, really cute, but playtime's over."

"Bobby," she said hesitantly and held up a pretty little hand. "Just turn around and leave. *Please.*"

"And you dressed up for me, I see. Terry cloth has always been my favorite." He shook his head from side to side. The mixture of drugs he had taken earlier was making his vision blurry, and he didn't want to miss a single second of the lovely vision in front of him. "Come here, Jazmine. Come to Daddy," he said, reaching out for her hand. Jazmine backed up and pulled the towel around her tightly. Bobby felt himself growing. How dainty his timid angel looked. He couldn't wait to hold her in his arms for the first time. "What's the matter? Don't back away from me. Come here."

"Get out!" she screamed and began to shake all over. She didn't know that she was only turning Bobby on more. He couldn't stand the tension any longer and grabbed out for her. The drugs had him groggy, but he held on to her even as she squirmed and tried to get loose. "Jazmine, Jazmine, Jazmine," was all he could say. "Sing me a song."

She could only cry, and when she did, her body seemed to relax into his. He kissed her neck and whispered again, "Sing me a song."

Bobby was beginning to get agitated. Games were okay, but he wanted what he wanted and it was taking too long to get it. "Sing, damn it!" he shouted into her face. He held her by the shoulders in front of him and shook her. "Now!"

Jazmine's head leaned back and she closed her eyes and began to stutter. "Am . . . amazing grace . . . how . . . how sweet the sssound."

That was better, Bobby thought. He pulled her to him and began to sway. Her tears stained his shirt, her trembles made him feel strong. "Don't be afraid, Jazmine. I won't hurt you. I love you."

They swayed together in the middle of the floor for what seemed an eternity. He loosened his grip and slid his hands down her back. The towel was making him too hot, so he flung it to the floor. Jazmine gasped, but didn't stop singing. She closed her eyes tighter. "I once, was lost . . ."

Her voice rang through Bobby's head as he caressed her back. He ran his hand over her hair and kissed her cheek, then her mouth. Jazmine continued to sing. He eased her down to the floor and covered her body with his. What a sweet, beautiful girl, he thought, as he began to undress himself. He scanned her body from head to toe as she lay there on the floor, eyes closed, singing her heart out.

When he returned to her, he kissed her forehead, her nose, and her eyelids. This was the moment he had been waiting for. If he hadn't taken so many drugs, he would have taken his time with her and absorbed every luscious minute of their first encounter, but he couldn't. He was ready for her now, and besides, there would be time for long intimate moments later. He had her now and he wasn't letting her go. He pushed her thighs apart with his knees and listened to her calming voice. But the more he listened, the less calm he became.

"Why did you have to leave me, Jazmine?" he asked and grabbed her by the neck. "Why?" he asked and pushed into her. Jazmine said nothing and kept her eyes closed, but Bobby could see the fear on her face. He pumped hard inside her, keeping his hand to her neck. "Why did you betray me, Jazmine?" He sighed as his strokes became more intense. "Jazmine, Jazmine, Jazmine."

.   .   .

I was on my last sip of J.D. when I decided to turn the car around and go back to Jazmine's. Being a punk didn't come easy, but Little Miss Redhead sho-nuff had me turning into the punk of the year. Fuck it. What did I have to lose? I had already begged her to take me back. Hell, I even cried.

Now that's a first. No woman had ever moved me to tears. But looking at Jazz and how hurt she was, how hurt I had made her, brought tears to my heart. I wasn't giving up on her, not yet. I wasn't giving up on myself. I had to make her see how much I needed her. I knew I had fucked up. But damn, who doesn't fuck up? If I had known I was gonna meet someone like her, I never would have gotten caught up with Eyeisha. But that was the past. There was nothing I could do to change that now. All I could do is say I'm sorry and try to be better. Shit, a man's only got his word and mine is as good as money. I was gonna go back there and let her know that, and if she didn't believe me, then fuck it. I'd wait for her. She'd see in good time that I was for real. I always said, I'd do anything for Jazmine. I meant it.

When I got to the security gate, I stood there for a minute, then decided to jump over. Jazmine was mad as hell at me and I knew she wouldn't buzz me in. But I was on a mission. No cast iron fence was gonna stand between me and my heart. I took my time making it up to her apartment. I needed time to calm down. I didn't want to rush in there throwing all this mess in her face. I wanted to be relaxed and talk to her like I had some sense. That way she could see I was serious, and whether or not she believed me, she'd at least know that I was for real.

When I made it to her floor the first thing that hit me was that she might not open the door. Scaling that gate was only the first obstacle. Actually getting in to talk to her was a whole 'nother thing.

I stood in front of the door and pulled up my pants and ran my hands over my face. This was it. Then I looked closer and noticed that the door wasn't completely closed and I wondered if I should knock or just let myself in. I decided to just go in. That way she won't have the option of locking me out and calling the police.

I opened the door and walked inside and I thought I was gonna jump out of my skin when I saw that fool Bobby on top of my girl. At first I thought I was dreaming or that I had walked into the wrong apartment, and to tell the truth I didn't know what to do. I flipped on the lights and that fool turned to look at me and I could tell he was high as a kite. His eyes were bloodshot and I knew he must have been out of his head 'cause he didn't even make a move to get up. I looked at Jazmine and she was just laying there with her eyes closed like she was in another world. I didn't know what the hell was going on, but I knew one thing. That nigga was about to get fucked up.

I ran over to the two of them and grabbed Bobby by the neck and pulled him up. All I know after that was that I couldn't stop ramming my fist into his face. And all the time I was doing that he just kept smiling. I finally threw him up against the wall. He stayed there for a minute like he was stuck, then slid down to the floor, laughing all the way. I threw his clothes at him and he was chuckling so hard that I picked up a vase and threw it at his head to make him shut up. The vase missed and he sat there on the floor grabbing his pants and snickering. I turned to Jazmine and my poor baby was still laying on the floor with her eyes closed. She was humming a song. It sounded like some church song, but I didn't know which one. And furthermore, I didn't know what the hell to do. She was spaced out, like she had taken a hallucinogen, and when I bent down to touch her face she didn't even respond. Just kept on humming and never opened her eyes. I turned to Bobby and said, "What the fuck did you give her?" And when I did, I noticed that fool had a gun pointed dead at me. I almost fell on top of Jazmine when he cocked that .45. I scrambled up from the floor and backed up against the wall. Bobby had me covered, and he was still smiling, like whatever drug he had sunk into his body was taking over him. I knew for sure that fool was completely out of it.

All I could do was freeze. He got up from the floor and stood plastered against the wall like he needed it to keep his balance. He looked over at Jazmine, then back over to me. I knew if I reached for my piece he would shoot. He started grinning again, and this time he pointed the gun down at Jazmine. My heart skipped about three beats, and I knew I had to stop that fool. He was crazy out of his mind, standing there, butt naked, laughing. He stared down at Jazmine like he was in a daze and started calling her name, "Jazmine, Jazmine, Jazmine." I reached in the back of my pants for my gun and felt the handle. He walked closer to her, pointing the gun up and down her body. I was shaking all over, but I managed to ease my gun out, keeping it behind my back. He looked up at me and said, "She's beautiful, isn't she?" He stumbled closer and closer to her. So close that I couldn't stand it. Thoughts of jail and the electric chair ran through my mind. But I had risked those things for lesser rewards before. Jazmine, my heart, was well worth whatever punishment I'd get for killing that bastard. His trigger hand began to shake and the expression on his face hardened. He looked sternly at me, but kept the gun pointed at Jazmine. "I love her to death," he said and started grinning again. "She's all I have. And I'm sorry, but I can't let you take her away from me." He looked back at Jazmine and I could see his finger begin to clutch. I pulled around my gun and shot two times. Bobby didn't fall. He kept the gun pointed down and shot at the floor just missing my baby's head. That was all the incentive I needed to empty the rest of my barrel into him. I shot ten more times and every shot pushed Bobby farther and farther backward until his head slammed against the wall and he slid back down to the floor.

I stood there watching his lifeless body, unable to believe I had just taken that fool out. I turned to look at Jazmine. Her eyes were open and she was smiling. But it wasn't a happy smile, 'cause there were tears running down her face. I went over to her and grabbed her arm. "You a'ight, Jazz?" She didn't answer. She kept looking up at the ceiling like there was something up there. I held her in my arms and rocked her. It was all I could do. Then she started singing again, "Amazing grace . . . ," and the tears from her eyes poured down like an ocean. "How sweet the sound . . . ."

"That's right, baby," I said, but I know she didn't hear me. "Sing from your soul," I told her and looked up toward the ceiling. "Sing from your soul and He'll hear you."

chapter twenty-two

monday

It's amazing what six months and five Grammy nominations can do for a girl's peace of mind, I thought, searching through my dresser drawer. I put on a pair of red polka-dot boxer shorts and a T-shirt and came out into the living room and sat down on the teal leather sofa and breathed a deep sigh. It felt so good to be in my own place. I didn't turn on the stereo or the television. I just sat taking in the silence and the scenery of my new condo and rested my head on the cushion of the couch. Life was good and it could only get better. My debut album had gone platinum yesterday, and I was so excited about returning to the studio to start work on my follow-up record. I guess because I felt so free, words and lyrics practically fell to the paper with virtually no effort. I felt great. But it had taken me a long time to get to that feeling. Time and a good therapist, that is. After Xavier shot Bobby, I was a basket case. I stayed in bed for days at a time. Dakota would come check on me every hour or so, but I didn't want to be bothered with her. I didn't want to be bothered with anybody. My daddy came to see me once everything had cooled down. He didn't say much. He just sat with me, like he used to do when I was a little girl. He came by every day, but he didn't preach to me. For once he was just my daddy, not Reverend Deems, healer of lost souls. He was the one who got me to see a psychiatrist. "People think they can just go to church and pray," he said.

"They drop a dollar in the collection plate, bow their heads, and think God will make everything okay. But God only helps those who help themselves." He was right, as usual.

After a month or so, I went back to the studio. Kirk had finally been promoted to president and the first person he hired was Dakota. He realized that she had been the driving force behind my career and decided to start her out in the promotion department, and of course she was great at it.

Within two months my debut was out. Everybody at Black Tie was so understanding and sympathetic. Just what I needed to help me through. It took a lot of rearranging schedules and meetings so that I wouldn't accidentally run into Xavier while I was there. He finally got his debut out too. It was a nice collection of rap music, though the one we collaborated on together didn't show up on his album. Every now and then, I hear one of his songs on the radio. I used to turn it off whenever I heard his voice seeping through my speakers. I didn't want any reminders of what we had between us. My therapist said I should see him so I can finally close the door on our relationship and move on. But that was totally out of the question. Memories of Xavier were best left hidden. Every now and then, Dakota will bring up his name. She sees him pretty often now that she's working at Black Tie. She tells me he's doing well. That he has finally been able to put his life in order and do something positive with his music. That's all fine and dandy, I tell her, but I still don't want to see him. There's no going back for me and Xavier.

Daddy phoned twice this morning to make sure I'd be at church tomorrow for the start of the revival. I'm doing a solo with the choir and the whole church is buzzing about it. They have my name and picture on a banner outside on the church wall. "Grammy nominee Jazmine Deems sings for the Lord. Sunday, eight o'clock service." The church will probably be a madhouse tomorrow, but it sure is going to feel good being back in the choir stands where I started out. For the first time, it feels good being me. I'm not scared, I'm not worried. It's as if I finally know who I am. Now I can march through the world with confidence.

When I heard a knock at the door, I knew it was Dakota. She stops by every Saturday for a cup of coffee, but mostly to check up on me. She still worries about me like I came from her womb. But now I don't mind so much. I realize it's not so bad to have people care about you. When I opened the door she breezed right by me and into the kitchen. "If I don't get my caffeine pretty soon, I'm gonna pass out." She prepared the coffeepot, then opened up the refrigerator. "Where's the creamer, girl?"

"I'm out, but there's some of that powder stuff in the cabinet."

"Girl, you know that stuff don't do nothing for me," she said, closing the refrigerator in disgust.

Too bad, I thought. This was my house, she'd have to make do. Besides, she was the one who used up the last bit of flavored creamer last week.

"So what's up?" she said, pouring us both a cup and sitting them down on the wet bar. "You ready to hit the studio again?"

"As ready as I'll ever be. I've been working on a couple of songs, as a matter of fact. I think I want this album to be a little more jazzy," I said and stirred a half packet of Sweet 'n Low in my coffee. "What are you so dressed up for?" I said and glided myself onto a stool beside her.

"Got a date," she said, grinning from ear to ear.

Dakota was back to her old self. This was her third relationship since she broke it off with Craig. She never explained why she started going out with him and I never asked. It was all water under the bridge now. For our friendship's sake, I didn't want to know the moral of that story.

"You wanna go with us?"

"Hell no. What do I want to go out with you and whoever it is you're seeing *this* week? Besides I got work to do."

"You really ought to get out, Jazz. You're a successful singer now. You need to be seen out in public. People love to see their favorite stars hamming it up in the limelight."

That was the businesswoman in Dakota talking. She knew good and well I didn't want to be bothered with no man. I had one goal and one goal only, and that was singing. Everything else would just have to wait.

"Saw Xavier yesterday," she said, taking a sip from her cup.

"So?"

"He asked about you."

"And?"

"And nothing. I'm just telling you. He's really coming along. He ain't no Ice Cube, but his music is really catching on. Positive rap music is the wave of the future. Don't nobody wanna hear all that 'bitch-bitch, fuck the police' shit no more."

"And what's your point, D?"

"No point. I'm just saying he got it going on these days. You wanna hear a sample of his new release?"

"No, Dakota, I don't. Can we change the subject?"

"Fine, but I might as well tell you, he's gonna be over here in about ten minutes."

She said the words so fast that I thought she was talking in another language. I could have slapped that coffee cup right out of her hand when it finally sunk in what she had said. "You didn't invite him to my house. I ought to kill you, Dakota."

"Chill out, girl. This is business. Kirk let me hear a sample of that duet you two did together and I had the idea for you guys to do a whole album together. People would scoop it up like government cheese."

"What?" I said, jumping off the stool. Before I could even get out a sentence my doorbell was ringing again. Dakota looked at me and I stared right back at her. I wasn't opening that door for nothing in the world. She got up and huffed over to the door and let Xavier in. He was dressed casually in a sweatsuit and tennis shoes. If it were anybody else I would have been impressed.

. . .

Damn. My baby, I mean, Jazmine looked good. Even better than she looked on her videos. I hadn't seen her in person since the night she came down to the police station after Bobby died. For a minute there, they were trying to pin a one-eight-seven on me, but Jazmine straightened all that out when she came down and backed up my story. I tried to tell her that Eyeisha had lost the baby but she wouldn't let me talk to her. Baby or no baby, she didn't care. It was like she wanted to forget everything. I understood. I wanted to forget myself. I had been dying to see her ever since, but Dakota told me to lay low. I knew she was right. Jazmine had been through too much and it was all because of me. So I stayed away in the physical sense, but not spiritually. A brother like me don't know shit about all that psychic shit, and I know this sounds like voodoo, but I never really left my baby—not really.

I needed to stay away for myself too. I needed to make sure my shit was fit before I tried to pass myself off on somebody else. I haven't been over to the hood in ages, and I ain't going back. I know everybody be talking about how when famous people get a little money, they forget about where they came from. Well, that ain't me, but sometimes you gotta know when to cut off ties.

After my record came out, I thought about calling up Rich. That was a stupid idea, and lucky for me, I had sense enough to know that. But it was more like I *couldn't* call him. Like if I heard his voice I'd somehow slip back into my old habits. I did hear that he did some time for beating up Eyeisha, but I also heard them two were planning to get married as soon as he got out. Huh. Things may change, but they always stay the same— in the hood, that is. That's why I keep my distance from them fools in the hood. People can say what they want about me, but fuck 'em. I know what's really up. I mean, I do what I can for my peoples, but that's all I can do. Just last month I went to the Crenshaw YMCA and talked to some kids about the dangers of gang life. I couldn't believe how those kids just sat and watched me with their mouths hanging open. They were looking at me like I was they father. I guess I'm a full-fledged role model now. Now ain't that some shit?

I liked to died when Dakota and Kirk approached me about doing a duet with Jazmine. I told them no at first, but that was just a front. Dakota didn't even pay attention to me. She knew I was bluffing. She told me to meet her at Jazmine's and gave me the address, then walked away. She knew I'd show up.

I had second thoughts when I walked up to the door. Not because I didn't want to see my baby, but because I didn't want to force her to see me. She had every right to still be angry toward me. I just hoped one day that we could be friends again. A'ight, I wanted more than friendship, but I wasn't gonna push. I'd take any old, dirty scraps Little Miss Redhead would throw my way.

. . .

"**How** you been, Jazmine?" he asked, casually.

I tugged at my T-shirt and sat back down on the stool. "Just fine, Xavier. And yourself?"

"I've been okay," he said, fixing his eyes on me.

"Yeah, yeah, yeah. He's okay, you're okay, now let's get down to business," Dakota said, walking into the kitchen to refill her cup.

Xavier walked over to the wet bar and rested his elbows on the counter. He kept trying to sneak a peek at me on the sly, and I must admit I couldn't keep my eyes off him either.

"Now, Kirk and I were thinking this track you guys laid down together could really take off. It has the right mixture of soul and rap. People eat that shit up." She looked at the both of us, waiting for one of us to respond, but neither of us said a word. We kept shooting each other looks, both of us trying to act unaffected by the other's presence. Dakota kept rambling on about us making an album together, but neither one of us were paying her any attention.

"Well, look. You guys think about it. I gotta get out of here or I'm gonna be late for my date."

She headed for the door and before she went out she turned around and looked at the both of us and giggled like a schoolgirl. "You two wanna tag along?"

"No," Xavier said. "I better be getting back down to the studio. I've got some work to do."

"All right. Don't say I didn't offer."

After she closed the door behind her, there was a long silence. Xavier looked at me, then down at the countertop and shook his head. "You don't have to do this if you don't want. I understand."

I stared at the kitchen wall, then back at him.

"Listen, Jazmine. I know I fucked up with you. I mean I messed up bigtime. I know I did a lot of things wrong and I'm sorry. Not that sorry means a whole hell of a lot now, but . . . I don't know. I guess if I were you, I wouldn't want to be anywhere near me either." He paused for an instant and looked down at his watch. "I better be going," he said and pushed away from the counter.

"I don't mind. Working with you, that is."

He turned to me and chuckled. "That sounds a'ight," he said, sticking his hands into his pocket. We stared at each other for the longest time and we both knew what the other was thinking. "I traded the Impala in for a Grand Cherokee," he said, smiling. "If we hurry up, we can still catch Dakota."

I got off the stool and walked closer to him. "No, not today," I said, and stopped in front of him. "But I'll see you down at the studio Monday morning."

"A'ight," he said, backing up to the door. "See you Monday."

He turned around and put his hand on the doorknob and paused. "You did say Monday, didn't you?"

"Monday," I repeated and smiled. "Now get out of here."

He chuckled again and opened the door. "I can't wait," he said and let himself out.

I stood there in the middle of the floor with a big, cheesy grin on my face. I couldn't wait either.

about the author

Sheneska Jackson was born in Los Angeles, California, where she grew up in South-Central and West L.A. She currently lives in Sherman Oaks, where she is working on her second novel.